Some Nerve

Some Nerve

||||||||||||||||||||||||||||||||||||||||||||||||||||||||||||||||||||||||||||||||||||

JANE HELLER

wm

WILLIAM MORROW

An Imprint of HarperCollins*Publishers*

SOME NERVE. Copyright © 2006 by Jane Heller. All rights reserved. Printed in the United States of America. No part of this book may be used or reproduced in any manner whatsoever without written permission except in the case of brief quotatons embodied in critical articles and reviews. For information address HarperCollins Publishers, 10 East 53rd Street, New York, NY 10022.

Designed by Paula Russell Szafranski

ISBN-13: 978-0-06-059927-0
ISBN-10: 0-06-059927-8

Printed in the U.S.A.

For Susan Shuman, who embodies the two
qualities every volunteer should: a huge
heart and a wicked sense of humor

ACKNOWLEDGMENTS

Thanks to Amy Schiffman, my agent at the Gersh Agency in Los Angeles, whose throwaway quip inspired this novel. Thanks to Carrie Feron, my editor at William Morrow, whose insights helped me write a much stronger book than I would have if left to my own devices. Thanks as always to Ellen Levine, Trident Media's agent extraordinaire, for never letting me down, personally or professionally. To say that I'm grateful to have her in my life is an understatement. Thanks to Drs. Dan Eisenberg, Ivan Strausz, Henry Spector, and Brenda K. Wiederhold for lending me their time and expertise regarding medical matters. Thanks to Catherine Bergstrom-Katz for sharing stories of growing up in the Midwest; to Ciji Ware for furnishing me with information about phobias and providing much needed moral support; and to Laurie Burrows Grad for either knowing the answer to every question I asked or directing me to others who did. Thanks to Bruce Gelfand, who never ceases to amaze me with his creativity and generosity. Thanks to Kristen Powers for keeping me up and running in cyberspace. And thanks to my husband, Michael Forester, for being my partner in life as well as my volunteering buddy.

Part One

Chapter One

|||||||||||||||||||||||||||||||||||||||||||||||||||||||||||||||||||||||||||||||||||||||||||

Things weren't going so well for the country that winter—the stock market was slumping and gas prices were rising and our soldiers were still at war—but they were going very well for Britney Spears, who was pregnant with her first child. She described the experience as "freaking awesome" during the two hours we spent together at her recently purchased nine-thousand-square-foot Malibu beach getaway, and she confided that sex with her husband, despite her swollen belly, was "crazy good."

No, the Britster and I weren't girlfriends sitting around having an afternoon gabfest, although there were moments when it felt like that. I was a thirty-year-old reporter for *Famous,* an entertainment magazine in Hollywood, and my beat was interviewing celebrities. Britney was an assignment for a cover story. She's generally viewed as a product rather than a talent, but she had a sweetness about her, I found, a giggly openness, and I enjoyed my time with her.

I enjoyed my time with all of them. I loved the feeling of gaining access to their private realms, loved trying to figure out for myself what it was that made them special. I'd been fascinated with famous people since I was a kid in Middletown, Missouri, a tiny place in the general vicinity of Kansas City. They were royalty to me—the beautiful ones with the beautiful clothes and the beautiful houses and the beautiful companions—and they were my escape from what was a dull and dispiriting childhood. I dreamed nonstop of fleeing Middletown and landing a job in L.A., and I'd made the dream come true. I'd really done it. So you could say that things were going very well for me too.

Well, you wouldn't say it if you're one of those snobs who thinks it's only news if it's on PBS or NPR. In fact, you're probably rolling your eyes right now as you picture Britney telling me about her morning sickness, her fluctuating hormones, and her cravings for pickles and ice cream, but I considered myself the luckiest woman on earth to be doing what I was doing. I could have been stuck in Middletown, where people get their kicks experimenting with different brands of snowblowers, eating casseroles made with cream of mushroom soup, and needlepointing pillows with bumper-sticker-type sayings on them, and where the biggest celebrity for a while was the guy who was cleaning his rifle and accidentally shot himself in the balls. I was bored out of my skull there, logy with the sameness of it all, convinced that if I stayed I would end up like my father, who died a slow and agonizing death, or like my mother, aunt, and grandmother, a trio of phobics who were too afraid of life to take risks and live it.

By contrast, I felt healthy in L.A., empowered, energized by the constant whirl of activity and by the people I met, most of whom were colorful and creative and the opposite of dull. I mean, I was attending movie premieres, film festivals, and Oscar parties, mingling with Clint Eastwood and marveling at the merry band of women who bear his children, waving at Penélope Cruz and admiring her ongoing battle with English, exchanging friendly glances with Meg Ryan and wondering why she looks so much like Michelle Pfeiffer now. It all seemed so glamorous to me, so Technicolor, especially in comparison with the grayness I'd left behind. Rubbing shoulders with exceptional people made me feel exceptional by osmosis.

Yes, the city was my oyster or, to be more L.A.-ish about it, my sushi. I had Leonardo DiCaprio's cell phone number, for God's sake. (Okay, his publicist's cell phone number.) It doesn't get much better than that, does it?

Not for me. Not then. When you grow up yearning to be in the orbit of movie stars and then actually hang out with them, albeit in the service of helping them promote their latest project, it's—well—freaking awesome.

And as far as I was concerned, there was nothing cheesy or demeaning about my career. I mean, I wasn't one of those tabloid creeps who picks through people's garbage. My methods weren't exploitative or intrusive. I had scruples. I didn't resort to underhanded tactics to score an interview. I didn't have to. I was a hard worker and a good reporter. The new and notoriously temperamental editor of *Famous*, fifty-year-old Harvey Krass, had been expected to clean house and bring in his own writers when he'd taken charge the previous month, and though he did fire some of the staff, he'd kept me on. I assumed it was because of my straightforward approach to the job, my integrity. He hadn't said as much—he wasn't big on compliments—but the fact that he'd asked me to stay at the magazine spoke volumes.

So, yes, things were going very well for me. I was living my dream, as I said.

And then, suddenly, a jolt.

Not an earthquake, although there was a cluster of tremors that winter. No, this was a much more internal, life-altering shift. A radical change in direction that sent me into an entirely new phase of my life. I went from Gutsy Girl to Gutless Wonder and back again, and what I learned from my journey was this: It's possible to be chasing the wrong dream and not know it.

"GOOD MORNING," I trilled to Harvey on Monday at nine twenty-five. His assistant had summoned me to his office for a nine-thirty meeting, but I was always early for things, unlike everybody else in L.A., where traffic is an extremely reliable excuse for being late for things or for missing them altogether. I'd been raised to believe it was rude to be late, and I certainly wasn't about to be rude to my new boss.

"It isn't good at all!" he shouted, brandishing a rolled-up copy of what appeared to be *In Touch Weekly*. *"This rag and its evil twins are eating into our sales and it's gotta stop! Right here! Right now!"*

As his temper flared, his short, stubby arms shot in the air, nearly knocking over the statue of the Buddha that was resting serenely on a table, courtesy of his feng shui master. He had an unfortunate habit of waving his arms around when he was irritated, which was most of the time. He'd bang into objects and send them crashing to the ground without so much as a backward glance and go right on ranting. Yes, I loved L.A., but borderline-personality disorder was rampant, even among those on a "spiritual path."

As I sat in one of his visitors' chairs, he began to pace in front of the window. His office had a spectacular view of the Hollywood sign on a clear day, but he was too wound up to appreciate it. "How can I help?" I said, because I wanted to be indispensable to him.

"You can interview Malcolm Goddard."

I laughed. "Malcolm Goddard doesn't do interviews. He hates the media."

"They all hate the media until their careers are in the toilet!" he yelled. *"Then they can't wait to talk to us!"*

A perpetually red-faced man with a pear-shaped body, a silly little ponytail, and the waddle of a duck, he was one of those Neanderthals who didn't get that it's not okay to scream at one's employees at the drop of a hat. He was also a heart attack waiting to happen, and there were many at *Famous* for whom it couldn't happen soon enough. But he'd been brought in by our parent company last month precisely because of his hard-driving style. Circulation at *Food,* our sister publication, had skyrocketed when he was editor in chief there, even as blood pressures did too.

"Right, but he's hot now and he won't talk to anybody," I said. The approach I'd adopted with Harvey was to remain focused and professional no matter what his decibel level. "He wouldn't cooperate for *People*'s Sexiest Man Alive cover, for example."

"I envision *Famous* as much hipper than *People*," he said with disdain. "We won't do stories about miracle quintuplets."

"Even if Charlize Theron gives birth to them?" I suggested. "Now that I think of it, why don't I interview her?"

Harvey wheeled around to face me, his cheeks florid with fury, his ears flaming. *"Because she's not the big get anymore. Malcolm Goddard is!"*

"Chelsea Clinton is a big get," I said. "Malcolm Goddard is a get-me-not."

"No, the Olsen twins are a get-me-not. I've told you my motto: If they're overexposed or over-the-hill, the only way they'll make it into *Famous* is if they croak. I want Goddard."

"He won't do it," I repeated. I wasn't trying to be negative, just realistic. I had nothing against Malcolm Goddard—I really did try to see the best in celebrities, even the ones who were reputed to be insufferable bullies—but he'd made it clear that he had no use for publications like ours. "Did you read that interview he gave *Vanity Fair* last year? He said it was his last. He sounded like an artiste with a sense of entitlement to match. He told the magazine—wait, let me quote his exact words—'Reporters are parasites who only want to feed off my vessel.'"

"What do you expect?" sniffed Harvey. "He's one of those Method assholes. Their vessel. Their instrument. Their whatever. 'The role took me places I never thought I could go.' They all spout that crap."

"But he seems to have a genuine distaste for the media, so who needs him?"

"We do!" Out went the flailing arms, just missing the hunk of crystal he'd been given by a shaman in Santa Fe. *"He's the 'it' guy now and millions of women are in love with him and I don't want to see his face in* Us Weekly *or* In Touch Weekly *or* Up My Ass Weekly! *He's ours and you're gonna make him ours, do you hear me?"*

The shaman in Santa Fe could probably hear him. I sat very still for a couple of seconds, my eardrums throbbing, waiting to see if he'd cool down again. Or fall to the floor and die.

"Look, Ann," he said. "You've been working here for—what?—three years?"

"Five."

I had arrived in Los Angeles shortly after getting my degree in journalism from Mizzou. Why journalism? I had a penchant for asking questions and digging for answers—a "busybody nature," my mother called it—and I'd always gotten As in English classes. Why celebrity journalism when a byline at the *New York Times* was so much more respectable? As I've said, I had an attraction to all things Hollywood, needed to place myself in the midst of that glitter. I could have taken my J-school degree and gone the Maureen Dowd route, ferreting out the truth and then penning withering Op-Ed pieces about wars and presidents and matters of real importance, but I was more interested in movie stars and TV stars and matters of no real importance. I actually cared when celebrity couples like Jennifer Aniston and Brad Pitt broke up. I wanted to know why they broke up and who said what when they broke up and did anyone threaten suicide while they were breaking up, not to mention whether a third party was involved. I know it makes me seem like a complete fluff ball to admit this, but I wanted to know who celebrities were underneath their designer clothes and nine-trillion-dollar haircuts and surgically altered faces, wanted to understand their specialness. Blame it on Don Johnson. He was born and raised in a small town in Missouri, just like I was. I was still a kid when he became a star on *Miami Vice,* and I guess it started me wondering why some people rise to the top and others don't. Yes, I could have taken my degree and covered wars and presidents and matters of real importance, but my need to know about George Clooney trumped my need to know about George Bush. So I headed for L.A., spotted an ad for an entry-level position at *Famous,* grabbed it, and scaled the ladder.

"Yeah, well, entertainment journalism has changed in those five years," said Harvey in almost an avuncular tone, as if he were suddenly my teacher as opposed to my tormentor. "The competition is uglier. Print. Television. The Internet. Celebrities are all over the place, so who cares about most of them? It's about the big get now—the person we fight over, the one who isn't accessible."

"I understand. Malcolm Goddard's a big get," I said, conceding the point. "But, practically speaking, how am I supposed to—"

"You just do it!" he bellowed, switching back to Bad Harvey, arms in the air. *"I don't care if he's a pretentious little prick! I don't care if he thinks we're parasites! I don't care if he never does another interview in his spoiled-brat life after he does this one, but he's gonna do this one and you're gonna make it happen!"* He paused to examine his hand. He had just singed it on the flame of the soy candle he'd been given by a Tibetan monk. "You're a good writer, Ann," he continued more softly, as if reminding himself to be Zen-ish, not churlish. "There was a reason I kept you on here: You know how to string sentences together and you know the right questions to ask. It's your killer instinct I'm not sure about."

"What do you mean?" I said, stung by the comment. Was he referring to the fact that I didn't embellish the truth the way some of my colleagues did? That I didn't turn in stories that were based strictly on rumor and gossip? That I didn't scheme and stalk my way into a subject's life? That I was raised to believe that if you were honest and trustworthy and worked hard, you were rewarded? My previous editor had never complained about my lack of a killer instinct. Okay, so I'd lost the Jane Fonda interview to *People* when her book came out, and Russell Crowe had decided to unburden himself to *Esquire* after his telephone-throwing incident. It wasn't as if I hadn't tried.

"Just what I said: You're not a killer." Harvey shook his head at me. "The business has changed and you haven't changed along with it. It's not enough to be nice to people. You need to toughen up, elbow everybody aside, show your edge, prove you're willing to do whatever it takes for a story." He sat down behind his big, stupid desk, a slab of antique mahogany that had been tested for termites by a holistic exterminator who hummed bugs away instead of spraying them with good old pesticides. "And right now, that story is Malcolm Goddard."

What was this? After five productive, thoroughly fun-filled years at *Famous,* I needed to prove myself? Prove, as in: change my style or else? Was he issuing me an ultimatum? Was my job suddenly in jeopardy? Did my career, my very identity, hinge on my ability to coax an interview out of Malcolm Goddard, who was not only media shy but downright hostile to reporters? It didn't seem fair, but I wasn't about to argue. I would put on my can-do face and continue to do things the way I'd always done them, and everything would turn out just fine. "Okay, sure, Harvey. I'll try to get him," I said with a big smile.

"Nope. Not 'try.' " He shook his head again. "There are plenty of wannabes ready and waiting to 'try.' Take a walk down to human resources and check out all their résumés." He leaned forward so he could regard me with his third eye. "You see what I'm saying, don't you, Ann?"

Now I did see what he was saying: Get the big get or get the hell out.

I felt an unfamiliar chill ripple down my spine, and my shoulders did this odd little shimmy. He was putting me on notice and I hadn't expected it and I wished I could go back to sleep, wake up again, and start the day over. But then I reminded myself that I had a track record. I had experience. I had credibility. I had nothing to fear.

"Ann Roth is on the case," I said jauntily as I rose from my chair. "One interview with Malcolm Goddard coming right up."

||||||||||||||||||||||||||||||||||||||||||||||||||||||||||||||||||||||||||||||||||||||||||||||||||||||||

Chapter Two

"I'm totally buying this sweater," said my best friend, Tuscany Davis, referring to a DKNY turtleneck that was not only her favorite shade of purple but had been marked down to half its original price. It was the day after my meeting with Harvey, and she had decided I needed retail therapy instead of lunch. At noon on the dot, we were in the giant bull pen of a dressing room at Loehmann's, where women of all sizes and zero modesty were trying on bargain merchandise, some of which was stained with lipstick.

"Go for the sweater," I said distractedly. I was staring at the woman next to us. The pants she had on were so tight they reminded me of sausage casing. They were also extremely low-rise, hitting her well below her navel and pushing her stomach up and out, the effect of which was that she looked about six months pregnant, just like Britney. Oh, and she was probably in her seventies. In L.A., there's no such thing as age-appropriate fashion.

"Aren't you getting anything?" asked Tuscany when she saw me standing there empty-handed.

"I'm getting Malcolm Goddard." I sighed. "Or I'm supposed to be getting him. I really can't concentrate on anything else. Sorry."

She put her right arm around my shoulder. Her sculpted, toned, buffed right arm. Tuscany, who was in the graphic-design department at *Famous,* spent many hours at the gym every week in a never-ending quest for the perfect body, which, in L.A., means a size 2. She'd grown up in Los Angeles and embraced the it's-all-about-how-you-look culture. How she wanted to look was as thin as a piece of dental floss. She wasn't a beauty—her nose was a little too broad and her brownish-red hair was kinky and cut so severely it resembled a clipped hedge—but she was rarely without a date.

She attributed her popularity to the fact that she was willing to sleep with just about anybody except actors (she and I both had a rule about them, actors being on the self-absorbed side and, therefore, lousy relationship material). She slept with the guy at the car wash, the guy at the coffee place, the guy at the farmers' market, whatever. People say it's hard to meet men in L.A. because of all the gorgeous babes who spoil things for the rest of us, but Tuscany met men left and right. Adorned with a pink rose tattoo on each ankle, she was a free spirit who wasn't raised with the strict Midwestern values that had been drilled into me.

I was often guilty of lecturing her about her promiscuity, but who was I to judge her? While I was holding out for Prince Charming, she was the one having a good time. I hadn't had a boyfriend since I'd been dumped by Skip Atwater, who was Denzel Washington's massage therapist. He said he loved me (Skip, not Denzel) and wanted us to move in together, and after we found a place we both liked, he broke up with me. I vowed never again to date a man who gave massages for a living. Since I already had a No-Actors rule in effect and since just about everybody else in L.A. gives massages for a living, I'd been spending most Saturday nights alone.

So in a way I envied Tuscany her free-spiritedness and laughed to myself as I remembered the day she'd shown up at *Famous* four years earlier. She'd introduced herself by saying, "In case you're wondering about the name, my parents conceived me thirty-two years ago while they were on vacation in Tuscany. Don't you think *Travel & Leisure* should do an article about that?"

"About what?" I'd said.

"About children who are named after the place where their parents did it. It's a trend. A woman in my Pilates class is named Kenya and a woman in my spinning class is named Mauritius, and all I can think about when I see them is that their parents had condomless sex under mosquito netting."

As it turned out, her parents never did stop traveling after her mother gave birth to her. Flush with the stock options her father had cashed in, they dumped Tuscany on her biker-chick aunt's doorstep in Topanga Canyon, then roamed the world, sending postcards and e-mails and enjoying a life of irresponsibility. Tuscany essentially raised herself. Maybe her obsession with physical love was really just a need for emotional love and she couldn't tell the difference. Or maybe she was, in her own words, just a natural-born slut. Either way, I couldn't help wishing she'd take her relationships more slowly instead of hopping from man to man, never settling down. But, as I said, I wasn't one to be giving anybody advice in the romance department.

My own background was stricter but just as messed up. I grew up with a father whose drawn-out battle with lung cancer reduced him to a wraithlike, barely-there, ghostly presence and reduced me to a person who equated sickness and death with helplessness, weakness, a lack of control. After Dad died when I was ten, my aunt Toni got divorced and moved in. Since my mother and I already had the long-widowed Grandma Raysa living with us, we were now four females sharing one house. It was an unorthodox arrangement and not always pretty. My grandmother had a powerful fear of germs and went around disinfecting everything.

Aunt Toni was petrified of enclosed spaces; she flat-out refused to take a shower in a stall instead of one with a curtain, for example. My mother became the most phobic of all, turning her grief over my father's death into a dread of heights, dogs, and dentists, and she would only ride on escalators if they were going up. At age twelve I developed a problem with peanut butter (I imagined it would stick to the roof of my mouth and make me choke) and clowns (they just scared the shit out of me), and I knew I'd better get out of there as soon as I was old enough or else I might really succumb to the family curse. Fleeing to L.A. and working for *Famous* had been my salvation as well as my dream.

"So you talked to Goddard's publicist?" said Tuscany as we walked out of the store and into the underground parking lot. It was unseasonably warm for L.A. in January—in the eighties. We were both wearing summery high-heeled sandals and they made clickety-clack sounds on the pavement.

"I've called Peggy Merchant, the überflak, three times in the last twenty-four hours, and she still hasn't called me back," I said.

"Maybe she's still mad at you for skipping that Winona Ryder thing last year."

"Peggy's not the easiest person to deal with, but I don't think she holds grudges." She had organized a handful of entertainment reporters to visit the Palm Springs set of the movie that Winona, a client of hers, was shooting. My editor had left it up to me to decide if I wanted to go and I'd passed. The plane Peggy had chartered was one of those dinky, single-engine prop planes and I didn't do prop planes. No sir. They were synonymous with death as far as I was concerned. Too terrifying to contemplate. Yes, I'd pretty much escaped the family curse except for a paralyzing fear of flying. I got the shakes even making the reservation for a flight, let alone taking one, and if I absolutely had to fly for business, I took jets—and consumed many, many Bloody Marys.

"Then maybe she's just busy," said Tuscany.

"No, she's ducking me," I said. "I left a message saying I wanted to sit down with Goddard as soon as possible. No call back is her way of telling me no interview."

"Isn't it possible that she's taking the time to try to convince him to do it?" said Tuscany. "*Famous* isn't exactly the *Star*. He could do worse."

"Are you kidding? To him, we're the same as a tabloid. We might as well be covering aliens and Elvis sightings."

"Why does he hate the media so much?" she asked.

"He thinks we're out to exploit his vessel."

Her eyes widened. "Is it that big?"

Tuscany was obsessed with the size of men's penises. As I told you, she was earthy. "I meant the vessel for his acting," I said. "He believes that he channels the characters he plays, that his body is merely the instrument through which these characters find their voice. He's one of *those*."

"Too bad," she said with a shrug. "He's incredibly hot."

I stopped walking and looked at her. "You think so?" Sure, he was attractive, but I honestly didn't see what all the fuss was about.

"Duh." She said it with a lot of blinks, which emphasized that I must be nuts not to feel Malcolm Goddard's heat. "He's got a great face—one of those classic, WASPy, chiseled faces—but it's the clothes and the hair and the eyes that make him so hot."

"Okay, I can understand the eyes," I said as we resumed the trek to our cars. "They're almost turquoise. I've never seen a blue like that; it's the color of a body of water in the Caribbean. And I admit, his black-leather look is very bad boy, sort of the flip side of Tom Wolfe's white suit. But the hair? It's just your basic brown."

"Don't be ridiculous. It's serious hair," she insisted, patting her own, which was as tightly curled as a Chia pet's. "It's thick and wavy, and there's a little lock of it in the front that falls in his eyes."

"Right. The signature lock of hair that every woman is dying to comb back with her fingers," I said, rolling my own eyes. "Personally, I'd like to take scissors and snip it off, because if it weren't for him, I wouldn't be so rattled right now."

We arrived at our cars. "You going back to the office?" she asked.

"Not right away," I said, opening the door of the Honda I'd driven all the way from Missouri five years before. It was old and ugly, especially by L.A. standards, with dents and dings and scratches galore. When the valet-parking attendants saw it coming, they actually looked away. Tuscany, on the other hand, leased a used ("pre-owned") Mercedes. The valet guys sniffed when they saw it coming too, but at least they didn't fight over who'd get stuck having to park it. "There's a press junket for the new Pierce Brosnan movie at the Four Seasons this afternoon. Peggy Merchant's his publicist, so my plan is to grab a minute with her to talk about Goddard."

"You're so lucky that you get to meet all the stars," she said wistfully. "All I get to do is airbrush their photos."

I hugged her. "You're the lucky one. Harvey didn't ask you to do the impossible."

PIERCE BROSNAN'S NEW film was yet another thriller in which he played a suave and sophisticated thief. Whether the character was a stealer of jewels or artwork or Sub-Zero refrigerators I couldn't tell you, but suffice it to say, I wasn't interested. Peggy Merchant was my target, and the instant I spotted her in the hushed, lavishly appointed hotel suite where she was greeting members of the press and setting limits on how long each of them would have with Brosnan and his costars, I made a beeline for her, stopping only to grab a fistful of crab cakes off a silver tray, stuff them into my mouth all at once, then chew and swallow them dry. Well, I hadn't eaten lunch.

The sixty-year-old doyenne of Hollywood publicists, with a client list that included dozens of A-list actors and directors, Peggy was an angel if she needed you and a barracuda if she didn't. At first glance, she disarmed you with how down-to-earth she seemed. Her short, pixie-ish blond hair was flecked with gray. Her face was lined and freckled in the manner of someone who lived anyplace other than L.A., where there's a law against lined, freckled faces. She wore human clothes—i.e., nothing that required a thong. And she smiled relentlessly, as if she were your long-lost grandmother. But, I'm telling you, she was tough. Having all those big clients gave her power, and she flaunted it. If you were a magazine reporter who wanted Pierce Brosnan, you had to sign a written guarantee that you'd put him on the cover, give him photo approval, and avoid asking him anything that would make him uncomfortable, which meant anything juicy. If you didn't sign the waiver, you'd lose him to someone who *would* sign it. She had you over a barrel. Still, there were times when she was desperate for positive publicity for her stars so she could rehabilitate their image—when their movie tanked or when they were arrested for drunk driving, shoplifting, or hooking up with a hooker—and it was under those circumstances that she'd be the one who'd come begging.

"Ann, dear," she said when I tapped her on the elbow. "What a lovely surprise. I thought *Famous* was sending someone else today."

I started to respond, but the crab cakes hadn't gone down after all. I looked around for a glass of something—anything—and found a flute of champagne on yet another silver tray. I drank up.

"Hi." I coughed, cleared my throat. "It's nice to see you too, Peggy. But I'm not here for the junket." I plunged ahead even though she started to turn her attention elsewhere. "It's about another matter. Since I couldn't reach you on the phone, I thought I'd try this."

She smiled. "Couldn't reach me? I didn't know you'd called, dear." Such a manipulator.

"Well, I did call, Peggy. Three times. *Famous* wants to interview Malcolm Goddard, as I told your assistant."

"*Famous* and everyone else." She smiled even wider. Her teeth were tiny, I noticed. Like baby teeth. "But Malcolm doesn't do interviews, Ann. He's a very private person."

Private? He once took off all his black-leather duds and dove naked into the pool at the Chateau Marmont, the occasion being a birthday party for that illustrious thespian Paris Hilton. "He did the *Vanity Fair* piece last year," I reminded her. "And he did *Inside the Actors Studio* on Bravo with James Lipton." I'd watched a tape of the show the night before, hoping it would give me some insight into Goddard, but all it gave me was indigestion. He sat on that stage not only mumbling about how he used his body as a vessel for his characters but insisting that he dreaded doing love scenes because they were so demanding technically. Please. The guy made on-screen love to the sexiest women on the planet. Even if there were a thousand cameramen watching, the scenes were hardly the chore he made them out to be. "I'll give him the star treatment he deserves, Peggy," I said, moving into grovel mode. "Naturally, he'll get the cover of the magazine and I promise I won't ask him about his little brawl at the Skybar, and I'm a fast interviewer, so I won't take up much of his time. We could do it at your office if he'd rather not have me at his house, or he could come to *Famous* and we'll chat in the conference room, or I could camp out on the set if he's shooting." I took a breath, then resumed my pitch. "Maybe he has a favorite spot in L.A. and we could do the interview there. How about Griffith Park if he goes hiking on Sunday mornings, or the beach in Malibu if he—"

Peggy held up her hand. "Ann, dear. There's no point in going on," she said. "You and I both know that Malcolm doesn't need any publicity. He's got the look, he's got the talent, and he's got more projects in development than he can count. His aversion to the media has made my job easy. All I have to do is say no to you people."

"It does sound easy, but what about his fans? Doesn't he owe them something?"

"His position is that he gives them one hundred percent when he's acting. Beyond that, he doesn't feel he owes them anything."

"That's pretty shortsighted, Peggy," I said. "It's because of the fans that he can afford to blow off the media. They're the ones buying the tickets and they want to read about him."

"Ann, Ann. You have such a refreshing take on the business." She smiled patronizingly. "Why don't we have lunch in the next few weeks and discuss some of my other clients? I'll have my assistant—" Just then, Pierce Brosnan stuck his head out of one of the suite's bedrooms and motioned for her. She nodded to him that she'd be right in, then turned back to me. "So sorry. Duty calls."

She served up one last phony smile and was about to dash off when I caught her arm and held it.

"Wait," I said, abandoning my professional tone for my desperate one. Suddenly, Harvey's words reverberated in my head and all I could hear was *I want Goddard and you're gonna get him!* "Couldn't you at least ask Malcolm if he'll do it?"

She wriggled out of my grasp and smoothed the fabric where my fingertips had made indentations. "I can ask," she said wearily, as if I were overtaxing her by merely suggesting that she do her job. "But I wouldn't get my hopes up. As far as he's concerned, you're all—"

"Parasites, I know," I said, feeling my heart sink.

"I might be able to help you with Pierce, though," she said. "I booked him with Diane Sawyer for next week." She beamed with admiration. "That woman is amazing when she wants a story."

"In what way?" I asked out of genuine curiosity.

She looked at me as if I were simple. "She courts people."

"You mean her producers court people."

"No, she does it herself."

"By calling and writing them notes and that sort of thing?"

"No, she gifts them." For the uninitiated, "gift" is a verb in Hollywood. "She does her research and finds out all the little things they love and then she sends the gifts as a surprise. Her strategy scores points. No doubt about it."

Harvey was right. Integrity was out and bribery was in, and the realization sickened me. Yes, of course, I knew all about the toadiness that went on in the industry, the buying of favors, the *swag*, but I suppose I'd turned a blind eye to it because I honestly thought that plain old hard work paid off in the end.

"Take care, dear," Peggy said with a wave as she hurried to attend to her client. "And don't fret about Malcolm. His animosity toward you isn't personal. He just hates the idea of you."

I lingered in that suite at the Four Seasons for a good ten minutes after Peggy Merchant abandoned me for Pierce Brosnan. Not that I blamed her for that. *I* would have abandoned me for Pierce Brosnan, who was handsome and debonair and didn't think media people were parasites. I didn't even blame her for allowing him to be bought. I had to face facts: It wasn't enough to be a good writer now; you had to be Santa Claus too.

As I sat on a very pouffy sofa contemplating all this, I inhaled another couple of crab cakes and about a dozen mini egg rolls, and washed them down with more champagne. Yes, free food was one of the perks of my job, and I'd never questioned the ethics of that. Had I been too rigid in my thinking? If members of the media were entitled to free food, why weren't celebrities entitled to free gifts? Maybe I needed to lower the bar just a little. So they didn't teach us gifting in journalism school. I was out in the big, bad world now. Like it or not, if I wanted to stay in the game, I had to play by the new rules.

Chapter Three

|||||||||||||||||||||||||||||||||||||||||||||||||||||||||||||||||||||||||||||||||||||||||||||||

So, naturally, I decided to gift Malcolm Goddard, as repellent as the idea was to me. The question was, what to gift him with? He always seemed so grumpy, so joyless, even when he was photographed with a pretty woman on his arm. What do you buy for a thirty-five-year-old superstar who couldn't possibly need anything? What product, what goodie, what treasure would convince him that I wasn't just some bottom-feeder who only cared about getting my get? Okay, yes, that's all I did care about, but I still wanted to think of something he'd really like, something meaningful to him as opposed to just a glitzy toy. And it had to be within the budget. Harvey was thrilled when I told him my plan for wooing Goddard—*"That's exactly the kind of killer stuff I'm looking for from you, but don't go overboard!"* he'd warned. *"No bling!"*

It was during my replaying of the *Actors Studio* tape later that night that inspiration struck. I was watching the tape in my bedroom, the warmest room in my ground-floor apartment, the lower rental unit of a Spanish-style duplex in West Hollywood. The apartment itself had character—wood floors, cove moldings, and arched doorways—but it got very little light and was cold all the time. Not Missouri cold, but cold enough that I wore socks and a flannel nightgown to bed. What I liked best about it was the residential feel of the neighborhood and its easy access to all sections of L.A. What I liked least about it was the noise that routinely seeped down the thin walls from upstairs. James, my friend and neighbor, was in charge of hair and makeup on *The Bold and the Beautiful*. He was a sweetheart except that he blasted disco music at two o'clock in the morning, particularly after a night of gay-bar hopping and ecstasy (the drug, not the feeling). I considered myself a reasonable person, but being awakened by Cher's "Believe," the most repetitive song ever written, wasn't fun. I'd stand on my bed and bang my broom handle on the ceiling, and that would usually prompt James to turn it down a notch. But the situation wasn't ideal. My dream was to save enough money to move to another duplex—a larger, sunnier, upper unit this time. The dream was totally doable if I remained employed.

So there I was, huddled under the covers in my socks and nightie, polishing off a bag of Fritos and replaying the tape of *Inside the Actors Studio*.

James Lipton, in his typically unctuous manner, was asking Goddard about his childhood. "And where did you grow up, Malcolm?" he said. "Here in New York on the Upper West Side," Goddard mumbled. His voice was distinctive because of his mumbling. It was soft, low, barely audible, his words running together. "Right down the street from Zabar's," he mumbled some more.

I hit Pause at that moment because there was a hint of a smile on Goddard's face when he mentioned the famous gourmet-food emporium. For just a second there, he didn't look so surly, so miserable, so tortured actor-ish, and I was sort of fascinated.

I let the tape continue. "Did you partake of any of the delicacies at Zabar's?" asked Lipton. "Oh, yeah," said Goddard. "I still do whenever I'm in town. Their cheesecake is the real deal, and there are nights back in L.A. when I actually fantasize about it. They don't know how to make it on the other coast. They know how to make movies—well, some of 'em do—but definitely not cheesecake."

As the audience laughed appreciatively, I realized with a wave of satisfaction that I had my perfect gift. All I had to do was figure out how to give it to him. I knew he lived in the Hollywood Hills, but his multimillion-dollar estate was tucked away behind wrought-iron gates and I couldn't exactly leave a cheesecake out in the street. Not only could it melt in the sun or be eaten by a coyote, but it was crucial for me to be present when he received it. He was supposed to see the cake, see me, put two and two together, and think, Wow, what a nice person to go to all this trouble for me and I'd be glad to return the favor by sitting down for an interview with her. How to make this happen? How?

I went to the office the next morning and called Peggy Merchant.

"It's about Pierce Brosnan," I lied to her assistant.

This time, Peggy came right on the line. When she thought you were pitching what she was selling, it was uncanny how accessible she was. "So you'd like to talk about interviewing Pierce?" she said cheerfully.

"Someday," I said. "But I'm calling about Malcolm, and please don't hang up."

There was a pained sigh. "In case I wasn't clear, Ann, Malcolm thinks the media—especially the print media—distorts the truth and takes what he says out of context and is all about invading his space. You may think he's being difficult or demanding or reclusive, but he just refuses to subject himself to all the scrutiny, except on those rare occasions when he respects and trusts the interviewer."

"Then I want him to respect and trust me," I said. "After we talked about gifting yesterday, I decided it couldn't hurt to buy him a little trinket. Just to make myself stand out from all the others and to show him my interest is sincere. You told me that gifting scores points with your clients, remember?"

Another sigh. "Yes, but I doubt it'll help in Malcolm's case, because he's so adamant."

"Why don't you let me try? What's the harm?"

She considered this for a second or two, then said, "Fine. Go ahead. Just don't count on anything."

"Yes. Okay," I said with new hope. "Now, tell me how I can deliver my gift. I'm sure you can set something up, right?"

"Have it sent here and I'll see that he gets it."

"No way, Peggy," I said, determined to stand my ground. I was making progress, I could feel it. "I need to deliver the gift myself, so that Malcolm and I can meet face-to-face. That's the whole idea. You said he does interviews with people he respects and trusts. He won't respect and trust a complete stranger."

"Look, Ann. He isn't going to meet with you and that's that," she snapped. "Have a lovely day."

She slammed down the phone. I marveled at her high-and-mighty attitude and felt utterly thwarted by her unwillingness to cooperate. Then I reminded myself that I was supposed to be a killer journalist now. Killer journalists didn't go through the proper channels. Killer journalists did whatever it took to get the story.

SINCE THE GOLDEN Globe Awards were being handed out that Sunday evening, out-of-town actors, producers, and directors of nominated films, including those who were foreign and, therefore, obscure to most Americans, had descended on Hollywood. German director Wilhelm Holtz, for example, was turning up everywhere. He was a favorite of young American actors, who admired his dark, brooding style (nobody so much as cracked a smile in a Wilhelm Holtz movie). One of those actors was Malcolm Goddard, who, in the *Vanity Fair* piece, had proclaimed himself Holtz's biggest fan. Was it possible that he and his idol would be getting together over the course of Globes weekend? For dinner at some trendy restaurant, perhaps? Could Goddard be hosting a dinner in Holtz's honor, and if so, where might it be? And when?

I decided to go digging. I bypassed the publicists and headed straight for the people who really knew what was happening in Hollywood: the maître d's at the hot spots. They were the ones with access to the reservation books. They gave the impression that they were secretive about their clientele so the celebrities would think they were being coddled, but they loved boasting about which star was sitting in which booth eating which specialty of the house. And they weren't above pocketing a wad of cash in exchange for the information. The paparazzi relied on them, and now I was relying on them too. Harvey had instructed me to stay within my budget, but that wouldn't be a problem. The cheesecake was less than fifty dollars, plus shipping. I had plenty more to spend.

I drove all over town, my wallet bulging. I hit the Sunset Strip and combed the "in" spots there. I hit Santa Monica and talked to everybody on my list there. I wasn't even going to bother with Beverly Hills, given how Goddard was so damn arty and Beverly Hills was so old farty, but on a hunch having to do with Wolfgang Puck being Austrian and Wilhelm Holtz being German, I hit Spago—and hit paydirt.

What I learned was that Malcolm Goddard was, indeed, hosting a party of six in the garden patio of the famed restaurant, although the reservation, I was told, was in the name of Luke Sykes in order to throw parasites like me off the scent. The dinner was set for Friday night at eight-thirty. Since it was only Wednesday, that left me just enough time to order the cheesecake from Zabar's and have it FedExed right to Spago, where, after Goddard's main course was cleared away, my dessert would be carted out with great fanfare and delivered to his table. From my own table a few feet away, I would be able to witness the surprise and delight on his face, and then I would make my move. I was very optimistic about this plan, mostly because it was the only one I had but also because it had come about as a result of my dogged detective work. I *was* a good reporter and Goddard would respect and trust me, even if I did have to grease the palm of every restaurant employee in town.

LATER THAT NIGHT I went to Bristol Farms, the upscale supermarket not far from my apartment. All the running around had made me hungry and I had nothing but an old jar of Dijon mustard in the refrigerator. I needed to stock up.

I wasn't alone. L.A. is a city filled with busy professionals and seven o'clock at night is prime after-work food-shopping time. The aisles at Bristol Farms were jammed. Carts were colliding. Gridlock reigned, particularly in the paper-goods aisle, where I'd gone after buying all the edible stuff. They say never to shop for groceries on an empty stomach because you end up buying more than you expected, but I was much too preoccupied with being a killer journalist to worry about that.

I steered my overflowing cart through the throngs of customers, past the tissues and the napkins and the toilet paper, and reached for a roll of Bounty. I was just about to grab it when the weirdest thing happened: My throat started closing up and the room started spinning. Not spinning as in after drinking too many margaritas, but definitely moving with the herky-jerkiness of a movie shot with a handheld camera. Feeling slightly faint, I gripped the handle of my cart to steady myself and waited helplessly for the wave of dizziness to pass.

It did pass after only a few seconds, but it left me wondering what the hell was the matter with me. Was I dying of cancer like my father did and was this an early warning sign? Or was I just hungry? Hunger made people light-headed, didn't it?

I didn't know what to think at first, but as I waited in the long line at the checkout counter, I reminded myself that I probably didn't have cancer—I was a bit of a hypochondriac. Okay, more than a "bit" of one. I subscribed to *Women's Health, Prevention,* and *Psychology Today,* and when they described a disease, I immediately convinced myself I had it—and that what I needed was to eat a decent meal and get a good night's sleep.

I HAD INVITED Tuscany to be my date for the big night—I thought I'd look too predatory and obvious if I sat three feet away from Goddard at a table by myself—and she was excited about tagging along. I was excited about the evening too. I even took extra care with my appearance, and attempted to look a little more glamorous than usual.

Glamorous. Ha. I was what is commonly referred to as "fresh faced." I had dark blond hair (shockingly, it was natural) that I wore shoulder length and parted down the middle in no particular style other than that it always looked clean. My features were even and well proportioned. My height and weight were average—perfectly healthy by Missouri's standards but borderline fat by L.A.'s. I didn't wear tops that exposed my midriff or bottoms that exposed my crack, but rather, dressed conservatively, if casually. I wasn't a tomboy exactly, but I was more comfortable in blue jeans than in ball gowns. When I covered industry events in fancy clothes, I always felt like a drag queen.

On that Friday night, as I regarded my reflection in the bathroom mirror, I groaned. James had given me makeup tips, and I'd tried to follow them. The result was that I had over-painted my lips and over-shadowed my eyelids and over-bronzed my cheekbones, chin, and forehead. I looked hideous and slathered the whole mess with cold cream and started over.

By the time I left my apartment, I was feeling better about myself. My charcoal gray pantsuit was businesslike but appropriate for an evening at Spago, as were the little diamond studs I'd stuck in my earlobes, and my makeup no longer looked like it had been applied by a cement mixer. I was good to go.

Tuscany, on the other hand, was dressed for Halloween.

"What's wrong with it?" she asked after she'd picked me up in the Mercedes.

"Nothing, if you're in your Goth period," I teased, appraising her raccoon eyes and black cape, the hood of which was draped over her head. "Or are you making a statement about the plight of women in certain Arab countries?"

She smiled mischievously. "It's possible that I could meet someone tonight," she said as she drove us to Beverly Hills. "I wanted to look dramatic, just in case."

"Well, you've achieved your goal," I said. "But tonight isn't about you. I'm the one who's supposed to make a conquest."

"He's gonna love that cheesecake," she reassured me.

"He should," I said. "I read a description of its ingredients on Zabar's Web site and it's as dense as he must be."

About ten minutes later, we pulled onto Canon Drive, where Spago has been serving upscale diners since its relocation from the Sunset Strip back in the nineties. There were three valet-parking attendants rushing around in front of the restaurant, but none of them rushed around to help us.

"It's not as if this car is a beater," said Tuscany of the Mercedes, which was only three years old.

"They ignore you if you're not in a Hummer limo," I said.

Eventually, one of the valets did come and take the car. We walked to the entrance of the restaurant and stood at the threshold. While Tuscany peeked inside, I checked my watch.

"Eight-thirty," I said. "You ready?"

"Very," she said with wide eyes. "Every man in this place looks like Johnny Depp and I'm taking one of them home."

"Tuscany," I said sternly. "We have a No Actors rule."

"Right."

I poked my head inside the restaurant. It was crowded, at maximum capacity, everybody laughing and talking animatedly. For some reason their voices started coming at me at an exaggerated, extremely loud volume, and I began to feel twinges of the same dizziness I'd felt at Bristol Farms. Again, I wondered what in the world was going on. Was it cancer? A heart problem? An acute infectious disease for which there was not yet a vaccine?

I took a few long, deep breaths and tried to focus on the matter at hand—at how relieved I'd be once the Goddard interview was in my pocket and Harvey was off my back.

"Hey, are you okay?" asked my friend as she held my arm. "You're kind of swaying."

"I'm great." I smiled, thinking of the cheesecake that was chilling in Spago's refrigerator right that very minute: Malcolm Goddard's fantasy dessert come true. I bet even Diane Sawyer hadn't thought of it. There was really nothing to all this do-whatever-it-takes-to-land-an-interview stuff, I decided. It was a piece of cake, no pun intended.

Chapter Four

||||||||||||||||||||||||||||||||||||||||||||||||||||||||||||||||||||||||||||||||||||||||

After I had a brief word with Henry, the maître d', confirming our little plan, Tuscany and I were shown to our table for two on the patio, a beautiful garden setting where a fountain trickled next to a pair of century-old olive trees. There was a reason celebrities loved to dine there. The atmosphere was charming, an oasis of calm in the middle of the city.

"Oh my God." Tuscany grabbed my arm across the table once we were seated. "He's even hotter than I thought."

She wasn't talking about Henry, who had a beaky nose and a recessive chin. No, she was swooning over Goddard. I'd seen him too, out of the corner of my eye as we had stepped onto the patio, and he was hard not to notice. He was holding court at a banquet-size table a few feet away. Wearing his customary black leather jacket and jeans, that curly lock of brown hair falling into his eyes, he was toasting Wilhelm Holtz and four other men and then throwing back a shot of whiskey. Even during what was clearly a festive occasion, he looked dour.

"How are we supposed to eat with him sitting right there?" said Tuscany. "I've lost my appetite already." She was employed by a magazine devoted to covering celebrities, and yet she was forever in awe of them. When I'd first come to L.A., I'd been in awe of them too, but I wasn't quite as reverent as I used to be. I was still keenly interested in them as a species, I enjoyed the challenge of getting them to discuss subjects they'd never discussed in public before, and I really did try to bring out the best in them, even the ones who took themselves much too seriously. But Malcolm Goddard? He seemed to take himself more seriously than most, and I was less sure about my ability to bring out the best in him.

"I thought he was dating Rebecca Truit," Tuscany mused, craning her neck to get a good look, "but she's not with him."

"It must be boys' night out," I said. Rumor had it that he and Rebecca were an item, possibly engaged. I intended to ask him about their relationship once I had my shot at him. "Now, revive your appetite and let's order. Harvey's paying, so pick something expensive."

After we each had a glass of Spago's best pinot noir, we focused on the main course. Tuscany went off her diet of yogurt and pine nuts and ordered the beef stew with spaetzle, while I chose the Wiener schnitzel. When the food arrived, neither of us could do more than pick at it. Try as we did to indulge ourselves, we were too distracted by what was going on at Goddard's table—Tuscany, because she decided her trophy for the night would be Wilhelm Holtz, who had slicked-back golden hair and rosy cheeks and looked like much more fun than the movies he directed; me, because I couldn't help glancing over to see how their meal was progressing, which was extraordinarily slowly. They seemed to be drinking more than they were eating, and I was getting antsy. I wanted to hit my target and win the prize and put Harvey's doubts about me to rest once and for all.

Eventually, our waiter ambled by. "Finished?" he asked, although our plates were full of spaetzle and schnitzel.

"No, we're still working on them," I said. And we'll continue to work on them until Goddard and his guests are no longer working on theirs, I thought.

As the hours crawled by, we played with our food, moved it around the plates, built little Prussian castles with it, but mostly let it sit there until it was hard and dry and very unappealing. I was beginning to think the night would never end when I saw the busboys finally clearing Goddard's table.

"This is it," I whispered excitedly to Tuscany. "Let the games begin."

Henry, the maître d', caught my eye and gave me a conspiratorial nod. We were on track. All systems were operational. Over at Goddard's table, it appeared that everybody was being served after-dinner drinks. Yes, it was dessert time.

I gulped down some water and sat there clutching and unclutching my napkin, nearly bursting with anticipation while trying to look nonchalant.

"Here it comes!" squealed Tuscany, who didn't understand the concept of nonchalance.

Sure enough, Henry reappeared, carrying the cheesecake on a large platter that had been garnished with a cascade of fresh flowers. He was beaming proudly, as if he were holding a baby.

He strode past our table, winked surreptitiously, then continued to his destination. When he placed the cake carefully down in front of its recipient, he announced, loud enough for the whole restaurant to hear, "A gift for you, sir. From Zabar's in New York."

Goddard looked totally taken aback. I leaned toward him and strained to pick up his response. "A Zabar's cheesecake?" he said as if it couldn't possibly be true.

"Yes, sir," Henry confirmed.

I sat up straighter in my chair and practiced different smiles. I had to be ready. I intended to project just the right balance of friendliness and professionalism. Oh, and modesty, as if I made benevolent gestures all the time but was a very humble person.

Goddard's own smile reflected the delight of a kid at Christmas. Gone was the morose expression. Suddenly, he was transformed. *I* had transformed him. It dawned on me that if making grumpy people like him happy was a by-product of being a killer journalist, maybe I wouldn't mind being one. "I love their cheesecake," he said in an adoring tone, not unlike the one he'd used in their recent movie when he told Jennifer Connelly he loved her. "I mean, this is incredible. You have no idea, Henry." I really had come up with the perfect gift, if I did say so myself. "If I were alone, I'd inhale the whole thing, but I guess I have to share it with my friends here." Everybody at the table chuckled and said what I assumed were hilarious German things. "How did Wolfgang even know that I—"

"The cake is not a gift from Mr. Puck, sir," said Henry. "It's from the lovely lady sitting over there."

All heads turned in my direction when Henry pointed at me. I quickly chose from among the smiles I'd been rehearsing and trotted one out for Goddard. He sort of stared at me for several seconds, as if he couldn't figure out what was going on.

"Apparently you told a television audience that the cake was your passion," Henry explained to him. "She knew you would be here tonight— she read about it in a gossip column, I guess—and, as an avid fan of your movies, thought it would make a great little surprise. Very generous of her, isn't it?"

God, Henry was good. But then I'd paid him handsomely. Well, *Famous* had.

Goddard nodded and waved at me. Then he said something to Henry, who scurried over to our table. "Mr. Goddard would like to invite you both to join him and his guests, so he can thank you properly," he reported with obvious satisfaction. "I'll have the busboys pull up two more chairs."

"Excellent job," I told him out of the side of my mouth.

After he raced off, I turned to Tuscany, who had removed her black cape only to reveal a pink slip dress that was slipping right off her shoulders, soon to be a wardrobe malfunction. "Listen, no flirting," I said. "This is business, okay?"

"You got it," she said, nevertheless reaching into her purse for a tiny bottle of vanilla and dabbing some behind her ears.

I gathered myself up and marched over to Goddard's table, Tuscany in tow. He was standing to greet me, extending his hand, welcoming me into his domain instead of shooing me away.

"Malcolm Goddard," he said in his trademark mumble as he pumped my hand. "Your name?"

My name. It wasn't a trick question and yet, without any warning whatsoever, my brain froze.

You know how I just told you that I was no longer awestruck when it came to meeting movie stars? Well, for some reason I was momentarily tongue-tied in the presence of this particular one. No kidding. Instead of introducing myself to Malcolm Goddard, I stood there gawking at him. Tuscany was right. He *was* better looking up close. Taller, maybe. Broader. And definitely more vivid in living color. Those turquoise eyes were freakishly beautiful, and it was impossible not to be awed by them. Still, let me repeat: This sort of thing hadn't happened to me in years.

"Your name?" he said, prompting me.

Tuscany gave me an elbow in the back.

"Oh," I said. "It's Ann. Ann Roth." I giggled idiotically. "Like Ross, only with a lisp."

Another shove from behind.

"And this is my friend Tuscany Davis."

"I love you," she said to him.

"I love you too," he said with a laugh. "Both of you. Now, join us. Please."

We sat down at his table—me to his right, Tuscany to Wilhelm's right because he was the one she'd been psyching herself up to snare—and he introduced us to the others. Then he refocused on the cheesecake and cocked his head at it in amazement.

"This is the sweetest thing a fan's ever done for me," he said, grinning, although the grin was slightly off-kilter. He'd had many, many cocktails, I realized. Now that I was within inches of him, I could smell the intensity of the alcohol on his breath. "You're terrific, Ann Ross with a lisp."

I giggled again, out of apprehension this time. A fan. Hardly.

"You're terrific," he repeated, as if he hadn't said it a nanosecond ago, the way people do when they have no clue that they're drunk.

"Well, you did rave to James Lipton about how much you love that cake," I said. "I thought it would be a great way to show you how much I admire your work."

"A better-than-great way," he said, slurring. "A super-super-super-fine way."

"Thanks," I said, wondering if I should order him some very strong coffee.

"How about I cut everybody a piece?" he suggested. "Like, before I eat it myself."

"Sure, unless you'd rather take it home and save it for another time," I said. "Zabar's told me it keeps well."

"I'm on a diet, so none for me," Tuscany volunteered, pulling her chair closer to Wilhelm, who fingered the strap of her dress and called her *Liebling*. She was moving quickly, even for her.

"Then there'll be more for the rest of us," Goddard said. He instructed the waiter to bring a knife and seven plates and forks. While we waited, he asked me to tell him which of his films I liked the best. Since I was such a fan.

"I guess I'd have to say *The Whistle Blower*," I replied, referring to the movie in which he'd played a corporate snitch who was kidnapped by the CEO's evildoers and held prisoner in a filthy Arizona shack, only to escape, testify before Congress, and die of West Nile virus. Malcolm

Goddard died in a lot of his movies, and his character was always brave and strong in those instances, never whimpering or whining or moaning in pain. I had a feeling that in real life, he was the type who moaned over a paper cut.

"*The Whistle Blower* is your favorite, huh?" He nodded, then blinked rapidly, as if summoning up the memory of the film. "We shot it in Romania in winter and I froze my ass off. And the food just sucked there."

"How interesting," I said. I would have my work cut out for me once I got him to sit down for the interview. I'd need more than his impression of Romanian cuisine to produce an in-depth piece.

"What's your second favorite of my movies?" he asked, soaking up the attention from his number one fan. I couldn't let this charade go on, but I didn't know exactly how to stop it.

"I liked all of them," I said. "In fact, I was hoping we could talk about them in more detail. At your convenience, of course."

He patted my shoulder. "I'd love that, babe, but I've got a tight schedule these days. If you go on my official Web site and click on the FAQs, you'll get my take on every film I've ever made."

"I'll do that," I said, "but I'd still appreciate it if we could have a substantive talk."

He leaned back in his chair, his arm dangling over the side. "We're talking now, aren't we? Substantiously?"

Yes, he was drunk, but he also wasn't getting it and why should he? I needed to be straight with him. No more stalling.

I took a deep breath, reached into my purse for my business card, and handed it to him with an air of pride, just as I always did when I was representing the magazine. "I write for *Famous* and I'd love an interview, Malcolm."

Okay, I knew he wouldn't be thrilled by this news, but I honestly thought the gift would have softened him up.

Not a chance. He took the card and stared at it, then he stared at me, then back at the card, then back at me. With each stare, his smile faded, until his lips formed a thin, tight line. He seemed too angry to speak.

"I should have figured," he growled finally. So much for the delight. In its place was disgust. He flipped the card into the air as if it were a Frisbee, and it landed in Wilhelm's water glass, where it floated and eventually sank. "You people just won't leave me alone, will you?"

"Please don't lump me in with other writers," I said, wanting to appease him and maintain my dignity at the same time. "I'm good at what I do. I'm not into gratuitous hatchet jobs. I don't cut and paste from other sources. I—"

"What you do is worm your way into restaurants," he said, glowering at me.

"Spago is a public place," I reminded him.

"My table is not public." He pounded it with his fist just in case I didn't catch his drift. The dishes and cutlery jumped. "You pretended you were a fan giving me a present, which is the only reason I invited you to sit here."

"I am a fan, but I'm also a journalist," I said, my knees beginning to knock in a very un-killerlike way. "And the cake was my attempt to show you that the readers of *Famous* would like very much to learn more about you. All I'm asking is that you let me tell them your story."

"You want to tell them my story, huh?" His blue eyes flashed with fury. "Well, here it is: I don't like your kind of *journalism* and I don't mind showing it."

What came next felt as if it were happening in slow motion, the way train wrecks do. Before any of us could possibly anticipate his next action, Malcolm Goddard rose from his chair, lifted up the entire cheesecake with his bare hands, and smashed it down on the table, a toddler having a tantrum. People nearby took a furtive look to see what all the commotion was about, then turned away with a shrug, figuring it was just another movie star misbehaving.

As for me, I wasn't joking earlier when I said the cake was dense. It was like a brick, sort of bouncing up after it hit the table and then breaking into pieces that flew everywhere. A very large chunk nailed me in and around my left eye. No one was spared—Wilhelm, for one, had bits of graham-cracker crust splattered across his face—but I bore the brunt of the dessert. Or should I say my charcoal gray pantsuit did—the one I'd had dry-cleaned and pressed especially for the evening. I stood up from the table and a cascade of crumbs fell to the floor, as if I were some gross pig with a coordination problem who couldn't manage to navigate my food directly into my mouth.

"Are you okay?" asked Tuscany as she came rushing over. She'd emerged relatively unscathed with only a small piece of cake dangling from her right breast. Wilhelm couldn't take his eyes off it.

Too upset to speak, I just nodded. I had never cried on the job, not even during one of Harvey's meltdowns, and I wasn't about to start now. No way. But it took all the effort I could muster to put the brakes on the tears. I'd never felt so humiliated, never felt so utterly out of control.

"Ann?" said Tuscany with growing concern. "You're doing that swaying thing again."

At that very moment the garden was, indeed, spinning, just as the paper-goods aisle at Bristol Farms had spun a few nights before, just as the entrance to Spago had spun earlier in the evening. And this time my heart began to pound and my legs turned to rubber and I became extremely short of breath. Oh, and sweat started to pour down my armpits and dampen the nape of my neck. Attractive, huh? Yep, I was a mess, literally and figuratively.

Dear God, what on earth is going on with me? I wondered as I grabbed the back of my chair to steady myself. My body was falling apart and I had no idea why or how to fix it. Sure, I was pissed off that Goddard had gone ballistic over the cake, but why the physical symptoms?

And then I knew. I recognized them.

It was anxiety that was overwhelming me, not an infectious disease. I'd experienced the feeling before, whenever I had to fly. The dizziness, the rubbery legs, the palpitations—they all showed up when I was at thirty-five thousand feet. But I wasn't aboard a 767 that night at the restaurant. I was on terra firma, surrounded by people who must have been just as baffled by my swoon as I was. Why was I coming apart there, of all places?

"Hey, I didn't mean for you or anyone else to get hurt," said Goddard, who seemed, if not apologetic, more subdued once he saw how wobbly I was. He actually reached out to touch my arm and then thought better of it. "I was just trying to make a point, um, uh—"

"It's *Ann*," I said, praying that the swaying, spinning, and sweating would cease and desist. I didn't need him seeing me in this condition. I wasn't some weakling. I was a killer journalist. I had to pull myself together and take charge of the situation.

Summoning all the strength I had, I picked up a napkin from the table and wiped my eye with it. The area was tender, and I had a hunch it would be black and blue the next morning. A cheesecake shiner. But at least the dizziness and palpitations were letting up, and I was immensely grateful for that.

"As I said, I was just trying to make a point," said Goddard in a more combative tone now that it was apparent that I wasn't going to pass out.

"And you made the point loud and clear, Malcolm," I said, my voice beginning to come back, along with my nerve. I had never mouthed off to a celebrity, but I was about to break my record. "You hate the media. We all know that. But here's a bulletin for you." I held my head higher, even though it was matted down with cream cheese. "The media hates you too. Precisely because of incidents like this. You're rude and boorish, and you should have thanked me for the cake instead of thrown it at me."

I was amazed by my outburst, which was so uncharacteristic for me. No, I hadn't viciously cursed him out—I was from the Midwest, remember—but as I said, I'd always been so careful not to offend or provoke a star, particularly a star I was supposed to court. There was something about Goddard that brought out the fighter in me, and I had a powerful desire to set him straight. He'd asked for it with his ungentlemanly actions. Besides, there was no reason to hold back. Once I told Harvey what Goddard had done, my boss would be incensed on my behalf, praise me for at least trying to get the interview, and then reassign me to some other celebrity. So why shouldn't I let this guy have it?

"Is that right?" he said with a derisive laugh, as if no one had ever had the audacity to call him on his bad behavior. "Well, first of all I didn't throw it *at* you. I'm sorry if you got some on you, but—"

"Sorry?" I said. "I could have you arrested."

He smirked. "For what? Assault with a deadly dessert?"

I looked at Tuscany for moral support, but she was trying to rub out the stain on her tit.

"Your problem, Malcolm, is that you don't know how to treat people," I said, my voice surprisingly cool considering the level of my emotion and the fact that my legs were still mush. "You surround yourself with the Peggy Merchants of the world and all they do is yes you to death, like a scene out of *The Emperor's New Clothes*. They're afraid to tell you that the things you do are unacceptable."

Another smirk. "But you're not afraid to tell me?"

"Obviously not. You may be Hollywood's hottest leading man, but you need to learn some manners." We were standing nose to nose now. I could see every pore on his face. And sure, I was afraid. But I wasn't backing down. I'd had enough of his crap.

"So let's see," he said, narrowing his blue eyes at me. "If I'm such a monster, what does that make you for sucking up to me? A parasite maybe?"

"Oh, please."

"Please what? You are." He downed the rest of the booze in his glass

41

and then threw his hands up, as if he were the one who'd been victimized. "Look, I didn't ask for this tonight. I was sitting here having a nice time with my friends. You're the one who intruded. You're the one who misrepresented herself. You're the one who wanted something from me— who tried to *buy* her way into my good graces—so don't you go making me the bad guy, babe."

I was all set to respond with a snappy, stinging retort, but I was stumped for one. His words had shut me down, because it occurred to me unexpectedly and with a horrible wave of self-loathing that they might be true. If he *was* such a monster, why *had* I gone there to suck up to him?

I continued to sort of stand there speechless as I let what he said sink in. I mean, the guy wasn't wrong. There *was* a predatory aspect to what I'd done, and for a split second I admired him for his own brand of integrity. But I had only been doing my job, the job my boss had commanded me to do. I was being a good soldier, following orders, working hard to earn a living. That wasn't wrong either, was it?

"Fine. I did want something from you," I admitted. "And I did try to buy my way into your good graces, not that you have any. I'm not proud of that, but your reaction was— Well, it was exactly what I should have expected. You really lived up to your reputation tonight, Malcolm. Great performance."

"And you lived up to the reputation of the media," he countered. "Always trying to steal my privacy. You should be ashamed of yourself."

"Not as ashamed as you should be. You just wasted a perfectly delicious cheesecake."

He glanced down at the cake, which looked as if it had exploded.

"I didn't waste it at all," he said as he sat back down and began to scoop up what was left of the cake with his fingers and eat it, caveman style, right off the table. He was an actor, all right, hogging the spotlight. "Hmm. It's the best. Want some?" He glanced up at me as he licked his index finger.

"I'd rather starve."

I turned to the Germans and fake-smiled. "Nice to meet you all." Then I stormed out of the garden, assuming Tuscany would follow on my heels. Instead, I waited outside the restaurant for ten minutes before she finally appeared.

"I was about to call a cab," I said impatiently. "Was making plans with Wilhelm Holtz really that important?"

"I wasn't making plans with him," she said. "I was telling him to fuck off for being Goddard's friend. He doesn't understand much English, so it took a while."

I smiled, and the movement of my cheek muscles made me wince. I could feel my eye starting to swell.

"Let's get you home," she said. "I'll put ice on it. By tomorrow, you won't feel a thing."

Chapter Five

||||||||||||||||||||||||||||||||||||||||||||||||||||||||||||||||||||||||||||||||||||||||||

But I did feel a thing on Saturday morning. More than one thing.

I felt ridiculous that I had an actual reddish-purple welt under my eye—the price I paid for being "fresh faced." My skin was fair and easily irritated, but why did it have to blow up from contact with something as benign as a chunk of cheesecake?

I felt enraged that Malcolm Goddard had pitched a fit instead of granting me the interview. Sure, he was drunk, but did that excuse conduct that could only be described as over the top?

But mostly, I felt a nagging, debilitating awareness that he had nailed me on the parasite thing. I *had* intruded on his dinner out with his friends. I *had* misrepresented myself by posing as a devoted fan. I *had* tried to worm my way into his good graces. But wasn't that exactly what Harvey wanted me to do? Expected me to do? Directed me to do in order to be a killer and keep my job? Of course it was. Still, the label ate away at me. A parasite wasn't the image I'd ever attributed to myself, not in the entire five years I'd been at *Famous*. I'd viewed myself as a good person and a good journalist, bringing news of the stars to their adoring public. No harm, no foul. In my eyes, it was the Malcolm Goddards of Hollywood who were the villains. Who asked them to punch out a photographer or tell an interviewer to shove it? Who held a gun to their heads and forced them to become celebrities? Why couldn't they be gracious when they were sought after by the media? Why did they have to get all belligerent and uppity and downright reclusive when all we wanted was a story in their own words? And yet, I couldn't ignore the accusation that had been leveled at me. It kicked up a sudden ambivalence toward my job, a discomfiting new uncertainty. I'd been uncertain about how to cope with a dying father as well as a mother, aunt, and grandmother who saw every event as a potential catastrophe, but I'd never been uncertain about my career.

Oh, and I felt exhausted, totally wiped out. James had been up to his old tricks the night before, blasting Donna Summer's "Hot Stuff" at 1 A.M. Instead of defaulting to my broom-handle-on-the-ceiling measure, I'd put on a robe and traipsed upstairs to threaten to rat him out to the landlord if he didn't turn down the volume. He took one look at me and my pathetic eye, said, "How on earth did we get that boo-boo?" and I caved. For the next hour, we sat on his couch, trading swigs from his bottle of Baileys Irish Cream while I told him the whole sob story. Donna was wailing, "She works hard for the money," at one point, and it seemed like the perfect soundtrack.

"Was it so awful of me to try to get Goddard to agree to an interview?" I asked glumly.

James, a slightly built forty-something who'd had the fat sucked out of his butt and injected into the lines around his mouth, shook his head, which had recently been implanted with hair plugs. "Absolutely not and don't let one jerk's opinion throw you. People want to read about the guy."

"I know, but you should have seen his face when I showed him my card," I said. "I swear, James, you would have thought I wrote for *Hustler*."

"Celebrity magazines like *Famous* don't cure cancer, but they do serve a purpose," he insisted. "When I'm reading about Lindsay Lohan's life, it makes me forget that I don't have one of my own."

"You do so have one," I said, thinking of all the years he'd been on staff at *The Bold and the Beautiful*.

"Really? Then why was I home dancing by myself on a Saturday night?"

"Same reason I was home sleeping by myself," I said. "Both of us are going through a phase during which we aren't seeing anybody, that's all."

He laughed. "Your phase has lasted over a year. And mine—" He rolled his eyes. He'd had them done too: the upper lids tightened and the lowers de-bagged. The surgery made him look vaguely Asian. "Reading about celebrities is a diversion. They wear great clothes and travel to exotic places and have sex with other celebrities. What's not to love?"

I exhaled a plaintive sigh. "All I know is that when I started in this business, it was fun for me. What happened last night wasn't fun at all."

He patted my knee. "Aside from the clothes and the travel and the sex, celebrities are just people, Annie."

ON MONDAY MORNING, I listened in astonishment as Harvey, pacing around his office like a tightly coiled tiger, ordered me not to back down from my mission, but rather to redouble my efforts. While he wasn't entirely unsympathetic about my eye and all the rest, he insisted that Goddard's outright hatred of the media made him an even bigger get.

"Think about it. Sales will go through the roof if we're the ones who land him," he said.

I couldn't believe it. I was sure he'd hear what had happened and then let me move on to somebody else. But no. Goddard's attitude was a turn-on to him, and I shouldn't have been surprised. It was as if the more the celebrity he coveted rejected him, the more he coveted the celebrity. And the theme carried over into his personal life. His wife had rejected him twice—she'd divorced him both times—but he'd chased after her like a lovesick pit bull and they were currently on their third marriage, to each other.

"Harvey, he's not going to do an interview with *Famous* or anybody else. He made that very clear. It's over."

"It isn't over until I say it's over!" His arms shot out. The left one belted the hand-hammered singing bowl that his kundalini yoga teacher had given him. *"Now is not the time to give up! So he trashed your cake! If you're a killer reporter, you dust yourself off and try again!"*

"But he's not likable," I said gently, the way you do with a deranged person. "I honestly think he might make statements in the interview that will repel the readers we're trying to attract."

"Oh, really?" he said, eyebrows arched. "Do you think Scott Peterson is likable? The guy murdered his wife and unborn child. But that didn't stop Diane Sawyer from interviewing him, and you know why? Because he was a big get."

Diane Sawyer again. I wondered if she'd sent Scott Peterson a gift and, if so, whether it was something he was allowed to take with him to death row.

"Honestly, Harvey, I don't see how I'm supposed to make this work after what—"

"Figure it out!" he thundered. *"Or I'll find someone who will!"*

End of meeting.

I walked back to my office feeling as if I'd been run over by a bus. I plopped down at my desk and sat there for several minutes, just staring at the ceiling and wondering how I could possibly make Malcolm Goddard change his mind. Killers weren't quitters. That much I knew.

I looked around my office, searching for answers, and my gaze rested on the framed covers that hung on the wall. There was the story I did on

Angelina Jolie in which she clarified that she did love her brother but wasn't "in love" with him. There was the story I did on Ben Affleck in which he revealed that he hired a Hollywood witch to remove the curse from the Boston Red Sox. There was the story I did on Kelsey Grammer in which he discussed openly and for the first time the agony of having to decide which of his four residences would get the Christmas tree each year. Yes, it's true that these candid offerings weren't earth-shattering in their importance. But for every goofball I'd talked to, there were the smart, articulate ones who spoke of their commitment to their family, of their battle with a serious illness, of their real feelings about being in an industry that values youth and beauty over all else. The point is, I'd had easy access to celebrities of all types until I'd hit the roadblock with Goddard. I'd be damned if I'd let him cost me my job.

"Okay," I said out loud with renewed determination. "Harvey wants a killer? I'm a killer."

I grabbed the phone with the aggressiveness of an athlete on steroids and dialed Peggy Merchant's number.

"It's Ann Roth," I told her assistant. "I'm calling about Malcolm Goddard. *Famous* is breaking the story that he's checking himself into an anger-management facility in Santa Barbara."

The assistant didn't even ask me to hold. Within a heartbeat, Peggy was on the line.

"Malcolm's not going to any facility in Santa Barbara. What the hell are you talking about?" she demanded.

"Maybe not right away," I said coyly. As far as I knew, there *was* no anger-management facility in Santa Barbara. "But it's only a matter of time before he does. In case you haven't heard about the stunt he pulled—"

"I heard," she snapped.

"Good," I said. "Now hear this. If you don't set up the interview I've been asking for, I'm running my own story about him. It'll be very juicy,

Peggy, I promise you. I'll write that he got drunk at Spago and threw a cake that found its way onto the face of Golden Globe–nominated director Wilhelm Holtz. I'll write that he verbally abused his dinner guests. And I'll write that the cake throwing was only his latest tirade and that Paramount—aren't they the ones who are paying him twenty million dollars to star in that action movie based on that video game based on that comic strip based on that children's book?—is rumored to have ordered him into anger-management rehab."

"But . . . but . . . that's patently false," she sputtered.

"Only the last little part about Paramount is," I said. "The rest is true. I was there. I witnessed it and so did everybody else at the restaurant."

Silence.

"I don't have to tell you how the press works these days," I continued. "As long as we print what's *mostly* true, we're in the clear. Our readers believe us and our subjects don't sue us, and it's all good. For us, anyway." I paused to let my words sink in. "Peggy? You still there, *dear?*"

After a few beats she said, in a much more conciliatory tone, "Okay, I'm very sorry about the incident at Spago. But don't write about it, Ann."

"Why shouldn't I?"

"Because it would be unfair. Malcolm was just having a bad day."

"Really?" I scoffed. "Does he have any other kind?"

"Sure he does," she said unconvincingly. "I admit he goes overboard when he feels cornered by the media—by anyone he thinks is trying to take advantage of him—but he's a sweetheart, deep down. Don't smear him. I'm begging you."

She was begging me. So the dirty tactics Harvey advocated really worked. And what a pleasure to have her over a barrel for a change.

"Just look the other way, won't you?" she pleaded. "As a personal favor to an old friend?"

I laughed. I couldn't help it. Now she was my friend? She was such a phony and so good at playing the game. But I was better. I had it in me to be better, and now I was about to get exactly what I wanted. "Set up the interview and I won't have to smear anybody," I said. "Malcolm can tell his own story. To *Famous*. Exclusively."

"All right, all right," she said. "I guess he owes you one after what he put you through."

"You guess?" Yes, I was starting to enjoy this.

"I meant that I can certainly see your point, and Malcolm will too," she said. "I'll talk to him as soon as we finish up."

"So I'll be hearing from you about a time and place for the interview? Within the hour?"

"I'll do my best."

"Not good enough."

"Fine. You'll hear from me within the hour."

"Great. Oh, and Peggy?"

"Yes?"

"Have a lovely day."

I hung up and pumped my fists in the air. And then I ran down the hall to the art department and recounted the entire phone conversation to Tuscany, who was sitting at her computer, Photoshopping the nose hair out of Michael Caine's nostrils.

"You did it!" she said, jumping up and hugging me. "You totally proved Harvey wrong."

"I know," I said. "Now maybe he'll give me that raise I've been hoping for."

"You bet he will," she said.

TWENTY MINUTES LATER, Peggy called back. I held my breath as I waited for her to determine my fate. My hands were clammy and my mouth was dry. For all my tough talk, I felt a sense of dread. If Goddard said no, I was done at *Famous*. If he said yes, I'd actually have to sit in a room and converse civilly with the guy.

"I've spoken to Malcolm and he agreed to do the interview," she said, rather subdued. "I hope you're happy, Ann."

"Very." Yes, of course I was happy. I would keep my job *and* get a raise, and I'd have the upper hand with Goddard this time. I was thrilled, in fact, my anxiety disappearing completely.

"He's still miffed that you horned in on his private dinner," she went on, "but he regrets that he reacted so childishly."

"Apology accepted," I said, aware now that I was grinning from ear to ear.

"He's going to make the time to talk to you," she said. "With a few conditions."

"Right, right." The usual. I was so grateful and relieved—I mean, the pressure was off! I had accomplished the impossible!—that I wasn't about to fight her on The Conditions. "I already told you, Peggy. He gets the cover. He gets photo approval. He gets me to sign a waiver with your litany of no-no questions. And he gets to choose the location of the interview."

"Yes. Speaking of which, he did the *Vanity Fair* piece while he was shooting *Sea of Dreams* in the south of France. The writer spent an afternoon with him onboard his sailboat."

"I remember," I said, recalling that the entire interview took place while they were cruising around the Mediterranean. "Hope nobody got seasick."

"Malcolm's not one for contrived Q and A sessions in hotel suites. The only way you'll get anything spontaneous or intimate out of him is if you catch him while he's focused on something else."

"Fine," I said. "I've already suggested that we go hiking or—"

"With him, it's important to select a location that'll open him up, help him communicate his passion about acting."

"All righty. Then how about a walk on the beach in—"

"The key is to lull him into forgetting that he's even talking to the media. So I think the location he picked is a perfect one."

"Great. Just name it already," I said, more than eager to move things along. Harvey wanted the interview done ASAP. He hoped to run it the following month, to coincide with Oscar madness. Goddard was nominated for best actor for *Famous Last Words*, the story of an out-of-work housepainter who's married to Jennifer Connelly. He wins the lottery only to learn he has lead poisoning.

"In case you didn't know, Malcolm is an avid flier," she said.

"And?" I said. So he traveled a lot, had accumulated a lot of miles. Not unheard of for a movie star.

"He keeps his Cessna at the airport in Santa Monica and takes it for a spin on Sunday afternoons when he's in town."

"His Cessna," I repeated, suddenly feeling my palms turn clammy again.

"Yes," she said. "He's got a Gulfstream, of course, so he doesn't have to go commercial, but he's not trained to fly it. It's the Cessna Skyhawk, his little single-engine prop, that he pilots himself. His Sunday jaunts in it are his way of unwinding."

Okay, I didn't like where this was heading. Not at all. My heart rate sped up, and my mouth was now without a single drop of saliva. "I'm glad to hear he has an outlet for unwinding," I said as my legs started to twitch. "We all need that. But let's get back to the location for the interview—and the date. Does he want to do it while we—"

"He wants to do it this coming Sunday afternoon. While you're up in the Cessna. The photo shoot can be done later in the week."

"While who's up in the Cessna?" This wasn't happening. This was not happening.

"You and Malcolm, of course." She paused and I thought I heard her stifle a giggle. "Is there something wrong?"

Wrong? Oh, let's see. How about *everything?* I had finally landed my big get, except that the only way I could get him was to fly in a contraption that was smaller than most cars? As I've explained, I simply didn't do prop planes. They were death machines. Seriously, doesn't it seem as if they crash a lot? Into trailer parks? Into bodies of water? Into remote rural areas where the remains of the passengers aren't recovered for days, even weeks?

I thought of my mother then. If I died in a crash, she wouldn't even be able to identify my remains because her fear of dentists would probably extend to the office where my dental records were on file and the mere smell of that cherry-flavored topical anesthesia would send her running for the door.

"My tape recorder won't pick up anything with all the engine noise," I told Peggy, trying to sound calm even though what I wanted to do was shriek. "We need to choose a quieter place to do the interview."

"Don't be silly," she said. "Haven't you ever heard the cockpit recorders on planes that have accidents? The pilot's voice comes through loud and clear."

Accidents. My point exactly. "Still," I said, "I'd hate to lose even a word, considering how important the interview is to the magazine."

"You can always take notes if you're so worried," she said.

So worried. She had no idea. Or—wait—did she? *Did she?*

Oh my God, she certainly did, I realized with a blow to the stomach. When I'd declined to take part in her Winona Ryder joyride, I'd confessed that I was phobic about flying, in prop planes especially. She'd acted all sympathetic and understanding, and I'd told Tuscany I didn't think she held grudges. But I was a fool. A naive, dumb-ass fool for buying her act. She was a master manipulator, and now she was playing me, punishing me.

"Peggy, you know very well that I'm afraid of flying," I said, wondering when she'd decided to use this little tidbit against me and why it was necessary to exact payback for the Winona incident. I wasn't the only reporter who'd blown off that Palm Springs trip, but I'd been honest about my reason for doing it. A fool, as I said.

"Yes, poor dear, I remember that you're one of those phobics, and I conveyed the problem to Malcolm. But he still wants to do the interview on the plane," she said, hardly concealing her glee. "It's out of my hands. He was insistent."

Malcolm. Ah. So this was *his* doing. I felt the fingers of my right hand curl into a fist.

So. He was the one who was looking for payback. He was still upset that I had invaded his space, that I had turned out to be a media parasite instead of a fawning fan, and now he was determined to test me, to make me twist in the wind. Peggy had tipped him off about my fear of flying and he was using it to both torture me and wriggle out of doing the interview. He figured I'd be so afraid of climbing aboard his damn plane that I'd take my parasite self and go wrap it around some other celebrity. He was a sadistic snake, and if I resented him before, I resented him even more now.

"He says it's the plane or nothing," Peggy prattled on, driving the knife deeper into my back. "He won't budge. He's offering you his free time on Sunday afternoon and he thinks that's a pretty nice concession."

Yeah, right. "He doesn't care if I go ahead and write the Spago story?" I said, making one final attempt at hardball. "This isn't an idle threat. I'll do it."

"Ann," she said, then lowered her voice into this nasty, hissing whisper. "Malcolm has asked me to relay the following to you: If you write a single word about the incident with the cake, he'll authorize me to leak it all over town that he agreed to the interview but that you refused, because of your—well—handicap. Your editor won't be pleased. We both know that. So it's up to you, dear. Do you want the interview or not?"

He was worse than I thought. He was determined to make me squirm, make me suffer, make me lose my job. I had never despised a celebrity—as I've said, I tried to see the best in all of them—but he was the exception.

"I told Malcolm I'd get right back to him, Ann," she prompted. "What's your answer?"

There was only one answer. I had to agree to her conditions. All of them. I'd say yes, sure I'll do the interview on his stupid plane, and then find a way to actually do it, in spite of my certainty that the plane would crash. Of course, when it did crash, he would be the one who'd get the giant obituary while I'd get barely a mention. Except in *Famous*, where they'd run a boxed item with a paragraph about how I perished heroically while on assignment for the magazine; it would be accompanied by a photo, which I hoped Tuscany would airbrush to make me look a tiny bit more—

"Ann? Are you there?" said Peggy.

"What time on Sunday?" I managed.

"Two o'clock," she said, as if she didn't know she was putting me through hell. "He'll meet you in the pilots' lounge at the airport and then you can walk over to the plane together."

"The pilots' lounge," I repeated, my body spasming out of control.

"Yes. He said it's in the building right next to Typhoon, the Asian restaurant there. You enter off the observation deck, go past the restrooms, and make a left."

The restrooms. Well, at least I'd be able to pee before I went up in the plane, crashed into the side of a mountain, and traveled down that long, lonely tunnel to The Other Side.

"So," she said, "you're all set. Weather permitting."

Weather per— Right! There was always the possibility that I'd be saved by rain or wind or fog!

"Although I hope the skies will cooperate," she added. "For your sake.

Malcolm will be out of the country after the Oscars, probably for a couple of months. If you want the interview to run sooner rather than later, Sunday will be your last stab at him."

No, I wasn't a violent person. But just for a split second there, I really wished I'd stabbed Malcolm Goddard when I'd had the chance.

Chapter Six

||||||||||||||||||||||||||||||||||||||||||||||||||||||||||||||||||||||||||||||||||||||||||||||||||||

"**Wait, listen to** this," I said to Tuscany and James, both of whom were sitting in my living room on Monday night, sipping wine and watching me torment myself. I was pounding away on the keyboard of my laptop, pulling up every word I could find on the Cessna Skyhawk in anticipation of my dreaded Sunday-afternoon flight. The devil you know, I figured. "It's described as a 'monoplane.'"

"As opposed to what? A stereoplane?" said James.

"Maybe it gives you mono if you kiss someone while you're in it," said Tuscany.

"This isn't funny," I scolded them, then felt sorry I had. They were trying to be supportive in their own ways. It's hard for people who aren't afraid of something to relate to those who are afraid of it, and I should have just been grateful that they were there for me.

I cleared my throat and continued to read from the manufacturer's Web site. "'The Skyhawk is an all-metal, single-engine piston, high-wing monoplane with a four-seat capacity. Its height is eight feet eleven inches.'"

"That's not much taller than a basketball player I once dated," said Tuscany.

"I think I dated him too," said James.

" 'The Skyhawk embodies everything exciting about flight,' " I pressed on. " 'Power. Styling. Adventure.' "

"You could use an adventure, Annie," said James. "Maybe you'll actually enjoy yourself up there."

"Please. I have plenty of adventure on the ground," I said, shutting down the computer. I couldn't take it anymore. Not only had I done searches for the exact make and model of Goddard's plane, I'd also checked to see how often it had crashed. I'd made myself sick with all the searching and wished I'd left well enough alone.

"Sit here," said James, patting the cushion on the couch next to him. "Let us help, would you?"

He and Tuscany had each come bearing drugs. Xanax. Valium. Ativan. Klonopin. They'd brought every antianxiety medication their doctors had ever prescribed for them, dumping their vials of pills on my big coffee table, which now looked like a counter at Walgreen's.

"Thanks, you guys," I said, sinking onto the sofa and resting my back against the pillow. "I appreciate the thought, but I can't take any of that stuff."

"Just one Xanax," Tuscany implored. "Put one under your tongue about forty-five minutes before you go to the airport and it'll calm you down. You'll see."

"I can't," I said. "I'm too afraid."

"That's what the Xanax is for," she pointed out.

"No, I'm afraid of medicine the way I'm afraid of flying," I explained, admitting to yet another phobia I hadn't been willing to face. "I know it sounds crazy, but I've convinced myself that I'll have a bad reaction to whatever the drug is and then die."

"I thought you convinced yourself that you're gonna die in the plane," said James.

"I did," I said with a shrug. I had traveled halfway across the country to escape the family curse, but here it was, popping out all over me like a nasty rash. Not only was I panicking about flying and pill taking, but I had panicked that night at Bristol Farms and again after Goddard had lit into me at Spago. I had no idea why I was suddenly having the attacks—Life was good! I was happy! I was living my dream!—but I could no longer deny that bouts of anxiety disorder were exactly what they were. "This is hopeless. I'm never going up in that Cessna with Goddard. Who am I kidding?"

"What about alcohol?" said Tuscany. "You drink Bloody Marys when you fly on jets."

"Yeah, but I have to get hammered or else I won't even go. I can't do an interview in that condition. I wouldn't be able to ask a single coherent question, let alone write down the answer." I sighed and put my head in my hands.

"Well, there are other solutions, but you always look down on my alternative therapies," said Tuscany, who, before becoming a regular at the gym in order to control her weight, had consulted a reflexologist, an acupuncturist, and a hypnotist, none of whom had reduced the size of her thighs.

"I'm from the show-me state," I reminded her. "We're not as gullible in Missouri as people are in L.A."

"Maybe, but you're not in Missouri anymore and you're desperate," she said. "I think you should call Dr. Qian."

"The acupuncturist?"

"No, the hypnotist. He just happens to be Chinese too. Chinese-American and very cute, by the way."

"As I recall, you didn't lose a pound when you were seeing him," I said.

"That's not true," she said. "His hypnotic suggestions worked great until I started dating the chef at the Daily Grill in Brentwood. Not even Dr. Qian can compete with free food."

I smiled. "What makes you think he can help me? Does he work with people who have a fear of flying?"

"Absolutely," she said. "Fears are his specialty. Fear of flying. Fear of spiders. Fear of whatever. You have nothing to lose, Ann. You should call him."

"Does he work with people who have a fear of commitment?" James asked. "Because I think I might have it. Either that or I'm just not meeting the kind of men who are life-partner material."

James met men at a dance club in West Hollywood called One-Night Stand, where there probably weren't a lot of men interested in becoming anyone's life partner.

Tuscany said she didn't know if Dr. Qian dealt with relationship issues, but reiterated that I should consult him as soon as possible. "You've only got six days until the flight," she said. "Maybe if you told him it's an emergency, he'd give you a double session."

She was right. What did I have to lose?

I vowed to call the doctor first thing in the morning. I was determined to cure myself and keep my job, even if it meant going to see every quack in town.

DR. QIAN'S OFFICE was in a small strip mall in Westwood, and the session itself took place in a dimly lit room furnished only with a La-Z-Boy-type recliner and a straight-backed chair. I went for the recliner, figuring I was the one who'd be going into a trance and reclining, but the doctor directed me to the other chair. He'd been having a problem with swollen ankles, he said, and needed to keep his feet up.

We sat. He began by asking me when I first became aware of my aviophobia.

"My fear of flying, you mean?" I said.

"Yes. That's the Greek term for it."

"Oh. I've always had it to some extent. Other fears too."

"Like what?" he said, making notes on a pad. He was a very thin, very short, very serious man who wore a white lab coat over his shirt and slacks, as if to convey just how serious. He wasn't my idea of "cute," but then Tuscany and I were rarely attracted to the same men because she was attracted to virtually all of them.

"Well," I said, "there's my fear of peanut butter sticking to the roof of my mouth."

"Arachibutyrophobia," he said with a nod.

"It started when I was a child, along with my fear of clowns."

"Coulrophobia."

"I come from a family of phobics," I said, "but it wasn't until recently that my own situation deteriorated."

He glanced up from his pad. "Have you tried any antianxiety medications?"

I shook my head sheepishly. "I have a fear of them too. They all have these hideous side effects. I can't even watch their commercials."

"Pharmacophobia," he said, nodding again. "You assume you'll develop a fatal allergy to them."

"Yes. And I'm afraid they'll make me vomit," I said. "Ever since Teddy Sloan threw up his bologna sandwich all over my desk in third grade, I've been afraid of vomit. Of doing it, seeing other people do it, smelling other people do it."

"Emotophobia," he said conclusively.

"Okay, but the reason I'm here is the flying," I said, eager to get down to business. "Today's Tuesday and I'm supposed to go up in a prop plane on Sunday. I need to be fixed by then."

He described the process by which hypnosis works and started with a relaxation technique. He asked me to close my eyes and concentrate on

the sound of his voice, which was high and nasal and not the sort of sooth-
ing tone that would lull anybody into an altered state of consciousness.
"I'd like you to imagine a blanket wrapping itself around your feet—a
very soft, very warm, very healing blanket. Your feet are becoming completely relaxed by this blanket. Deeply relaxed. Every muscle in your feet
is becoming limp and relaxed."

I visualized my feet as limp and relaxed. I also visualized Dr. Qian's
feet, which he'd said were so swollen they had to be elevated.

I opened my eyes. "Maybe there's too much salt in your diet," I said.
"Excess sodium can cause edema in the feet." As I've said, I was a hypochondriac who spent way too much time reading up on medical conditions I'd never have.

Dr. Qian thanked me, but suggested that I close my eyes and refocus
on my own feet.

He moved the imaginary blanket up my body, then counted down
from twenty-five, assuring me that I would be drowsy and limp by
zero.

"Now," he said, "I'm going to paint a picture of exactly how you'll feel
on Sunday afternoon when you take a ride in your friend's plane."

My eyes flew open again. "He's not my friend," I said. "He's the last
person I'd—"

"Ann," said Dr. Qian. "Please."

"Sorry." Down went my eyelids.

He said I'd be smiling and laughing on Sunday, filled with joy as I
soared above the earth. He went on and on, and at the end of his rosy
scenario, he brought me back from my supposedly altered state.

"As I count to three you're going to slowly, gradually wake up," he
said. "You'll be refreshed, as if you've taken a nice little nap. Now, start
waking up . . . one, becoming more alert . . . two, getting ready to wake
up . . . three, wake up."

On "three," I opened my eyes.

"How do you feel?" asked Dr. Qian.

"I wasn't hypnotized, if that's what you're asking." I didn't want to insult him by calling his expertise into question, but his routine simply hadn't done the job. I was still petrified of flying.

He leaned forward in the recliner. "I recommend that you seek out a competent psychotherapist."

"But psychotherapy can take years," I said, my spirits sagging. I hadn't really expected the hypnosis to work, but there was always the chance it might. Now I was more discouraged than ever. "And its success rate isn't very high in dealing with people who have phobias and panic attacks. I've done a lot of research on the subject lately. No, I need something that will help me and help me fast."

Dr. Qian considered my dilemma. "You might give virtual reality therapy a try," he said. "There's a clinic not too far from here."

"Oh, you mean one of those places where they use a computerized headset to simulate being in a plane?"

"Yes," he said. "The patients who can handle it do well."

"The patients who can handle it?"

He nodded. "Some find it too overwhelming. You have to be willing to immerse yourself in the fear in order to get over it."

I was willing to immerse myself in cow dung if it cured me by Sunday. "Do you have their number?" I asked.

"CAN'T YOU SQUEEZE me in sooner?" I said, my voice cracking as I spoke to the receptionist at the Virtual Reality Treatment Center (aka VRTC). Their first opening wasn't for three weeks.

"Sorry, but there are a lot of people with panic and phobia disorders," she said. "It's only gotten worse since nine-eleven."

"I understand," I said, not wanting to act like those overbearing types who think their problem should take priority over everybody else's. Still, there was a ticking clock here: only six days until Sunday. "Can you at least put me on a waiting list in case you get cancellations?"

"Sure, but it takes eight to ten sessions with the therapist to see results. One appointment isn't enough."

"One appointment will be just fine," I said, figuring that I didn't have to *like* flying by Sunday. I just had to do it.

MEANWHILE, I PINNED my hopes on Walter Riddick, the self-proclaimed "healer with the magic hands." Angelina Jolie had told me about him when I interviewed her. She said she'd been afraid of fire—something about getting burned as a kid while toasting marshmallows—and how he'd come to her house and unblocked her. In desperation, I called him.

At nine-thirty that night, he rang my doorbell. He was an attractive blond man in his thirties wearing a clinging black T-shirt, blue jeans, and two gold hoop earrings, one in each nostril.

"So Angie gave you my name?" he said as we stood in my threshold.

"Yes. She told me how you got rid of her fear of fire."

He beamed. "She's a trooper now. Even lights her own candles."

So she used to—what?—hire someone to light them? "How do you accomplish your, um, unblocking?"

He nodded at the large folding table and duffel bag he had set down on the floor. "I detoxify the system through the art of deep body work, which you probably think of as massage."

He was a massage therapist? Like my old boyfriend Skip, who never healed anybody? I had pictured a laying-on-of-hands type of person, someone more evangelical.

"Deep body work gets at your issues," he said. "It attacks the stuff that congeals, and brings you to a place of courage."

Courage. Exactly what I needed. I ushered him inside.

He set up his equipment in my living room, pulling freshly laundered sheets and blankets from the duffel and turning the massage table into a comfy bed. Then he said he'd leave the room while I undressed.

"Take everything off," he instructed.

"Everything?" I called out after he was too far away to hear me. I was thirty and still ridiculously modest about my body. I bought bras online. I doubled up on those paper gowns they make you wear in doctors' examining rooms. I shaved my legs and "bikini hair" as opposed to subjecting myself to the scrutiny of a waxer. It was probably the influence of my mother, the catastrophizer. When I was growing up, she told me that women who "showed themselves" either caught fatal diseases or were murdered.

I was stark naked and hiding under the blankets when Walter returned. He dabbed a few drops of oil into his palms, rubbed them together vigorously, and told me to turn over on my stomach.

"For the next hour I'm going to work on your blockages," he announced. "When I'm finished, you'll feel great about flying."

I closed my eyes and prepared for a relaxing massage if nothing else.

Suddenly, Walter was climbing up onto the table, his legs straddling me, his hands swooping down and grabbing the skin around my lower spine and pulling it—hard—causing me to practically levitate. I yelped. The pain was searing, hot.

"Keep breathing," he said as he twisted and tugged on my back. "Allow the pain. Surrender to it. If you fight it, I won't be able to destroy your toxins."

He ended up nearly destroying my sanity. He tore at every body part, claiming my "hardened structures" were making me rigid and that his work would have a profound effect on me.

It did. By the time he was finished, I was so sore I couldn't walk. Or talk. He had applied his magic hands to my chin and cheek muscles too, the result of which was that I had lockjaw. Worst of all, I was just as afraid of flying as ever.

I was about to send him on to his next sucker when James started blasting Gloria Gaynor's "I Will Survive." It was only eleven-fifteen, not his usual middle-of-the-night concert, but I wasn't sure *I* would survive if he didn't turn down the volume. Every nerve ending was throbbing.

"Could you do me a favor?" I asked Walter in this weak, faraway voice I hardly recognized. I was leaning against the wall so I wouldn't fall down. "Could you go upstairs and ask my neighbor to kill the music? He's very nice. He just forgets he doesn't live in a soundproof recording studio."

"Will do," said Walter. "And don't hesitate to call if you need me again."

Right.

In the morning, I dressed very slowly for work and limped out of the apartment to my car. James came running over. I assumed he wanted to apologize for the music; he was always so guilt ridden after the fact. He took my hands in his and kissed them.

"Okay, okay. I forgive you," I laughed, aching everywhere. "Why so dramatic?"

"Walter," he said, as if it were obvious. "You sent him to me."

"Yes," I said, "to get you to turn down the—"

"He's The One, Ann." He sighed like a lovesick fool.

"I hope you'll both be very happy," I said and eased myself into my Honda.

ON THURSDAY MORNING, the receptionist from VRTC called me to say she'd had a cancellation for that very afternoon.

"I'll take it," I said with profound gratitude and relief.

The office was located on the fifth floor of a mid-rise building on Sepulveda Boulevard. As I sat in the waiting room, I filled out a questionnaire intended to evaluate the intensity level of my fear of flying. On a scale of zero (not at all disturbing) to eight (extremely disturbing), I was asked to rate everything from standing in line on the boarding ramp to experiencing turbulence during the flight (I gave that one a ten, even though the scale didn't go that high). The average score for people with aviophobia was 130. I scored 148.

The doctor, Hilary Horner, was a babe, reminiscent of those reality-TV bachelorettes who claim they're in it for true love, then pose nude for *Playboy*. She was in a slinky navy blue dress and matching high heels with pointy toes. And she kept flicking her long blond hair off her face with her manicured fingers, one of which—her left ring finger—was adorned with a diamond the size of my head. "Have a seat," she said.

My "seat" in her therapy lab was a replica of an airline seat. It was affixed to what I would later learn was a vibrating platform.

"All set," I said after buckling up. "But before we get started, I should explain that what I need is an accelerated treatment." I told her about the flight on Sunday and how essential it was that I get over my fear by then. "You'll be cramming a lot of virtual reality into a short amount of time, but I can handle it."

She shrugged, as if to say, "It's your funeral," and hooked me up to a biofeedback machine. Little sensors were taped to my wrists, fingers, and waist in order to keep track of changes in my heart rate, breathing patterns, and skin temperature. Her giant diamond nearly got stuck in all the adhesive.

Then she showed me how to breathe properly—from the abdomen, not the chest—and attempted to correct my misconceptions about flying.

"What you have is an irrational fear," she said.

"It's very rational," I said. "Planes do crash."

"Most planes don't," she said. "You're catastrophizing."

Well, I knew where that came from. "Still, I do feel that flying can have disastrous consequences," I said.

"I see we need to do some reframing of your thoughts by replacing them with positive probables." Sounded like a board game. Or maybe a children's snack. "For instance, the odds of dying in a plane crash are one in eight million. That's a positive probable."

"It's not so positive if you're the one in the eight million," I said.

She flicked her hair. "Here's another one. Statistically, a traveler would have to fly every day for more than eight thousand years to be in an accident where there are multiple fatalities."

"What about non-multiple fatalities?" I said. "On Sunday I'll be flying with only one other person. If we crash, maybe I'll be a fatality but he'll survive. What are the statistics for a situation like that?"

Another flick of the hair. "Let's move on, since we don't have that much time," she said. "I'll give you a card with additional positive probables on it and you can practice them when you get home."

"Will do."

"We'll begin the in-vivo exposure." She retrieved the bulky black headset from a nearby table, the one with the earphones attached. It was a very science fictiony gadget, complete with this 3-D screen that jutted out and fit over the eyes. She strapped it onto my head, then dimmed the lights in the room. "I'm going to project some environments onto your screen that will provoke anxiety. You'll use your breathing technique and I'll monitor your reactions."

"Okay," I said. "Let it rip."

I peered into the screen. Suddenly, it was as if I was sitting in a window seat on an actual commercial plane filled with other passengers. It was only a computerized movie, but it felt incredibly real. I could see us taxiing to the takeoff area, and my heart raced.

"Breathe from your abdomen!" Dr. Horner commanded.

Inside my headset, we were now lifting off from the ground! Up we went. Over buildings. Over freeway traffic. Into lots and lots of clouds, which produced not only raindrops on my virtual reality window but *turbulence*. Apparently, Dr. Horner had arranged for me to fly into a virtual reality storm.

"Breathe!" she said.

I couldn't. My seat was vibrating and it felt as if the plane kept dropping in altitude. I gripped the arms of the chair for dear life.

"Uh, this is Captain Jenkins up here in the flight deck," intoned the virtual reality pilot. He spoke in that generic, world-weary voice they all have. "We're passing through some choppy air, so I've turned on the seat-belt sign. Please remain in your seats with your seat belts securely fastened."

Just then, Dr. Horner turned up the vibration on the platform, and my seat started rocking and bucking and rattling so badly that I actually screamed. I was terrified. Stricken. In a complete panic.

"Breathe from your abdomen!"

"Breathe out your ass!"

I whipped off my headset and threw it onto the floor. I'd immersed myself in my fear, but enough was enough.

After I apologized for being impolite and abusing her equipment, I thanked her for trying to help.

"You didn't give me a lot of leeway because of your Sunday deadline," she said.

"I know," I said. "It's not your fault."

I sighed despondently as she disconnected me from the biofeedback machine. I felt like a failure and a chickenshit and a person who was running out of options—and time.

She put her hand on my shoulder as she walked me out the door. "When you wake up on Sunday morning, reframe your thoughts with the positive probables. Remind yourself of the odds."

I thanked her again and promised I'd repeat her positive probables over and over until they sank in. As a professional writer, I could certainly appreciate the power of words. I would use her words to strengthen my resolve. And I would get on Goddard's plane, conduct the interview, get off Goddard's plane, and lead a long and happy life.

||||||||||||||||||||||||||||||||||||||||||||||||||||||||||||||||||||||||||||||||||

Chapter Seven

I spent several hours on Saturday writing up my interview questions for Goddard. Peggy Merchant had forbidden me to ask about his rumored engagement to Rebecca Truit, his occasional run-ins with photographers, and especially his estrangement from his father, a sometime actor who was said to have pocketed his superstar son's money instead of managing it. But there were plenty of other topics to cover, and I compiled a long list of them. Some examples . . .

Q: Tell me about your childhood in Manhattan, Malcolm. Did you like growing up in the city or did you envy kids who lived in the suburbs?

Q: Were you a jock or a geek as a kid? Good in school or good at avoiding it?

Q: Your parents split up when you were twelve. What impact did their divorce have on you?

Q: What's your earliest memory of wanting to become an actor?

Q: Were you intrigued by movies as a boy? Which ones?

Q: What kinds of jobs did you take to support yourself while you were auditioning?

Q: Did you ever consider giving up acting in those early days? And, if so, what field do you think you would have gone into instead?

Q: Tell us about your first big break. It was a part in a Sidney Lumet movie, wasn't it?

Q: How did that film change your life?

Q: Since then you've gone on to become one of America's most accomplished and successful actors. How do you choose your roles? Is it a good script that pulls you in? A director you've wanted to work with? A genre that appeals to you?

Q: Is there a movie you wish you hadn't done? A performance you aren't proud of?

Q: How do you prepare for your roles?

Q: Which are your favorites of your films and why?

Q: Are you one of those actors who loses himself in a role? Is that part of the pleasure of acting for you? To become someone else?

Q: You're nominated for an Oscar this year. How do you feel about awards for acting? Are you a competitive person?

Q: You have many female fans, and I'm sure they'd like to know what you're looking for in that special woman. What attracts you to certain women? What turns you off to others?

Q: Do you see yourself settling down, getting married and starting a family at some point? Do you think about becoming a husband and father?

Q: Are you close to people in the industry or are your friendships with people you knew before you became a star?

Q: Is there anyone, living or dead, whom you particularly admire?

Q: What's a typical day like for you when you're not acting in a film? How do you enjoy spending your time off?

Q: Speaking of hobbies, here we are in your private plane today.

When did you get your pilot's license and what motivated you
to do it?

Okay, that last question made me queasy, but it had to be asked. I, for
one, wanted the answer, because I couldn't imagine why anyone in their
right mind would voluntarily take to the skies.

I came up with lots of questions, as I said, but in the end the key to getting
a good interview was not only to be prepared but to be spontaneous—to take
advantage of openings in the conversation and pounce on any off-the-cuff
revelations.

Of course, my prowess as an interviewer meant squat if I didn't have the
nerve to get up in that plane, and by Saturday night I wasn't sure if I could
do it. For every one of Dr. Horner's positive probables that I pounded into
my head, there was a what-if hovering right over it like a dark shadow. I'd
think positively about the one-in-eight-million statistic and then imagine a bird wandering into the Cessna's fuselage, causing us to explode in
midflight. Or I'd think positively about how I was more likely to die in an
avalanche than a plane crash and then picture Goddard pulling the wrong
lever, sending us plunging into the pool at the Hotel Bel-Air.

But I was determined that the positive probables would outmuscle the
what-ifs, so I made an audiotape on which I reeled off all the reasons why
I would survive the flight, and listened to it again and again in the hope
of reframing my thoughts. I even fell asleep to the tape. When I awoke on
Sunday morning, I was actually feeling a little better and decided to take
a jog/walk around the neighborhood. One of my favorite things about
living in L.A. was the great weather, and Sunday was a great-weather day.
It was early February, and while the temperatures were below freezing in
Missouri, they were in the high seventies outside my front door. I loved
the fact that the bougainvillea bloomed all year long and the grass stayed
green and the birds continued to chirp. I also loved that there was an
honest-to-goodness French patisserie just blocks from my apartment. I

planned to exercise for an hour or so and then reward myself with one of their buttery croissants. Hey, if it really was my last day on earth, some sunshine and a fattening breakfast were the way to go out, I figured.

I bought the croissant (okay, a croissant *and* a blueberry muffin), jogged/walked back to my apartment, and made some coffee. As I sat down to eat, I picked through the sections of the hefty Sunday edition of the *L.A. Times,* pulled out the front section, and set it on the table beside me.

Hmm, this muffin is delicious, I thought as I sank my teeth into some blueberries and scanned the headlines. There was a story about Iraq. There was a story about social security. There was a story about the latest CEO to be indicted for fraud. I took another bite of the muffin, congratulated myself on how well I was doing in terms of my anxiety, and took another bite. Sure, I was afraid, but I was coping. One in eight million. That's what I kept telling myself.

And then I flipped over the paper, intending to read the headlines that were below the fold, but a photo stopped me cold.

"Oh my God!" I said out loud when I saw the image of the wreckage. *Airplane wreckage.* A tail here. A wing there. Police officers everywhere.

"Oh my God!" I said again after processing the accompanying headline: "Couple Dead in Crash of Small Plane."

I spit out the unchewed morsel of muffin, since my throat had immediately closed up and I knew I'd never be able to swallow it. And then, with great trepidation, I read the article.

I won't gross you out with all the gory details, but the plane was a Cessna Skyhawk, the same model as you know who's. It had been flying south of Los Angeles the previous afternoon, making its descent into the Fullerton airport in crystal-clear weather when it struck a radio tower, killing its two occupants, who'd been torched after the plane burst into flames. The FAA and the National Transportation Safety Board were investigating.

I let the paper slip out of my hand, onto the floor, and sat there with my mouth hanging open, my mind reeling. My thoughts veered dangerously beyond what-if. They were now haunted by what-was. Two poor, unsuspecting people had gone up in that plane on a bright, sunny day, and now they were—

You're right to be afraid, I told myself, feeling no further inclination to cling to the positive probables, leaving me with my aviophobia as well as the conviction that flying really wasn't safe. Those stupid little planes *did* fall out of the sky, and Malcolm Goddard was a bastard for forcing me to become a casualty of his recklessness.

I bolted up from the table, paced around my combination living room/ dining room, and called Tuscany on her cell phone. She'd had a date the night before with a guy she'd met at the dry cleaner's and I had no idea if they'd ended up at his place or hers.

"Did you see the paper this morning?" I said when she answered.

"Yeah," she said. "I thought of you right away. It's a good thing you're getting Goddard before he goes out of the country."

"Getting— What are you talking about?" I said, as puzzled as I was frantic.

"It was in the Calendar section," she said, referring to the entertainment section of the *L.A. Times.* "There was an item saying that Malcolm Goddard is leaving for Canada after the Oscars. I guess he's shooting a movie there."

"Tuscany," I said. "I meant the *front page* of the paper." It wasn't that she was callous about real news. It was just that she always went for the lighter stuff first. "There was a crash of a Cessna yesterday. The two people onboard were killed."

She expressed the appropriate outrage, then paused. "I just realized that if the virtual reality doctor you went to had her numbers straight, you're totally in the clear now."

"What?"

"She told you the odds were one in eight million that you'd crash. Well, those people in Fullerton were your 'one.' You're off the hook, Ann. Everything will go great."

I didn't see it that way. Not at all. I hung up feeling worse than before I'd called her. No matter how many times I replayed the audiotape of the positive probables, I just couldn't shake the image of that wreckage or the sympathy I felt for the victims. As the clock ticked, I grew increasingly anxious and became the epitome of a catastrophizer. In my mind, there was no question whatsoever that if I went up in Goddard's plane, I wouldn't make it down alive.

Nevertheless, with a sense of doom and inevitability, I showered and applied two coats of moisturizer to my skin (I thought maybe a little lubrication would make it more fire resistant). And I dressed in blue jeans, a beige turtleneck, and sneakers (I wanted to look casual when they found my body, as if I were the sort of nervy, adventurous person who not only flew on small planes but climbed mountains and rode horses bareback). And I gathered my tape recorder and yellow legal pad and reams of notes and put them in my tote bag (I hoped that the investigators picking through the debris would find my interview questions and decide I must have been a killer journalist who did whatever it took to get a story). I left the apartment about one-fifteen, got into my car, and drove west to the Santa Monica airport.

I don't remember much about the drive except that my hands shook so forcefully that it was difficult to steer. And, of course, the wheel was soaking wet from my clamminess. Still, I made it to the airport. Early as usual, right to the end. I had twenty minutes to spare, in fact—twenty minutes to pull myself together and then die with dignity.

THE SANTA MONICA airport is a small facility for private planes. With its low-rise buildings and quaint little runways, it has the feel of an era when air travel wasn't about mammoth structures and jumbo jets and security pat-downs. It should have made me less anxious, given its "relaxed" atmosphere, but it didn't. From my perspective, it was as terrifying as LAX.

I parked where Peggy Merchant had told me to park, in the lot next to Typhoon. I turned the ignition off and hunkered down in the Honda for ten minutes, psyching myself up. *You can do this, Ann,* I coached myself. *You have to do this. You have no choice.*

After another five minutes of psyching, plus an additional two of vilifying Goddard, I grabbed my tote bag, got out of the car, and locked it. As my feet met the ground, I couldn't feel them. I was that numb with fear.

I managed to walk toward the cluster of wood-frame buildings in front of me. One was Typhoon; another was the observation deck and pilots' lounge. I felt myself moving forward but I wasn't in control of my body. Somewhere between West Hollywood and Santa Monica, I had lost the ability to tell it what to do.

I stepped up onto the observation deck and took in a huge gulp of air as I regarded the lineup of planes only yards away. One of them had to belong to Goddard, that son of a bitch. If it weren't for him, I'd—

I felt dizzy then—a true vertigo, where every turn of my head produced an uncontrollable whirling of my surroundings—and my stomach seemed to have lodged itself in my neck. I started to weave as my legs buckled, but I remained upright. Upright and sweating profusely. My face and hair must have looked like I'd been out in a torrential rain.

I tried to snap myself out of what was quickly becoming the most monstrous panic attack I'd ever had. *Come on, Ann. Go die and get it over with already,* I repeated to myself over the course of several minutes. No, it wasn't a positive probable, but at some point everything finally stopped spinning.

I looked at my watch. Two o'clock on the nose. Time to make my rubbery legs carry me into that pilots' lounge.

As I turned toward the door, two men emerged from the building.

"I hear they smashed right into that radio tower down in Fullerton. Never saw it coming," said one of them.

I stopped in my tracks and listened, my heart thumping so hard I thought it would poke through my chest. They were talking about the dead people, the poor casualties of the crash I'd read about that very morning.

"Clear skies like today's can be the toughest," said the other.

"Especially for weekend pilots," said the first. "Not enough flying time. Not enough experience."

"Bad scene all around," said the second. "That couple got crushed *and* fried."

Okay, that did it. That did it! We all have our breaking points and "crushed and fried" was mine!

I staggered back and flattened myself against the wall of the building, trying desperately not to catastrophize but doing it anyway. I had totally lost what little nerve I had. I was done, finished, wiped out emotionally. No matter how much I wanted to hang on to my job, no matter how badly I wanted to prove to Harvey that I was a killer, no matter how ferociously I wanted to show Goddard that I was not someone to be toyed with and kissed off like every other reporter he'd managed to scare away, I was helpless, out of control, incapable of doing what I'd come here to do. My fear had won. I was officially *not* conducting the interview in an airplane. No more vacillating. No more torturing myself. No more scrambling to accommodate a man who didn't deserve accommodating. I simply couldn't do it. If you've ever suffered from panic and phobia disorder, you get this. I'd been a happy, productive grown-up who'd just been reduced to a big, stupid baby.

As the two men disappeared into the parking lot, I lingered where I stood, just forcing myself to breathe. Yes, of course I would love to have marched into the pilots' lounge and given Goddard a piece of my mind, loved to have confronted him for putting me through hell for his own perverse amusement, but I wasn't doing any marching. I couldn't even talk. My lips were stuck together in a bizarre seal of terror-induced dryness.

Besides, what was the point of confronting him? So he could taunt me again about being a parasite? Make me feel even more beaten down than I already did? No. I would be lucky just to make it out of that airport without falling to the ground in a heap.

Tears dribbled down my cheeks then—tears of anger and frustration and self-flagellation—as I took a last look at the planes and then trudged to my car. When I passed one of those large metal trash bins, I stopped and dumped my entire tote bag into it—interview notes, tape recorder, and all. The bag landed at the bottom of the garbage bin with a thud, which was all too reminiscent of my once promising career.

Fine, Malcolm, I thought as I pressed on toward the parking lot, my eyes flooded and my chin quivering. You were victorious in your battle against this reporter, but someday you'll get yours. And if there's any justice in the world, I'll be right there to see it.

Chapter Eight

|||||||||||||||||||||||||||||||||||||||||||||||||||||||||||||||||||||||||||||||||||||||||||

I awakened early on Monday morning with a sense of unfinished business, a powerful need to rebound from my collapse at the airport and strike back at Goddard. But since he was chronically unavailable to me, I decided that Peggy Merchant was the next best target. I would speak to her face-to-face, get everything off my chest, tell her what I really thought of her client, and maybe give myself a boost of confidence, a feeling of vindication, before having to deal with Harvey.

At nine o'clock, Peggy was to be the keynote speaker at the annual Women in Media breakfast in one of the ballrooms at the Beverly Wilshire. I scowled as I sipped my coffee and fingered the invitation. The topic was: "How Hollywood Publicists and Entertainment Journalists Can Improve Their Relationship." I wasn't interested in improving my relationship with Peggy. Not anymore. I was interested in giving her a piece of my mind.

I had originally intended to skip the event, because it sounded like a waste of time, plus the eggs are always cold at breakfasts for five hundred people, but I dressed quickly and left my apartment in plenty of time to get to Beverly Hills.

There were considerably more than five hundred women in the ballroom, I estimated when I arrived. An excellent turnout. I felt a twinge of anxiety as I stepped between the tables in search of an empty seat, and prayed I wouldn't have another panic attack. Crowded spaces seemed to trigger them. *Focus on the conversation you'll have with Peggy,* I told myself. *Remember why you came.*

I did find a seat just as the cold eggs were being served. I picked at them and made polite conversation with the women on either side of me, neither of whom I'd met before. They were assistants who'd been sent in their bosses' stead, either as a perk or a punishment.

"Good morning, ladies, and thank you all for coming," said Kristen Charney, the president of the organization. Everybody yelled, "Louder!" so she adjusted the microphone that had been set up at the front of the room, on the podium. "Is this better?" Everybody yelled, "Yes!" The program was under way. She welcomed us again and said she was thrilled to be a member of such a wonderful, caring, supportive community of women. I tried not to choke on my ice water during her lavish introduction of Peggy, whom she described as the most caring and supportive of all. "When a reporter needs a story, Peggy Merchant has been and continues to be our go-to gal. None of us would be able to do our jobs without her leadership and her"—pause—"love."

I did choke on my ice water. People turned to look.

"Thanks for those special, special words, Kristen," said Peggy after settling in at the podium. She assumed an expression of humility as the audience applauded. She was the angelic Peggy, not the barracuda. She should have been an actress instead of a publicist, I decided.

The gist of her speech was that given the overheated celebrity culture in which we were living, there was a new frenzy about getting the big get, and that we all needed to take a deep breath and cooperate with each other.

Yeah, right, I thought as I zoned out and replayed my conversations with her about Goddard. Had she been cooperative? Had he? Hardly.

I replayed the cheesecake incident, practically feeling the sensation of the cream and the crumbs against my cheek. It was still that vivid for me. And then I replayed what Goddard had said to me at the restaurant and what I'd said back to him; how Peggy had tipped him off about my fear of flying and how he'd used it to rid himself of me and my inquiring mind. And the more I replayed these events, the more emotion bubbled up to the surface—the more anguish and humiliation and rage—and before I could stop myself, I leaped up from my seat. She was talking about the role of a good publicist when I stuck my hand in the air and said, "Here's a question for you, Peggy. Is it possible to be both a good publicist and a good person, or are they mutually exclusive?"

I had planned to have a showdown with her after the breakfast, without an audience of five hundred plus, but something, some powerful force, overtook me. Necks were craned and all eyes had turned in my direction, including Peggy's.

"Ann Roth?" she said, peering into the audience. "Is that you?"

"Yes," I said, determined not to let my voice crack even the slightest bit. It was suddenly imperative that I defend my honor to her (and, by proxy, to Goddard), and I no longer cared who heard me. I actually hoped she would respect me more if I spoke my piece. At the very least, maybe *I'd* respect me more. "I think it's very touching that as a 'good publicist' you try to protect your clients from an overzealous media. But who protects us from your clients? Don't you have a responsibility there too?"

There was a lot of murmuring now and many puzzled glances. "I don't know what you mean, dear," she said, fingering her pearls.

"Let's take one of your clients as an example," I said. "Malcolm Goddard." Even uttering his name sort of made me sick. "He treats reporters badly, Peggy, and yet instead of reining him in, you coddle him, encourage him, pretend he can do no wrong. Is that really what a good publicist should do?" I was amazed by my own boldness. Apparently, fear of public speaking wasn't one of my phobias.

She chuckled, but Kristen Charney looked on nervously.

"Ann, dear," she said, indulging me. "Wouldn't you rather discuss this later? When it's just the two of us?"

"Nope," I said and continued to stand. The other women at my table stared up at me as if I might be psychotic. "Malcolm should apologize to me for taking advantage of my personal problem. I'd like you to tell him that instead of letting him off the hook."

Peggy sighed heavily and said, not to me, but to the audience at large, to fill them in, "Ann was granted an interview with Malcolm for *Famous*. They arranged to do the interview on his plane yesterday, but Ann was a no-show. He waited at the Santa Monica airport for well over an hour, but she never came. She's the one who owes him an apology."

"That's ridiculous!" I said, my voice rising. "Malcolm knew I wouldn't be able to fly on his plane. Or at least he was willing to bet that I wouldn't be able to. He was testing me, goading me, using my fear to see how badly I wanted the interview, but all he did was prove what a nasty, self-important jerk he is." Yes, I had just admitted to everyone within earshot that I had blown my once-in-a-lifetime opportunity to interview America's biggest get, but it seemed more important to expose Goddard for the dirtbag he was.

"Now *that's* ridiculous," said Peggy, whose expression had hardened. What's more, Kristen was leaning over and whispering something to the person next to her, and that person waved to the security guard stationed off to the side of the room. "What Malcolm proved was that you didn't want the interview badly enough."

"Oh, I wanted it," I said. "I just didn't realize the kind of man I was dealing with, the kind who has his own warped code of ethics."

"Ann, Ann. You're taking this so personally," said Peggy as the security guard moved toward my table. "I told you once before. He doesn't hate you. He hates the media. If he can find a way to elude reporters, he will."

I shook my head. She made what he did sound so benign, like a friendly game of cat and mouse. "He's a talented actor, Peggy, but he needs a course in humanity. There will come a time when even you won't be able to spin his behavior."

"Perhaps the real issue," she said, "is that you don't have what it takes to do your job."

"That's not true," I said defiantly. "And just so you know, Peggy? This business doesn't have to be cutthroat. It's 'good publicists' like you who've helped make it that way."

I had just completed the sentence when the guard took hold of my arm and said, "Please come with me, miss."

I smiled at him. "I wasn't planning on staying. I'm finished now."

As the room buzzed with the unexpected drama of my outburst (you would have thought a gun-wielding nut had busted into the ballroom and held these women hostage), I walked out on my own, making sure not to slouch or otherwise look shriveled or defeated. But I couldn't deny that what I'd told the guard was true. I was finished now.

"I DIDN'T DO the interview yesterday," I told Harvey as he hovered over me. He had summoned me to his office at ten-thirty, expecting details of how well everything had gone between Goddard and me. So I gave it to him straight. I didn't have much choice. He would have found out anyway.

"What?" He stepped back to look at me, as if to determine whether I was kidding.

"I have a phobia about flying," I said, hoping that maybe all his crystals and candles and singing bowls weren't merely an affectation, that maybe he did have a spiritual side, a forgiving side. "When I got to the airport, I lost my nerve and came home. I just couldn't make myself get on that plane."

"You let Malcolm Goddard slip through your fingers because you were

scared of his plane?" he yelled, his right fist colliding with a photograph that hung on his wall—the one of him embracing the Dalai Lama. Nope. No spiritual side. No forgiving side either.

I nodded. "I'm sorry. So very sorry."

"Well, I'll tell you what else you are!"

I clutched the arms of the chair, bracing myself for the inevitable.

"You're fired!"

No, it wasn't a surprise, obviously. I would have fired me too. I wasn't someone my boss could depend on.

"I doubt it'll make any difference to you," I said after swallowing hard, "but I tried every way I knew how to get rid of my phobia in time for the interview. I did hypnosis, deep body work, virtual reality therapy, but none of that helped. I was supposed to meet Goddard in the pilots' lounge, and I didn't show up." I swallowed again, feeling sort of emboldened that he'd been silent for half a second. "I just want to assure you that this isn't about me being irresponsible or lackadaisical or even the least bit flaky," I continued. "I could still do a hell of a job for you and this magazine, Harvey. If you'd reconsider."

He didn't say anything for an entire minute, and I didn't know what to make of it. A quiet, contemplative Harvey was a rare occurrence, almost as intimidating as the shouting, combustible Harvey. His expression was blank too. He looked at me without moving a muscle, a poker face. "You should have told me all this when Goddard set the location for the interview," he said finally, in a voice that seemed more disappointed than angry. "I would have put somebody else on the case."

"You're right," I acknowledged. "But I really wanted to prove to you that I was up to it, that I was the killer you keep talking about, that I would do whatever was necessary to get the story."

"That didn't happen," he said. "You're not a killer and you didn't get the story." He started pacing around his office, and I anticipated the breakage of his various artifacts. But he surprised me by remaining calm,

without any arm flailing, and turned to meet my gaze. "Look, you're a nice person, Ann. We've established that. And you write better than plenty of the hacks around here. Why don't you go back to that little town in Mississippi and get your head together—"

"Missouri," I corrected him. "Middletown, Missouri."

"Missouri," he said unapologetically. "They have a local paper in the town, right? Probably even a magazine. With your experience, they'll grab you in a heartbeat."

"And I would—what?—interview bank presidents? Mall managers? High school drama teachers?" I heaved a disconsolate sigh. "I don't want to go home, Harvey. I came to L.A. because an entertainment journalist is all I've ever wanted to be." I pictured my old bedroom, off the kitchen of my family's ranch house. The walls were plastered with photos of movie stars that I'd clipped from magazines just like *Famous*. "There's an electricity in Hollywood. Things *happen* here. The biggest thing that happened in Middletown recently was that a cat jumped out of its owner's minivan and ran away, and it took the cops three whole days to find it. Oh, and a kid came in fourteenth in the national spelling bee." I gave him a pleading look. "Please don't send me back to that."

He shrugged. "You could try landing with another magazine here, but it wouldn't be worth the effort," he said. "Once the Malcolm Goddard fiasco gets out, they won't return your calls."

The Malcolm Goddard fiasco had already gotten out, thanks to my performance earlier that morning.

"I hate to say it, but you're toast in this town, Ann."

He put his hand on my shoulder, and the small gesture of kindness, so out of character for him, made me realize how pathetic I must have seemed. "Go home, chill for a while, get it together. Then who knows, huh?"

"Who knows?" I repeated, my spirits lifting a tiny bit. "Are you saying there's a chance you'd hire me back?"

He removed his hand and walked toward the door, opening it to let me out. "Listen, if I'm still running this rag and you can show me what you're made of, anything's possible."

Wow. So he might take me back. All I had to do was grow a spine. And maybe Middletown was just the place to do it. I could pull myself together in the peace and quiet and moral rectitude of the Midwest and return to L.A. as a totally fearless, ready-for-anything killer journalist—if I didn't die of boredom first.

Part Two

Chapter Nine

IIIIIIIIIIIIIIIIIIIIIIIIIIIIIIIIIIIIIIIIIIIIIIIIIIIIIIIIIIIIIIIIIIIIIIIIIIIIIIIIIIIIII

"**How old were** you when you first realized that you wanted to be a chimney sweep?" I asked a twentyish man named Bud Goober, who was wearing bib overalls and had extraordinarily long, soot-encrusted fingernails. We were sitting in a Naugahyde booth at Kyle's drugstore, a pharmacy and soda fountain located on Middletown's main drag, at the intersection that boasted our lone traffic light. I was interviewing him for the local paper, the *Town Crier* (everybody called it the *Crier* for short). Bud had just won a John Deere lawn tractor—the zero-turn, SST-15 model—in a sweepstakes sponsored by Middletown Lumber and Lawn. He was, therefore, a celebrity, and I, newly hired by the *Crier* as a free-lancer, had been given the plum assignment of bringing his story to our readers. He was a big get, relatively speaking. My first one since leaving L.A. two weeks ago.

"Gosh, I dunno," said Bud, as my tape recorder continued to pick up the long silences between his answers. "I guess I was about ten. My daddy is a chimney sweep and his daddy is a chimney sweep and his daddy is a chimney sweep too. Never thought about being anything else."

"Very interesting," I said, nodding. "So you're carrying on the family tradition." No, he wasn't carrying it on in the manner of, say, Drew Barrymore, but actors were not my beat for this temporary gig of mine, and I was okay with that. I just needed to fill the time while I pulled my life together and got over my panic and phobia disorder, just needed to keep my writing and interviewing skills sharp for my return to *Famous*.

Still, leaving L.A. was a downer and I'd done my share of sobbing. I'd sobbed arranging for my garage sale, sobbed clearing out of my apartment, sobbed saying good-bye to Tuscany and James. But the sobbing had really kicked in during the trip across the country. Somewhere in Kansas, I'd run out of tissues and was forced to blow my nose into my AAA map.

I'd also managed to block out the fact that it was winter in Missouri, which didn't help matters. When I'd reached the outskirts of Middletown on February nineteenth, the weather was as grim as my mood—28 degrees and snowing.

And then there was the cultural disparity between L.A. and Middletown. The closest thing to an arts festival in our little hamlet of five thousand people was the county fair in July with its demolition derby, mud marathon, and horse-and-mule show. Moving home was an adjustment for me, in other words. I hadn't had a full-blown anxiety attack since I'd arrived on my mother's doorstep, not like the one at the Santa Monica airport, but I was still fighting off moments of out-of-the-blue sweating and light-headedness and palpitations—moments of low-grade fear that were so hard to anticipate and even harder to ignore.

"HOW OLD WERE you when you first realized that you wanted to be a retailer of women's intimate apparel?" I asked Betty Nettles, the forty-year-old owner of Bettina's Fancy, Middletown's answer to Victoria's Secret. Her idea of sexy lingerie was a pair of tube socks, but she was my

second profile for the *Crier,* following the one on Bud Goober the week before. The occasion was the grand opening of her shop, which was located between the ribs joint and the tanning/hair salon.

"I've been wanting to do this ever since I started watching *Oprah,*" Betty said, winking at me. "She taught me the value of lifting women up." She started laughing hysterically and pointing at all the bras hanging on a nearby rack. She was laughing so hard she could hardly catch her breath. "I'm lifting them up all right, aren't I? Lifting and separating."

"You are," I said, shutting off my tape recorder and wondering if interviewing people for the *Crier* was really such a hot idea. Yes, I was keeping my hand in, but I'd be lying if I said I was fully engaged.

OVER THE NEXT month, I interviewed a girl who trained her parrot to recite passages from her favorite Harry Potter book, a man who built a snow figure on his front yard that vaguely resembled the Virgin Mary, and a woman who peeled so many carrots at one sitting that her palms turned orange permanently. Yes, I tried to bring out the best in all the people I interviewed, but my eyes crossed whenever I'd actually have to write up these stories. I'd sit with my laptop at the Caffeine Scene, Middletown's answer to Starbucks, where every table offered Internet access along with a cup of joe, and dwell on how much I missed my old life. Eventually, I'd snap out of my funk, force myself to make the profiles as entertaining as possible, and e-mail them to the *Crier.* I kept reminding myself that I wasn't there for excitement. I was there to get my head together.

And then something happened that not only broke the monotony but changed the course of events in ways I could never have imagined. An understatement, as you'll see.

It all started when the *Crier* assigned me a profile of Richie Grossman, a former classmate of mine from elementary school through high school, not to mention the only other Jewish kid in town.

"So, Richie, how old were you when you first realized that you wanted to be a doctor?" I said as I sat in his cushy corner office at Heartland General, the hospital that served the residents of north-central and northwest Missouri, as well as metropolitan Kansas City. It was the largest employer in the area, and Richie had just been named assistant chief of staff, the youngest one they'd ever had.

"People call me Richard, now that I'm a big boy," he said with a chuckle, fingering his bow tie. "And I was ten when I knew I wanted to play doctor with you. Jeepers, what a crush I had." He was the kind of person who said "Jeepers." The kind of person who wore bow ties too.

"Come on." I waved him off. "You were too busy getting As to pay attention to me or any other girl." I remembered him as a nerdy kid who aced every subject. I also remembered that he'd been desperate to be popular, to be accepted by Middletown's version of the "in" crowd. He'd tried and failed to make the basketball team, tried and failed to be elected class president, tried and failed to date me. That was his problem, I thought as I appraised him. He'd always tried too hard.

"Okay, I'll answer your question truthfully," he said, with a mock-serious expression. "It was just the other day when I thought, Well, I don't look like the kind of Hollywood stars Ann Roth hangs out with, so I might as well go into medicine."

"Richie," I said, then corrected myself. "I mean, Richard." When he was young, his "look" could be summed up in one word: acne. But as an adult, he was fairly handsome. The acne was gone, his nose had receded into a less prominent role on his face, and his once dark, shaggy hair was now clipped neatly and conservatively. But he was still gawky—well over six feet tall and thin, with broad shoulders and an extremely erect posture—and he couldn't hide the inferiority complex that continued to hover over him. "Obviously, I'm not hanging out with Hollywood stars anymore," I said, trying to put him at ease. I went on to tell him I'd been pink-slipped by *Famous,* but I withheld the gory details.

"Well, their loss is our gain, and I, for one, am glad you came back to town," he said. He glanced down at the pile of papers on his desk, shuffled them around, didn't meet my eyes. "You must think we're all a bunch of hicks compared to Ashton Kosher."

"Kutcher." I laughed, not knowing whether his mistake was intentional. "I'll admit it's been an adjustment, especially living with my mother, aunt, and grandmother. But I'll be going back to L.A. one of these days. I'm just taking a little time-out here, preparing myself for the next chapter. In the meantime, it's really good to see you again, Richard. I'm so proud of you for what you've accomplished." I *was* proud of him. Happy for him too. I sort of liked the guy in spite of his tendency to push too hard. After all, he'd been around when I went through braces and pigtails. He was at the playground the day I'd gotten my period and stained the back of my white shorts. He'd even come to my father's funeral. We shared a history.

"Proud of me?" He seemed surprised, but pleasantly so.

"Absolutely."

He sat back in his swivel chair and started spinning around in it. He was making me dizzy, but that didn't take much these days. "Okay, ask me all those questions you've written down on your legal pad," he said when he completed his last rotation. "Maybe you'll be so fascinated by my rise to power at Heartland General that you'll have dinner with me tonight. Or maybe we could do a movie."

Was he asking me out? On a date? Richie Grossman?

He must have read the ambivalence on my face because he said, "Cancel that about the movie. Jeepers, what an imbecile I am. You've probably seen every single one. Been to the premieres. Interviewed the actors, the directors, the producers, the screenwriters. Forget the movies. Just forget I even came up with that idea. I don't know what I was thinking. We could—"

"Richard," I said, before he whipped himself into a lather. "I'm the same Ann Roth who went on that class camping trip with you. The teachers ran out of supplies, remember? I sneaked away on a little investigation and came back to tell everybody which leaves made the best toilet paper. I may have gone to Hollywood, but I didn't *go* Hollywood. Understand? There's no reason to put me on a pedestal."

"Sure." He nodded vigorously. "I'm just overeager." He held up his left hand and wiggled his left ring finger, which was not adorned with a wedding band. "I'm not married. You're not married. I'm in Middletown. You're in Middletown. I guess I see this as the big chance I never had when we were in high school."

I smiled. I had no romantic interest in Richie Grossman whatsoever, but it had been so long since a man had shown romantic interest in me that I couldn't help but be flattered. Still, I wasn't about to lead him on. I hadn't done it in high school and I wouldn't do it now. "We can make plans to have dinner or a movie or whatever you want," I said. "As *friends*. I'm just not in the market for a relationship right now, and I need to be up front about that. Okay?"

He shrugged. "What choice do I have?"

"Good. Now, let's do the interview," I said, turning on my tape recorder.

"Right, and *then* we'll go have dinner."

I laughed. He was nothing if not persistent.

"ANN, THERE YOU are!" my mother exclaimed, pouncing on me the second I walked through the door. "Oh, sweetie. I was so worried. All I could picture was a terrible accident, what with the slick roads and your funny car. It could have been a complete disaster."

So worried. Terrible accident. Complete disaster. You can see how I might have turned into a catastrophizer, right? As for the *funny car,* no one in Middletown drove foreign cars except communists. When I bought the Honda, my mother had to change our phone number.

"I called and told Aunt Toni that I wouldn't be home for dinner," I said. "Didn't she tell you?"

"Yes, but she said you didn't tell her *why* you wouldn't be home for dinner. We were frantic."

Frantic. I wrapped her in a protective hug. A squishy hug. Linda Roth was an attractive fifty-one-year-old woman—shiny reddish-brown hair in the same bangs-and-flip do she'd worn forever, dimpled smile, rosy cheeks—but she'd gained weight since my father died and become rounder, puffier, more matronly. And then there were the clothes; she used to wear them. In the past few months, her anxiety had progressed way beyond heights and dogs and dentists, and she didn't leave the house anymore. Instead, she padded from room to room in her pink terry-cloth bathrobe and matching slippers. She still cooked professionally, baking pies and cakes and breads for local grocers and bakeries and the occasional catered party, but now she hired people to deliver them to her clients so she wouldn't have to set foot outside. Her life had gotten smaller and sadder, and while I loved her very much, I was determined not to become her.

"I had dinner with Richie Grossman," I said as we walked arm in arm into the living room and sat down on the sofa together.

"You're kidding," she said. "Where on earth did you run into him? I hear he's practically running Heartland General now."

"I know. I interviewed him for the *Crier*. He invited me to dinner and I accepted." I giggled at the memory. "I suggested we grab a quick bite in the hospital cafeteria, but he insisted on driving me all the way to Center Creek to a restaurant that served 'sophisticated fare.' "

She chuckled. "That boy always did turn himself inside out to impress you."

"What boy?" said Aunt Toni as she stomped into the room. She was four years younger than Mom and strikingly similar in terms of coloring and facial features. But she was harder, more angular. Where my mother was doughy, Aunt Toni was crusty. She spoke in a hoarse, husky voice from the many years when she smoked, and she was bitter toward men after her husband, Mike Benvenucci, the owner of three auto-body shops, dumped her for Claire Honeycutt, a cheerleader at Middletown High when I went there, which made her young enough to be his daughter and caused a scandal that was our equivalent of Brad and Angelina. Aunt Toni was the tart-tongued, blunt one in the family—the "businesswoman," my grandmother called her because she worked as a paralegal for Stan Orwell, Middletown's most successful slip-and-fall lawyer—but she was as fearful as the rest of us. As I've mentioned, her specialty was freaking out in enclosed spaces. She had taken to leaving her bedroom door wide open at night so she would feel less confined, and her snoring reverberated throughout the house.

"Richie Grossman," said my mother as my aunt joined us on the sofa. "He asked Ann on a date and she went."

"It wasn't a date—"

"He's a big shot at Heartland General now," Toni interrupted me.

"A catch," my mother cooed.

Toni rolled her eyes. "There aren't any catches in Middletown, Linda."

"That's not true," said Mom. "I managed to find one."

Toni's nostrils flared. "Are you saying I could have found one if I'd had your impeccable taste?"

"Of course not," said my mother. "I was only pointing out that Jim was a wonderful husband and he was from Middletown, so it's possible that Ann will—"

"Right, but Mike was a piece of shit, and if Ann stays around here, she's liable to end up with someone just like him."

"Ann isn't interested in marrying the owner of body shops, pardon your language. She deserves better."

"Oh, and I didn't? Is *that* what you're saying?"

I forgot to mention that in addition to having panic attacks and phobias, my mother and her sister had arguments. On a regular basis. They bickered the way spouses bicker—unconsciously, reflexively.

"No, Toni," said my mother. "You're so defensive."

"Okay, okay. That's enough out of both of you girls."

Our heads turned as Grandma Raysa entered the living room, wincing in pain. She was a wrinkled, silver-haired, seventy-eight-year-old version of my mother. Her recent hip-replacement surgery caused her to walk with a slight limp and had made her cranky.

"Hey, Gram," I said as she plopped down in her favorite chair. Even from a few feet away, I could smell the Clorox on her. My guess was that she'd been forced to shake a stranger's hand within the past hour. Whenever the Jehovah's Witnesses came knocking, for example, she'd let them speak their piece, then head straight for the laundry room and scrub herself raw. She had nothing against the "JWs," as she referred to them. She was just terrified that people might bring plague and pestilence upon her house.

"Hey, yourself," she said. "We were all wondering why you didn't come home for dinner. Your mother made that chicken casserole you used to like. The one with the potatoes, the bisquits, and the cheese sauce."

The low-carb craze hadn't reached Middletown. Consequently, I'd gained a few pounds while I was trying to get my life together.

I explained about Richard and let the three of them debate his virtues versus his flaws, and eventually excused myself and went to bed.

As I was brushing my teeth in the bathroom, with its flowered vinyl wallpaper and carpeted toilet-seat cover and can of Glade air freshener atop the vanity, I stared at myself in the mirror—peered at myself between all the little blue decals—and thought, Don't panic. It's only temporary.

Don't panic. If only.

Chapter Ten

‖‖

On Sunday night, the last Sunday in February, the Academy Awards were being presented at the Kodak Theatre in Hollywood. If I hadn't been fired from *Famous*, it would have been my busiest day of the year. I would have been all over L.A., scrambling for stories about the nominees, writing them up and e-mailing them to Harvey at a feverish clip, and then covering all the hip and trendy parties into the wee hours. Instead, I was home with the girls.

My mother, aunt, and grandmother always watched the Oscars in the den, which, like the rest of the fifties, ranch-style house, was straight out of an old Ethan Allen catalog and was, therefore, the antithesis of hip and trendy. They had a ritual for the occasion, which began with tray tables in front of the TV, whose screen wasn't much bigger than my computer monitor, and continued with my mother's special "red-carpet dinner" (beef tenderloin slathered in béarnaise sauce, baked potatoes stuffed with cheddar cheese topped with bacon bits, and hearts of palm buried under Russian dressing), and ended with my grandmother demanding to know why everybody who won an award had to thank Jesus for it.

I tried to be thrilled to have the night off from work for the first time in five years—thrilled to be wearing jeans and a sweater instead of some designer knockoff that required holding in my stomach. But about an hour before the show, I got very fidgety. I kept thinking, What am I doing *here* when I should be *there*? More than ever, I felt as if I'd been drop-kicked right out of the splashiest event on earth, and before I knew it, I was focusing on Malcolm Goddard and his contribution to my fall from grace. All the humiliation and anger came thundering back, and I realized there was no way I could sit in my mother's den and watch that pompous pain in the ass on television, watch him look all tortured-movie-star-ish in his tuxedo, watch him be pawed by Rebecca Truit while the best actor nominations were read, watch him walk up to the podium to receive— Nope. The very thought of hanging around for the spectacle made me ill.

So I spent that Sunday night at the Caffeine Scene, writing up my interview with Richard for the *Crier* and drowning my sorrows in bad coffee. My fingers were running along the keyboard of my laptop when the doctor himself suddenly materialized over my shoulder.

"Fancy meeting you here," he said cheerfully. Without waiting for an invitation, he eased himself down into the chair opposite mine and deposited his laptop on my table. When I'd last seen him at the hospital, he'd been all dressed up under his white lab coat, but he was in more casual attire this time. Well, casual for him. No bow tie, but a button-down shirt and pleated slacks with cuffs. I wondered if he even owned a pair of jeans.

"Fancy meeting you too," I said, amused by the coincidence. "I was just typing up the piece about you."

"I would have thought you'd be hosting an Oscars party," he said as he plugged his computer into the Internet connection and booted up. "I pictured you doing something glamorous and exciting tonight."

"Not this year." I smiled ruefully, not bothering to add that there wasn't anything glamorous or exciting to do in Middletown. "What about you? What brings you here?"

He nodded at his laptop. "Work. I have research to do for the hospital. Just trying to find solutions to problems. As assistant chief of staff, it's up to me to deal with our lack of funds, our inability to hire doctors away from other hospitals, our nursing shortage, and our need to recruit more volunteers to pick up the slack for the nurses and offer an extra pair of hands. We're a terrific facility—just rated in the top five percent in the nation for cardiac-interventional procedures—but we're nonprofit. We rely heavily on donations, and if we don't get more of them, we'll go under, just like a lot of hospitals are going under these days. We've got to have more paying customers too. The growing number of uninsured patients is killing our bottom line."

Almost without taking a breath or even blinking, he went on and on about his responsibilities at the hospital, and I found myself tuning out. And it wasn't because I didn't care deeply about the health care crisis in this country. It was because he'd already told me all of this stuff during our interview—in excruciating detail. He'd wanted me to understand what an important job he had, and I'd gotten it. I'd really gotten it.

"Oh, jeepers. I'm boring you, aren't I?" he said at one point, hitting himself on the side of the head. "I bet you'd much rather talk about Jude Lawson."

I didn't correct him this time. So he wasn't up on his Hollywood references. So what. "You're not boring me at all," I said. "As I told you, I'm very proud of what you're doing with your life. It's very admirable."

"Thanks." He looked around the café. It was pretty dead that night; only four other people hunched over their computers. "Maybe after we finish working, I could whisk you off to that new jazz club in Center Creek. Or, if jazz isn't your thing, we could drop in at the Hole in the Wall and grab a late snack."

The Hole in the Wall was a bar and grill of the type whose menu featured buffalo chicken wings prominently. It wasn't my favorite spot, but that wasn't the point. I didn't want to get Richard's hopes up. He and I were not going to have a relationship, and that was that. "I appreciate the offer, but I think I'll just finish up your article and get a good night's sleep."

He sighed, frustrated. "Jeepers, I should have come up with something more enticing than the Hole in the Wall." He brightened. "Wait. I just remembered. There's a place that just opened over in Lakeville. A club. A real nightclub. It's got a DJ and dancing and it's supposed to be very cool. I heard all the best people go there. No celebrities, but quality people, you know?"

"Richard," I said, wishing he would just calm down and stop trying so hard. "I'm—"

"Oh," he said, cutting me off. "Maybe you don't like to dance. Do you like to, Ann? Dance, I mean? If you don't, we could skip the club and take a drive and—"

I stood up and patted his left forearm. "I'm going home after I finish up here," I said gently. "But first I'm getting another decaf. Can I bring you anything?"

"I'll have whatever you're having," he said, clearly discouraged, the same way he'd been discouraged when we were in high school.

When I returned to the table with our coffees a few minutes later, I found him sitting in my seat, poring over my computer screen.

"What are you doing?" I asked, genuinely taken aback.

"Just making sure you wrote nice things about me," he said with a chuckle.

THE FOLLOWING WEDNESDAY night, I was back at the Caffeine Scene, writing up an interview I'd done with a woman whose Ford Expedition had flipped over into a ravine and trapped her there for twenty-four hours. Unhurt but extremely hungry, she'd subsisted on the family pack of Reese's peanut butter cups that she happened to have in her purse. She was a nice lady, but, God, did I want to go back to L.A.

"We meet again," said a voice that turned out to be Richard's.

"Oh," I said, surprised to see him and even more surprised when he and his computer made themselves right at home at my table, just like the last time.

"I'm not stalking you, if that's what you're worried about," he said, fingering his bow tie. "Great minds think alike, that's all. Besides, even if we're not compatible, our computers are. Not everyone outside Hollywood has a PC; I've got a Mac too."

"Right." I nodded. We'd already had the Mac-versus-PC discussion on Sunday night, and I had no interest in having it again.

I was about to make polite but brief conversation with him, then go back to work on my story, when he leaned across the table and said in a dramatic whisper, "I have a secret and it'll knock your socks off."

"Can it wait until after I finish this?" I said, really trying to make the point that I was there to work, not to be dragged into yet another attempt by him to impress me.

He shook his head. "You're going to flip when you hear. Jeepers, I nearly flipped myself."

"Richard, I'm on deadline for the newspaper. I'd love to chat, but—"

"It's completely out of bounds for me to tell you this," he went on, continuing to lean in and speak very furtively, looking over his shoulder to make sure no one was eavesdropping. "I'll lose my job if you repeat it. It's that big, that incredible."

I sat back in my chair and sighed. He wasn't giving up. The man was incapable of giving up. I had no choice but to listen to whatever it was he was dying to get off his chest, act fascinated by it, and then go back to work. "Okay," I said, forcing my eyes to widen with a curiosity I didn't feel. "What is it?"

He cupped his hands around his mouth, to absolutely ensure that he wouldn't be overheard or even lip-read. "A celebrity is coming to the hospital."

I laughed. I couldn't help it. I didn't mean to be rude, but he was going way overboard in his attempt to ingratiate himself with me. "A celebrity?" I said, glancing down at my laptop and picturing the woman whose interview I'd been writing up. *She* was Middletown's idea of a celebrity. So was the chimney sweep. So was Richard, for that matter. What was he getting all riled up about?

"That's right," he said, smiling and nodding now, like the proverbial cat who swallowed the canary. He had what he thought was a juicy piece of gossip, apparently, and he was bursting to share it with me. "We have a strict confidentiality policy at Heartland—we never give out information about a patient—but this is pretty amazing. I had to tell you, Ann. You of all people."

"So who is he? Or she?" I said, trying to keep my skepticism in check. "Oh, wait. Let me guess. It's the guy whose cousin in Boston was on *Jeopardy!* I'm supposed to interview him next week for the *Crier*, so I hope he's not sick. Or is it the cousin who's sick?"

"Neither," said Richard, maintaining his air of hushed urgency, as if he were about to hand over classified CIA documents. "This is a major celebrity. A Hollywood celebrity."

Now he was really stretching it. There *were* no Hollywood celebrities in Middletown. Not ever. Yes, Don Johnson grew up in Missouri. So did Brad Pitt, in fact. But they didn't show up in my town. Why would they? "Why don't you just tell me who it is and then we can both get on with our work," I said as patiently as I knew how.

He leaned so far across the table that I thought his neck might snap. "It's Malcolm Godman."

I blinked. "Who?"

"Malcolm Godman," he hissed, checking again for interlopers.

I narrowed my eyes at him. I couldn't be sure, not absolutely sure, to whom he was referring, given his butchering of movie-star names. Still, I felt my pulse quicken and my breathing speed up. It couldn't be . . . No, of course not . . . Why would . . . And yet I had to ask. "You aren't talking about Malcolm Goddard, are you?" I ventured.

"Shhhh." He pressed his finger against his lips.

I swallowed, then whispered ever so softly and tentatively, "You can't possibly mean Malcolm Goddard. Right, Richard? *Right?*"

He nodded, and I nearly died. Really. My tongue fell out of my mouth and drool started dribbling down my chin, and I was too stunned to wipe it off.

"I knew you'd be impressed," he said, beaming now.

Impressed? I was blown away. Goddard coming to Middletown? To Heartland General? How? Why? He had just gone off to shoot a film in Canada! (He'd lost the best actor Oscar to Tom Hanks, by the way; I was thrilled.) He was scheduled to be out of the country for months! I'd read it in *Famous,* so it had to be true!

"We got a call from his cardiologist in L.A.," said Richard, positively gleaming with pride because he'd not only been privy to this tidbit but had now deposited it at my feet, a doggie with a bone. "Seems Mr. Goddard developed a heart problem and needs further testing, diagnosis, and treatment. He doesn't want the media finding out about his condition, for some reason, so he asked his physician to find him the best cardiac facility in the middle of the country, away from all the hubbub. Heartland fit the bill. He's being flown in the day after tomorrow. Or maybe it's the day after that. Okay, I'm not sure when he's coming, but I do know that Jonathan White, our top heart man, will oversee his care when he does come. Oh, and we'll be admitting him under an alias. How's that for discretion?"

I kept staring at Richard, searching his face for a sign that he was only joking, that he was making up the whole story. But why would he pick Goddard to joke about or brag about? He had no knowledge of my resentment toward him, of the fact that I might still be working at *Famous* if it weren't for that snake. Besides, fleeing media scrutiny was Goddard's

MO, and it was logical that he'd want to hide out. God forbid the parasites discovered that he wasn't the virile, healthy star everybody thought he was and then unleashed the truth on his adoring public. As for the alias, my assumption was that he would most likely trot out the "Luke Sykes" cover, just as he had at Spago.

Spago. The mere thought of that night made me—

"Did you ever interview him?" Richard asked as I kept trying to process his bombshell. I must have looked like a deranged person the way my jaw hung open and my eyes bugged out. But I was floored, dumbstruck. His news was huge and who could have predicted it?

"No," I managed. "Never."

"Well, you'd probably fall for him if you did."

"Fall for him?" I said. "He's—"

"I know, I know. Handsome and talented and rich," said Richard with an envious sigh. "I keep telling myself I have a lot to offer you, but how can I compete with guys in his league?"

I started to respond, then stopped myself. If Richie Grossman hadn't gotten the hint by now that he wasn't and never had been in a competition for my affections, then he'd never get it. Not after all these years.

"Anyway, it's all very exciting, even if nobody but you and I and Jonathan will be in on the secret. And it *is* a secret, as I said. He'll be treated like just any patient." He chuckled. "Except that he'll have the money to pay for his care. And we do need paying customers."

The irony. Malcolm Goddard was the last person I ever wanted to see again. The absolute last. And yet he was coming soon. To a hospital near me.

Or, to put it in more classic movie terms, of all the medical facilities in all the towns in all the world, he walks into mine.

Chapter Eleven

On the drive home, I reached into my purse for my cell phone to call Tuscany, my mind racing, my fingers trembling. I figured she'd still be at the magazine, given the time difference, and punched in her extension there. Her phone rang once and I clutched, then hung up before she answered.

It's completely out of bounds for me to tell you this. That's what Richard had said. *I could lose my job.* He'd said that too, citing the hospital's strict patient-confidentiality policy. But if it was so strict, why was the assistant chief of staff shooting his mouth off to me about Goddard? Yes, yes, he was trying to impress me the way he always did, but he was the one who was breaking the rules, not me. He was the blabber and I was simply the blabbee. I wasn't bound by any patient-confidentiality agreement, was I?

I dialed Tuscany's number again. There was no way I couldn't tell her.

But after one ring, I hung up a second time. I didn't want to get anybody in trouble. Richard was a decent person, just mildly annoying. I certainly didn't want him to lose his job on my account.

I surrendered to my misgivings, dragged myself and my laptop into the house, and chatted with my mother, aunt, and grandmother, who were sitting in the den watching a rerun of *Everybody Loves Raymond*. At one point, my mother commented that I seemed "all keyed up."

"Was it running into Richie Grossman at the coffee place?" she asked with a twinkle in her eye. "Are you seeing him in a new light, sweetie?"

Aunt Toni groaned. "She sees him in the same light as everyone else sees him, Linda. He's smart, granted, but a little too ambitious, too eager."

My mother cast her an exasperated look. "I was only wondering if there might be sparks, now that they're older, more settled in their lives."

"Ann isn't settled," said Toni. "I know you love having her here. We all do. But she's itching to get back to Los Angeles, in case you haven't noticed."

"Maybe if she became interested in a local boy, she'd—"

"Stay?" Toni scoffed. "She came home as a temporary measure, to try to face her fears head-on instead of avoiding them like we do."

Mom looked bewildered. "What fears?"

My aunt rolled her eyes. "I've got mine and Mother has hers, but you, Linda, are afraid of your own shadow. You won't even set foot outside this house."

"Nonsense," said my mother, turning up the volume on the TV remote. "I've told you over and over. I can leave anytime I want. I just choose not to. This has been a snowy winter and I—"

"Cut it out, you two," said my grandmother, nipping this latest tiff in the bud. "And quit talking about Ann as if she doesn't know her own mind. She's a tough cookie deep down. She'll find her way."

"Right." I faked a big, noisy yawn. "Actually, I'm kind of pooped. I think I'll turn in, you guys. 'Night."

I found my way, all right—straight into my bedroom, where I called my best friend on her cell. I couldn't *not* call her, I'd decided while my mother and aunt were busy picking each other apart. Tuscany and I had been in touch regularly, but she always did most of the talking because she had the more interesting gossip. Now I finally had something juicy to tell her. Something that would rock her world. Besides, I knew I could depend on her. She would keep Richard's secret if I asked her to.

She was at her place getting dressed for a dinner date by the time I caught up with her. "I have to look my best, so I'm trying on everything I own," she said.

"Where'd you meet this one?" I said, thinking of all the men she'd gone out with once and dumped. "At the Mercedes dealership? Office Depot? A traffic light?"

"For your information, I was introduced to him by James," she said.

"James?" I was surprised, not only because he had never introduced me to a straight man but also because Tuscany tended to dismiss fix ups in favor of pickups.

"Yeah, I'm going out with an actor on *The Bold and the Beautiful*," she said. "His name's Don Carerra and it's our second date."

Well, now I was really surprised. For one thing, she rarely had second dates. For another, she had sworn off actors, just as I had. But I was too wired about my own news to obsess about hers. "Look," I said, "I found out something tonight, something so incredible you won't believe it."

"I bet I know. You're adopted."

"What?"

"Okay. Your next-door neighbor turned out to be a serial killer."

"Come on."

"Then it's that your aunt is really your mother."

"No! Stop!"

"Well? Things like that happen in small towns. You hear about them all the time."

"Tuscany," I said, adopting a tone I hoped was serious, somber. "What I'm about to tell you is extremely confidential. Richard could lose his job if you repeated it."

She laughed. "Richard? Dr. Dork?"

"Don't make fun of him. He's not a bad guy." I'd given her the back-story on Richard and she always teased me about him. "I really don't want to get him in trouble. So promise. What I'm about to tell you has to stay between us. Has to."

"Okay, okay. I promise. But if this is about some patient who's suing because they yanked out the wrong—"

"It's about Malcolm Goddard."

"Coincidence that you brought him up," she said matter-of-factly. "I heard he walked off the set of the movie he was supposed to start shooting in Canada. That nasty publicist of his claims there were creative differences, but rumor has it he came back to the States and checked into Betty Ford."

"No, Tuscany." I took a long, deep breath in an attempt to calm down. My mother was right. I *was* all keyed up. "He came back to the States and is flying here."

"Where?"

"Middletown."

"*What?*"

"And not for rehab."

I told her the little bit I knew. "I assume 'Luke Sykes' will be admitted in the next day or so."

"But why your hospital, of all places?" she said, as dumbfounded as I was.

"I guess he got sick on the set, went to his doctor, and said, 'Send me to the middle of the country, where I can disappear.' Heartland General has a great reputation for heart-related problems, so his doctor probably said, 'I'll send you there.' "

"This is *too much*! The privacy freak is going where he thinks no one will hound him! Oh my God!"

"Amazing, right?"

"Totally. Did you ever think your shot at getting your job back would come this soon? It's only been a month since you left."

"My job back?" I said. "What do you mean?"

"Helloooo? Anybody home? You've just been handed the opportunity of a lifetime, Ann. The guy checks into that hospital, a stranger in a strange land, not a friend in the world. Then you show up all sweet and sympathetic. You make him like you and trust you. You change his bedpan if you have to. And before you know it, he'll tell you everything about himself and you'll write a fabulous piece about him for *Famous*. Harvey will be ecstatic and you'll be back in L.A., earning double what he was paying you."

I laughed. "Are you stoned or something?"

"No, I'm just so excited for you." She squealed, forcing me to hold the phone away from my ear. "Is this perfect payback for the way he jerked you around or what!"

"Wait. Just hold on," I said. "I can't go running over to the hospital to visit him. He hates me as much as I hate him. He'd have me thrown out of his room."

"Oh, like he'd even recognize you? He met you once. For a few minutes. He was drunk. It was dark on the patio at Spago. You had cheesecake on your face."

"I remember," I said, remembering too well.

"Plus, you were just one of a million reporters who've done battle with him. Even if you were wearing a name tag, he still wouldn't make the connection."

She had a point. Several points. Still. "So I'd—what?—just appear at his door and pretend I'd walked into the wrong room?"

Tuscany sighed. She was frustrated with me. "Wasn't this Harvey's beef with you? That you wouldn't do whatever it took to get the big story?"

"I— Okay, yes. But there *is* no story. Not that I can—"

"Oh, there's a story, all right, and you're sitting on it. It's your chance to prove him wrong, Ann."

I didn't say anything. I was overcome by the magnitude of Richard's announcement and by the sudden possibilities it raised for me, for my future.

"You *do* want your career back, don't you?" she prodded. "I thought it was your dream to have it back."

"It is, it is," I said. "But I don't even know how long Goddard will be hospitalized. He could be in and out before I even have a crack at him. And then there's the issue of *how* to have a crack at him. I'm not a nurse. I can't just waltz in and draw blood, as much as I'd like to." I allowed myself a laugh. "I don't have access to the patients there."

"Look," she said. "You're the same person who came up with that cheesecake scheme. You figured out a way to get close to him even when the publicist was telling you to back off. So you'll figure this one out too."

IT WAS WONDERFUL to have a best friend, and I appreciated her faith in me. But the cheesecake stunt was a Hollywood ploy, a gifting thing. Nobody in Middletown gifted. Sure, I could dig around and find out the names of Goddard's favorite flowers, stop by the local florist, pick up a cheery get-well bouquet, and present it to him at the hospital, once I tracked down the room where "Luke Sykes" was taking cover. The problem was, *why* would I be bringing him flowers? I wasn't supposed to know who he was. I couldn't just show up like some long-lost relative.

On the other hand, she was absolutely right about Goddard's reappearance in my life: I'd be an idiot if I didn't capitalize on it. I had prayed I could prove to Harvey that I was a killer journalist, and now my prayer had been answered. The more I thought about it, the more I realized that I *had* to find a way to take advantage of this quirk of fate and get my job back, which meant that I also had to come up with a good reason for being at the hospital.

No small challenge for someone like me, given my phobia of sick and dying people. After watching my father wither away, I'd developed the fear of catching the helplessness, the frailty, the pain of the sick and dying. I was very close to my dad when I was little. Adored him. He'd take me to the recreational lake in Middletown and we'd sit on the beach and he'd spin tales about the sea and the sky and the planets. I'd be mesmerized. He worked at the bank, was a numbers cruncher, but he had a dreamy, ethereal side. I was his only child and he doted on me, and I was devastated when he disappeared without an explanation that my ten-year-old mind could comprehend. Yes, as an adult I'd read enough articles in *Psychology Today* to know that my fears—and my mother's—were probably linked to his death to some degree; that it wasn't uncommon for anxieties to surface as the result of a loss. But to place myself in a hospital setting for a story, place myself in the very building where I last saw my father alive? No, the idea wasn't nearly as traumatic as having to fly on Goddard's Cessna, but I wasn't exactly embracing it. The day I'd interviewed Richard in his office was the first time I'd been back at Heartland General since Dad died there.

So. To put this in perspective, I had a fear of sick and dying people, a case of hypochondria, *and,* let's not forget, a fear of vomit. Patients in hospitals vomited fairly often, didn't they? Why else would all the rooms have those little kidney-shaped pans around?

Still, I had to get in there. I believed in destiny, in the cliché that things happen for a reason. Perhaps Goddard was about to land in my town precisely because I was supposed to write a story about him and return to L.A. in a blaze of glory. There was no question that I had to follow that destiny, do whatever it took to *make* it happen.

Plus, I really did despise the guy. Finagling an interview out of him without his permission would give me enormous pleasure. He'd played me. I'd be playing him right back. I just needed a way in.

And then I lit on it. Just lit on it. The idea floated into my consciousness and stayed there, filling me with immense satisfaction because I'd managed to conjure it up.

I'd been thinking about the hospital, about Richard, about what he'd talked about—droned on about—during our interview. He'd been all worked up about the hospital's financial crisis and he'd specifically mentioned the shortage of qualified nurses—and the effort to recruit more volunteers.

Volunteers. Yes. Heartland General needed more of them.

I would become a volunteer and gain access to Goddard easily. I'd have security clearance, wear a uniform, and roam the hospital as freely as if I belonged there. Well, why not? I didn't have a job, other than the occasional freelance piece for the *Crier.* I could devote myself to volunteering without the slightest scheduling conflict.

I was too old to be a candy striper, but I wasn't too old to walk around smiling at people and pointing them in the direction of the cafeteria, assuming that was all that was required of me. I probably wouldn't even come into contact with a sick and dying person. It would be a snap. I'd get Goddard to talk on the record without his knowing it, prove to Harvey I was a killer, and life would be good again.

God, yes. It was a brilliant plan, if I did say so myself.

Chapter Twelve

IIIIIIIIIIIIIIIIIIIIIIIIIIIIIIIIIIIIIIIIIIIIIIIIIIIIIIIIIIIIIIIIIIIIIIIIIIIIIIIIIIIIIIIIIIIII

"I see that you've had a career in journalism, but have you had any experience interacting with patients?" asked Shelley Bussey, Heartland's director of volunteers, as she read over the application I'd filled out. I was sitting opposite her in her cubicle of an office on Thursday morning in March, my face flushed from the gale of dry heat that was blowing through the vent over my head.

"No," I said, "but I've interacted with movie stars and they require more hand-holding than any patient ever could."

She smiled awkwardly. I'd managed to make a joke that was both inappropriate and insensitive, particularly since she'd told me she was a colon cancer survivor and had undoubtedly required plenty of hand-holding. But she maintained her sunny disposition. In her late fifties, she'd been running the department for over ten years and was one of those people who radiates goodness without being sanctimonious about it. With her nearly six-foot height and infectious laugh, she would have been a standout even without her shock of frizzy white hair, which had grown in that way, both in color and texture, after her chemo treatments.

"Okay then," she said brightly. "We've covered your educational background, and we've established that you've never been convicted of a crime." She scanned the application, running her finger down the page. "Oh." She looked up. "There's a question you forgot to check off." She passed me the document. "It's just under the space where you filled in your mother's name and address. 'Do you have any physical or mental disorder that would impair your ability to perform as a volunteer at Heartland General?' See it?"

I hadn't forgotten to check that one off. I'd simply avoided checking it off, thinking maybe she wouldn't notice the omission. "Physically, I'm fine," I said, figuring I might as well be open about my "handicap," as Peggy Merchant had dubbed it, in case it reared its head while I was on the premises. "But I've been dealing with anxiety lately. I'm not psychotic or anything, I swear. I just have panic attacks at inopportune moments, like when I'm in a crowd or about to board an airplane."

She didn't say anything, so I rushed in to fill the dead air.

"I can give you a personal reference," I offered. "I went to grade school with Richard—sorry, Dr.—Grossman, the assistant chief of staff. I'm sure he'd vouch for me." I hadn't told him yet about my sudden impulse to volunteer, but I assumed he'd be pleased and would, indeed, provide a reference.

She sat back in her chair and smiled. "First of all, you can call him Richard or you can call him Dr. Grossman or you can call him Tight Ass. It's all the same to me."

I laughed. "Tight Ass?"

"Well?" She arched her eyebrow mischievously. "He's all business around here, all hustle. Not exactly the class clown."

I decided not to tell her I was afraid of clowns too. I really liked this woman. She was kind and caring but a straight shooter. And I appreciated her sense of humor. It felt like an eternity since I'd worked for someone who had one.

"Second of all, there are a lot of reasons people choose to volunteer their time and energy," she said. "Some are on a crusade and believe it's their duty to serve others. Some are lonely and need a place to come to on a regular basis. Some have been sick, like I was, and want to give back to the hospital that saved their lives. And then there are some"—she paused, her eyes shining with compassion for me—"who are trying to find themselves or find their strength of character or conquer their demons. You'd be surprised how a gesture as simple as reading to a patient can make a volunteer feel heroic. Giving to others does that for people. It's more rewarding than you can imagine."

I also decided not to tell her that, while I certainly admired people who came away from volunteering feeling heroic and all that other good stuff, I wasn't wild about getting close to the patients, plural. I was only interested in getting close to one patient, and once I got my story about him, I was gone. I know that sounds callous, but it was true. I would do my very best to help out at the hospital as long as it didn't involve anything too creepy, but I had a career to salvage. "So you're not blackballing me for losing it every now and then?" I said instead.

She shook her distinctive white head, which reminded me of a tropical bird. "We all lose it every now and then. I'm much more interested in your ability to keep our patients happy than I am in whether you get a bad case of flop sweat whenever you fly."

"Thank you, Shelley," I said, touched by her willingness to overlook my shortcomings. Well, the ones I'd been honest about.

"You're welcome," she said, turning to her computer screen. After a few clicks, she pulled up a page that looked like a schedule. "Let's begin by assigning you a shift. Shifts are in four-hour blocks. Do you like mornings? Afternoons? Weekdays? Weekends?"

"My date book is wide open."

"Good. For beginning volunteers, I don't recommend taking on too much. I'll start you with two shifts per week and see how it goes."

On one hand, I was relieved when she said I didn't have to come more often. On the other hand, I didn't know when Goddard was being admitted or how long he'd be a patient. I didn't have the luxury of time. "How about Friday and Tuesday afternoons?" I said. "That way, I could start tomorrow."

"I like your spunk," she said, typing the information into her computer. "Fridays and Tuesdays from one to five." She turned back to me. "Now, which of our programs would you like to try?" She ticked off a list. There was a program where volunteers with dogs brought them in to boost patient morale, but since our family didn't have a dog, given my mother's fear of them, that one was out. There was a program where volunteers with musical talents performed for the patients, but since I couldn't carry a tune or play an instrument, that one was out. And there was a program where volunteers with strong religious backgrounds provided patients with spiritual counseling, but since I was the sort of Jew who celebrated Christmas, that one was out too.

"We're full up in the gift shop," she added. "But, considering your background, maybe we should put you in the magazines program. You'd be perfect."

"You want me to interview the patients?" My God, did she somehow sense I was there under false pretenses?

"Interview them?" She laughed. "Lord, no. As a matter of fact, I need to tell you about HIPAA, which stands for the Health Insurance Portability and Accountability Act. Basically, it's a federal law regarding privacy. It mandates that any breach of confidentiality about a patient's medical condition will land you in big trouble. We're talking about a fine and possible imprisonment."

"Wow. You could never have that law at hospitals in L.A.," I said. "Everybody's frantic for information when a movie star is admitted there, right down to the diagnosis. The paparazzi stake out all the entrances."

"They do have that law at hospitals in L.A.," she said. "They have it at every hospital in the country. But I'm sure it's tougher to enforce when celebrities are involved. We don't have much of a problem, fortunately, not being a magnet for the movie-star set."

If you only knew, I thought as she went back to her computer. Of course, it occurred to me then that Richard's blabbing to me about Goddard was more than a harmless attempt on his part to dazzle me; it was a serious breach of ethics that really could land him in big trouble. It also occurred to me that writing about Goddard while he was a patient and I was a volunteer could land *me* in big trouble—unless I avoided any mention of his medical condition and stuck strictly to his life and career prior to his hospitalization. Yes, I would write the story without even a passing reference to Heartland, with no information about where I'd interviewed him or under what circumstances. I would say we met at an "undisclosed location." It would give the piece a hint of mystery. Harvey would love that.

"So. We'll put you in magazines," said Shelley. "You'll be in charge of the cart that has new issues of all the major ones. You knock on the patients' doors, ask if they'd like anything to read, and give them a copy of *Famous* or *People* or whatever else they want. If they ask you to read to them, you read to them. If they ask you to sit with them, you sit with them. If they ask you to talk to them, to be their companion for a little while, you do that too. How does that sound?"

It sounded like an odd juxtaposition. I used to write pieces on the entertainment world. Now I would be reading somebody else's pieces on the entertainment world—to people with tubes sticking out of every orifice. I realized there was no getting around it: I'd have to do more than stand around looking useful. "It sounds incredible," I said, bursting with positive energy. I intended to convey to Shelley that I was looking forward to a wonderful, horizon-expanding adventure. I would touch lives and, as a result, become a stronger, more courageous person who would go on from this experience and reach great heights. Or whatever.

THAT AFTERNOON I stopped in at the hospital's lab to obtain my health clearance, then underwent three hours of orientation in a conference room with a half dozen other would-be volunteers. I learned that Heartland General had 250 private rooms and 1,500 employees, and catered to every conceivable medical specialty. I also learned that my mode of dress as a volunteer would be white pants, white shirt, white shoes, and a pink-and-white-striped smock; that we should always use the staff elevators, not the visitors' elevators; that it was imperative that we leave it to the nurses to both examine the patients and escort them in and out of bed; and that my mission as a volunteer was to treat patients with compassion, dignity, and respect, no matter what their demeanor.

Blah blah blah, I thought, wishing we could just dispense with the formalities so I could start my campaign to track down Goddard. But *no*. Jeff, our leader, a pleasant-looking man in his forties with a receding hairline and one of those walruslike mustaches that curls up at the ends, was frustratingly thorough. He even asked us to introduce ourselves and say which program we'd chosen. Ethan, a muscular twentysomething with a mullet, was volunteering in the ER because "that's where the real action's at." Nadine, a woman in her sixties who wore a nun's habit, wasn't offering spiritual services but rather musical ones; she was going to play the harp for the patients. Hank, a tiny, wrinkled man in his eighties, was participating in the puppy program along with Tillie, his cocker spaniel. And then there was Jeanette, a conservatively dressed blonde about my age—the very essence of the wholesome, corn-fed Midwestern gal. When asked what had brought her to Heartland, she said, "I got drunk and fell down a flight of stairs while I was pregnant. I lost the baby. My husband left me. I had a complete breakdown. My therapist suggested that by working with sick and needy children in pediatrics, I would feel better about myself." Everyone applauded.

"How about you?" asked Jeff, nodding in my direction. "It's Ann, right?"

"Yes, Ann Roth," I said, nervous suddenly. "Like Ross, only with a lisp." It was a silly line and I vowed that minute to stop using it, but Jeanette was a tough act to follow and I felt pressure to top her on the schmaltz meter. "I'll be working in magazines, because, um, magazines are the literature of hope, the people's poetry. I've seen how they offer a distraction for the sick and needy and help take their minds off their problems. And, like Jeanette, I've had my own personal crisis, my own breakdown of sorts. I came to volunteer here so I could heal myself in the process of healing others." Oh God.

"That's beautiful," said Nadine, the nun, while Ethan, the one with the mullet, pumped his fist in solidarity.

"Thank you all for being so forthcoming," said Jeff. "Now we'll be turning our attention to serious matters. Matters that affect the health and safety of our patients. Matters that could, if not handled correctly, trigger panic and fear."

Panic and fear. My two least favorite words in the English language. I felt my palms moisten.

"We'll start with the emergency codes," he went on. "Code blue is a life-threatening situation involving cardiac arrest or respiratory failure. If you're with a patient who's exhibiting signs of either condition, your job is to determine if the patient is breathing and/or has a pulse and, if not, to find the nearest hospital phone and dial 111, our equivalent of 911. Then—"

"Excuse me, Jeff," I interrupted, raising my hand. Shelley hadn't mentioned cardiac arrest and respiratory failure, had she? "You told us never to examine the patients ourselves."

"Right," he said. "I misspoke. In a code blue situation, it's really up to you. If you'd rather get a nurse to check the patient for unresponsiveness, do that. And thanks for the question, Ann."

"You're welcome," I said, somewhat reassured that I would not have to make the decision as to whether or not a person was dead, let alone touch that person.

"When a code blue is announced over the paging system, a specially trained team will exit the staff elevator and rush to the scene," he said. "As a volunteer, you must remember to stay out of their way, which is why you should always use the visitors' elevators."

My hand shot up.

"Yes, Ann?"

"You told us to use the staff elevators."

He thought for a minute, then nodded. "I guess it's more practical to use the staff elevators, except when there's a code blue emergency."

"But we won't know in advance if there's a code blue emergency," I said. "We could be on a staff elevator, minding our own business, and— bam—the code blue team shows up."

He nodded again. "Then use the visitors' elevators unless you're transporting a patient in a wheelchair."

Up went my hand.

"What is it, Ann?"

"You told us to let a nurse escort patients in and out of bed, so why would we ever be transporting them in a wheelchair?"

Jeff twirled the ends of his mustache. "In special cases, you might be transporting them, but I wouldn't worry about it. *Okay?*" He said that as if to mean: "Will you shut up now?"

"Got it," I said.

Jeff moved on to other codes, including code gray, which related to "suspicious unknown individuals."

"I'm not here to alarm you," he said, immediately alarming me, "but because we're a highly visible entity in the area and our doors are open day and night, there's always the possibility of a confrontation with an abusive or even dangerous person."

Up went my hand.

"Ann?"

"Are we talking about a terrorist?" I said, which elicited gasps.

"It's unlikely," said Jeff, "but don't hesitate to call 111 if you're afraid."

If I'm afraid? I started to feel more and more dizzy as I listened to Jeff warn us about things like hazardous-materials spills, abductions of new-borns, and lapses in infection control, which could lead to contact with contaminated blood, which could lead to—

"And finally, we need to talk about code red," he said. "Fire is the worst thing that can happen at any hospital."

"What should we do if we smell smoke?" asked Hank, the man with the cocker spaniel.

"Your first priority is to remove the patient from danger," said Jeff. "Then you—"

"Sorry to repeat myself, but you told us not to escort a patient in or out of bed," I reminded him without bothering to raise my hand this time.

"Fire is a different story, Ann. Your job is to get him out of the room, close the door, pull the nearest fire alarm, and call 111."

"What if he's not ambulatory?" I said, hearing myself sort of screech.

Jeff yanked on his mustache. Hard. "Just find the fire alarm and pull it," he said curtly. "And then get a nurse to move the patient."

I sat back in my chair and felt my knees knock, my mind filled with visions of all the ways I could fuck up as a volunteer.

"Psst."

I glanced to my left. Jeanette was leaning over to speak to me. "What?" I whispered.

"You ask a lot of good questions," she said. "You should be a reporter for one of those magazines you'll be giving out."

"Actually, I used to be," I said, "but I was fired."

"I hear you." She patted my hand. "You're doing this to prove that you have what it takes to get your job back."

"Exactly," I said. Well, maybe not the way she meant it, but close enough.

Chapter Thirteen

On Friday afternoon at ten minutes to one, early as usual, I reported to the volunteers office outfitted in my uniform and photo ID card, which hung from my neck on a lanyard. As I appraised myself in the full-length mirror on Shelley's office door, I thought with intense pleasure, Goddard won't have a clue who I am and he'll spill his guts to me willingly.

I couldn't help grinning. I mean, I really couldn't.

Shelley laughed at the way I was admiring myself. "Little Miss Hollywood is getting a kick out of this, isn't she?"

"You have no idea," I said.

She surprised me by reaching out and hugging me. She was so tall that I ended up wrapping my arms around her hips.

"Just remember that you can come to me with any problem, large or small," she said after letting me go. "That's what I'm here for. So whenever you're confused or in the mood to vent, my door's always open. Don't forget that, Ann."

"I won't," I said. I smoothed out my smock and retied the laces on my white shoes. "So, Shelley. I'm ready to roll. Just point me in the direction of the magazine storage room and I'll get to it." I was dying to find out if Goddard had been admitted yet. During the orientation, Jeff had explained that the sixth and highest floor of Heartland General was the so-called VIP floor, and I figured he'd be up there somewhere. Its rooms were more spacious and more luxuriously appointed—they had bathrooms with both a tub and a shower, as well as a sofa bed where visitors could spent the night—and they had a distant view of the lake as opposed to the roof. My plan was to head straight up there and offer the guy a copy of *Famous*. Ha-ha.

"I do love your spunk," she said with a smile, "but we have to rein it in just for today. We don't send our volunteers out solo, not for their first shift. We have you shadow one of the other volunteers, so you get the hang of things."

Swell. How was I supposed to interview Goddard as someone's *shadow*? Unless I found a way to shake him or her off and go my own way. Maybe I'd get lucky and be assigned one of the octogenarians who'd want to leave early and let me finish up the shift by myself. Maybe I could request—

"Ann?"

A high-pitched, oddly familiar voice pierced my reverie. I turned. And then I did a double take. "Claire?"

"Bet you didn't expect to see me," said the brunette who was standing very close to me.

"No, I sure didn't." Claire Honeycutt was the cheerleader/slut in my high school class who grew up to become Aunt Toni's ex-husband Mike's second wife. I hadn't seen or spoken to her in years. I'd only heard that she'd brought her Ford Taurus into Uncle Mike's body shop one day following a fender bender, lured him into a room at the Middletown Best

Western, and destroyed his happy marriage. That was my aunt's version anyway.

I backed away so I could get a better look at Claire. She wasn't the perky cheerleader anymore—gone was the ponytail, gone were the gold hoop earrings, gone was the lithe little body that did splits and somersaults and other contortions I could never do—but she was still smiley and fairly trim and short (the top of her head came up to my nose). She wasn't unattractive, just unremarkable looking, someone you'd never figure for a home wrecker. She wore her brown hair in a haphazardly cut, layered style that was messy as opposed to flattering. She painted her full lips in a retro peach color and applied too much concealer under her eyes. And her body was thicker around the middle now; she was trim, as I said, but there was a pouch sticking out of her smock.

Yes, the smock. Claire Honeycutt—Pardon me. "Claire H. Benvenucci" was how her name was printed on the ID badge that dangled from her lanyard—was a volunteer too. But not just any volunteer, apparently. *My* volunteer. Such was life in a small town. People from your past were always turning up.

"Shelley asked me to train you today," she said, bouncing up and down on the toes of her white sneakers. "She had no idea we were semi-family until I told her a few minutes ago."

Semi-family. Aunt Toni would flip if she heard that. "Just curious, Claire. How long have you been in the magazines program?" She couldn't be all bad if she was motivated to donate her time to the hospital.

"About a year," she replied. "I was arrested for forging one little check, can you believe it? Anyhow, they let me do my community service by volunteering."

Lovely. But then, who was I to talk? I too had another agenda for being there.

"Shelley wants you to shadow me today," she went on. "So you gotta stick to me like glue, okay?"

THE STORAGE ROOM where the magazines were kept under lock and key was a short walk down the hall from the volunteers office. Issues of the publications were stacked on shelves by title and included everything from *Redbook* and *Martha Stewart Living* to *Popular Mechanics* and *National Geographic.*

"But the most popular ones are right here," said Claire as she pointed to the shelf where copies of *Famous, People,* and *Up Your Ass Weekly* were piled. "We always run out."

"So even patients in hospitals want to know what's going on with Jessica Simpson," I mused.

"Oh, yeah," she said. "You'll see. They want the light stuff when they're recovering. It takes their minds off the pain."

So I hadn't been exaggerating in my speech at the orientation. The patients did need the distraction that the celebrity magazines provided.

"Your biggest trick will be to keep *Famous* and the other Hollywood ones away from the nurses," said Claire. "Sometimes they steal 'em off the cart when you're not looking."

Speaking of the cart, it was a longer but no less clunky version of your basic metal shopping cart, with partitions for each category of reading material (fashion, news, sports, cooking, etc.). Once we loaded it with fresh issues, it weighed as much as my Honda.

"How are we supposed to push that thing around the entire hospital?" I asked, since I hadn't anticipated that there would be strenuous physical labor involved in my pursuit of Goddard.

She answered by grabbing the handlebar of the cart and shoving it out the door. "It's hell on your back," she said through gritted teeth, "but Mike gives me a massage after my shift."

Men who gave massages. I couldn't get away from them.

She steered the cart to the visitors' elevator and in we went. "Why don't we start on the sixth floor?" I suggested. Yes, I'd have to stick to her like glue, but at least I could get a glimpse of Goddard, I figured, get a sense of how receptive he'd be to a visit from a volunteer.

"Sure," she agreed. "We can work our way down. Shelley says to cover as much of the hospital as possible during our four hours, but the key thing is bonding with the patients, not giving out magazines. Nobody's gonna yell at you if you come back with a full cart."

Claire seemed to be relishing her role as my teacher. Either that or she was just paying her court-mandated debt to society.

"Here we are," she said as we exited the elevator on six. She pushed the cart down the hall, waving to a passing nurse like an old pro, while I walked beside her, smelling the hospital smells and hearing the hospital sounds and suddenly feeling afraid. My hunt for Goddard notwithstanding, who knew what lurked inside those rooms? Gross things. Upsetting things. Things I might catch. "Okay, a few don'ts before we start." Claire parked the cart in the hall, against the wall. "If the door is marked with a sign that says 'Must Wear Gloves Before Entering,' you don't go in. If the door says 'No Visitors,' you don't go in. If the door is completely closed, you don't go in, because the patient could be sleeping or getting examined by a doctor."

"What if it's open?" I said in the grip of fear and stupidity.

"You go in." She laughed. "They don't bite, although some of them can be snippy. Just try not to take it personally."

Goddard didn't know how to be anything except snippy, and I'd tried not to take it personally. But he'd made it personal. The minute he'd insisted on doing the interview in his SUV with wings.

"How about the do's?" I asked, praying they didn't include offering a patient a magazine while he or she was projectile vomiting.

"You always knock on the door and ask, 'May I come in?' Once you have their permission, you go in and introduce yourself. Depending on what shape they're in, you try to get them to talk. Ask how they're feeling. Ask how long they expect to be in the hospital. Ask if they want something to read." She laughed. "A lot of the men want *Playboy,* but Shelley doesn't let us carry skin."

"No point in arousing them for nothing," I said, trying not to recoil at the image of a guy on a ventilator springing a boner.

"Right." She motioned for me to follow her into the first room whose door didn't signify a don't. She knocked, asked for permission to enter, and received the okay. We approached the bed. The patient was a beautiful woman in her forties with her leg in a cast.

"How're you feeling?" Claire asked.

"Not bad, considering I broke it in three places," said the woman, nodding at the cast.

A broken leg, I thought, relaxing a little. I can deal with that. Not contagious. Of course, the reporter in me had lots of questions for her. "How'd it happen?" "Where were you when it happened?" "Did you fall in your kitchen or on a ski slope?" But I remembered Shelley's warning: We weren't supposed to ask about the specifics of a patient's condition. If they chose to discuss the details with us, fine. Otherwise, confidentiality ruled.

Claire talked to the woman for several minutes, then offered her a magazine.

"I brought a book, but it's hard to concentrate," said the patient. "Do you have *Famous* or one of those?"

I couldn't help smiling when she singled out the name of my old employer. I felt proud, oddly enough, even though the issue she ended up with was published after I'd been booted out of the company.

Claire and I proceeded down the hall from patient to patient. There was the man with an ulcer who didn't want to talk but did want a copy of *Smithsonian.* There was a woman with a ruptured disk in her back who didn't want a magazine but did want to talk about how she suspected her husband of having an affair with their daughter's second-grade teacher. And there was a woman with no discernible illness or injury who didn't want to talk and didn't want a magazine but did want to inform us that she would have been discharged that morning if she'd been able to move her bowels.

"We always get the shit report when they're about to go home," said Claire after we'd made our escape. "I don't know why they like to give us the turd-by-turd, but they do."

I thanked her for the tip. As she was about to wheel the cart back into the elevator, I held her arm. "Are you sure we've been in to see every patient on this floor?" Almost all the doors to the rooms had been open. No Goddard. No Luke Sykes either. Not a trace of him.

"Yeah. Why? You looking for someone in particular?" she asked.

I shook my head much too vehemently. "Just didn't want to miss an opportunity to spread that Heartland General good cheer."

We took the cart down to the fourth floor, the "women's wing," which included patients who'd just had hysterectomies as well as mothers who'd just delivered their babies. We found ourselves lingering in maternity, because the newborns were so cute.

"This isn't hard at all," I said with relief when our shift was over.

"Not hard at all for me," said Claire. "I was looking at three months in the county jail. I got off easy."

ON MY WAY back to the volunteers office, I ran into Richard. Literally. He was walking backward, reeling off instructions to some underling, and crashed into me.

"Ann! I'm so sorry! What are you—"

Naturally, he was surprised to see me in uniform. I had intended to stop by his office after I signed out that afternoon so I could tell him I'd become a volunteer, but there was no need now.

"Hey, Richard. I bet you're wondering about this," I said with a big smile, fingering my smock. "Well, what you told me during our interview about the need for volunteers really resonated with me. Since I'm sort of at loose ends at the moment, I thought why not help out?"

"Jeepers. This is great," he said. He was carrying a medical chart and looked very authoritative in his lab coat. Still geeky but definitely in charge. "Great for the hospital, of course, but great for me too. How about dinner tonight?"

"Oh, thanks for the invitation, but I promised Mom I'd—"

"She'll understand," he interrupted, taking my arm and leading me off to a quieter corner of the hall. "We could drive over to Center Creek for the Ice Capades show. Do you like to watch skating, Ann? Or would you rather do something else? Maybe just dinner and a brisk walk in the snow? I bet you were one of those exercise nuts when you lived in L.A.— yoga and who knows what else, right?"

He was exhausting. "I can't, Richard," I said. "I'm kind of tired after my first day of volunteering, and I did promise my mother I'd be home to help. She's got a big order of brownies to deliver to Sallie's Groceries. Besides, I think you should ask somebody else to go to the Ice Capades. There must be dozens of women at this hospital who'd love to be your date."

"Okay, okay," he said with a sigh. "You only want us to be friends. You've told me that. But, jeepers, can't friends go out every now and then?"

"Of course," I said, too worn out to pursue the conversation further. "Just not tonight."

"Then I'll try again," he said, straightening his already straight posture.

Fine. What I really wanted was news of Goddard. Had he arrived yet? Had he been admitted? Had his heart condition been diagnosed? Would he need surgery? So many questions, but I was uncertain as to how to ask them. I really didn't want to get Richard in trouble or make him suspicious about my motives for asking them.

I was mulling over these matters when he put me out of my misery. He leaned in very close to me, much too close given the garlic on his breath, and whispered, "Godman's not here yet, by the way."

I pretended to be blasé about this. "Mum's the word, right?"

"Right, but now that you're a volunteer, you might get a peek at him."

"I hadn't thought of that," I said without so much as a blink. "And if I do, I'll make sure he gets the care he deserves."

Chapter Fourteen

|||||||||||||||||||||||||||||||||||||||||||||||||||||||||||||||||||||||||||||||||||||||||||||||

The women of the household were panting with excitement when I got home. They'd been more than a little bewildered by my decision to become a volunteer, seemingly out of the blue, although my mother reminded the others that I'd always been a "good girl," but they were starved for entertainment and were eager to hear about my first day at the hospital.

"Start from the beginning," Mom said as we all sat at the dinner table eating foods whose main ingredient was butter. She was wearing a bathrobe I hadn't seen before. New slippers too. No, it wasn't as if she'd put on real clothes and decided to stop holding herself hostage in the house, nor had she copped to suffering from agoraphobia, but maybe my living at home was having a positive impact on her. I liked to think so, anyway.

"Very well," I said. "The person who trained me gave me a list of do's and don'ts, and I met some of the patients and handed out magazines."

"Who trained you?" Aunt Toni pounced, as if she had a sixth sense about anything having to do with her ex-husband.

I can't say I didn't anticipate the question. I'd even rehearsed the answer. "Oh, just one of the other volunteers," I replied. "She's been there for about a year."

"And she told you how important it was to wash your hands?" asked Grandma Raysa.

"Yes, Gram. She told me. She even showed me where they keep the Purell. It's industrial strength."

"Is she from Middletown?" asked my aunt, homing in on the facts like a reporter. I may have inherited my phobias from my mother, but Aunt Toni had the same inquisitive nature I did.

"As a matter of fact, she is," I said. I had given myself permission to be vague and evasive, but not to lie. There was enough denial in this household.

"What a coincidence, sweetie," said my mother. "What's her name?"

"Her name?" I repeated, hoping I could keep dancing around the subject until it went away. I really didn't want to start a war or open old wounds. "Actually, I'm not allowed to reveal the names of the patients. There's this thing called the HIPAA law that mandates privacy and confidentiality."

"She meant the name of the volunteer who trained you," said my aunt. "We might know her or her relatives."

I crossed and uncrossed my legs. Oh, they knew one of her relatives all right. "Hang on. Don't you want to hear more about my shift?" I said as a diversionary tactic. "I thought you guys were so interested."

Mom clapped her hands giddily. "Yes, yes. Tell us more."

I regaled them with tales of the man with the ulcer and the woman with the broken leg and the beaming mothers with their beautiful infants. And then I finished up the story with a flourish, expressing my high opinion of Shelley Bussey and the wonderful work she was doing at the hospital.

"Bussey?" said Grandma with an arched silver eyebrow. "Is she Jewish?"

As I've explained, we were lapsed Jews in that we celebrated Christmas and didn't belong to a temple, but we were cultural Jews in that we rooted for Jewish baseball players and Jewish politicians and Jewish Miss Universes. Oh, and my grandmother was always speculating about who might be Jewish despite a gentile-sounding name, the way people in Hollywood speculate about who might be gay despite a lead in a romantic comedy.

"I have no idea," I said.

"Is she from Middletown?" she followed up.

"I don't think so," I said.

"How about the one who trained you? Is she a local?" asked Aunt Toni.

That again. Now what? I could only skirt the issue for so long.

Oh, the hell with it, I thought and braced myself for the inevitable.

"Yes," I said. "The person who trained me today was Claire Honeycutt."

There was a collective gasp. I watched Aunt Toni's jaw go slack.

"That tramp is a volunteer at Heartland General?" she said finally, her voice quivering with rage. "They let her into the rooms of those poor, vulnerable people?"

"Look, I know she's public enemy number one around here," I said, "and I'm not sticking up for her. It's just that she was pretty decent to me, and I—"

"Did you hear that?" she said, leaning over me so she could speak directly to my mother. "Your daughter is all chummy with that trashy girl who stole my husband."

"Ann didn't say they were chummy," Mom replied, leaning over me so she could speak directly to my aunt. "And it isn't her fault that Claire was the one who trained her today. There's no reason to get testy with her."

"I'm not testy with her," said a testy Aunt Toni. "I'm testy with you, Linda. All you care about is smoothing everything over, making it all nicey-nicey. There are times when things can't be nicey-nicey."

"Enough!" said Grandma Raysa, clinking her spoon against her glass for emphasis.

Satisfied that she had put an end to her daughters' bickering, she rose wearily from her chair, limped into the kitchen, and started spritzing the countertops with Lysol—her way of dealing with stress.

We weren't your typical family, obviously, but we were all we had.

"YOU SURE YOU'RE ready to go it alone?" Shelley asked on Tuesday afternoon when I arrived at the volunteers office. She was wearing a bright red dress, which, together with her imposing height and her white frizz, created a startling impression. She loved to dress colorfully. She said that every day of her life was a celebration of her victory over cancer and that, by God, she was going to make us all sit up and take notice. She was the opposite of my father, who succumbed to his cancer without a fight. There wasn't a hint of weakness or frailty about her.

"Oh, I'm definitely ready," I said. I'd spent the entire weekend wondering about Goddard, picturing him stretched out in a bed on the sixth floor, rehearsing my entrance into his room and my first words to him. He'd be all alone, so lonesome, so ready to unburden himself to a sweet new friend.

"Well, then have at it," said Shelley, continuing to enjoy my enthusiasm.

And I was enthusiastic. Just not for the reason she thought.

I headed for the storage room, refilled the cart with fresh magazines, including as many issues of *Famous* as I could stuff into the "entertainment" divider, and set off on my first solo act. I felt chipper in my crisp uniform and enjoyed the smiles I got from passersby. Under my breath, I even hummed a little. I was optimistic about my future, just like I used to be.

I went straight to the sixth floor, hoping to find Goddard right away but trying not to appear obvious about it. I was supposed to be interested in *all* the patients.

When I got off the elevator, I spotted the same nurse I'd seen on Friday and waved to her, just the way Claire had. She was a bosomy Pamela Anderson blonde, and if I were Richard I would have put the moves on her instead of me. Actually, I did put the moves on her. I hoped she'd be able to tell me if there were any new admissions on the floor. Any new admissions with turquoise eyes and wavy dark hair and rotten manners.

"Pammy, right?" I said as I parked the cart in the hall.

"Right," she said without interest. She was undulating around the nurses' station, looking way more slutty than Claire.

"I'm Ann, and I'm a new volunteer," I said. "I was wondering—"

Just then a voice came over the loudspeaker, and Pammy held up her hand to silence me. "Gotta go," she said.

"But I only have one question," I said.

She glared at me. "They just announced a code blue on the ninety-year-old guy in 605, so make yourself scarce."

"Oh, sorry," I said, feeling really lame. Suddenly, there was heightened activity around us. Nurses, orderlies, technicians—they were all rushing toward the patient's room. Pammy muttered as she bustled past me, but she did take a second to glance at my cart. Probably to see if I had the latest issue of *Famous*.

Not wanting to be anywhere in the vicinity of a dying person, I turned the cart around and headed for the other end of the floor, which was much quieter. I parked the cart in the hall, arranged my face into my kindest smile, walked toward the patient rooms, and knocked on the first open door. "May I come in?" I asked.

No answer, so I peered into the room to see if the patient was asleep or in the bathroom.

"Oh," I said when I saw a perfectly healthy-looking sixtyish woman sitting up in bed. Aside from the IV fluids dripping into the vein in her hand, I wouldn't have figured her for a person who needed hospitalization. "Maybe you didn't hear me knock." I moved closer, my confidence bolstered by how un-sick she seemed. "I'm Ann, and I'm a volunteer at Heartland General. How are you feeling today?"

Her large brown eyes stared vacantly at me. Her mouth too was non-committal.

I repeated my greeting loud enough to wake the code blue guy down the hall. Still no response.

"Well, I just wanted to say hello and ask if you needed anything to read," I said. "I'd be glad to bring you a magazine."

Her expression never wavered. I wondered if she might be from another country and we had simply hit a language barrier. I knew a little Spanish—Well, okay. I knew *Que pasa?*—so I tried that. Nothing.

I kept going, groping for anything that might be a conversation starter. "We have magazines about cooking and gardening and—"

"AHHHHHHHH!" screamed the woman, scaring me in that primal way that people scare you when they sneak up from behind and go, "Boo!"

After practically leaping into the air, I flattened myself against the door, pulsating with fear, wishing I were back in L.A. getting screamed at by Harvey. "Are you in pain?" I said in a small voice.

"AHHHHHHHHH!" she screamed again. It was a bloodcurdling scream that brought a harried nurse into the room.

"What's going on in here?" she demanded, as if I were a thief, even though it was obvious from my uniform that I hadn't done anything wrong.

"I was just asking if she wanted a magazine," I said.

"Didn't they teach you the rules?" she said, dragging me out of the room by my arm, then pointing at the sign on the door. "'No Visitors' means no visitors."

Oh God. I hadn't seen the sign. In my zeal to find Goddard, I'd just barged right in without bothering to read it. Not only that, I'd forgotten to get the patient's permission to enter—one of Claire's don'ts. I *had* done something wrong. Two things. I was a fool. I apologized to the nurse, who gave me a withering look and walked away.

"But why was she screaming?" I called out to her. "Does she have dementia? Or some other sort of neurological problem?"

The nurse, who was as fat as I was going to be if I kept eating my mother's casseroles, said, "In case they didn't teach you *anything,* you don't ask about a patient's medical condition and I don't tell you about it. Got that?"

"Okay, sure." Three things wrong.

I pushed my cart down the hall, hoping my next patient would be Goddard. But when I came to an open door, I was careful to check it for warning signs before entering. There weren't any, so I knocked. "May I come in?"

"Whatever," said a female voice that wasn't Goddard's but sounded just as irritable as I expected his would be.

I waltzed in. The patient had a splint on the bridge of her nose that was held in place with a wad of adhesive tape. "I'm Ann, and I'm a volunteer at Heartland General," I said. "How are you feeling today?"

"How do you think?" she snapped. "I look like a monster."

"No, you don't," I said, since it was my job to cheer her up. "You look lovely considering what you've been through."

"How the hell would you know what I've been through?" she said, narrowing her eyes at me.

I figured I'd better stick to the script. "I have some magazines in the hall, and I'd be happy to bring you one."

"I don't need a magazine," she said, continuing to be cranky. "What I need is a bowel movement. The doctor won't let me out of here until I have a really good one."

A shit report. Well, Claire said I'd be getting them.

I wished the woman a speedy recovery and hurried out of the room. Unfortunately, I wasn't watching where I was going and collided with a harp. I hit it in such a way that as I fell to the floor, my leg passed over its strings, causing an actual *twang*.

"Nadine! I'm so sorry!" I said, recognizing the nun from my orientation as I picked myself up and smoothed my smock. "I hope I didn't break anything."

She smiled and plucked a few notes to test out the instrument. "Fit as a fiddle," she said. "I play those too, you know."

We talked briefly about our respective volunteering experiences thus far, and it was comforting to hear that I wasn't the only one who'd encountered a couple of tough cookies. The difference between Nadine and me, however, was that she welcomed the challenges brought by the patients who were out of sorts. "Those are the ones we need to help the most," she said.

I admired her loving, forgiving nature, and wished I could follow her example when it came to Goddard. But I wasn't a nun. I was a killer journalist.

With a renewed sense of purpose, I pushed my cart farther down the hall, in search of my prey.

"May I come in?" I said after knocking on a door that was open but only just a crack. When the patient didn't answer, I tried again. "Hello? Anybody there?"

"Uh, yeah. I'm here," said a man sounding a little winded, "but just give me a second to get pretty."

My God! I'd found him! It had to be Goddard in that room! I'd recognize that mumble voice anywhere!

Get pretty. I rolled my eyes. Who else would be so vain? And it made sense that he'd sound winded. He was having heart problems, according to Richard.

I took lots of deep breaths as I prepared to act charming so I could ingratiate myself with him and coax him to talk. This was my moment. My once-in-a-lifetime opportunity. More deep breaths. Inhale, exhale.

Okay, what's the holdup, I thought as I waited for permission to enter. "May I come in now?" I said when I couldn't wait any longer. I was crazy with anticipation and, yes, anxiety.

When he answered in a low moan, "Oh, yeah," I was trembling slightly but eager. I opened his door wider and stepped brightly into the room. "Hello. I'm Ann, and I'm a—"

I froze in my tracks when I realized my mistake—the latest of what would be many mistakes. Goddard was nowhere in sight. The patient was a middle-aged man who was lying on his back stark naked, receiving a blow job from a middle-aged woman who had purple hair.

What will always stick with me was the fact that they didn't stop what they were doing when I caught them going at it. Either they were too carried away to care that they had an audience, or they were exhibition-ist types who enjoyed having an audience. All I can tell you is that I was deeply unnerved by the situation, wracking my brain to remember if Jeff, the leader of the orientation, had covered the subject of patient sex and, if so, how we volunteers were supposed to handle it.

"Sir, I really think you . . . It's important that . . . Your health should be your primary concern," I stammered, averting my eyes as the woman's head continued to bob up and down over the man's remarkable hard-on. I wondered if she'd smuggled him some Viagra. "This is a hospital, and while I don't know anything about your medical condition—not that I'm asking—I'm sure that engaging in . . . Well, it can't be good for you at this time."

They ignored me. The woman accelerated her efforts and the man stepped up his "Oh, yeah"s.

"You need to stop now!" I said with more authority. "You could be-come a code blue, and it would be my fault if anything bad—"

"Faster, faster," he moaned to the woman, who seemed to me to be going fast enough.

"I'm not kidding," I said, fearing the guy might flatline on my watch and that I would be held responsible. "Please stop."

Of course, I should have fled the room and flagged down Pammy or one of the other nurses, but they already thought I was a doofus, so I guess I felt compelled to take charge. But how?

I flashed back again to the orientation and ticked off all the codes Jeff had told us about. Which code did fellatio fall under? Not red for fire. Not orange for hazardous materials. Not pink for abducted babies. Code gray for security? Close enough.

I grabbed the phone next to the man's bed and dialed 111. The female operator answered in a gruff voice: "State the nature of the emergency." All I could think of to say was: "Dangerous conduct on the part of a patient." I meant "dangerous to himself," obviously, but I was so flustered I made it sound as if he were a threat to me.

Before I knew it, there was a SWAT team in the room. I know, I know. I can hardly recount this anecdote without cringing.

Suffice it to say that the security guys were furious with me for dragging them up there for what was basically just rude and lascivious behavior, not to mention hearsay. (By the time they arrived, the woman had long since swallowed the evidence, so it was her word against mine.) The nurses were furious with me for causing a scene and adding unnecessary drama to their already hectic routine. (I offered them magazines and they rebuffed me.) And the patient was furious with me for exposing him as an adulterer. (It was his mistress who'd paid him the visit, not his wife.)

"Okay, so you overreacted," said Shelley after she was paged to the sixth floor to witness the spectacle that one of her volunteers had created. "Try to calm down."

"I am trying," I said, red-faced and sweaty, "but I screwed up and I'm so sorry."

"You did screw up," she acknowledged. "But here's the rule of thumb: Always get a nurse. Don't take these things on by yourself."

"I understand," I said sheepishly, grateful she didn't kick me off the team.

She patted me on the shoulder. "Now put the incident behind you and jump back on the horse." She checked her watch. "Two more hours to go on your shift. Better get moving."

Chapter Fifteen

||||||||||||||||||||||||||||||||||||||||||||||||||||||||||||||||||||||||||||||||||||||||||||||||||||||||

I was tempted to bolt from the sixth floor and peddle my wares elsewhere in the hospital—anything to avoid the snarky giggles and sideways glances from the staff after what had happened. But Shelley had advised me to put the incident behind me and jump back on the horse. So I sucked it up and kept going on six. Somewhere, Goddard was lurking. It was only a matter of time before I found him.

"Hello? May I come in?" I said after knocking on a half-open door.

"Of course."

A female voice. Damn.

"I'm Ann, and I'm a volunteer," I said to a young woman with a giant turban dressing wrapped around her head. When I entered her room, she was watching television and laughing. "What's on?" I looked up at the screen that was mounted on the wall. I doubted that I would have been laughing if I'd been swaddled in that bandage.

"*Butch Cassidy and the Sundance Kid,*" she said, lowering the volume. "My mother loves Paul Newman."

I said my mother did too, and asked her how she was feeling.

"Great," she said, smiling. "This was my third brain surgery, so I hope they got all the cancer this time."

She'd had three brain surgeries and she was smiling? I'd had zero brain surgeries and I was moping. "I hope they did too," I said, amazed by her positive attitude.

"I always have hope," she went on, her eyes shining with optimism. "It's what keeps me going."

My God, she probably wouldn't live to see her next birthday, but she hadn't given up. I have to say, I found this more than a little inspiring.

"Well, I should leave and let you get back to your movie." I didn't even bother to offer her a magazine or feed her one of the sappy speeches Claire had scripted for me. I mean, what do you say to a woman who's dying? How could I possibly help her?

And then it came to me. A way to make conversation that wouldn't sound too Hallmarky but would allow me to talk about what I knew best. "Before I go, I heard a funny story about Paul Newman," I said. "Your mother will get a laugh out of it."

Her eyes widened. "Tell me."

"Well, there's a Baskin-Robbins near his house in Connecticut," I began. "He went in one night and there was a woman in line in front of him. She was determined not to be one of those gushing fans who embarrass themselves by fawning over movie stars, so she overcompensated and acted as if she didn't even notice that he was standing right behind her."

"And?" said the patient, eager for more.

"After she paid for her order at the counter, she started to walk out of the store, not even glancing in Newman's direction. Then she felt someone tap her on the shoulder. She turned, and there he was. 'Madam,' he said, 'you just put your ice-cream cone in your purse.'"

It was an old story and no one at *Famous* could confirm if it was New-man or Redford who'd delivered the line, since both men had houses in

Connecticut, but the patient thought it was hilarious and couldn't stop giggling.

A story she'll tell for years, I thought as I waved good-bye. She didn't have years. What she had were moments, and my story had provided her with a lighthearted one. I felt oddly gratified by that.

"May I come in?" I asked when my cart and I reached the next room that had an open, signless door.

"Sure," said a male voice.

It was too high for Goddard's, I thought, but I was on heightened alert just in case.

"Hello," I said after entering and finding not a movie star but a man who couldn't have weighed more than a hundred pounds. He was a skeleton splayed out on the bed, and I'd be lying if I said I wasn't afraid of him, of going near him. He had that look—the one my father had. The look of death. I swallowed hard and forced myself to launch into my spiel.

"I'd love a magazine," he replied, somehow summoning enough strength to rouse himself up on his elbow and play the gracious host. "Something Hollywoody."

"You got it." I hurried out to the cart and came back into the room with the latest issue of *Famous,* the one with Leonardo DiCaprio on the cover.

"People say I used to look like him," he said. "Before AIDS turned me into a beanpole."

Yep, he was wasting away, just like my father, and I started to feel the same old impulse to flee, to escape the panic I was feeling. But I stuck it out. I was there to be helpful, not cowardly. Besides, he was the one who was suffering. It was up to me to distract him from his symptoms, not obsess about my own.

"So you were Leo's twin, huh?" I teased, focusing on the twinkle in his eyes.

"I was," he insisted. "I'll show you." With a great deal of effort, he reached into the top drawer of the little bedside dresser and pulled out his driver's license. "That was taken four years ago."

I studied his picture and shook my head. "Nope. You're much better looking than Leo. His photo in *Famous* was airbrushed." I nodded at the magazine. "My friend works there. She made every one of his zits disappear."

"Really?"

"I swear."

I reeled off another celebrity factoid, but he was so weak his eyelids started drooping. When I tried to tiptoe out, he begged me to stay, explaining that his family was in Oklahoma and couldn't fly up to see him. "And most of my friends are gone," he lamented. "Some dead, some not interested in watching me die."

What do you say to that? *Oh, come on. Cheer up?* I think not.

I decided not to say anything and to simply do as he asked, which was to stay with him for a while. I watched him drift in and out of sleep, watched his bony arms tense and relax, gave myself over to his needs, and realized, after twenty minutes at his bedside, that I hadn't thought about Goddard once. Not for a second. Was this what Shelley meant whenever she waxed poetic about how rewarding it was to be a volunteer? This sense of feeling useful, of being completely at someone else's disposal, of having the experience be about them, not about you? I had never considered myself a selfish person—I was Ann Roth, the journalist who wasn't cutthroat enough for Harvey—but there was something about offering a patient a tiny window of comfort that felt, well, unselfish. And satisfying.

When I finally started to leave, he pointed to the cover of *Famous* and said with a mischievous smile, "Airbrushed."

I laughed. "That's right, and yours was the real thing."

"See you again?" he asked.

"Count on it," I said, knowing that someone with his disease couldn't count on much.

I was almost buoyant as I continued down the hall on six. When I spotted one of the nurses on the floor, I didn't shrink away because of the code gray incident; I waved to her. And, miracle of miracles, she waved back.

"I'm Rolanda," she said as I approached with my cart. She was a pretty black woman with intricately woven dreadlocks. "I'd stop and talk but we're really busy today." She shrugged. "Same as every other day."

"Then I can be an extra pair of hands," I said, parroting a phrase Richard had used when describing volunteers.

She sighed wearily. "Extra hands would be great."

"Any room in particular?" I said, thrilled that a nurse was actually talking to me instead of snickering about me. I felt like one of the gang instead of an outcast.

"Oh, yeah," she said. "The guy in 613 is a new admission, and he's a handful already. He's complaining that his room has a draft. I've gotta call engineering."

A new admission. A handful already. Complaining.

Here we go, I thought, feeling my newfound self-confidence evaporate in an instant, only to have it replaced by a case of performance anxiety. Yes, this was showtime, I just knew it. Goddard had finally been admitted to the hospital and he was giving everybody some don't-mess-with-my-vessel attitude and I was about to begin my campaign to win back my job. Excitement and dread. The twin demons. They were both lodged in my throat at that moment.

"You okay?" asked Rolanda. She looked up at me after scribbling on a patient's chart.

"You bet," I said. "See you later."

When I reached room 613, I peeked inside and saw that a couple of doctors were hovering over the patient. As per Claire's don'ts, I remained in the hall, waited for them to leave, and knocked only after the coast was clear.

"May I come in?" I called out.

"Jesus. Now what?" was the response. "I just got here and everybody's harassing me."

Okay, I thought, wiping my now sweaty palms on my smock. He's here. No mistaking that mumble or the grouchy tone. This is it, Ann. Your big chance. Don't screw it up.

"I'm a volunteer," I said brightly, still standing in his doorway since he hadn't given me permission to enter. "I'd like to see how you're doing, find out if you have any questions, offer you something to read."

"Who can read with people barging in here every two seconds?" he barked.

I was determined to remain pleasant and courteous. I hated the guy, sure, but I would have to be just as good an actor as he was if I had a prayer of getting him to open up. "You sure you wouldn't like a magazine?" I said with a perky lilt. "I've got the latest issue of *Field and Stream*." Well, it was a favorite with male patients, according to Claire.

He laughed derisively. "A big no."

"Well, then how about a visit from a harmless volunteer who won't stick you with a needle or take your blood pressure?" I tried again, hoping some medical humor might do the trick. "It can be pretty disorienting when you first land in a hospital. Maybe I can ease the transition for you."

"What I want is an extra blanket. This place is a meat locker."

There it was, all right. The low growl, the whispery mumble, the arrogant tone. Apparently, our tough guy wasn't taking to Missouri weather, poor dear. "I'll track one down and be right back," I said.

I went to the nearby supplies closet, got him his blankie, and stepped inside the room, trying not to let the enormity of the situation overwhelm me. "Hello," I said as I approached the bed and, careful not to disturb any of the electrodes attached to his chest, spread the white polyester number across his body. "I'm Ann and I—"

I stopped. No, not because I was awestruck, like the first time I'd met him at Spago. This time, it was because the man in that bed, as handsome as he was, looked different to me, like Goddard only not quite. It wasn't because he was wearing a hospital gown instead of his customary black leather or because he was hooked up to a heart monitor instead of a posse of hangers-on. There was something else that was off, something—

"You're staring," he snapped. "Is that what you do as a volunteer? Knock on doors and stare at patients?"

"Oh, gosh no," I said, recovering. I couldn't let him suspect that I knew who he was. "It's just that you remind me of someone. My cousin. Yes. You remind me of Cousin Zeke. He's about your age and works at a hog farm down in Arkansas." Well, why not. I loved the image of Goddard sloshing around with a bunch of pigs in a puddle of mud. "I'm Ann Roth."

"Luke Sykes."

"Nice to meet you. So how are you feeling today, *Luke*?"

Instead of answering my question, he cocked his head at me. "Hey, I'm from out of town, so I'm curious: Are you Midwesterners on the level with all this 'How are you feeling' stuff or are you all a little on the Stepford side?"

I was offended, of course, but held my smile. "We're not Stepford, just friendly." I peered at him and tried to figure out what was different about his appearance. It wasn't his face exactly. He still had that nose—one of those chiseled, upturned marvels of nature that people pay plastic surgeons a fortune to duplicate. But the hair was—Yikes. It was receding a few inches off his forehead! There was absolutely no adorable lock that tumbled down over his forehead, into his eyes. It simply wasn't there! And speaking of his eyes, they weren't turquoise. They were a very unmemorable, very nondescript shade of brown!

"You're friendly, huh? Well, maybe you could go be friendly someplace else. I'd like some peace and quiet."

What a delightful person. "I understand, but I really do want to know how you're feeling," I said, trying to sound sincere while I was also barraging myself with questions. Where were the gorgeous baby blues? Had the big phony been wearing contact lenses throughout his career? And did the doctors make him remove them when he checked into the hospital or was taking them out his idea, so he'd be less recognizable? And what about the famous curls that always fell into his *brown* eyes? He must have been parading around in a hairpiece all this time, just like Bruce Willis and Ted Danson used to before they decided to go au naturel. Was he following their lead or was he letting his baldness show for the sake of preserving his anonymity? Obviously, he'd do anything to keep the media from knowing he was sick, even if it meant losing the movie-star accessories. Why else would he choose to have his heart monitored at Heartland General instead of at a facility in L.A., our hospital's excellent reputation notwithstanding? Why else would he fly all the way to Missouri for treatment? Why else would he materialize in the middle of nowhere? Because he was pathological about anyone invading his privacy. He was afraid that the minute the paparazzi and the reporters got wind of his health problem, they'd be swarming like—well—parasites. But he needn't have bothered with the alias. Without the lenses and the hairpiece, no one would have recognized him. I wasn't even sure I would have.

"I feel normal, that's how I feel. It's ridiculous for me to even be here. If it weren't for overprotective doctors, I'd be in—" His lips pursed.

"That's okay. I'm a good listener," I said, heavy on the sympathy, even though I was still stupefied that I was standing there next to him. As I've indicated, we didn't get many—make that *any*—celebrities in Middletown. The fact that we'd somehow snagged this one and that this one also happened to be the celebrity of my nightmares wasn't easy to process. Sure, he blended right in with the patient population now—a brown wren instead of a peacock—but I knew about the riveting performances he'd given on-screen and the international acclaim he'd garnered for them, and it was hard to just block all that out. "You'd be where?" In Canada shooting your movie? Ordering everyone around on the set? Making your costars miserable?

"Never mind," he said. "They'll probably discharge me tomorrow anyway. I mean, I fainted. Big whoop. I was working long hours and partying too much. So what?"

Interesting. There certainly hadn't been any items in the press about him fainting. According to Tuscany, all the rumors had to do with him going into rehab. Peggy Merchant was a genius in the way she'd managed to keep his condition under the radar. "Fainting is nothing to ignore," I pointed out. "And the doctors here are first rate—especially for cardiac problems."

"I don't have cardiac problems," he said as his heart monitor continued to beep. "I already told you."

"Yes, you did. Hopefully, you'll be okay, but in the meantime, is there anything I can do for you? You mentioned that you're from out of town. Do you need me to contact anyone? Make travel arrangements for a family member? Get in touch with your boss?" I was suddenly enjoying this. He was pretending to be someone he wasn't? I'd pretend to be someone I wasn't. Perfect symmetry.

"My boss?" He smirked. "No, thanks." He shivered and burrowed under the blanket. "Man, do I wish I could be home where it's not below zero—inside."

"Where's 'home'? if you don't mind my asking." I was dying to see how far he'd go with his charade. "Someplace with a warm climate, I guess."

"Florida," he said with a straight face. "Miami. I'm in real estate development down there. Residential. Commercial. You know."

"It's definitely warmer there," I conceded. "But I bet people aren't as friendly in Miami as they are in Middletown."

"It's too soon to tell, since I just got here," he said. "But from what I've seen, you all have this very upbeat, have-a-nice-day thing going on. Is it in the drinking water or are you as sincere and *real* as you seem?"

I didn't feel very real at that moment, but I was energized by the fact that I'd gotten him to speak civilly to me. "Some places are just more down to earth than others. Here in Middletown, we grow up without the superficialities you find in other parts of the country. Like Hollywood, for example. Now *that* must be a difficult town for making friends. Have you ever been there or do your, uh, real estate ventures keep you too busy in Miami?"

God, this really was fun. And easier than I'd expected.

"I've been there a few times," he said. "And you're right. It's a weird place. Everybody's a walking résumé. They don't have friendships. They have 'business relationships.' I have a buddy who acts in the movies and he's never met a single person who didn't want something from him, talk about shallow."

Wow, I thought. He sounded almost sincere himself, despite the "buddy" bullshit. But how could he be? He was one of the shallow Hollywood types he was denigrating. And since when didn't he have any friends? Every time he was spotted coming into or out of a nightclub, he was surrounded by an entourage that often included his sweetheart, Rebecca Truit. Which prompted me to wonder: Did she know he was in the hospital? Had he confided in her that he left the set where he was shooting, not to go into rehab but to have his heart monitored?

"Whenever I read magazines like *Famous,* I get the feeling it's one big party in Hollywood," I said. "Maybe they all want something from each other, but they look like they're having the time of their lives in those pictures."

"*Famous*?" He shuddered, and it wasn't from being cold. "That's the worst of those parasites."

"Parasites?" I said, feigning surprise. "I kind of like the magazine. So do most of the patients. It's a distraction for them."

He shook his head. Even without the add-on hair and enhanced eye color, he was uncommonly great looking, I had to admit. "Don't be suckered in by those entertainment rags," he said. "Against his better judgment, my buddy out there agreed to an interview with *Famous* and the writer didn't even show up. Can you believe that?"

Suddenly, the humiliation of that day at the airport came flooding back and I had to force myself not to slug the guy. "Does your buddy have a name?" I asked sweetly. "Maybe I've heard of him."

"I can't tell you his name, because he's a very private guy," he improvised. "He's the one who told me how hard it is to be in the public eye. He says he can't even walk his dogs without the media there to cover it."

Goddard had two dogs: Sam, a golden retriever, and Lucy, a collie. He'd made this declaration in his interview with *Vanity Fair*. "Does this actor enjoy any aspect of his success?"

"Hey, success is great, but it's lonely too. According to *him*."

"Because of everybody being so shallow?"

"Yeah. If a guy like him has a problem, who's he gonna call? His agent? His manager? His publicist? They all want something from him, so he can't trust any of them."

"If you're his buddy, why doesn't he call you?"

He was stumped by that one, and I gave myself a silent pat on the back for asking it. "Look, he has a hard time trusting anybody," he said. "His father, who was responsible for managing his money, ended up stuffing it into his own pocket. His mother, who was against him going into show business in the beginning, turned into a user, selling personal stuff about him to the tabloids. It's not a stretch to figure out why this guy keeps to himself."

Okay, a tiny part of me felt sorry for him after that speech, because I knew it wasn't a fabrication. He'd gone on record that his father and mother had sold him out. My family members had their "issues," but they'd never done anything to shake my trust in them.

"Doesn't he have a wife or girlfriend he can turn to?" I asked, picturing the veddy veddy British Rebecca in one of her skimpy little frocks. She was the latest in a string of actresses from the UK who were beautiful but boyish.

"He's not married, but he's been seeing someone," Goddard confirmed. "I think he'd like to make a commitment and settle down, but he's not there yet."

Well, so much for breaking the news of their engagement, I thought. Still, I was making progress. He was telling me things without realizing it. He was giving me material that could form the basis for a fabulous piece in *Famous*. I was totally on track.

I was about to ask another question when he started complaining about his accommodations. The room was too cold. The mattress was too thin. The sheets were too starchy. Blah blah blah.

"I don't even know why I'm here," he said petulantly. "I had flip-flops in my chest and dizziness and nausea, but that was four days ago. I don't see why I'm being hooked up to this TV screen."

"Isn't it better that they're being cautious?" I said, since I was supposed to be a representative for the hospital. "You wouldn't want anything serious to happen once you're back in . . . Miami."

As if on cue, his heart monitor suddenly started beeping loudly and with urgency. I jerked my head at the screen and even I could tell there were wild fluctuations in his beats or his rhythms or whatever the monitor was recording.

"Not again," he moaned, grabbing my arm, pulling me closer to the edge of the bed.

"Not again what?" I said, wishing I could extricate myself from his grip. Coaxing information out of a movie star was one thing. Getting too close to a man in the throes of *cardiac arrest* was quite another. "What is it? Luke? *Luke?*"

He didn't answer. Instead, his eyes sort of rolled back in his head and his color turned a sickly yellowish-green.

"Do you want me to get the nurse?" I said.

"It's the same damn thing I had the last time," he whispered, breathless. "It came on fast, from out of nowhere. Man, I'm so dizzy, so nauseous. I feel like I'm gonna—"

Hurl. Yes. He felt like it and he did it—on the sleeve of my freshly laundered smock. I'd been dreading a patient vomiting on me. I just didn't expect the patient to be Malcolm Goddard. But then, he'd been hurling things at me since we met.

I felt very close to puking myself, naturally. Panicking too. But I couldn't fall apart. Not in front of Goddard or in front of Rolanda, who had hurried into the room.

"Yeah, there's the arrythmia," she said, nodding at the monitor as if she'd been waiting for it to reveal what was wrong with her patient. She turned to him, examined him quickly, told him she was calling the doctor, and promised she'd be back to clean him up.

What about me? I wanted to ask her. I wasn't exactly smelling like a rose. In fact, I was dying to rush off to the restroom to clean myself up. But I didn't think it would be ethical to desert someone in need, even if that someone was a snake.

"How are you feeling now?" I said to a slightly groggy but otherwise alert Goddard. It sounded like "How are you feeling *dow*," because I was kind of holding my nose.

"Just go!" he commanded.

Yep, commanded. I was stunned. Who did he think he was? He should have been apologizing instead of ordering me around. He was the one who'd puked on me, wasn't he?

"I'd like to make sure you're okay first," I said, keeping a lid on my anger, but only barely.

"What are you now? A nurse?" he said with a sneer. "Leave me alone."

"I'm not a nurse, but I care about your health." I did. Sort of. I wasn't completely single-minded.

"My health is nobody's business," he muttered, turning his head away. "Don't let the door hit you on the way out."

"But—"

"What part of that sentence didn't you understand?"

Okay, he was sick. He had some kind of heart condition, and he wasn't happy about it. I got that. But I was trying to help (well, right then I was trying to help), and I did not deserve to be treated so rudely. His attitude was infuriating, just as it had been infuriating back in L.A., and I couldn't stand there and not call him on it. Sick or no sick.

I moved to exit his room, shaking my head at his ability to push my buttons yet again. "Just a little advice," I said, breathing in my own foul fumes now. "If you want friendly Midwesterners to stay friendly, try not to throw up on them if you can avoid it."

||||||||||||||||||||||||||||||||||||||||||||||||||||||||||||||||||||||||||||||||||||||||||||

Chapter Sixteen

"**Come on, it'll** be okay," said Tuscany after I called her to report on my first encounter with Goddard. "He was probably embarrassed because he hurled on you. He's a macho guy, remember? He'll let you back in to see him once he gives his big movie-star ego a rest."

"I hope so," I said. I was sitting in the Honda, parked in front of my mother's house. I had just gotten home from the hospital. The sleeve of my smock was still damp; I'd washed it with Purell in the sixth-floor ladies' room. "But I don't volunteer again until Friday. That's three days from now, Tuscany. Maybe they'll cure him by then and he'll be gone when I get there."

"Doesn't sound like it," she said. "From what you described, he could be there awhile."

"Well, as much as I hate the guy, I don't wish him any harm," I said. "I want my job back, but not if it means somebody has to languish in a hospital."

"Everything will work out," she said. "You're just a little down right now."

I *was* down, and watching the snow pile up on my windshield and wishing I was on the beach in Malibu weren't helping.

"You'll figure out a way to get the interview," she said, trying to pump me up. "You're gonna make this happen, Ann. I know you are."

"Love you," I said, grateful to have her in my life, even long distance.

"Love you too," she said.

I FORCED MYSELF to get out of the car and trudged into the house, careful to remove my shoes first. The only thing worse than germs, according to my grandmother, was dirty footprints.

I'd been home for only fifteen minutes when Richard called. He invited me to an impromptu dinner with one of his doctor friends and his wife. "We're all in the mood for Hop Woo and I'm hoping you'll join us."

Middletown had two "ethnic" restaurants: a taco stand next to the Mobil station and Hop Woo, the Chinese place whose chef was a local boy named Brady Finnigan and whose specialty was hamburger chow mein. I wasn't a Hop Woo fan, but mostly I didn't want to encourage Richard, who seemed incapable of taking no for an answer. Going out with him as part of a foursome—on a double date—might be sending the wrong signal.

"You're hesitating." He sighed. "But, jeepers, Ann. You said we could spend time together as friends. We'll have an early night if you want. A little dinner, a few fortune cookies, and that's it. Of course, if you decide you find me irresistible while you're gazing at me across the table, we can always head back to my place afterward."

"Richard."

"Okay, okay. Strike that last comment. I'll be good, I promise." He chuckled. "And I think you'll enjoy meeting Eleanor and Jonathan White. Eleanor volunteers at the hospital too, in the gift shop. And Jonathan's our top cardio man."

I sat up straighter. Jonathan White was the doctor who was overseeing Goddard's care. Richard had mentioned him that night at the Caffeine Scene when he'd dropped his bombshell. Jonathan would certainly know how long his patient would be hanging around, what the treatment plan was, all of that. I wasn't allowed to ask him a million questions—not even one question—but things had a way of slipping out, especially after a glass or two of wine. Yes, maybe dinner with Richard wasn't such a bad idea after all.

"What time should I be there?" I said.

"THIS IS A LOT nicer than the cafeteria," Eleanor White remarked, surveying our surroundings at Hop Woo, where the lights were low, the décor was red, and the tables were wobbly. There was nothing especially nice about it, but she was right: It beat the hospital cafeteria. She was my mother's age—a matronly blonde on the order of Lynn Cheney—and she smelled faintly of Bengay. She was also, I was dismayed to discover, one of those women who exhausts you with her breathless, brainless, nonstop chatter about food.

"It is," I agreed distractedly. I was more interested in the conversation the doctors were having about a certain patient of Jonathan's: a young man who'd recently been admitted with arrythmia. Obviously, the patient was Goddard. Jonathan had described him as a hothead who kept insisting he was fine and was resisting treatment.

"Although their meat loaf isn't bad," Eleanor droned on. "I have it about twice a week. Sometimes I get the mashed potatoes with it. Sometimes I'll try the squash. And if I'm really feeling adventurous, I'll ask for the Spanish rice with those little slivers of red peppers in it. Oh. Wait. Is it Spanish rice or Mexican rice?" She pondered as she scratched her chin, which, by the way, had a blond whisker on it. "I just can't keep their Hispanic dishes straight. Or should I have said their Latino dishes?"

"Either way, I'll make a point of trying the meat loaf," I said, wishing she'd shut up and let me eavesdrop.

"Yes, do try it," she said. "And try their roast chicken. They season it with lemon. Parsley and garlic too. The thighs are the—"

I tuned her out and strained to hear what Jonathan, a short, thin man with delicate fingers and wrists and, very likely, extremely low cholesterol, was reporting to Richard.

"After he had the episode, I told him we suspected the ventricular tachycardia," said Jonathan. "And his response was: 'Great. Just give me some medicine and let me go home.' I explained that medicine wasn't the answer and that his abnormal heartbeats could kill him. That got his attention, temporarily. I said we'd have to do the electrophysiological study tomorrow and that everything would be okay once we confirmed the diagnosis. He said, 'I don't want any study. I want out of here. I've got to get back to work.' He's quite a character."

Yep. Sounded just like my boy Luke.

Richard gave Jonathan one of those wink-wink looks. "He's used to having everything his way, don't forget."

"I understand that," said Jonathan, "but I reminded him that his life was more important than his career. Bottom line: He's having the test tomorrow."

"Good," said Richard. "Hopefully, you'll be able to induce the ventricular—"

"Ann," said Eleanor, tapping my arm. "How's your moo goo gai pan?"

I glanced down at my food, having forgotten all about it. "It's delicious," I said, eager to get back to news of Goddard. So his heart condition was life threatening but treatable. Amazing. Everybody in the entire world thought he was battling a booze problem. Maybe he would mellow out now that he realized he was as vulnerable as the rest of us.

"My Mongolian beef is a little tough," said Eleanor. "Not terrible, just chewy, stringy, hard to digest. I think if they'd marinated it longer

or used a more pungent sauce, maybe more so
been a tastier—"

"How are the kids?" Richard was asking
broke free of her restaurant review.

Damn, I thought. I'd missed the end of the Go
have to wait until Friday to find out more. I planned to go ba
shift and get the story for myself. Right from the horse's ass's mouth.

I WASN'T PLANNING on stopping to chat with Shelley that Friday afternoon, but she beckoned me into her office with her big, hearty laugh, so
I could hardly refuse. She was great, don't get me wrong. It was just that
I was dying to load up the magazine cart and head straight for six for
my next shot at Goddard. And yes, of course, I was concerned about his
health. As I said, I didn't wish illness on anybody, not even him.

"How'd you make out on Tuesday after all the fireworks?" she asked.
"You came back today, so that's a good sign."

"Did you really think I'd quit?" I asked.

She shrugged. "I wasn't sure. Were there some positive experiences
for you after the adventure with the porn couple?"

"Actually, there were," I said, and I wasn't talking about our celebrity,
although I'd already typed notes about my conversation with him into my
laptop, recording his answers to my questions, especially those regarding
his take on Hollywood. No, when Shelley asked about positive experiences, I was thinking about the woman with brain cancer and the man
with AIDS—how I felt I'd lifted them up just a little and, in the course of
doing that, lifted myself up too.

"Just what I wanted to hear," she said. "Now I know you spent your
entire shift on six last time, so today you need to visit patients on other
floors. I like our volunteers to spread the good cheer around."

No six? Well, she couldn't mean that, I decided. She just meant that

start on the other floors and work my way up, which is exactly
I intended to do.

After loading up the magazine cart, off I went. On three, I visited
the kids in pediatrics, figuring I'd just hand out copies of *Woman's
Day* to the mothers and *Sports Illustrated* to the fathers and scram.
Instead, I found myself totally entranced by the children. Many of
them were cancer patients, according to Jeanette, whom I'd met at my
orientation and who was volunteering on the floor twice a week. And
despite the obstacles they faced and how awful they felt, they giggled
with me and asked me to read to them and told me about their dreams
for the future.

"They're pretty inspiring, right?" said Jeanette. "They're changing
my life, I can tell you that."

"They're wonderful," I agreed, realizing yet again that my problems
were so trivial in comparison with those of others.

"There's one I'd really like you to meet," she said. "Her name's Bree
Wiley and she's a cutie."

Bree, it turned out, was a ten-year-old girl in dire need of a liver transplant. She was an adorable, precocious child with deep dimples on both
cheeks. She was also the only daughter of parents without insurance—the
sort of people Richard said were responsible for the hospital's diminish-
ing profits. Both Mr. and Mrs. Wiley had been laid off from the chemical
plant in Center Creek and were working part-time jobs that left them unavailable to see their daughter very often.

"Hi, Bree," I said. "I'm Ann, and I'm a volunteer like Jeanette."

"Hi," she said. She was sitting up in bed writing in her diary, a hot
pink vinyl-covered book with a lock and key, just like the one I had at her
age. Her hair was a tangle of golden blond ringlets and, despite her sal-
low complexion and overall listlessness, she was flashing me a smile that
would melt anyone's heart.

"Want some company today?" I asked.

She nodded, then cupped her hands around her mouth, preparing to whisper. "Jeanette told me something about you."

"Oh?" I said, whispering back. "What was it?"

"That you know movie stars," she said, her eyes wide with her discovery.

I laughed. "She told you that, huh?" After the orientation, Jeanette had asked me which magazine had fired me and I'd told her. So much for volunteer confidentiality.

"I love movie stars *so* much," said Bree, clutching the diary to her heart. "Even the ones my parents' age. I have a million pictures of them at my house, some of them even autographed. I wrote to fan clubs and got them. I have more pictures than any of my friends."

She really did remind me of myself when I was ten. I too had the faces of celebrities plastered on my walls. "Do you have a favorite movie star? Hilary Duff, maybe?"

Bree crinkled her nose in disdain. "She's big with *kids*. I meant *grown-up* movie stars. My mom won't let me see their movies until I'm older, but that doesn't stop me from thinking about them." She giggled. "I *love* Orlando Bloom."

"I bet he'd love you too." I tousled her hair.

"Do you know him?"

"No, honey. Sorry. I did meet movie stars when I worked for a magazine, but not him."

She pouted for a second, then perked up. "Are you friends with the ones you did meet? Like, is there any way you could get them to visit me?"

"I wish I could," I said, "but they're busy people. They're always off shooting their movies." Of course, if Goddard had checked into the hospital under his own name and not been such a nut about his privacy, I could have brought him to meet Bree. Not that she'd recognize him any more than I did at first.

She sighed and rested her head on the pillow. "When I get my new liver, my parents will take me to Hollywood and I'll meet movie stars every single day. That's my dream."

"Perfect," I said, knowing full well that she could die before making it to the top of the donor transplant list. What's more, her parents didn't have the money for a trip to Hollywood or anywhere else. "You hold tight to that dream and never let it go."

"What's your dream?" she asked. "Or don't you have one?"

Oh, I had one, all right. But it suddenly seemed ridiculous, petty. And so I answered, "To see you healthy and out of this place, Bree Wiley. That would make me the happiest person in the history of Heartland General."

On four, I stopped in to see both the mothers of newborns and the patients who would never have newborns. Regarding the latter group, I found it disturbing that so many women—some in their thirties like me—were having to undergo surgery that robbed them of their chance to have children. So many hysterectomies were being performed at the hospital, and it didn't seem right.

One such patient was a woman in her late thirties. She was stocky, with a thick neck and massive forearms, her brown hair pulled back in a loose ponytail. She looked like a bulldog and I half-expected her to jump down off the bed and gnaw on my leg.

"How are you feeling today?" I asked.

"I'm in a lot of pain," she said. "The doctor told me I'd feel this way for another week. Then I'll be fine."

"Sounds like the worst is over then," I said. "You've had the surgery. Now you just have to heal."

She shrugged. "Still, they took everything out. I can't have kids."

I pulled up a chair and sat beside her. I had no personal experience whatsoever when it came to having children other than hoping I'd have a few of my own someday, but I knew a sad lady when I saw one.

I brought up adoption. She said she didn't know anyone who'd ever adopted. I pointed out that Angelina Jolie had adopted two orphans. She smiled and thanked me for reminding her about that. (I'm telling you, the celebrity stuff really came in handy.)

"Once I'm done with the abdominal pain, I'll speak to my husband about it," she promised. "Thank you for the talk. You're a very nice person. What's your name again?"

"Ann," I said, suddenly very pleased that I seemed to be representing Heartland General so well. "Ann Roth."

On five, I met a handsome white-haired man who only spoke Russian and, therefore, wasn't a candidate for *Field & Stream* or anything else I was peddling. But he'd just had a stroke—or so it seemed, given his limited use of his right arm—and was very gloomy about it. I couldn't leave without at least trying to lift his spirits.

Through a combination of sign language and overly enunciated English, I told him that my great-grandmother was Russian. "From *Odessa*," I said.

His expression brightened. "Odessa. Beautiful, beautiful." He chattered away in Russian after my announcement and I pretended to understand what he was talking about, and by the time I left he seemed less discouraged, more hopeful.

Damn, I'm not bad at this stuff, I thought, suddenly feeling less discouraged and more hopeful myself.

Chapter Seventeen

|||||||||||||||||||||||||||||||||||||||||||||||||||||||||||||||||||||||||||||||||||

When I finally arrived on the sixth floor, I made a very showy demonstration of stopping in to see each and every patient; I didn't want anybody getting suspicious of my keen interest in the patient in 613. And it was keen, all right. I was dying to know if he'd died. Or if he'd had that study Jonathan White had told him to have and was now improving quickly enough to be discharged soon. And I wondered what sort of reception I'd get when he saw me, given our last encounter.

Once again, I steadied my nerves as I knocked on his door.

"May I come in?" I said. "It's Ann, your favorite volunteer. I'm ready to call a truce if you are."

"Oh, jeez." A pause. "Yeah, sure. Come on in."

It wasn't the most gracious welcome, but it could have been worse.

"Hello, Luke," I said, striding merrily up to his bedside. He had dark circles under his eyes, his hair was matted to his head, and there was stubble lining his jaw. He was still handsome but he needed a shave and a shower badly. If only the paparrazzi could see him now, I thought. "How are you feeling today?"

"You don't have to wear a rubber suit around me, if that's what you're worried about. I'm over the upchucking."

I smiled. "I'm not worried about that at all." Well, maybe just a little.

"Actually, I'm glad you're here."

"Oh?"

"Yeah. I'm sorry I barked at you after I—" He shrugged. "I reacted like a dumb kid. You were very decent about it, Ann."

An apology and a compliment? And he remembered my name? I was amazed, but then I reminded myself that he had no idea he was conversing with a bona fide media parasite. "Believe me, I can relate. I've certainly felt humiliated once or twice," I said, having been humiliated once or twice by him.

"This whole thing has been so weird for me," he said, ignoring my comment and keeping the focus on himself, the way all actors do. "I mean, I've never been sick in my life and all of a sudden they tell me I have a heart condition? It sucks. It totally sucks."

"It does," I said. "But I'm sure the doctors will find a way to—"

"They found a way all right," he interrupted. "On Wednesday morning they wheeled me into the 'cath lab' for this test where they sedate you and stick wires up your veins."

"Did it hurt?"

"It didn't hurt so much as blow my mind. They got my heart to do its out-of-rhythm thing and then they had to *shock* it back to normal. I had no idea what was going on until I saw a guy coming at me with paddles. He was yelling, 'Clear!' just like on *ER*. Then I felt this jolt of electricity and I must have blacked out. Afterward, I said, 'What the hell was that?' The doctor goes, 'You were dead for half a second and we brought you back.' Talk about a nightmare. I'm still trying to shake it off."

No wonder he looked as if he'd been through an ordeal. "So now they know why your heart was out of rhythm?"

He nodded. "But the remedy's even worse. Tomorrow morning

they're dragging me back into that lab and implanting this little defibrillator into my chest so it can shock me automatically, whenever my heart needs that jolt. It stays in there forever, except when the battery runs out." He rolled his eyes. "Me. Walking around like a character in a science-fiction movie."

He was being overly dramatic, but I didn't envy him his condition. "So that's why they're running an IV," I mused, noticing the bag of fluids dripping into a vein in the hollow of his arm. As a card-carrying hypochondriac, I knew that antibiotics were routinely administered before and after surgery.

"Yeah. Getting stabbed and pricked and poked is just another fun thing about being here."

"Come on, look on the bright side," I urged. "Once they do this procedure, you'll never have to worry about your heart again. You can go back to Miami and it'll be as if this whole experience never happened."

"True. They'll do the implant tomorrow and I'll be home the day after. That's the good news."

Good news? Maybe for him, but not for me or my story. I'd have to get some good quotes out of him fast or else. "What's the bad news?"

"I'll have a small scar."

"And that bothers you?"

"Sure, it bothers me."

"Because you're vain?"

"I'm not vain," he said, as if the notion were inconceivable.

"You sound defensive," I said.

"No, I'm just not *vain*."

"Then why would you care about a little scar?"

He regarded me with puzzlement, probably because he wasn't used to anybody questioning him, challenging him. He was an A-list celebrity and nobody ever challenged A-list celebrities. Now, some volunteer at a hospital in the Midwest had the audacity to do just that—a volunteer who used to ask celebrities questions for a living—and he obviously didn't know what to make of it. "It's not cool in my line of work to have a scar, that's all," he said.

In his line of work? I could hardly conceal my delight. I'd caught him in his lie. "I didn't realize that men in real estate go around baring their chests in order to close a deal."

"I *meant* that in real estate you're supposed to look and act confident," he said, becoming flustered, "and this scar, which will be right under my collarbone and visible if I wear an open shirt, might tip off my clients that there's something wrong with me."

"Don't be silly," I said. "People aren't that shallow. Well, except the ones in Hollywood that you talked about. But since you don't live in Hollywood, what's the problem?"

"Okay, fine. Forget the scar," he said. "There's all this other stuff I've gotta deal with after they put the gizmo inside me. How would you feel if your doctor told you your battery had to be changed every five years or so? That you had to hold your cell phone at least six inches away from your defibrillator? That you had to avoid metal detectors, slot machines, amusement-park rides, and anything else that generates a strong magnetic field? You'd feel like a freak, that's what."

"I probably would at first," I conceded. "But you know, Luke, there are patients in this hospital who'd be so thrilled to have their hearts fixed and their lives saved that they wouldn't complain about the annoyances."

"Annoyances?" He propped himself up in the bed and sort of glared at me. "Are you saying I'm a complainer?"

Yes. "No, I just think your priorities might be skewed. You came here with a serious medical condition, but you're going to get well. If you can't take a ride on a Ferris wheel because of the defibrillator, it's a small price to pay, isn't it?"

No immediate response, except for that glare. The color of his eyes may have been a run-of-the-mill brown without the blue lenses, but the intensity of their gaze was as unnerving as ever. "So, Florence Nightingale," he said finally. "Are you always so blunt?"

No, I wasn't always so blunt. I'd hardly ever been blunt with Harvey. But for some reason Goddard brought out the fire in me, the emotion in me, the fighter in me. I had planned to be on my best behavior when I visited him—to flatter him, pamper him, do whatever it took to make him like me and confide in me. Instead, I was succeeding only in pissing him off.

"Sorry," I said. "I didn't mean to be rude. I was only suggesting that— Well, I see a lot of patients when I come to the hospital and many of them aren't as fortunate as you. They won't be going home in another day or two. They may not be going home at all."

He nodded begrudgingly. "Okay. I get that. You're right. I should shut up and count my blessings. Thanks for the reality check."

"You're welcome." Wow, I thought. Two semi-apologies in one visit. Maybe when they shocked his heart, they also shocked his brain. "Speaking of going home," I said, "what brought you to Middletown in the first place? It's a long way from Miami."

"I was scoping out property," he said without missing a beat. "I'm always in the hunt when it comes to areas that are ripe for development."

"I see," I said. "So you were—what?—looking at farmland while you were here?"

"Exactly," he said. "I was standing in a cornfield when I felt the palpitations and fainted."

I had to turn away for a second or he would have seen me laughing. "That's so interesting," I said. "I'm not aware of any cornfields in Middletown and I've lived here all my life. Wheat, but no corn."

He hesitated, stymied briefly. "Yeah, well, it's all the same to me. I'm from a blue state."

"Didn't Florida go for Bush in '04?"

He fiddled with a snap on his hospital gown. "Yeah, but Miami's pretty liberal. Personally, I'm a libertarian. I don't want the government interfering in my life."

"That's because you can afford the most expensive health care," I said. "You wouldn't be on the sixth floor if you couldn't. But there are patients on other floors who'd be very relieved if the government would help them out."

He regarded me with another quizzical look. "Do you lecture those patients too?"

I had to laugh at that one. "Not unless they ask for it. Mostly, I bring them magazines. Are you sure you wouldn't like something to read?"

He lowered his head back down onto the pillow and exhaled. "I'm too tired to read. Whatever they injected me with on Wednesday morning kind of knocked me out." He pointed at me. "But I'm not complaining! I swear I'm not!"

I smiled. "That's okay. You're allowed to be tired."

He smiled too. "To tell you the truth, I'm glad you reminded me of how grateful I should be that I'll be walking out of here as good as new. But all this has been tough for me to absorb. I'm in my thirties, I've been healthy all my life, I've got more money than I'll ever need. It never dawned on me that I could drop dead from some heart thing I didn't even know I had."

"So you felt invincible before this?"

"Yeah. I always figured I'd die of old age—a crabby guy with nobody but a paid companion to watch over him."

A Hollywood hermit to the end. "That's a very sad image. Why crabby? Why a paid companion? Why no wife or children?"

"I'm a loner. It's a character flaw." He narrowed his eyes at me. "Did I mention that you ask a lot of questions?"

I laughed nonchalantly, scolding myself for not being more subtle. "I'm just curious about people, I guess." Especially famous people who've made themselves inaccessible to journalists.

"The difference between you and those parasites who write for the entertainment magazines—the ones my buddy in Hollywood can't stand—is that you aren't out to exploit people. You genuinely care about them. You wouldn't give up your time to volunteer here if you didn't."

Okay, so I felt like a fraud and an impostor and a rat at that moment. But he wasn't exactly authentic himself, checking in under a fake name and trying to fool everybody by masquerading as a civilian. "Volunteering is incredibly rewarding. I really enjoy talking to the patients." That part was absolutely true, I realized. I may have signed up for the program in a desperate attempt to get my job back, but I was reaping other dividends from it. I hadn't had a panic attack in days, for one thing.

"What do you do when you're not at the hospital? Do you have a paying job somewhere?" he asked.

I *would* have one if it weren't for you, I thought. I'd even let my freelance gig at the *Crier* slide once Goddard had come to town. "Actually, I'm between jobs," I said. "A high school friend—he's the assistant chief of staff here—told me the hospital was looking for volunteers so I decided to help the cause."

He whistled. "The assistant chief of staff, huh? Is this guy a boyfriend? Or are you married?" He glanced at my left hand. "Nope. No ring. And I always thought you Midwestern gals with your Midwestern families and Midwestern values went for the husband and kiddies right out of the womb."

"That's a little patronizing, isn't it? We're not as stereotypical as you make us seem." Not quite, anyway.

"I'm reacting to the statistics I've read, that's all."

"Maybe you need to get out of Miami more."

He held up his hands in protest. "Hey, look. No offense intended. I just figured that a beautiful woman like you would be married by now."

By now? Like I was a hundred years old or something? And since when did he think I was beautiful? Not when he was throwing that cheesecake at me. "Well, I'm not married, so there goes your stereotype."

"You sound defensive." He was mimicking the charge I'd leveled against him and enjoying it.

"No, I'm just not of the opinion that women have to be married by a certain age."

"Duly noted." He arched an eyebrow at me. "So what's up with this doctor? Are you two . . ." He interlocked his fingers.

I laughed. "Hardly."

"Ah, come on. I bet you've got it bad for him."

"No, I don't. We're just friends."

"So why no ring?"

"I haven't met the right man." I thought of Skip then, of how he'd told me he loved me and wanted to live with me, then dumped me. "I've spent too much time around guys who break their promises. I'm holding out for one who doesn't."

"Ouch. Sounds like you've had some heart problems yourself."

He didn't like it when reporters pried into his personal life, but he had no qualms about prying into mine, apparently. "I have, but let's get back to you," I said, pulling up the chair next to his bed and sitting down, hoping for more interview material. Tuscany had suggested I stick a tape recorder in the pocket of my smock, but I have a good memory. I just needed to get him to open up and then enter every morsel into my laptop. "What's your life like in Miami? Do you have hobbies, for instance?"

He yawned, stretched his arms. "Listen, I'm exhausted. Whatever they're putting into me is sapping all my energy. How about we talk tomorrow, after my procedure?"

Damn. I wasn't volunteering on Saturday, although I didn't see why Shelley would mind if I did. It would be my last chance to pull an interview out of Goddard. I had to come back and see him before he went home. Amazingly enough, he'd actually invited me to come back.

"You sure you don't want me to stay?" I tried. "You can take your nap and I'll keep this chair warm and we can talk when you wake up."

"Nah." He yawned again. "There's no telling how long I'll sleep. Wouldn't want to keep you dangling."

He was already keeping me dangling, for God's sake.

I got up from the chair and smiled sweetly, even though my frustration was building. I'd had two shots at him and neither had produced enough for a magazine profile. "Then get some rest and I'll be back tomorrow," I said resignedly. "After they've installed your battery-operated vibrator."

He laughed. "Vibrator. Defibrillator. You're right. No difference. See you tomorrow."

I had turned to go when he called out to me, his tone more serious than before. "Ann?"

"Yes?"

"I know what you're up to."

I felt my throat tighten. "Excuse me?"

"All the grilling, the baiting, the kidding around. I know exactly what you're doing and why you're doing it."

My face burned. My ears too. Had I given myself away somehow? Had he suddenly remembered me from our one encounter in L.A.? Had somebody at the hospital tipped him off that I used to work for *Famous*? What? "I was only—"

"Trying to distract me, take my mind off the heart thing, lift me out of my own head." His expression relaxed into a smile. "I didn't get it when you first knocked on my door, but I do now. I get it and I appreciate it. You're good at your job."

The circulation returned to my body and I heaved a huge sigh of relief. "I'm giving it my best, Luke."

It was while I was sitting at the Caffeine Scene a little later, reread-ing what I'd just typed into my computer about him, that I smiled and thought, This guy is actually starting to let me in.

No, I hadn't elicited headline-worthy stuff from him yet or even more than half a page worth of quotes, but we'd established a connection. A tentative, fragile connection, maybe, but it was a whole lot more than any-thing Diane Sawyer had come up with.

Chapter Eighteen

||||||||||||||||||||||||||||||||||||||||||||||||||||||||||||||||||||||||||||||||||||||||||||||||

"**So nobody has** a clue where Goddard is?" I asked Tuscany when I reached her at home on Saturday morning. Surprisingly, she was alone. She was still dating the actor from *The Bold and the Beautiful,* but they had yet to spend the night together. She said he wanted to take it slowly, and I was delighted to hear that she had agreed.

"Nope," she said. "Rumors are flying and reporters are staked out at every rehab facility in the country, but no one knows where he's hiding."

"Amazing," I said. "And I suppose Peggy Merchant is 'No comment'-ing everybody to death?"

"You got it. So is Rebecca Truit, although she did tell *Access Hollywood* that she and lover boy are still devoted to each other."

He probably called her and told her not to come to Middletown, I realized, since her appearance would bring him unwanted attention. On the other hand, they couldn't be that devoted. I had it from his own lips, right there on my computer screen: He wasn't ready to make a commitment to her. "Harvey must be going nuts trying to dig up something on him."

"He is. Goddard's a bigger get now than he was before."

And I have him, I thought with a sense of both personal and professional justice. Well, technically, I didn't have him; I had Luke Sykes.

"But since he's AWOL," she continued, "Harvey's making do with Seamus Farrow."

"Who?"

"Well, I think they named him Satchel when he was born, but now he's Seamus," she said. "You know. The only biological child of Mia Farrow and Woody Allen. He's speaking out for the first time about how it felt when his father became his brother-in-law. He's our cover story next week."

"Does he have a relationship with Woody or are they still estranged?" I asked, because, as I've already confessed, I cared about stuff like that.

"He never really addresses their current relationship," she said. "Of course, if you'd been the one asking the questions, we'd have a lot more info. Which is why I can't wait for your story on Goddard. Just think, Ann. You're on the verge of being the hottest reporter in this town. In the world!"

"Down, girl," I said. "The doctor's discharging him tomorrow. I don't have much time left with him."

"Ann, Goddard's the guy everybody wants to read about, and you're the only writer he's talking to," she said. "Whatever you get will be the scoop of the century."

"He doesn't know I'm a writer, Tuscany. That's the thorny part."

"Thorny part? Since when?"

Yeah, since when? My words had surprised me too. Was I having a twinge of conscience all of sudden? And if so, why? I was a killer journalist with access to the biggest star in Hollywood. What was there to be ambivalent about? Well, except that he was a patient and I was a volunteer, and I had started to take my duties more seriously than I'd expected to.

"I guess I can't help thinking how sick he is. Richard called his condition life threatening."

"*Was* life threatening," she pointed out. "They're gonna fix him up today and send him home tomorrow."

"True." Then was my hesitation because Goddard had been fairly pleasant to me for once? Because he'd thanked me and told me I was beautiful? Was I that easy? "You know what? There *is* no thorny part," I said, reassuring her and myself.

"Good. I can't imagine a more spectacular way to make a comeback than turning in an exclusive on Malcolm Goddard."

"Neither can I," I said as I allowed myself the fantasy of Harvey offering me a huge raise and of me renting a West Hollywood duplex on a sunny, quiet, upper floor.

She sighed. "I still can't believe you're the only one at that hospital who knows his real identity. Maybe the nurses are keeping quiet about him just like you are."

"I don't think so. He really looks different, Tuscany. Also, people often don't recognize actors out of context. I just got lucky."

"You did, my friend, so don't blow it."

"GOING TO THE hospital on a Saturday, sweetie?" asked my mother a few minutes later. She was in the kitchen, lifting a sheet of brownies out of the oven. She looked startled when I appeared in my volunteer uniform instead of my jeans.

"I thought I might be needed," I said, popping a chocolate crumb into my mouth and burning my tongue on it.

She regarded me with a smile. "Are you sure you're not going there to see Richie?"

"Oh God, Mom. You've got to give that up, okay?" I hugged her. Her belly protruded from her bathrobe and her flesh was rubbery from lack of exercise and too much snacking.

"When I was dating your father, I always found ways to see him." She chuckled. "We couldn't stay away from each other."

"I know how much you miss him, Mom. You never talk about it, but the way he died—I mean, how drawn out it was—must have been traumatic for you. It was for me."

She shook her head, as if I'd just suggested the earth was flat. "No, sweetie. I have my happy memories of Jim, so I don't dwell on the unpleasant ones."

It occurred to me that Aunt Toni was right when she'd accused my mother of always trying to make things "nicey-nicey," of putting an unrealistically positive spin on them, of avoiding the negative at all costs. While Toni's glass was half empty, Mom's was filled to the brim, and maybe it was hers that was the unhealthy approach to life. Where was the sadness? The grief? Even the anger? In the years since Dad died, I'd never once seen her express those emotions. It was as if she'd buried them along with him, and now here she was, agoraphobic and not doing anything about it.

"How do you think Daddy would feel if he knew you couldn't leave the house?" I asked, not to guilt her but to try and pull her out of her self-imposed confinement.

"I can leave the house, sweetie," she replied. "I choose not to, as I've told you time and again."

I took her hand and looked her in the eye. "Then if I got married, you'd come to the wedding?"

She laughed. "Of course I would. What a question."

"And if I were in an accident, you'd be there to visit me in the hospital?"

"Ann. You know I would."

"What if I needed you to walk outside to the mailbox? Would you do that?"

Her smile faded and she slid her hand out from my grasp. "Now you're just being foolish."

"You didn't answer me, Mom," I persisted. "There's no snow. The weather's beautiful—for Missouri in March. If I held your arm very tightly and promised to bring you back inside the house the minute you felt panicky, would you walk out to the mailbox with me? Just to the curb? We could take it as slowly and gradually as you want."

"I . . ."

She looked at me with pleading eyes that were saying, Don't make me do this. I knew the look. I knew the feeling. I'd been there. That afternoon at the Santa Monica airport still plagued me.

"I'm going to leave for the hospital now," I said. "But one of these days, we'll take a short walk to the mailbox. Just the two of us. If you decide you're too shaky to make it to the curb, we'll turn around. It'll be your call. Okay?"

She thought for a few minutes. In the end, she didn't say no, which I considered a tremendous victory. What she said as I was rushing out the door was, "Drive carefully."

"YOU MUST BE running for volunteer of the year," Shelley teased when she spotted me signing in at the office. "I've heard of dedication, but on a Saturday?" She laughed. "At least I'm getting paid to be here."

"I hope it's okay," I said. "I know my shifts are supposed to be on Tuesdays and Fridays, but there are a few patients I wanted to check on. I'd like to be there for them until they're discharged."

"Oh, Ann," Shelley cooed. "What a lovely thing to say. You *should* be volunteer of the year."

Yes, I felt shabby. I wished I were as noble and heroic as she thought I was.

As we stood next to each other at the reception desk, she smiled down at me as if from a mountaintop covered in fall foliage. The color of her pantsuit that day was bright orange, a shade that only people who don't give a damn about fashion can pull off. She was the opposite of the Hollywood phonies I used to deal with. I respected her and craved her respect in return.

But I needed to have my career back and move out of my mother's house. Malcolm Goddard and whatever pearls of wisdom I could extract from him were beckoning.

I went straight to his room, but he was still down in the cath lab having his defibrillator implanted. The procedure had been delayed, according to Rolanda.

I busied myself until he returned to 613, roaming the hospital with my magazine cart. I stopped on three to see Bree Wiley and ended up reading to her from *Gone with the Wind*. Yes, she was only ten but very precocious, as I've said. She'd seen the movie and asked her mother to take the book out of the library for her. She was much too tired to read it that Saturday, let alone lift it, so I was happy to oblige. At one point, she interrupted and asked me how long I thought it would be before she got her new liver. I tousled her golden curls and told her I was sure it would be very soon. I was full of shit, since I had no idea when they'd find a donor match for her. I only knew that my answer seemed to soothe her for the moment, which was the best I could hope for under the circumstances.

On four, I arrived just in time to say good-bye to the woman who'd had the hysterectomy—the one who reminded me of a bulldog. She was dressed in overalls and seated in a chair, waiting for her doctor to come and discharge her. She was clutching her handbag as if it had millions of dollars in it. For all I knew, it did.

"You must be excited about going home," I said.

"I am," she said with a shrug of her strong, solid shoulders, "but I'm still in a lot of pain."

"It takes a while for the tissue inside the abdomen to heal," I said, sounding silly even to myself. I was a volunteer and a recovering hypo-chondriac, and neither qualified me to make medical pronouncements. "But before you know it, you'll be back to your regular routine."

She nodded. "You're so nice, Ann. Every time you visit me. I won't forget you, I swear."

I was oddly touched by her comment. I'd never considered myself unforgettable.

Eventually, I was back on six again. I was so keyed up about what might be my last chance at Malcolm that I wasn't watching where I was going and T-boned an oncoming gurney with my magazine cart. Luck-ily, the gurney was on its way to pick up a patient, not in the process of dropping one off, so nobody was hurt. Still, I reminded myself to calm down.

"Hey, you're all defibrillated," I said, greeting a fully conscious and extremely good-humored Malcolm, judging by the big smile. Maybe they were giving him happy juice along with the antibiotics, or maybe he was just relieved the procedure was over.

"All wired up and ready to rock." He tugged on the neck of his gown to show me the proof: a small bandage just under his left collarbone. "They put the thing in, shocked me a few times to make sure it was working, and sewed me together. I can have the stitches out when I get home." He nod-ded. "Yep, by this time tomorrow, I'll be outta here."

Okay, hotshot reporter, I said silently. This is it. No time to waste. It's now or never. Get to work.

"Mind if I pull up a chair, since this will probably be our last visit?" I asked, already pulling up the chair and planting myself in it before he could tell me not to.

"As long as you don't try to force a magazine down my throat," he said. "But all bitching aside, this place is great. A definite must for the sophisti-cated traveler, although they need to put less starch in the sheets."

"You can sleep in your Frette linens when you're back in Miami," I said. "Heartland General is interested in making people well, not bathing them in luxury."

He shook his head. "There you go again, lecturing me."

"Right. Sorry." Why did I keep doing that? I was supposed to be softening him up.

"No, actually, I like it," he said. "It's kind of refreshing. It's that honest, Midwestern sensibility of yours. Don't ever apologize for it."

My honest sensibility. Sure. "Well then," I said, settling into the chair. "Why don't we have a little chat?"

"What would you like to *chat* about? The Middle East? Gun control? Social security?"

"All worthy subjects, but I was thinking more about you, about your life. I meet so many people in my capacity as a volunteer, and each person has a story, a set of experiences that makes him or her unique. Since you're just passing through and we'll never see each other again, I was hoping you'd talk about yourself, about where you grew up and the events that shaped you. Did you watch movies as a child, for example?"

He arched an eyebrow. "Why would you ask me that?"

Oh God, I thought. He suspects that I recognize him, and why wouldn't he? I sounded just like James Lipton. "Probably because most people tell me they watched movies as kids," I said casually. "I, on the other hand, was raised in a very strict household without any sort of mass media—a total hayseed. I never went to the movies. Still don't. I vaguely know the names of celebrities, but only from the magazines I've got in my cart."

He seemed to go for it, relaxing his head onto the pillow. "The truth is, I was mesmerized by movies as a kid. I grew up in New York City and there were theaters on every block."

"Really? What drew you to them?"

"Escape. I was an only child with parents who couldn't stand each other. I wasn't much of a student and I never wanted to go home after school, so I'd hang out at the theaters and watch whatever was playing. As soon as the lights went dark and the images popped up on the screen, I was hooked, every time. I loved being swept away into other worlds, other lives." He rolled his eyes. "Big cliché, I know. Every Joe Blow says he grew up losing himself in movies."

"No. Lots of men say they grew up losing themselves in sports," I pointed out.

"Not me. I didn't like the competition. It felt too much like my parents arguing." He laughed. "Of course the movies I'm most attracted to are heavy dramas involving people in conflict. I guess we gravitate toward what's familiar. My shrink says that's why I create my own dramas, because it's all I learned."

He doesn't need a shrink to get him to stop creating dramas, I thought. He needs a walk around this hospital so he can see what real dramas are— people with brain tumors and rotting livers and AIDS. His dysfunctional family was small potatoes in comparison.

Still, he was definitely opening up to me. The interview was going well so far. Better than I'd hoped.

"You said you weren't much of a student," I continued. "And yet here you are, a success in real estate."

"I didn't say I was stupid. I just said I didn't like school."

"Why was that?"

"I was the type who sat in the back of the classroom and prayed I wouldn't get called on."

"Because you didn't do your homework?"

"No, because I was painfully shy."

Oh, please, I thought. Almost all actors claim they're shy, and then they go out and perform in front of millions, sometimes with their clothes off. "You don't look shy now," I said, trying to keep my cynicism in check.

"What does 'shy' look like?" he said. "Should I stutter, blush, stare at the floor when I talk to you? Shy is a state of mind, an internal disability.

Others can't always see it, but that doesn't mean it's not there. Fears don't have to be visible to other people."

Well, he had me there. I'd tried to get by without anybody knowing I suffered from phobias and panic attacks. I knew firsthand that it *was* possible to have fears and not broadcast them. "What sort of fear brings out shyness?" I asked, sort of amazed that I was having this conversation with the almighty Malcolm Goddard. Who would have guessed that we had anything in common?

"Fear of being scrutinized, exposed, criticized. It can be very debilitating to be shy. You overcompensate for it by acting like an arrogant jerk. Well, some of us do."

So he'd been Hollywood's biggest brat because he didn't want anybody to know how frightened he was inside? Was that why he had such an aversion to the media? Because he was afraid of revealing how self-confident he wasn't?

"You're not an arrogant jerk," I said in what was *my* best acting performance to date, because it was his arrogance and his jerkiness that had cost me my job.

"Thanks." He flipped over on his side and faced me. "Now let's talk about you. About *your* life and the events that shaped *you*."

I waved him off. "I'm much too boring, believe me. I've spent my whole life in Middletown doing the usual things." I needed to get back to him. The clock was ticking, and all I had so far was some stuff about his parents' crummy marriage, his early interest in movies, and a lifelong shyness that he masked with bravado. It was all usable, but not enough.

"So? Let's hear," he insisted. "It's not as if you're conducting an interview. You said we were having a chat."

"An interview," I said with a dismissive laugh. "Fine. I'll talk about myself, but it'll put you right to sleep."

"Try me."

"Well, I grew up here in Missouri, as I said."

"Siblings?"

"Nope. The apple of my parents' eye."

"What's your dad do?"

"He used to work at the bank."

"Laid off?"

"Lung cancer."

His face sagged. "He died?"

"He did." What were we doing talking about me, for God's sake?

"You miss him, huh?"

"Yes. Yes, I do, Luke, but—"

"But you Midwesterners don't moan and groan about everything, I know. You just pick yourselves up and do what has to be done. I admire that, Ann. I really do."

Sheesh. Now he admired me. Or admired who he thought I was. I didn't know what to say, was flustered by his interest, so I stood up, fluffed the pillow behind his head, tried to look very busy. When I'd found my equilibrium, I started asking him questions again. I was in the middle of the one about his favorite movie when a voice came over the loudspeaker.

"Code red. Code red," said the voice, indicating that there was a fire hazard on the floor.

Crap. I knew code reds didn't necessarily mean that the hospital was about to go up in flames. Sometimes, they merely indicated that a drill was in progress. Still, my job at that moment was to reassure Malcolm that everything was okay and then march out to the nurses' station and find out what I was supposed to do. My interview with him would have to be put on hold, in other words.

"You have to evacuate," said Rolanda. "Now."

"What about my cart?" I said.

"Leave it in the hall," she said. "Take the stairs to the ground floor, and exit the hospital. There's no fire, but you still have to follow the code rules."

"I don't understand," I said into the air after she ran off and abandoned me. "If it's just a drill, why can't I stay with the patients?" As in: one particular patient. A patient who is being discharged tomorrow and will no longer be able to tell me his life story.

"Those are the rules for volunteers," snapped one of the other nurses. "Deal with it."

"Okay, okay, but can I come right back?" I said, again to nobody in particular. I was at a crucial point in my conversation with Goddard. If I left now, I might never get another crack at him.

"Go!" somebody scolded me. "And use the stairs!"

Fine, so I used the stairs. When I reached the ground floor, I joined the other "nonessential personnel" of the hospital and hung out in the plaza in front of the main entrance, waiting for the prescribed period to be over.

As soon as it was, twenty minutes later, I rode up in the elevator to six hoping to pick up with Goddard where we'd left off. Unfortunately, Jonathan White was in with the patient, having some sort of consultation. I waited in the hall, leafing through the various magazines in my cart, rehearsing the questions I would pose once we resumed the interview. And waited. I figured that Jonathan was examining Malcolm after his procedure earlier and discussing the plans for his discharge the next day. There had to be details to work out, especially since Malcolm would be going from the hospital to the airport. Perhaps he was asking Jonathan what would happen when he went through the metal detector. Perhaps he was asking whether he would require aftercare once he got home. Perhaps he was complaining about the starch in the sheets. All I knew was that they were taking forever.

When Jonathan finally emerged and spotted me lurking, I said hello and asked him to say hello to his wife, Eleanor, and made the requisite small talk.

"It's great that you're keeping up with the volunteering," he said, patting me on the shoulder.

"I enjoy it," I said.

I had launched into a cheesy speech about what a do-gooder I'd become when I noticed that Rolanda was taping a "No Visitors" sign on Malcolm's door. I was so rattled by this development that I could no longer focus on Jonathan. "I know I'm not supposed to ask," I blurted out to him, "but is everything all right with the patient in 613?"

"Oh, sure. We're sending him home tomorrow," he said. He didn't wink. He didn't give me a nudge. He didn't show any indication that *he* knew that *I* knew that the patient was a big fat superstar. Richard must not have told him I knew. He leaned in and whispered, "Sort of a handful, that one. Says he needs his beauty sleep and doesn't want to be disturbed for the rest of the day."

Doesn't want to be disturbed? For the rest of the day? I was dumbfounded. Malcolm and I had been communicating, connecting, clicking—or so he'd led me to believe. How dare he issue a directive to shut me and everybody else out of his room? Did he think it was okay to pull a diva act now that he was in the clear, healthwise? Or did he mistake Heartland General for the kind of hip hotel where he probably put a "Do Not Disturb" sign outside his door as a matter of course? Well, Heartland General wasn't a hip hotel, and *beauty sleep* wasn't the point.

Fuming. I was absolutely fuming. Stupidly, I thought he had actually come down off his throne with all that talk about being shy and afraid, but his sense of entitlement was as huge as ever. Yes, it was his perfect right to be left in peace if he chose, but he'd told me he found me refreshing! He'd seemed engaged in our dialogue! He'd given me the impression—gullible me—that he liked me!

"Ann?" said Jonathan. "I know volunteers don't work shifts on Sundays, but if you really want to visit with him, I'd come back tomorrow. I'll probably be discharging him midmorning." He smiled. "Eleanor makes me egg-white omelets on Sunday mornings. She adds just a touch of low-fat cheese along with turkey bacon, and I have to tell you, it's as good tasting as it is good for you."

So he was just as boring as his wife. But my bigger concern was Goddard. If I didn't get to him before he left in the morning, I'd be writing for the *Crier* for the rest of my pathetic life. I'm not saying chimney sweeps aren't fascinating, but— Well, yes I am.

Chapter Nineteen

||||||||||||||||||||||||||||||||||||||||||||||||||||||||||||||||||||||||||||||||||||||||||||

On Sunday morning, I put on my uniform and stole out of the house before anybody was up. I didn't want to have to answer the big question: Why was I going to the hospital on a Sunday when volunteers didn't work on Sundays? I figured I'd deal with it later, hopefully with a computer full of meaty new material. The important thing was to hop into my Honda and get to the hospital fast—before Malcolm was given a clean bill of health and escorted out the door and into a waiting limo.

I was zooming along at a brisk clip, about five minutes into my drive, when I was pulled over for speeding. Yep. I was so worried about missing Malcolm that I'd pushed it.

"You were doing fifty in a thirty," said the cop, who turned out to be Ken Culhane, a boy I knew from high school. Even back then, he was sort of cop-ish with his thick neck and crew cut—the type who was always keeping kids in line by beating them up.

"Do you remember me, Ken?" I asked, fumbling in my purse for my license. I was totally unnerved, both by the fact that the class bully was now a member of Middletown's Finest and by the delay he was causing me. I had to get to the hospital right away. I didn't need a ticket. Or a knuckle sandwich. "I'm Ann Roth. We went to school together."

"Sure, I remember," he said with a snicker. "Miss Hollywood with the stars in her eyes."

"Listen, Ken," I said as I gazed pleadingly at him through my open car window. "I was driving too fast. I acknowledge that. But, as you can see from my uniform, I work at Heartland General now. I was on an urgent mission to see a patient who, sadly, is on his way out." No lie there. "Can you cut me a break just this once and let me go? For old time's sake?"

He appeared to consider my request. For several long minutes. I was so antsy I almost drove off without waiting for his answer. But he finally gave me one: No. Speeding was speeding, he said, and wrote me a ticket for seventy-five bucks.

SINCE THE VOLUNTEERS office was closed on Sundays, I didn't have to sign in, didn't have to make conversation with Shelley, didn't even have to tell her I'd come in. I could simply sneak in under the radar, not have to exchange pleasantries with any of the other volunteers, and get my big get once and for all.

Unfortunately, the elevators were annoyingly slow. The volunteers may have been off duty but the friends and families of the patients were very much on duty, and the hospital was filled with visitors toting flowers, balloons, and teddy bears.

I was standing there at the bank of elevators, pressing the Up button for the thousandth time, when somebody tapped me on the shoulder. I turned.

"Ann?" said Claire, who bounced on the toes of her shoes and would have been an interesting diversion on another day but was an unexpected roadblock on this one.

"Claire," I said, my heart thumping with adrenaline as I tried to smile at her. She was not in uniform. She was wearing a fleecy sweatsuit, the kind with a hood. "Uh, what are you doing here?"

"I could ask you that too," she said, taking my elbow and steering me away from the others. She was pretty strong for a small person. "What's the deal?"

"The deal," I said, dying to fling myself into the elevator that had finally arrived in the lobby, "is that I wanted to say good-bye to a patient who's going home today. After that, I'm off to the lake. This is the first warm day since I came back to town, and I'm planning to take a chair, soak up the sun, and relax." I really was planning to go to the lake. Much later.

"Are you going with *Richie Grossman?*" she asked in a singsong voice.

"What?" I said, shaking my head. "Why would you think that?"

"He's telling everybody you two are dating."

Oh God. "He's a very nice guy, but we're not dating, Claire. I had dinner with him a couple of times. As friends."

"If you say so."

"I do." I surreptitiously checked my watch. Nine o'clock. There was no telling when Jonathan White would show up in Malcolm's room. Some doctors made their rounds at the crack of dawn. Others were more leisurely about it. How was I supposed to know when Eleanor would feed her husband his egg-white omelet with low-fat cheese and turkey bacon? He'd said he'd be around "midmorning." But what did that mean? He could be up on six right now. More heart thumping.

"Aren't you gonna ask what I'm doing here on a Sunday?" said Claire.

"Yes. Sorry," I said. "Why are you here?"

She rolled her eyes. "Mike got into a fight at the Hole in the Wall last night. Ten stitches on his chin. He looks like Harrison Ford now. I wish."

"I hope he'll be okay," I said to the accompaniment of the *ding* of the elevator arriving—the elevator I needed to be on.

"Hey, I bet he'd love to see you," she said. "Why don't you stop by his room and say hello. He's in 510."

"Oh, gosh. I'd like to but—"

"No, really. He always said how he thought it was cool that you went to Hollywood and all."

"Right, but it's that patient I mentioned," I said quickly. "I have to make sure I catch him before he's discharged. I really do want to wish him luck."

"Whatever." She nodded and steered me back to where we'd started. "I'll ride up with you."

I couldn't lose her. Swell.

We entered the next elevator. She pressed five, then asked me which floor I wanted.

"Six, please," I said.

The doors closed. Up we went.

"Which patient on six?" she said.

"I forget his room number," I said, because we weren't supposed to discuss the patients among ourselves and because I didn't want to even hint that Malcolm might be more than your average local *and* because more than anything in the world, I didn't want her tagging along.

Mercifully, it was a quick trip to the fifth floor. As the doors opened, Claire held them for a second and looked back at me. "If it's the guy in 613, I doubt he's in the mood for good-byes. He's cute but what a sourball." She stuck her tongue out. "I tried giving him a magazine the other day and he said, from out of nowhere, 'Media people are parasites!' Weird, huh?"

"Incredibly weird," I agreed and asked her to send Mike my best regards. My aunt would have killed me for that.

When I got to six, I went straight to 613. The door was open just a crack and there wasn't any sort of sign on it, so I knocked. No answer. I knocked again and said, "Hi, Luke, it's Ann. May I come in?" Still no answer. I knocked a third time and said, louder, in case he was in the bathroom and couldn't hear me, "It's Ann! I wanted to give you a friendly Midwestern bye-bye before you go back to Miami!" Not a peep.

Violating one of Claire's cardinal rules, I opened the door without an invitation and stepped inside the room. And then I gasped.

No, the patient wasn't having sex like the last time I'd walked in on somebody without permission. On the contrary. The patient wasn't there.

The second I saw the empty bed, I didn't even bother to snoop around the room. I flew out into the hall in search of a nurse, a tech, Jonathan, someone who could tell me whether Malcolm had left the building, as I feared. Just as I was cursing myself for stopping to talk to Claire, for getting caught speeding, for allowing myself to fantasize about staging a comeback at *Famous,* I spotted my prey. He was way down the hall, still in his hospital gown but minus the IV pole, walking slowly toward me. I experienced a bizarre feeling: I was happy to see someone I detested.

He's still here, I thought with enormous relief, telling myself to breathe normally. I haven't missed my once-in-a-lifetime opportunity after all.

"Hey," he said when he finally made it back to the room. He looked winded and pale as he grabbed hold of the doorknob to steady himself, but he was smiling. "I was just stretching my legs while I wait for the doctor to give me the thumbs-up. He told me he'd be here this morning, but no sign of him so far. When's checkout at this place?"

"It varies," I said. We were standing face-to-face for the first time since he'd been admitted, and I suddenly felt winded myself. Even in the drab gown, even with the grubbiness, even with the brown eyes and receding hairline, Malcolm Goddard radiated the kind of star power that had flustered me at Spago. But I recovered quickly. The memory of that night snapped me right out of it. "Why don't you sit in the chair until he comes and we'll have a last visit?"

"Why not?" he said cheerfully. "I'm so glad to be a free man that I'll talk as long as you want. There's definitely something to be said for being handed a new lease on life."

Talk as long as I wanted? I could hardly contain myself. "Let's get you settled first," I said, hoping Jonathan was only beginning to sink his teeth into his omelet and that I'd have an uninterrupted one-on-one with Malcolm. "At Heartland General, we like our patients to be comfortable right up until they leave us."

He started to walk toward the armchair next to the bed, but instead he stopped and cocked his head at me, as if he were trying to size me up, the way he'd done before. "Can you keep a secret?" he said, lowering his voice a bit.

Well, I wasn't expecting the question, obviously. I reacted by saying that yes, of course I could.

"I thought so," he said, still standing, still appraising me. "You strike me as the trustworthy type. No pretenses. No angles. No agendas. Just straight talk. You don't want anything from me, except my good health, and you just might be the only person on this earth who doesn't."

"That's very nice of you to say," I managed, "but I'm not perfect or even close to—"

"See that? You're modest too. It's that Midwestern thing, I guess. You're real. You're authentic. You're grounded. You're not all about how you look."

Instinctively, I reached up to touch my face and hair. So he thought I was—what?—hideous?

He laughed. "I think you misunderstood me. You're a beautiful woman. I'm just saying you don't parade it out there, and it's such a switch from what I'm used to."

I didn't have time to process the compliment. I was trying desperately to follow where this was going. "The women in Miami are different?"

"The women in *L.A.* are different." He took a step forward in my direction. We were face-to-face again.

"L.A.?" I said, utterly bewildered. "But I thought—"

He placed his forefinger across my lips. He was that close to me. "Shhhh," he whispered. "Here's the secret. I'm only telling you because you don't care about the movies or Hollywood or any of that. Well, and because I'm leaving any minute, so none of this will matter anyway."

"None of what?" I said, although I knew. I knew but I didn't believe it.

"My real name is Malcolm Goddard," he said proudly, as if he'd announced that he was the king of a major monarchy.

As the thumping in my chest came in faster, louder beats, I tried to figure out how to respond. Surprise? Excitement? Reverence? Nonchalance? I was completely thrown by his disclosure and what its implications for me might be.

"So then you're not really Luke Sykes?" I said, going with a combination of surprise and nonchalance. What *were* the implications for me, for my plan? What did all this mean?

He shook his head. "I use that alias when I don't want the media to know where I am. I'm one of those reclusive movie stars you read about, so don't tell anybody until after I'm gone, okay?"

"Sure, sure," I agreed, trying not to look as if my whole world had just caved in. Which it had. The realization hit me the instant he'd said the word "reclusive": My shot at getting the big get was over. Yes, he'd blown his own cover, because he was leaving and because he figured I didn't give a damn who he was. But now that he had, he would never open up to me, not about anything worth putting in a magazine. That was the irony. His guard would be up—the same stupid resistance that had made interviewing him impossible in the first place. When I'd posed my questions to Luke Sykes, he'd found them innocuous enough to answer. But posing them to Malcolm Goddard? Forget it. Malcolm Goddard didn't let people in. Malcolm Goddard didn't believe anybody had a right to ask him about his thoughts and feelings. Malcolm Goddard was an asshole, and at that very moment I had an urge to set his hospital gown on fire.

"Might as well sit down," he said, turning back toward the chair and shuffling away from me. "I'm kind of tired from my little marathon. Maybe you could ask the nurse to bring me some juice or something. I think her name's Rowanda."

"*It's Rolanda,*" I said, more sharply than I intended. Well? I was crushed, absolutely reeling from defeat.

"I'd love some OJ," he said as he approached the chair. "Or maybe some cranapple, if they have it."

He's giving me his drink order like I'm his personal assistant, I seethed as I watched him take another step and then fall.

Fall?

Oh my God! He sort of swooned and then crumpled to the floor in a heap!

I ran over to him, careful not to do anything that was against the rules. But I had to see if he was . . . dead. Oh my God!

His eyes were closed and his jaw was slack, but he was breathing. At least it seemed that way when I held his wrist and felt a pulse. Or was it only my own that was throbbing?

"Help!" I said, getting up off my knees and scrambling to the phone next to the bed. I'd made my share of procedural mistakes since I'd started volunteering, but this wasn't a fire and it wasn't a security breach. That much I knew. With trembling fingers I punched in 111.

"State the nature of the emergency," said the operator.

"Code blue," I said.

Chapter Twenty

‖‖

"He'll be all right. He just fainted," said Jonathan after Malcolm was back in bed and resting. We were standing in the hall at the nurses' station. The crisis was over and the patient was stable, but I was a wreck.

"I thought he was dead," I said wearily, propping myself up against the wall. "One minute he was walking around, champing at the bit to go home. The next he was down on the ground. I didn't know what to do."

"You did what you were supposed to do," he reassured me. "Now we'll take over."

"But what's wrong with him? Why did he faint? Is there a problem with the defibrillator? Did he have more palpitations?" Questions. Lots of questions, as usual. It wasn't my place to ask them, but I did anyway.

"His heart seems fine," he said. "The EKG looks good. The chest X-ray looks good. The device's leads are in place. The rhythm is normal."

"Then what's the matter?" I said.

"We'll know more when the blood work comes back. Not to worry."

As he continued on his rounds, I decided I'd had enough of Heartland

General and left the patient in the hands of the professionals. As I drove home, I called Tuscany with the bulletin that Malcolm had confessed his true identity and then taken a dive.

"I nearly died when 'Luke' told me who he really was," I said wearily. "But, as it turned out, he was the one who nearly died."

"What? Why?" she said.

"He passed out right after letting me in on his big secret," I said. "He's stable, but they don't know what's wrong with him. Looks like he'll be staying with us longer than he expected."

"That's awesome!"

"Tuscany."

"Not that he's sick. Just that you'll have more time with him." She squealed. "It's like he wants to give you the interview without even realizing it."

"No, the only reason he told me the truth is because he thought he'd be back in L.A. by now. And because he thinks I'm *real*."

"You are real," she said. "A real reporter who's determined to get her story."

"The story is that he's Malcolm again, the guy who will go to any lengths to keep inquiring minds away. Which means I'm washing my hands of the whole thing. I won't humiliate myself by chasing after him. Not anymore. I'm abandoning my little project."

"Like hell you are."

"I have no choice. He won't open up to me now."

"Ann, you're the only journalist in the world who knows where Goddard is. That's still huge."

What was huge right then was my headache. I couldn't wait to get home, change my clothes, and head to the lake for some peace and quiet. The sun was shining, the breeze was light, and the temperature was climbing to a forecasted high of seventy degrees. Perfect conditions for trying to figure out what to do with the rest of my life, now that *Famous* and I really were history.

WHEN I ARRIVED at the state park, I was further bummed to find that I had lots of company. With all its recreational opportunities—boating, fishing, camping—the area had always attracted hundreds of people, but I hadn't anticipated that they'd all be there so early in the season. Then I remembered that "the season" started as soon as the snow melted. Or, as my father used to say, the four seasons in Middletown were: Snow, Almost Summer, Summer, and Still Summer.

I positioned my canvas folding chair in the sand facing the water, set my tote bag next to the chair, and plopped myself down, exhaling a disconsolate sigh as I did. I was wearing shorts and a T-shirt and my arms and legs were an unsightly fish-belly white, but I didn't care.

I sank into an exhausted person's nap, dozing off for about twenty minutes. I felt fairly renewed when I woke up—so renewed that I thought, Oh, go ahead and play with your laptop. I pulled it out of my tote bag and rested it on my legs. Yes, I was finished with the idea of duping Malcolm into giving me an interview, but I hadn't entered my last real conversation with him into the computer, so I decided it couldn't hurt to type it in. Just to tie up loose ends.

My fingers were moving quickly over the keyboard when I suddenly felt a shadow cross my body. I looked up, expecting to see a cloud obscuring the sun momentarily, but there, instead, was Richard. He was in baggy white shorts and a pink polo shirt, and he was wearing white socks with his brown sandals. He had a large towel under one arm and his computer under the other, and his face was slathered with white sunscreen that he hadn't managed to rub in.

"Mind if I join you?" he asked.

Well, yes, I did mind. I'd been enjoying my solitude. Sure, there were lots of people around, but I didn't have to actually talk to them. "I'm not very good company today," I said, because I couldn't just come out and hurt his feelings. "I'm kind of doing my own thing."

"I understand completely," he said, planting himself right down next to me, spreading out his towel and making himself comfortable. "I'll let you get back to whatever it is and *give you your space*." He chuckled. "That's a very Hollywood expression, isn't it?"

A thousand years ago, I thought. Clearly, he didn't understand, but what was I supposed to do?

"I'll leave you alone, Ann. Really," he promised. "It'll be fun just to sit together."

I smiled and went back to my laptop. I was typing up the part where Malcolm/Luke had confided that he was shy.

"Quirky weather, isn't it?" Richard said only seconds later. "I mean, jeepers, Middletown is so strange. We can go from heat to air-conditioning in the same day and how about all this bright sun? But then you probably got used to the sunshine when you lived in L.A. Heck, you probably went to the beach every chance you got. Or did you lounge around the pools of the rich and famous? Everybody has a pool there, don't they?"

Okay, maybe I could ask him to put a sock in it without hurting his feelings. "You know, Richard, I was hoping we could each concentrate on our work and not have to—"

Just then his cell phone rang. It had one of those incredibly irritating ring tunes better suited for a child's birthday party.

"Dr. Grossman," he answered in his authoritative voice, as opposed to his "jeepers" one. The signal he was getting while splayed out on his towel must have been bad because he got up and kept asking "Can you hear me now?" until he finally found the right spot.

"It was the hospital," he announced when he came back and sat down again.

"Everything all right?" I said, wondering if they really needed him on a Sunday or if he just wanted me to think he was indispensable.

"It will be. The risk-management department was calling about a patient who's making noises about suing. It happens all the time."

"Does it?"

"At every hospital in the country. People want somebody to pay for their pain and suffering."

"Is there any merit to this patient's complaint?" I asked, figuring that if he'd been so cavalier about sharing Malcolm's personal information, he would probably be just as indiscreet about a lawsuit.

"Of course not. She had a hysterectomy three months ago. Now it's sunk in that she can't have kids and she's lashing out at us. I feel for the woman, I do, but jeepers."

"It does seem as if Heartland performs a lot of hysterectomies," I said. "More than I would have thought."

"Ann." He chuckled. "You've only been a volunteer for—what—a week?"

"True. I was only saying that—"

He patted my knee. I noticed that I'd missed a section shaving. There was a tiny island of leg hair just below the hem of my shorts. "Why don't you hand out magazines and we'll handle the medical evaluations, okay?"

"Sure." He was right. What did I know?

A while later, I decided to go for a walk along the water to escape my relentless companion. "I need to stretch my legs, but I'll be back soon," I said, hoping he would take the hint and not jump up to come with me.

"Have a good walk," he said with a salute.

I was about to go when I suddenly remembered the time we'd been together at the Caffeine Scene. I'd gone to the counter to get us coffee and had returned to find him poring over my computer screen.

I knelt down and shut the computer off this time, then went on my way. Yes, Richard was an okay guy, but, as I knew only too well, he had privacy issues.

ON TUESDAY AFTERNOON, I put on my uniform and headed to the hospital for my regular shift. As I was signing in at the volunteers office, Shelley stuck her head out of her cubicle and waved me inside.

She was holding a yellow Post-it with "Room #613" written on it. "This patient made a special request," she said, handing it to me. "He'd like some magazines."

I couldn't hide my surprise. For one thing, I thought maybe Malcolm had gotten better since I'd last seen him and been discharged. For another, I certainly didn't expect him to ask for magazines.

"Did he say which type?" I said, knowing he had nothing but disdain for the sort of publications we offered.

"No, but he asked for you by name."

Interesting, I thought. What could he possibly want with me? Well, there *was* the fact that I could have saved his life by calling the code blue. "Then I'll load the cart and start my shift on six," I said.

She smiled. "You're developing quite a fan club around here."

"I wouldn't call one patient a fan club," I said.

"How about two patients?" she said. "Actually, this one's a former patient on four. She called this morning and left a message asking for 'Ann, the nice magazine lady who talked to me about adoption.'"

"Oh, sure," I said, nodding. "She went home last week after surgery." Yeah, I thought. Another patient who'd had a hysterectomy. I wasn't crazy. There were a lot of them.

"You must have made quite an impression, because she wants you to call her." She handed me another Post-it, this one with the name "Isabelle Sawyer" written on it, along with a phone number. "Some of them view the volunteers as friends and try to keep in touch. It's entirely up to you whether you reciprocate."

"I'll think about it," I said, not sure that Isabelle and I would have much more to talk about. "See you later, Shelley."

I restocked the cart with magazines, then took the elevator up to the sixth floor. I can't deny that my heart was beating just a little faster as I approached 613. Yes, the project was dead, but I was curious about Malcolm, about why he'd asked for me. Maybe he did want to thank me or maybe he wanted to threaten to break my kneecaps if I told anyone he was a celebrity.

"Knock, knock," I said as I tapped on his door. "It's Ann, from volunteer services. May I come in?"

"Please do," croaked an astonishingly weak voice.

I parked the cart in the hall and ventured inside the room. What I saw stunned me. Malcolm, who had looked relatively robust when he'd first been admitted, was deathly pale—a shade of whitish gray. His eyes were glassy and his lips were parched, and when he lifted his head to acknowledge my entrance, the small physical act seemed to sap all his energy. Despite my antipathy toward him, I was deeply concerned.

"Hello," I said in a soft, low voice. "*Malcolm.*" He had the lights turned off and the curtains drawn. This was a sickroom now, not a pit stop between movie shoots, I realized. It looked and smelled like a place where life was ebbing away. "How are you feeling?"

He nodded at the IV bags on the pole next to his bed. "They're giving me blood," he said almost in a whisper. "Lots of bags of the red stuff."

Blood? Oh God. "Because you fainted on Friday morning?"

"I guess." He blinked his eyes slowly. He was a little disoriented, I noticed. Groggy. "They found out I'm bleeding internally."

"From the fall?" I asked, even though he'd only slid to the floor rather than made a crash landing. He hadn't hit his head, hadn't collided with the chair, hadn't gone down hard at all. It didn't make sense that he was bleeding.

"No," he said. "It probably happened—" His eyes closed again. He was out for a few seconds, then revived. "During the implantation of the defibrillator last week, they might have nicked a vein somewhere. They came up with this theory after they checked out my blood tests. My hemoglobin was, like, six."

"Oh," I said. I had no idea what was normal for hemoglobin—ten? twenty? a thousand?—but clearly six was not. "I'm sorry to hear it. But hopefully the transfusions will fix you up and you'll finally get out of here. I know how eager you were to leave."

"No, you don't," he said as his eyes closed again. I waited silently until he had the strength to continue talking. "I was about to shoot a movie when all this happened. They had to shut down production because of me. I'm costing them money, screwing up the schedules of the other actors, giving the media more reasons to attack me."

No mention of my keeping quiet about his identity. Either he really did trust me or he was delirious. "Your health is more important than any movie," I said, because it was true and because my compassionate side overtook my I-hate-Malcolm side. "You'll get better and you'll pick up your career where you left off."

"If the morons at this hospital can figure out where the bleeding's coming from," he said, his old hostile attitude returning. The difference was that I could understand his anger this time. If some doctor had clipped one of my veins during a routine procedure and I'd started bleeding internally, I wouldn't have been too thrilled about it either. I wondered if risk management would be calling Richard about Malcolm's case.

"What are they doing to find the bleeding?" I asked.

"CAT scan, other tests. Meanwhile, I'm stuck here wondering what I did to deserve this nightmare."

He deserved plenty for all the grief he'd put others through, but not this. Not even overpaid, self-absorbed actors deserved this. "Sorry," I said again, feeling the need to apologize for *my* hospital. "Is there anything I can do? You didn't really want a magazine, did you?"

"No. I wanted a friendly face." He sighed heavily. "I don't know anybody here. I'm totally lost. You're the only one who seems to care about me."

"Everybody in this building cares," I said. Again, I felt an allegiance to the hospital, an allegiance to Shelley's core of volunteers too. They all cared, even Claire. Even me.

"Then why am I still here?"

"I don't know."

I needed to get to the bottom of why Malcolm Goddard was "still here," of who was responsible. I was a reporter and I wanted answers.

"I've got to run an errand on another floor," I told him, "but I'll be back to see you a little later. Okay?"

"Promise?" he said, his voice barely audible.

"Promise."

If anyone had told me that Malcolm Goddard would be depending on me for moral support and that I would freely give it, I wouldn't have believed them. But, as I was discovering daily, life was full of surprises.

||||||||||||||||||||||||||||||||||||||||||||||||||||||||||||||||||||||||||||||||||||||||

Chapter Twenty-one

I stowed my cart back in the storage room and marched down the hall to the administrative offices where Richard's was located. His was a spacious corner office, as opulently decorated as Harvey's, minus the spiritual aids. With its marble desk and cushy leather chair and abstract paintings on the wall along with all the diplomas, it befit the man of authority that he had become. I knew his duties didn't include micromanaging the doctors, but on this particular Tuesday I needed him to do just that.

"I hope I'm not interrupting," I said after his assistant told me he was off the phone and free to see me. He'd been in meetings for most of the morning, and I'd had to leave and come back several times.

He rose from his chair and greeted me, fiddling with his bow tie, self-conscious yet preening. "You've been looking for me?" he said with obvious delight.

"Sorry, but it's not a personal visit," I said, not wanting him to get the wrong idea yet again. "I'm worried about a patient." I moved closer to him so I could whisper, "Malcolm Goddard."

"You mean Luke Sykes," he whispered back, nodding at his assistant, who sat well outside his door and couldn't have heard me.

"Fine, then it's Luke Sykes I'm worried about," I said, playing his silly game.

"Jonathan's on the case. No need to be worried. Unless—" He wagged a finger at me. "You met our special patient. You're smitten."

"Richard." He talked like somebody's grandfather.

"Well? He's very handsome and quite the muscular specimen. Should I be jealous?"

"This isn't funny," I said, surprising myself by how earnest I was, by how I had come to serve as an advocate for Malcolm, of all people. "It turns out that he's bleeding internally. He told me it probably happened while they were implanting the defibrillator." I paused. "But then you must know that. You know everything that goes on in this place, don't you?"

"Pretty much."

"I was wondering if the hospital could have been at fault. With his bleeding."

"The hospital?" He chuckled, the way he had at the lake when I'd mentioned the hysterectomies.

"Isn't that a possibility?" I said. "That's why Heartland General has a risk-management department, isn't it?"

Another chuckle, this one accompanied by a shake of his head. "Ann, you still think like a reporter. I bet you were terrific at that magazine the way you—"

"Richard, can't you just answer my question without all the flattery?"

"Of course. Risk management contacted me about Mr. Sykes's situation a little while ago. Because they're thorough. Because we have checks and balances at this hospital. Because things happen during invasive procedures, especially when you're running a catheter up into the heart area. That's why the patient signs consent forms, because things happen even under the best conditions."

"And?"

"And a member of the department just came back from interviewing him about what might have caused his bleeding." He waved a hand at his desk. "The report is over there."

"What does it say?"

"That someone *was* at fault."

"Oh God," I said with dread in the pit of my stomach as I thought about the monumental lawsuit Malcolm would undoubtedly file, even if it did create a media circus. I felt terrible for him, terrible that he had come to Middletown and gotten more than he'd bargained for. "You have to fire the doctor responsible, Richard, or at least conduct an investigation. Was it Jonathan? Or someone less experienced? A nurse? Who?"

"Mr. Sykes did this, Ann. To himself."

"I don't understand."

He nodded again at the file. And then he explained. It turned out that after being pressed by risk management, Malcolm suddenly remembered that he'd had a headache the day before the procedure and, against his doctor's orders, had swallowed a couple of the aspirin that he'd stuffed into his jeans pocket before leaving L.A.

"Aspirin causes bleeding, which is why we strongly advise against taking it prior to surgery," said Richard. "Mr. Sykes may have forgotten he took it until we jogged his memory, but the bottom line is that he caused his own complication. Jonathan warned me that he was a hothead."

I was dumbfounded. Absolutely stunned. How could Malcolm have disobeyed his doctor's warning? Was he so arrogant that he thought he knew what was better for him than a trained cardiologist did? Did he think he was above the rules because he was a celebrity? Was he so reckless, so *hotheaded,* that he believed he could do anything without consequences?

Richard sat back down behind his desk. He opened the folder and skimmed what was in it. "Jeepers, it's completely out of bounds for me to share this with you, but his CAT scan shows a retroperitoneal bleed."

"Could you be a little less technical?" I said, still wondering how Malcolm could have jeopardized his own health.

"It means there's a hematoma—a clot—in his back, near the kidneys. They're giving him medications and he'll be fine in a few days."

"Oh. Good." I was so relieved. If Malcolm had died— Well, I'm just saying that the film community would certainly have missed him.

I SPENT AN hour in the cafeteria, drinking bottled water and trying to cool off before returning to Malcolm's room. I'd promised him I'd come back, but I had to get control of my emotions first. I was angry with him for putting himself at risk, but regardless of how he'd gotten that way, he was sick and I had to be mindful of that.

When I arrived at 613, he seemed glad to see me and even looked a little less pale, less toxic. Maybe the drugs and transfusions were having the desired effect and he would, as Richard predicted, be well enough to go home soon.

"Here you are." He straightened his gown, which had twisted in the sheets. "There's been some good news. The CAT scan showed the doctors where the bleeding is."

"I know," I said, standing at the foot of his bed. I was afraid that if I stood any closer I'd strangle him. "I also know that you took aspirin before they put the defibrillator in. You were pretty quick to blame this hospital, Malcolm."

He lowered his eyes, like a guilty child. "I totally forgot about those aspirin when everything went downhill and they started sticking needles in me again," he said. "I was focused on how lousy I felt. That's why I screwed up."

"But why did you take the aspirin in the first place?" I said, my exasperation building in spite of myself. "Your doctor specifically warned you against it."

He shrugged. "I honestly didn't think it would be such a big deal. Obviously, I was wrong, and now I'm paying the price."

"That's it?" I said, throwing up my hands. "That's your excuse?"

"Hey, you're supposed to be my friend," he said. "The only one I've got around here. Why are you so mad about this? Why do you even care? It's not as if I did it to you."

He had a point. He'd done other things to me, but not this. Still, he needed a tongue lashing—had been crying out for a tongue lashing—and in my capacity as kindly, clueless, down-home Midwestern gal, I was just the person to give it to him. I'd waited months for the opportunity. Now here I was, all pent up with someplace to go.

"It's your attitude I'm mad about," I said.

"What are you talking about?" he said.

"Since you're a movie star, you probably surround yourself with yes people, right?" I began, reprising my Spago speech.

His eyes narrowed, as if he wasn't sure what was coming next. "I have people who handle stuff for me, yeah."

"And they tell you whatever you want to hear, right?"

"I wouldn't put it like—"

"For instance, you probably have a publicist," I went on, reliving how shabbily Peggy Merchant had treated me over the years.

"I do."

"Has he or she ever been critical of anything you've done?"

"No, but it's her job to—"

"Promote you to others," I said. "But what about in your private conversations with her? Has she ever questioned your judgment? Challenged your actions? Suggested that you might be wrong about something?"

"I— Well, not that I recall," he said warily.

"And there must be someone who picks out your wardrobe and someone who buys and cooks your groceries and someone who drives you around. Oh, and someone who watches over all your houses, however many you have. They don't challenge you either, right?"

"No, because they work for me."

"I see," I said, nodding like a prosecutor in a courtroom. "So you have all these people who tell you you're wonderful—people you *hire* to tell you you're wonderful. At the same time, you avoid contact with the outside world."

"No. *No.* It's the media I avoid."

"Right, but when you avoid the media, you're also avoiding us regular folks who want to know more about you. Take coming to this hospital, for example. You eluded the media, but you also lost the support you would have gotten from your fans, who don't have any idea what you're going through. Plus, you told me you're estranged from your parents and aren't ready to commit to your girlfriend. So that brings us back to the yes people, the only ones you listen to."

"Okay, just hang on a second there." He pointed his finger at me, the one with some digital medical contraption taped to it. "You're making it sound—"

"Like the truth," I said. "I don't know anything about Hollywood, as we've established, but from what I've read, it seems to me that you and other celebrities are so insulated, so pampered, so removed from reality that you think the rules don't apply to you. You behave badly and there's always someone on your payroll to clean it up, to *spin* it. Well, not at Heartland General, Malcolm. You behave badly and you end up with an IV pumping blood into your body."

He didn't say anything. Not for several seconds. He just stared at me with this odd, completely bewildered look on his face. If I'd been the one in that bed, I would have stared at me too. Who was I, anyway? Yes, I'd been dying to tell him off, but I was my mother's daughter. I'd spent too many years making "nicey-nicey" with everybody. For some reason, though, I didn't hold back when I was with Malcolm. I let him have it without worrying about whether he'd like me. Of course, while I was standing there waiting for him to say something, I did wonder whether he'd yell for a nurse and have me tossed out of his room.

He exhaled deeply, his head sinking into the pillow. "I have no illusions that the people I surround myself with are friends, Ann," he said finally. "But once you've achieved a certain level of fame, you don't know which ones you can trust. So you don't trust any of them. You just pay them and let them perform their services and get on with it. That's the way the game is played in Hollywood. Has it warped my sense of reality? Maybe so. Has it given me the feeling that I can do whatever I want and there will always be someone to clean up after me? You could make a case for that too."

"How sad," I said, ignoring the tiny detail that I wasn't someone he could trust either. "But there must be a better way to live, even for famous actors. Isn't there?"

He turned away and gazed out the window. The afternoon sun was peeking out from behind a cloud, casting a golden hue across the bed. "I appreciate your attempt to reform me, and you can tell the doctors I'll be a good boy from here on out, but I don't feel like debating my lifestyle anymore," he said, his voice weak but unwavering. "Not with you or any-one else. So no more questions."

Ah. There he was: the Malcolm Goddard I knew and loathed; the man who didn't answer questions; the man who shut everybody out. As he continued to stare off into the distance, I did wonder if I'd gone too far, spoken too brazenly. Yes, I'd lost my shot at interviewing him, but he was a patient and it was my job as a volunteer to treat him with respect and dignity. On the other hand, he'd asked for it with that crazy aspirin stunt of his. Someone had to unload on him, and it might as well have been me.

"No more questions," I agreed, moving toward the door. "I'll let you get some rest. I really hope you'll be able to go home soon."

I started to leave.

"Hey," he said, turning away from the window to look at me.

"Yes?" I said, suddenly clinging to the slim chance that he'd changed his mind and did want to answer my questions after all. Just a few. Enough for a *Famous* article. Nope, part of me still hadn't given up the dream.

"Did you ever see the movie *One Flew Over the Cuckoo's Nest?*" he asked.

Of course I'd seen it. It was thirty years old, but a classic—the winner of numerous Oscars. "No," I said, since I was supposed to be a dummy when it came to movies. "Why?"

"There's a character named Nurse Ratchet," he said with a straight face. "You remind me of her."

"I—" I was on the verge of pointing out that I was nothing like the evil, sadistic monster in that movie, but I muzzled it. "Thank you," I said instead and retreated.

Chapter Twenty-two

Okay, so I'd been forced to abandon the idea of writing the scoop of the century about Malcolm, but I wasn't happy about it. Thanks to Tuscany and her urgings, I'd allowed myself to imagine returning to *Famous* and demanding my due as the journalist who'd reeled Goddard in, and I'd invested more of my heart and soul in the fantasy than I'd realized. Legally, I couldn't write about his medical condition, but I'd managed to accumulate other bits and pieces and I was planning to add more, enough for a whole profile. When I got home on Tuesday night, I couldn't resist rereading the e-mail I'd composed to Harvey and left in the Drafts folder, where it waited to be completed and sent. It was meant to be the cover letter accompanying the story, and it was full of exclamation marks. ("You said I didn't have what it takes to get the big get! Well, feast your eyes on the attached document, Harvey!") I laughed ruefully as I thought how exuberant I sounded in that e-mail, how vindicated. But then came Malcolm's admission about who he was and the abrupt end to the possibility of my questioning him about his life. I had to let it go, let the fantasy go, once and for all. The upside of all this was that I now had the time and energy to focus on other things, on other people.

My mother, for instance. On Wednesday morning, I tried yet again to coax her outside to the mailbox.

At first, she claimed that she had a cough and that the spring air would bring on full-blown pneumonia. And I thought I was a hypochondriac. I assured her that spring air doesn't cause pneumonia and that her cough was audible only to her. Then, she remembered the lemon bars she had supposedly promised to bake for Sallie's Groceries. I reminded her that she'd sent the lemon bars over to Sallie's on Monday; I knew because I'd dropped them off myself. Excuses, always excuses. Of course I understood them, understood the whole psychology of fear and panic. How many times had I called the airlines to make reservations for flights, only to cancel them a day later, giving Harvey a laundry list of "reasons" why I couldn't possibly have flown—from phony sinus blockages to funerals of relatives I didn't have. I knew what my mother was going through better than anyone, which was why I was determined to push her out the door.

"Just a few steps," I said, once I'd actually gotten her to the threshold and we were on the verge of venturing out. She was holding on to my arm for dear life. I could feel her fingernails digging into my skin.

"What if my legs buckle?" she said, looking at me with the same deer-in-the-headlights expression I must have worn at the Santa Monica airport the day I had doomed myself to ignominy and unemployment. I did miss L.A., did miss the excitement, but I sure didn't miss the panic attacks. Since I'd moved home and become a volunteer, they'd disappeared. Well, not completely. I don't think you're ever cured of fearfulness; you develop an acceptance of it, then a gradual management of it. I still felt shaky in crowds on occasion, but I didn't feel the need to bolt from them or avoid them altogether. I hadn't been on a plane, granted, but I had every intention of flying at some point, I really did. Bree Wiley dreamed of flying to Hollywood, but she needed a new liver first. I had no such impediment. I was lucky. The patients at Heartland General were beginning to teach me just how lucky I was.

"If your legs buckle, you'll fall down," I said as my mother gripped my arm even more tightly. "And then you'll dust yourself off, get back up, and keep going. You won't die and the neighbors are too busy with their own problems to notice and the world won't come to an end if you fail, Mom. I promise."

She nodded. Putting what felt like all her considerable weight on me, she walked with me out the door.

"I'm only doing this for you," she said as we took our first steps—slow, deliberate, baby steps—down the brick path. "Because you asked me if I'd come to your wedding."

I laughed. "It was a hypothetical invitation. Nobody's proposed to me yet."

"Maybe getting me out of the house will bring you that proposal," she said. "Good deeds bring good things."

"You're not a good deed," I said. "You're my mother."

We proceeded at a snail's pace down the path, one foot at a time, until she announced that she'd had enough. We'd only made it halfway. "I'm very light-headed," she said. "We have to stop."

"We can if you want to," I said, then pointed to the mailbox. "But it's only a few more steps. And you're doing great."

"No, I'm not. I'm panicky," she said, her breath coming in short spurts. "This all feels—I don't know—dangerous."

I thought of some of the patients with their shaved heads and bandaged limbs and infectious diseases. They were proof that life was dangerous, that none of us was guaranteed a safe passage.

"You're doing great," I repeated, cheering her on. "Incredible, in fact."

I managed to talk her into continuing. When we reached the curb, she let go of my arm so she could fling herself onto the mailbox. She rested her head on it, cradled it, and then the tears came. I hadn't seen her cry since my father died. But these were tears of victory, of sheer joy at having done what had seemed impossible. If you've never been disabled by panic disorder, you're rolling your eyes right now and thinking, *The woman didn't win a marathon; what's the big deal?* If you have been a sufferer, you're clapping for my mother because you know exactly how big a deal it is.

LATER THAT MORNING, I decided to return the call from Isabelle, the former patient who'd contacted the volunteers office and asked for me. Although Shelley had left it up to me whether or not to call her back, I didn't want to be rude and ignore her.

"It's Ann from Heartland General," I said when she answered the phone. "How are you feeling, Isabelle?"

"Bad, very bad," she said. "That's why I called you. You were so sympathetic and understanding. So I'm asking for your help again."

"I'm not sure how I can help," I told her. "Have you spoken to your doctor?"

"I've tried to speak to him," she said. "Over and over. He won't pick up the phone."

So she's a complainer, I thought. Just like Malcolm. "It hasn't been that long since your surgery," I reminded her. "There's bound to be some leftover soreness."

"My doctor said my problem would be gone by now, but it isn't."

"Your problem?" I said, getting sucked into this conversation in spite of myself.

"He said I had an infection in my tubes," she explained. "That's why he did the hysterectomy. But if he took everything out, why do I still have such pain?"

Okay, I knew Richard was right when he told me to leave the medical stuff to the pros. I also knew he was right when he said that some patients liked to blame the hospital for their suffering, the fiasco with Malcolm being a prime example. And he'd explained that women who've had hysterectomies often had emotional aftereffects once the reality of losing their reproductive organs set in. But this woman was entitled to an answer from her doctor, wasn't she? A follow-up exam at the very least?

"Call your doctor and say you want him to check you out," I offered. "Don't just complain. Tell him you need to come into his office immediately."

"I already did that," she said. "The receptionist insisted I didn't have to come in for three months."

That didn't sound very conscientious on the part of the doctor, not if the patient was in severe pain. But I couldn't get involved, couldn't start rushing off to Richard with accusations. Not again.

"I still don't understand why you're telling me all this," I said. "We hardly know each other."

"You were the only one at that place who listened," she said.

Listening was one thing; interfering in hospital business was another. Still, it wouldn't be terrible of me to make a suggestion or two, I figured. "Here's what I'd do if I were you," I said. "I'd ask questions and I'd keep asking them until I got answers. If your doctor won't return your calls, you should fax a letter to his office asking for your medical records. Then you should take those records to a new doctor and get a second opinion."

"I don't know," she said. "Doctors can be so intimidating."

"So can patients. You should ask for all records relating to your surgery, including the pathology report," I said. "You have a right to that information."

"Yes, yes. Okay," she said, sounding more hopeful. "Thank you for speaking to me, Ann. I knew I could count on you."

"My pleasure," I said, hoping I'd given her the right advice.

When we hung up, I kind of puffed out my chest and smiled. This volunteering stuff really was rewarding. The fact that Isabelle had sought me out—me, of all people—was a surprise. I hadn't expected to be helpful to any of the patients, let alone a former patient. But even handing out copies of *Famous* was helpful to them, I saw, and I understood now that entertainment really does uplift. I used to be ashamed to say I wrote for the magazine, in certain circles, but not anymore. It did serve a purpose in its own way.

But how do I get back there, back to *Famous*? I wondered as I sat in my old bedroom, on my old bed. How do I return to a town that chewed me up and spit me out? Was there still a place for me in L.A.? If so, I certainly wasn't seeing it.

"YOU JUST MISSED all the excitement," said Shelley as I signed in for my shift on Friday afternoon. Part of me had considered bailing out on the program, given that the Malcolm story wasn't going to happen, but the other part of me wanted to continue volunteering as long as I stuck around in Middletown. So there I was, smiling at Shelley in her black pants and screaming yellow sweater. She looked like a very tall bumblebee.

"What excitement?" I asked.

"A dozen members of the Royals stopped by for their annual visit to the physical-therapy wing," she explained.

"The Royals, as in the baseball team?"

"Yep. The patients loved it. It's amazing how a handshake from the players just perks them right up and makes them work harder on their rehab."

"Too bad they can't come here more often."

"Don't I know it."

She was in the middle of filling me in about the team's PR person when her phone rang. She excused herself to take the call, and I went off to the storage room.

While I was stocking the cart, I thought about starting on a low floor and working my way upstairs, but who was I kidding. Story or no story, I had to find out how Malcolm was.

When I got off the elevator on six, I spotted Jonathan standing at the nurses' station, scrawling instructions on someone's chart. He spotted me too and waved me over. I prayed he wasn't going to ask if Richard and I could join him and Eleanor for dinner.

"Hello, Ann," he said, and steered me into the corner by my elbow. "I wanted to talk to you about the patient in 613, the code blue from the other day."

I nearly rocketed out of my white shoes. Did Jonathan think I'd told anybody about Malcolm's identity? Was I about to get in trouble? "Is he being discharged?" I said innocently.

"No, he's had another setback."

"Setback?"

"Yes, and I'm only telling you so you'll be prepared when you visit him. Yesterday he started running a fever and experiencing acute pain in his back. We've determined that the blood clot has spawned an infection."

"Oh." It was all I could manage. I was too alarmed by the news to say anything else. "Is it serious?"

"All hospital-borne infections are serious," said Jonathan. "This place is full of bugs, some of which are resistant to common antibiotics."

I swallowed hard, trying to process this ominous new development. "What happens now?" I asked, feeling like Jonathan's colleague instead of a volunteer.

"We'll watch him over the next week or so, until we're sure we've got the right drugs. In the meantime, he's been asking for you."

Asking for me? Again? In spite of the way I'd scolded him the last time? "Is he still running a fever?"

"Yes, but he's lucid. Very talkative, in fact."

Talkative.

Well, of course I zeroed in on a possible interview when he said that. I just couldn't seem to give it up.

Chapter Twenty-three

Malcolm wasn't the pale, wan patient this time; he was flushed, vivid, expansive, animated. He welcomed me into his room as if I were his best friend in the world, telling me how I was the only bright spot in this whole mess; how I made him feel less isolated when I visited; how he missed my honesty, my realness when I wasn't around. He announced that once he stopped blaming himself and everybody else for his predicament, he realized for the first time how fortunate he was to be alive. "I was never in touch with my mortality before," he said. "Now I'll never take it for granted."

And that was just the opening act. What came next really shocked me.

After asking me—asking me!—to pull up a chair and sit next to him, he said he needed someone to talk to, someone who knew his true identity, someone who wouldn't mind if he purged himself of all the thoughts and feelings he'd kept bottled up inside for so long, the highs and lows of his career included. "I could die from this infection, who knows," he said, his eyes sort of crazed with fever. "I could die in this hospital out here in the middle of nowhere, with no friends or family around me, nobody to care, and it would be my own damn fault. I didn't let people in, didn't let them get close. But now I want at least one person to know who Malcolm Goddard is before it's too late, and that one person is you. I want to talk to *you* about my life, Ann. I want you to know what it's been like to be me, because I value what you think. If it's not a huge imposition, would you be willing to just sit there and listen to my ravings?"

I could almost see Tuscany standing behind Malcolm's head, jumping up and down and squealing, *"Duh."*

"Of course I'll listen," I said gently, at the same moment my brain was spazzing out with anticipation. I was finally landing the big get, and I wouldn't have to ask him a single question. Ironic.

First came his childhood: the parents who never should have gotten married and who never hid their contempt for each other; the lonely, painfully shy boy who wandered off after school to find solace in movie theaters; and, most poignant of all, the two-year-old sister who'd died before Malcolm was born.

"Her name was Lily," he said, wiping a tear from his eye. "She fell out of my parents' fourth-floor apartment window, can you believe that? I mean, yeah, this was before they required everybody to put up those bars, but for my sister to be left alone and slip on the ledge and fall all the way down—"

He stopped himself. He was too choked up to keep going. Instinctively, I reached out to touch his hand, to try and comfort him.

"It must have been awful," I said. "The worst thing imaginable."

He nodded, wiped away another tear. "But it was compounded by the fact that I didn't know she even existed until I was eighteen. Can you believe *that*?"

"No," I said softly. There were no skeletons in my family closet. Everybody's neuroses were right out there in the open.

"My parents must have been so wracked with guilt that they swept Lily under the rug, kept her a deep, dark secret."

"I'm so sorry," I said, beginning to understand even more clearly why Malcolm had such a difficult time trusting anybody. After he became an actor, it was his father who stole his money and his mother who sold him out, but they both kept the secret of his sister, and he called that the most painful betrayal of all.

"I started acting in college," he said, his mood brightening when he turned to the early days of his career. "I had no business even being there, because I was such a lousy student, but the drama department saved me. I did everything from Shakespeare to *Oklahoma!* while I was there."

I laughed. "Somehow I can't picture you singing 'The Surrey with the Fringe on Top.'"

He laughed too. "I sounded like a cat in heat. No voice whatsoever. But my Shakespearean roles were beyond bad." He had me giggling when he delivered a line from *Twelfth Night* in the loopy, over-the-top, overeager style he'd adopted back then.

I'd never witnessed this self-effacing side of him, and I enjoyed it, enjoyed his mimicry of a young actor who hadn't yet learned his craft. He even joked about his postcollege auditions, which inevitably ended in rejection, and the numerous jobs he'd taken to pay his rent, the worst being a ditch digger for a cemetery on First Avenue. He told me all this with surprising wit, and it occurred to me that despite his success as a dramatic actor, he might actually have a flair for comedy. Yes, this same guy who'd never given any indication that he had a sense of humor was making me laugh, and I found myself being stupidly charmed by him.

His big break, he said, was the part of a rookie cop in a thriller that was shot in New York and directed by Sidney Lumet. It led to more movie roles and his eventual relocation to Los Angeles. All old news and fully documented. But what captivated me were his thumbnail sketches (again, often funny) of the legendary directors and actors with whom he'd worked. He did impressions of them, recounted anecdotes about them, served up the ways in which each had had an impact on his life and his art. He swept me away with his descriptions of the exotic locations where some of his movies had been filmed and explained how he prepared for each role, studying specific periods of history if the story warranted it, working with speech coaches to perfect accents and dialects, training with stunt coordinators to be able to take on action sequences without a double. He threw himself into acting, he said, because each role represented the opportunity to lose himself in that character, to put himself in another person's shoes, to escape his own emptiness. He repeated over and over how much he loved being an actor. What he didn't love was being a movie star. It was when he used the phrase "evil media parasites" that I shifted in my seat and tried to steer him back to more pleasant topics. But here, again, he surprised me. He said that his brush with death had given him a new perspective on the media; that he understood now that having to put up with interview questions, idiotic and intrusive as they might be, was much less onerous than having a serious medical condition; and that if he ever escaped from Heartland General, he would lighten up with reporters and resign himself to their demands. Needless to say, his declaration was even more motivation for me to run home, write up his story, and e-mail it to Harvey. I wasn't about to lose the big get now that he was willing to talk to *Famous* or even *Up My Ass Weekly*.

He seemed to tire at one point, and I assumed he was finally out of gas. But then he spotted an airplane out the window and became rapturous on the subject of flying—from recounting the day he earned his pilot's license to chronicling his first solo trip in the Cessna.

"Flying is all about freedom for me," he said.

"It's all about fear for me," I said. Of course if he'd remembered me from L.A., he would have known that.

"Someday I'll take you up in my plane and show you there's nothing to be afraid of," he said, almost protectively.

Promises, promises, I thought, reminding myself that timing was everything in life.

It was during his account of a flight to Colorado that I noticed how his face was perspiring. I reached over to feel his head, which was hot from the fever. As he kept talking, I got up and went to his bathroom, ran a washcloth under cold water, and came back and laid it across his forehead

"You're very sweet," he said, gazing up at me. "You're a straight shooter but you've got a tender side too."

"Just lie still," I said as I made sure the compress didn't drip all over his pillow.

He smiled. "What's the matter? Can't take a compliment?"

"Of course I can." What I couldn't take at that moment was being so close to Malcolm. Every time I was within inches of him, going back to the night we'd been nose to nose at Spago, I seemed to lose my sense of balance, my ability to concentrate on anything but my proximity to him. It was odd and distracting and made me extremely uncomfortable.

"You must be wondering," he said, touching the washcloth and, by extension, my hand.

"About what?" I said.

"The hair, the eyes. What my deal is."

"Your deal?" I said as if I didn't know. I did wonder when or if he'd get around to explaining why he wore the contacts and the hairpiece.

"Hollywood's a tough town," he said. "There's a law against being old or ugly."

"You're hardly either of those, Malcolm."

"No. I was young, in my late twenties, when my hairline started going the route of Ron Howard. I was fine with it, didn't even think about hiding it under a baseball cap. But in the Sidney Lumet film I did, the character I was playing had a full head of hair, so I wore a piece. The movie was a hit. I got noticed big-time. My agent suggested I keep wearing it. I was impressionable in those days. I did what I was told. Same with the eyes. It was in the script: The character had piercing blue ones. What I'm saying is that my career clicked with that picture and I didn't want to jinx it. It must sound bizarre to someone who's not in the business, but being a good actor isn't enough in Hollywood. You have to look the part of a star. If you don't, you're demoted, from leading man to best friend."

He wasn't overstating it, sadly. A few wrinkles, a bad face-lift, a balding head. Career over.

"I feel like a fraud a lot of the time," he said. "An impostor. Maybe that's why I never wanted to be interviewed. But as I told you, I love acting, so I thought it was a decent trade-off—if I wore the contacts and the hairpiece, I'd get the good scripts. Actually, I took my cue from Sean Connery and his amazing career. He had to wear a rug when he played James Bond and it kept him working for a long, long time."

"But now? Will you continue to wear it?"

He shrugged. "We'll see."

I turned the washcloth over and placed its cooler side back on his forehead. "I bet your audience is loyal enough to handle a few cosmetic changes."

"It would be liberating to be myself, whoever that is."

"I think you know exactly who that is," I said. "It has nothing to do with appearance and everything to do with perseverance."

His smile widened. "Is Nurse Ratchet paying *me* a compliment now?"

"She might be."

While we sat together in silence as he let the cool cloth soothe him, I replayed all the stories he'd just told me and realized that a theme had emerged—the theme of a man who took risks and succeeded on his own, without the support of his parents or the security of a group of close friends. I was impressed by his determination, his grit. If I'd clawed and scraped to become an actor the way he had, I would have hung on to the blue eyes and the wavy hair too, plus anything else that would have allowed me to keep the dream going. I knew where he was coming from. All too well.

"Hey, enough about me," he said, taking off the compress and picking his head up to look at me. "I've gone on way too long. Tell me more about you."

"Oh, like my stories will be as interesting as yours? I don't think so."

"Please? I want to hear what it was like growing up in Middletown, Missouri."

I laughed even though he seemed quite serious. "Well, there are only five thousand residents of Middletown," I said. "When you get a postcard in the mail, about four thousand nine hundred and ninety-nine people will have read it before you do."

He smiled, settling back onto the bed. "What else?"

I told him that vacations consisted of trips to Six Flags; that everybody thought deer season was a national holiday; and that if someone had out-of-town guests, their names made the local paper. "And nobody's ever met a celebrity," I said. "You picked the right place when you decided to get sick in Middletown. They wouldn't recognize you around here even if you did wear the hairpiece and the lenses."

He looked at me almost adoringly, as if I were the most wholesome, genuine, *real* person in the world. "Tell me more about your family," he urged. "You're an only child and your father died. Are you close to your mother?"

"Actually, I am," I said, thinking that despite our long-distance relationship over the past five years, we'd spoken on the phone several times a week, always treated each other with affection, never had the kind of mother-daughter power struggles that were all too common among women and girls. "I've been living with her since I"—whoops, I almost gave myself away—"started doing construction on my own place. I'm putting in a new bathroom."

"What's it been like moving back in with her?"

"Noisy," I said with a laugh. "My aunt and grandmother live in the house too, and they can't agree on much. But I'm lucky. What they do agree on is that they care about me and want what's best for me."

"I'm envious."

"Well, I didn't mean to make it sound like we're a *Leave It to Beaver* family. We're hardly that."

"But you're there for each other," he said. "I wish I had that in my life, that kind of unconditional love." He sighed. "Maybe I should have grown up in Middletown instead of Manhattan."

I smiled. "It's not the most exciting spot, but people here do tend to pull together. After my father died, everybody rushed in to help out. Of course, the only thing I wanted was for one of them to bring him back."

Again, Malcolm gazed at me with a tenderness I'd never believed he was capable of. He was about to speak when there was a knock on the door.

"Hello? It's just me, Mr. Sykes," said Rolanda as she bustled into the room. "Time to check vitals and all that good stuff."

Not a moment too soon, I thought with relief. If she hadn't come along when she did, I might have blabbed something totally maudlin, not to mention incriminating, to Malcolm. I couldn't blow my cover any more than he didn't want me to blow his.

"I should go," I told him as Rolanda was fiddling with his IV. "I'll come see you again if you want to talk some more." I'd finally gotten what I needed for the story, but I couldn't just leave him in the lurch. I was all he had. He'd said so. He depended on me.

"I'm not going anywhere." He rolled his eyes at the bags of medicine hanging from the pole.

I stood at the foot of his bed and patted his feet. "Get some rest and fight this infection, okay?"

"Hey, Ann?" he said as I'd started for the door. "I've decided you're not Nurse Ratchet after all."

"No?" I said, giving no sign that I'd understood the reference in the first place.

"No. I'm thinking you're more like the heroine of another classic movie you've probably never seen. It's called *Coming Home* and it was one of the best antiwar movies of the seventies."

One of my favorite love stories too. But why was he bringing it up now?

"Jane Fonda played a volunteer at a veterans' hospital and Jon Voight played an angry, pain-in-the-ass patient," he said. "It was her compassion, her willingness to listen, that pulled him through."

I didn't react at first. I was too flustered. Jane Fonda was willing to listen to Jon Voight because she was hot for the guy as well as compassionate toward him. I was willing to listen to Malcolm Goddard because I was memorizing every word for a magazine piece—a piece I was about to run home and write. Big difference. On the other hand, I'd been there for him when no one else was, regardless of whether I had an ulterior motive. The visit had been a win-win for both of us.

I WALKED INTO the house, kissed everyone, begged off dinner claiming I'd stuffed myself with cafeteria food and couldn't eat another bite, and disappeared into my room for the rest of the night, practically chaining myself to my laptop.

My first draft of the story was rough—basically, just a transcript of the conversation as I remembered it. By the second draft, I was starting to shape the story, to give it a beginning, middle, and end. And by the third, I was cutting and pasting and punching it up, editing it into a crisply written profile of a man who'd overcome a rocky childhood to become one of Hollywood's most gifted stars.

I smiled as I reread my handiwork. It was damn good, if I said so myself. It had all the elements Harvey looked for in a story. Demanded in a story. Well, everything except a heavy dose of dish about the subject's sex life. Malcolm did touch on the fact that he'd had numerous relationships since he'd moved to L.A., and admitted to being leery of commitment, even as he claimed to want the kind of solid, unshakable marriage his parents lacked. But he didn't utter a single syllable about Rebecca Truit, not a word, which led me to believe that they had broken up and that her sound bite on *Access Hollywood* had only been the usual Hollywood bullshit. If they'd been engaged or living together, he would surely have included her in his delirious ramblings, wouldn't he? Not that I ever thought she was right for him. She was beautiful, sure, and spoke with an aristocratic British accent, but she was one of those skinny, brittle types with a little-boy body and a little-boy haircut, and I couldn't picture her as the woman who would be on his arm when he finally took the walk down the aisle. Of course, I didn't *care* if he married her or not. Not from a personal standpoint. Why would I? It was none of my business whether he ever married anybody. I was only interested from a professional perspective, naturally.

God, Harvey will be thrilled when he gets this, I thought as I gave the piece one more read, attached the document to the e-mail message I'd already typed out, and moved the whole thing to my Drafts folder.

Yes, the Drafts folder. I didn't send the story right that second. I wanted to let it sit and marinate awhile. I would read it again over the next few days and make any necessary changes. That's how I always worked.

Oh, hell. I'll be honest. There was also the matter of my suddenly conflicted emotions. After all my plotting and planning, I was now officially ambivalent about whether I should go through with the story. Yes, yes, it was my ticket back to *Famous* and I really thought it was a valentine to Malcolm, who came off as both vulnerable and dynamic. But something else kept me from hitting Send Now on that computer, and I couldn't identify it.

Did I have feelings for him that went beyond writer and subject and were *they* inhibiting me from sending it? Had his gradual personality changes turned my head? Was I starting to

Ridiculous. I detested the guy. Okay, "detested" was no longer accurate. But I certainly wasn't interested in him romantically. How could I be? He was the man who'd cost me my job. What's more, I had a No Actors rule when it came to boyfriends.

No, the "something" was just a case of nerves, I decided. The kind of butterflies you get when you're on the brink of getting what you think you really want.

Chapter Twenty-four

|||||||||||||||||||||||||||||||||||||||||||||||||||||||||||||||||||||||||||||||||

On Tuesday, Malcolm's fever was still slightly elevated, but he was in good spirits. Better than good. He spoke to me with affection, as if his confessional a few days before had cemented some sort of bond with me. He said he was happy to see me and told me I looked pretty and asked if I could stay and *chat*. When I agreed to hang around for a while, he actually beamed. I had never seen Malcolm Goddard beam.

Was he so chipper because he liked me? Liked *me* as a woman as opposed to me as a volunteer whose job ran the gamut from getting vomited on to giving tongue lashings? Had he thought about me at night with the same intensity that I'd thought about him? And I *had* thought about him. Forget about sleeping. I'd spent hours tossing and turning and stressing about whether I should or shouldn't send the story to Harvey. In fact, maybe my lack of sleep was making me delusional. Maybe Malcolm wasn't beaming because he had feelings for me. Maybe he was just mellow from the medications they were pumping into him.

But then we were in the middle of discussing his health when he begged me to tell him more stories of life in Middletown.

"Please," I protested. "I've already told you enough. My life isn't nearly as glamorous as yours."

"Did I say I wanted glamour?"

When I realized that Malcolm was not to be refused, I sat down and talked about my early memories of screen doors slamming and men hand-washing their cars and everybody gathering on the porch on a hot summer afternoon to watch a thunderstorm. "Although my aunt Toni's afraid of lightning," I added, then gave him the short version of her split with Uncle Mike.

"He married Claire? Our Claire?" said Malcolm after I mentioned that she was a volunteer. "The short one who bounces in here offering me two-year-old issues of *American Heritage*?"

I nodded. "We're one big happy group."

Again, he looked at me as if I were wearing a halo. He seemed to be as charmed by my homespun stories as I'd been charmed by his glittery ones. "How about you, Ann," he said, leaning over to tap the arm of my chair. "Are you happy here?"

I was totally caught off guard by the question. "Me? Of course. Wouldn't live anywhere else," I said, hoping I was convincing.

"You're in your—what?—thirties, I'm guessing. You said you're between jobs. What sort of job did you have?"

The moment of truth. Or, more accurately, another moment of untruth. "I was a dental hygienist," I said. "I got downsized."

"That's too bad," he said with so much sympathy that you'd think I'd told him I'd been run over by a truck. "Do you want to keep working in that field? If you do, I'd be glad to talk to the dentist I go to in L.A. He's got a big practice and he's always looking for good people."

I was floored. He was offering to help me get a new job—the same man who'd helped me lose my old one. "That's very kind of you," I said, "but I'm sure something will open up soon."

He smiled. "I guess it was silly of me to suggest it. You'd never move to

Tinseltown. You'd hate the traffic, hate the whole environment. Nobody washes their own car in L.A."

There was a car wash on every corner. Celebrities had their own personal car washers.

"But maybe you'll come out for a week and experience it for yourself," he said. "I'll show you around, take you to the hot spots."

My God, he was flirting with me, asking to spend time with me. How weird was that? What's more, he was moving his eyes up and down my body as if I had no clothes on. I felt my face turn beet red and stared at my feet.

"Ah, I've embarrassed you," he said. "Sorry about that. It's just that you've been such a friend to me that I wanted to return the favor."

A friend to him. Well, yes and no. "You needed a friend because you were all alone in a strange town, that's all," I said.

He inched closer to the edge of the bed, and put his hand on mine. Right smack on top of mine. I sort of made this gulping sound and hoped he didn't hear it. His hand was hot, and I told myself it was due to his fever. But the longer he left it there, the hotter my face was too. What was the matter with me? Why was this guy always getting to me?

"I couldn't have managed without you, Ann," he said in a more serious tone. "You kept showing up even though I treated you badly. You didn't hesitate to take me to task when I deserved it. You let me bend your ear with an entire episode of *Biography*. Oh, and let's not forget that you also saved my life when you called everybody in here for that code blue. I've never met anyone quite like you." He looked down at our clasped hands, then back up into my eyes. "I don't know how this happened, but in a very short time you've become very important to me."

Just so you know, my face was flaming red by the end of that speech and my palms were sweat city. I was so uncomfortable, I wanted to bolt up from my chair and run like hell out of that room. *Was* he telling me he felt something for me? Something romantic? And if so, how was I supposed to handle it? He was just a story to me. A career move, nothing more. I had shown up again and again simply because I needed him to spill his guts. I didn't feel anything for him except gratitude—he was responsible for getting me fired but now he'd be responsible for getting me rehired. Of course, I couldn't deny that having Malcolm Goddard say such beautiful things to me, such loving things to me, was rather thrilling in a perverse way.

I was about to express just how thrilling when he made it clear that he wasn't finished.

"Remember when you told me how I lived in an isolated world and didn't let anyone in, not even those who were close to me?" he asked as he returned his hand to his lap, releasing mine, which was soaking wet.

"I do," I said shyly, modestly. So he'd really taken my words to heart. I *had* become important to him.

"And remember how you said that by keeping my illness a secret, I was isolating myself even more?"

I nodded, speechless.

"Well, I've decided that you were right. I don't want to be alone through this thing."

So he wanted me to be with him every minute of his hospitalization! Maybe even sleep in his room at night! The sixth-floor rooms had comfy sofas, and visitors slept on them all the time. He was into me, all right, and who could have predicted it? I couldn't wait to tell Tuscany.

"So I have a favor to ask," he said. "You've done so much for me already, but there's one more thing."

My head was spinning with possible responses to his request for me to stay with him overnight until he was discharged, absolutely spinning. I could explain that the sofas were strictly for family members, not hospital volunteers. I could explain that I wasn't supposed to show one patient preferential treatment over another. I could—

"The favor is, I'd like you to smuggle my girlfriend in here."

I blinked and said, "Excuse me?"

"I've been going out with an actress named Rebecca—maybe you've read about her in your magazines. She wanted to come and be with me, but I kept putting her off. I still don't want the media getting wind of all this, and I was sure her being here would tip everybody off." He beamed again. "But you told me how wrong it was to shut people out, so I called her and told her to come tomorrow."

Now my head was spinning with thoughts of what a total fool I was, a complete airhead. He wanted Rebecca, not me, for God's sake.

But when I calmed down and stopped feeling humiliated by my misinterpretation of the situation, I realized it was a relief. Yes. His revelation that Rebecca was, in fact, his girlfriend and that they hadn't broken up after all was a big fat relief. Now I didn't have to concern myself with anything other than The Story. I mean, really. What was I thinking?

"But we need your help," he continued. "Can you think of a way to get her in here without anybody noticing?"

"If I remember her photograph correctly, she's extremely thin," I said, narrowing my eyes as if I were trying to conjure her up from memory. "It's hard not to notice someone who weighs four pounds."

He laughed. "Most actresses are 'extremely thin' compared to the average woman."

The average woman was a hippopotamus compared with Rebecca. "I stand corrected."

"Look, it would be great if you could figure out a way to sneak her in here."

"Why 'sneak'? Nobody will recognize her, just like they haven't recognized you. I'm telling you, Malcolm, people in Middletown wouldn't recognize a celebrity if they drove their lawn mower over one."

"I'd rather not take any chances. I'd be very indebted to you if you'd do this. Rebecca and I both would be."

How sweet. "Okay. Sure, I'll help," I said. "Far be it from me to stand in the way of true love."

"Great. I knew I could count on you."

"Call me old reliable," I said.

"She's in the middle of a movie shoot and only has one day off, so she's arranged to fly into the Kansas City airport by private plane for a ten A.M. arrival. I was hoping you could pick her up, drive her to Middletown, rig up some sort of disguise for her, and then bring her to me. She'll be flying out later that night."

"Some sort of disguise," I mused. "I take it she can't just ditch her hairpiece and contacts like you did?"

He laughed, not minding my little jab. "No, she's the real thing."

"If you like the type." Okay, I was being catty and it wasn't like me and I was immediately sorry. I chalked it up to feeling put out by having to be Malcolm's errand girl. Apparently, I was resenting him again. "I'd be happy to help. It'll be good for you to have her here."

"They say love is the best medicine."

They also say misery loves company. "Give me her flight information and I'll take care of the rest," I said.

REBECCA TRUIT WAS even skinnier in person. She was wearing a miniskirt that wasn't much bigger than a napkin. She was a beauty, with a pert little nose and big round eyes and the requisite inflatable lips, but on the boyish side, as I've indicated, complete with a cleft in her chinny chin chin.

"So nice of you to come 'round for me," she said, her voice eerily similar to that of Princess Diana.

"My pleasure," I said as I escorted her to my waiting Honda in the airport parking lot.

As I drove, she asked about Malcolm, naturally, and I threw all sorts of medical terms at her. It seemed odd to me that she never said in response to my technical jargon, "What's that?" Not even when I dropped "ventricular tachycardia" on her. She had a distinctive lack of curiosity. She seemed more interested in telling me about her film. "It's sort of a feature-length sequel to *Dynasty*," she said, pronouncing the word "Dinasty."

I considered adding a few paragraphs about her to my Malcolm story, since she continued to provide me with all sorts of tidbits, but I'd already tinkered with it enough. Maybe once I was back at work at the magazine, I would ask Harvey to assign me a profile of her, now that I could see what a talker she was.

When we arrived at my house, I told her to stay in the car since I couldn't let anybody in my family know what was going on.

I raced inside, put on my uniform, and grabbed my spare pants and smock, the ones I wore whenever I forgot to wash the others. Rebecca had brought her own white shoes and white T-shirt, as per my instructions, so all she needed to do was change into my pants and smock once we got to the ladies' room at the hospital.

We were about to take off for Heartland General when out popped my mother, who, flush with the triumph of her trip to the mailbox with me, was now walking to the mailbox by herself.

"Ann?" she said, knocking on the car window. "Who's in there with you?"

I whispered to Rebecca to pretend that she was playing an American in a movie. Then I rolled down the window and said, "Just a friend who works at the hospital, Mom. Her uniform got bloodstains all over it—occupational hazard—so I'm lending her mine."

Rebecca waved to my mother and said, "Yo, mama. What's shakin'?"

I suppose I should have told her I meant a Caucasian American. Obviously, Malcolm hadn't chosen her for her brains.

My mother looked startled—no one in Middletown used the greeting "Yo"—but then she smiled and said, "It's wonderful that you're volunteering on your off day, sweetie. Maybe you'll run into Richie and the two of you can have dinner together again."

"Who's Richie?" asked Rebecca.

"A *friend*," I said, loud enough for my mother to hear it and, hopefully, get it.

I drove off to the hospital, parked in the lot, whisked Rebecca past the people milling about the lobby, and pulled her into the first ladies' room I saw. "Here," I said, handing her the clothes and checking under the doors to make sure there was no one in any of the stalls. "I'll be waiting outside."

When she emerged, I had to force myself not to feel like a hippo again. My pants were swimming on her and much too short, and my smock would only have fit her if she were seven months pregnant. But we were improvising. The important thing was that she was wearing a volunteer's uniform, which was as close to a disguise as I could come up with.

After a quick conference during which I advised her to tell anyone who asked that she was in a special program informing patients of the importance of living wills, we took the elevator up to six. I made sure the coast was clear and slipped her into Malcolm's room. He extended his arms, laden though they were with IV needles, to embrace her, his face having lit up at the sight of her.

"Oh, Mal!" she said, rushing to his bedside. "My poor, poor Mal."
Mal.

I took one last look at the adoring couple—watched them hug and kiss and act as if they were the long-lost, love-starved children of rival clans finally reunited. And then I put my tongue back in my mouth, retreated from the room, and closed the door to allow them their privacy.

Chapter Twenty-five

||||||||||||||||||||||||||||||||||||||||||||||||||||||||||||||||||||||||||||||||||||||||||

At eight-thirty that night, I drove Rebecca back to the airport. During the trip, she went on and on about how Malcolm had changed; how he seemed less distant, less angry, less inclined to keep his guard up. "As we were kissing good-bye, he told me he had had an epiphany," she said. "Whatever that is."

"It's sort of a moment of self-discovery," I said. "A revelation."

"Right. Right," she said and continued talking. "He told me he understands now, on a deeper level, that life is short and that he shouldn't waste an instant of it." She giggled. "I thought he was about to spring a proposal on me, but I guess he's waiting to buy me the ring."

I made noises about how wonderful it all was, but mostly I played the part of the silent chauffeur, nodding and listening and eagerly anticipating the time I'd have to myself once I unloaded my cargo.

"You know, Ann, Malcolm was spot on about you," she said as we shook hands at the terminal. "You're a treasure."

"Glad to be of service," I said, even more glad to be done with the Cupid routine. "Take care."

"You too," she said. "If you ever come 'round to L.A., you must ring me."

And off she flew, without bothering to give me her phone number.

On the ride back, I felt oddly depleted, low on fuel, listless. Not depressed in the manner of those awful days when I'd first shown up on my mother's doorstep. Just sort of wrung out.

As a pick-me-up, I pulled out my cell phone and called Tuscany at the magazine.

"I'm on my way home from the airport," I reported, having told her about Malcolm's rendezvous with Rebecca and my role in it. "She thinks he's gonna pop the question as soon as he's discharged."

"At least somebody's happy," she said. Earlier in the week, she and Don, the soap star, had broken up. It turned out that the reason he'd been giving her so much space was because he was sleeping with another woman—an actress on the show who was married to the executive producer, who was having an affair with a man. Things like that didn't happen in Middletown. Well, they did, but there were usually guns involved before anybody found out what was what. "Although *you* don't sound very happy, Ann. What's wrong?"

"Nothing. I'm just tired."

"Tired, my ass. You're upset. I can hear it in your voice."

"I'm not upset."

"And I know why," she said, ignoring my denial. "You've had Goddard's full attention since he's been in the hospital, but today you saw him with Rebecca and you couldn't handle it."

"Tuscany."

"It's true. You want him for yourself."

I laughed. "I don't want him. I hate him."

She didn't laugh back. "Used to hate him. Lately, whenever you talk about him, you go all dreamy. Admit it. You're so into him."

"That makes no sense," I insisted. "He's getting better and he'll be heading home in a few days. To marry *her*."

"Since when does love make sense?" she said. "Goddard gets you firing on all cylinders. I saw it that night at Spago. There was something going on between you two even then."

"Yeah, mutual rage."

"No, chemistry. Look, Ann, if you hadn't fallen hard, you would have e-mailed the story to Harvey by now. Instead, you've been dragging your heels on it. Why? You're afraid of losing Goddard."

"I've never *had* Goddard."

"Doesn't mean you don't wish you did. Come on. Be honest."

Okay, I *had* been dragging my heels, because every time I imagined Malcolm finding out that I had exploited his words for my own self-interest, I was convinced that he would despise me the way I'd once despised him. And I *couldn't* handle that. She was right again.

"Oh, crap," I said as the tears started dribbling down my cheeks. Too dazed to determine where the moisture was coming from, I flipped on the windshield wipers instead of grabbing a tissue.

"Annie," she said soothingly. "It's okay. Really it is."

"It's not okay!" I shouted, scaring myself. "For one thing, he's practically engaged to Rebecca. For another, he thinks I'm a sweet, trustworthy hospital volunteer, not a media parasite. And for still another, I have a No Actors rule! Your breakup with Don is proof that the rule should remain in effect!"

"Whoa, girl. Slow down. He's not engaged to Rebecca yet. He doesn't know you wrote a story about him and if you don't send it to Harvey, he never will. And your No Actors rule is bullshit. You can't decide the profession of the person you fall in love with or you would have snapped up that dorky doctor who's been slobbering all over you."

I didn't say anything. I was too busy trying to cry and drive.

"My advice is, get a good night's sleep," she said. "It'll all be clearer in the morning."

"What's already clear is that without the story, I have no leverage with Harvey," I said.

"Then you'll find another way to make a living. In the meantime, go home and go to sleep."

"I will," I said resignedly. "Are you gonna be okay with all this Don stuff?"

"Yeah. I'm thinking it was a blessing that I met him. Kind of the way people with cancer are always saying it's a blessing that they got an incurable illness. Bad experiences make you appreciate the less bad ones. So I went back over the guys I've dated and dumped, and decided that some of them were less bad. I'm going out with one of them tonight."

I rolled my eyes but wished her luck.

WHEN I SIGNED in at the volunteers office on Friday afternoon, Shelley said I looked beat. Being the sweetheart that she was, she added that even when I looked beat, I looked better than most of the female population.

"Flatterer," I said. "You just want me to work harder."

"You work hard enough," she said. "Which reminds me." She peeled off a couple of Post-itss from the edge of her desk and handed them to me. "Your public awaits."

Before I read the messages, I said a silent prayer that one of them was from Malcolm, begging me to come to his room because he realized he loved *me,* not Rebecca. Pathetic, right?

As it turned out, neither was from Malcolm. One was from Bree Wiley, asking me to bring her some movie magazines. The other was from Isabelle, the disgruntled patient I'd advised to seek a second opinion. With a heavy heart but an obligation to push forward, I went about my day.

Bree, who was moving up the list for a liver but hadn't yet received one, was her usual precocious self, wanting to know everything about Hollywood.

"My mom said she'd find a way to take me," she declared while she leafed through one of the issues of *Famous* I'd given her. "The minute I'm better, I'm there."

"And you'll have an awesome time," I said, and launched into what I thought would be the perfect itinerary for her.

"I have no interest in Disneyland," she said with the discriminating tone of a grown woman. "I'll be going to the Walk of Fame, where the stars put their handprints."

"Of course you will," I said, hoping she'd live long enough to walk out of the hospital.

I PUT OFF calling Isabelle and instead continued to wheel my cart to the other floors. As I waved to the nurses and the other hospital personnel, who were now as familiar to me as any of the entertainment reporters I used to run into, I realized that I'd become an actual member of this community. I may have joined it for the wrong reasons, but I found myself wishing I could volunteer 24/7 and never have to deal with whether or not to send Harvey the story.

I visited a woman that day whose violent hand tremors prevented her from brushing her hair and applying her lipstick. I did the honors for her and by the lavish words of praise she heaped on me you would have thought I'd cured her illness.

I visited a man with a bad case of macular degeneration along with his diverticulitis. He couldn't read his dinner menu, so I read it for him and circled the items he wanted. He kissed my hand and told me I was an angel.

And I visited a teenage boy with a broken back who told me he'd lost his iPod. I asked him which song he missed the most and he said "Falling," by Alicia Keys. Luckily, I happened to know that one and sang it to him. I am a white Jewess with no blues, soul, or Motown in my blood whatsoever, never mind a decent voice, but I'd managed to distract him from his pain and he asked me for an encore. Yes, I wanted to be back in L.A., but it hit me with shimmering clarity that day: Ministering to the patients was more fulfilling than anything I'd ever accomplished in the magazine world.

How was that possible? All I'd ever wanted to do was write about celebrities, and yet suddenly I wanted to do more, make a bigger contribution, direct my energies toward giving rather than getting. I'd experienced a shift. I didn't know how it would change the course of my life. I only knew that it would.

Feeling reenergized, I knocked assertively on Malcolm's door. Rolanda had let it slip that his fever was gone and his condition much improved, so I was happy about that too.

"It's Ann," I said. "May I come in?"

"Not if you're allergic to flowers," he said.

I entered the room to find a spectacular arrangement of tulips and roses and every other spring flower I could think of, along with greens and some baby's breath. It was gorgeous—spectacularly colorful—and I tried not to let my jealousy rear up when I realized that Rebecca must have ordered it for him from the florist before she left.

"Looks like you have an admirer," I said, proceeding right to the table where the flowers rested regally in their glass vase. I leaned over to smell them. "I take it the visit went well yesterday?"

When he didn't answer, I glanced at him and noticed how much healthier he looked. His eyes were clear, his complexion less flushed, and he was sitting up in bed instead of reclining against the pillow. "Malcolm?" I said. "Don't you like the flowers?"

He curled his index finger at me, summoning me over to the bed. When I was standing beside him, he said with a shy grin, "You're the one with the admirer, Ann. They're for you. I was hoping you'd show up before they wilted."

"For me?" I shrugged, mystified, and then I got it, got that this was a gesture of gratitude. He and Rebecca wanted to express their thanks for yesterday, for my part in successfully sneaking her into the hospital without the media catching on. "You two didn't have to do this. I was glad to help."

"Sit down, please," he said, nodding at the nearby chair.

I sat. "I love the flowers," I said, in case he thought I didn't.

"Great, but they're from me. Just me."

So it was Malcolm himself who wanted to show his appreciation for my bringing his beloved to him. Very gallant. "Well, either way they're beautiful and it was fun pulling a fast one on everybody." Not really, since Shelley would have dismissed me if she'd found out.

"What if I told you they had nothing to do with Rebecca's visit yesterday?" he said. "What if I told you I just wanted to buy you flowers?"

I thought of what Rebecca had said in the car: Malcolm was waiting to propose until he could buy her a ring. I guessed he liked buying women things. "Actually, volunteers aren't supposed to accept gifts from patients. No gifts. No tips. Nothing. They told us that in the orientation."

He looked wounded. "So you won't take them home?"

I shook my head. "We'll keep them here. That way everybody can enjoy them."

"Right." He cleared his throat, scratched his chin. He was awfully fidgety, but it was probably because he was dying to leave the hospital now that he was feeling better. Still, he kept looking at me funny and then turning away. He just couldn't seem to maintain eye contact.

"Did you and Rebecca have a good time together?" I asked, trying to break what had become an awkward silence.

He stared at his lap, then over at me. "I was thinking. I've never seen you in regular clothes. Only in the uniform."

Talk about a nonresponse to a question.

I reached down to touch the collar of my smock, self-conscious suddenly. "I asked you about Rebecca," I said, wondering if maybe his fever wasn't gone after all.

"She's not you."

Yeah, the fever was back. "Malcolm, you're not making sense. Should I get a nurse?"

He shook his head, all business. "I was looking forward to spending time with her, but after about fifteen minutes, I knew."

"Knew what? That you wanted to marry her when you got home?"

Another shake of the head. "That she was self-involved and not very bright and one of those yes people you mentioned."

I didn't understand. Yes, Rebecca was everything he'd just described, but I didn't think he'd noticed. "So you don't want to marry her?"

"No, and I tried to tell her that." He looked at me again, his eyes soulful, tender. "She isn't you."

Isn't you? What was he talking about?

"She's fine as a friend, someone to take to a party, but she's not especially smart and she's certainly not genuine or down to earth," he said, his emotion swelling with each word. "Instead of being a straight shooter, she tells me whatever she thinks I want to hear. She's not you, Ann. And what I realized after being with her yesterday is that I won't be happy with someone who's not you."

I tried not to let my jaw drop open, but I'm sure it did anyway. How could it not? I was blindsided by Malcolm's declaration. Yes, I'd fantasized about it, allowed myself to imagine it, but never dreamed he would actually *say* it. And now that he had said it, what was I supposed to do about it? Confess my feelings for him? And if I did, would I also be required to tell him I wasn't so genuine after all? "I'm not sure what you mean," was all I could manage.

"I've been profoundly changed by this experience," he said, echoing my own thoughts about my work at the hospital. "It stands to reason that what I'm looking for in a woman has changed too." He smiled, the dashing leading man now. "You know how patients think they're in love with their doctor? Well, I think I'm in love with my volunteer."

"But you hardly know me," I said, my heart beating so fast I nearly called a code blue on myself.

"Then let me get to know you," he said.

"How?" I croaked. My throat had gone dry.

"They're taking me off the intravenous stuff tomorrow and I'll be on oral antibiotics for a couple more days after that—just until they say it's okay to travel."

"And?"

"And I thought maybe we could have a date tomorrow night. A good old-fashioned Saturday-night date. If you're not busy, that is."

"A date?" I know. I wasn't bringing anything to the dialogue except monosyllabic answers, but I was freaking out inside. Everything was happening so fast and I wasn't prepared. Sure, I had pictured just such a scene, as I've indicated—the words he would say, the way he would say them—but in a ridiculous oversight I'd forgotten to rehearse my own lines.

"Nothing fancy, obviously," he said, gesturing at his hospital room. "But I could clean myself up and you could leave the uniform at home and we could have dinner together at the table over where the flowers are. They'll make a nice centerpiece."

"So you want me to share your tray of scrod and Jell-O?" I said, starting to recover and actually deal with this new reality.

"Leave the dinner to me, okay?"

"Okay."

"Since I'll be disconnected from all the needles, we'll be able to take a stroll." He shrugged. "Well, maybe a short one. We wouldn't want me to faint again."

"You really should clear all this with your doctor," I said, thinking I should clear it with Tuscany. On the other hand, she would squeal and tell me to forget about my duplicity and encourage me not to overthink the situation.

"Not to worry," he said. "Just tell me you'll be my date tomorrow night and I'll do the rest." He leaned over the side of his bed and took my hand in his. It felt as hot as the last time, even without the fever.

"I do worry a little," I said. "There's something I should tell—"

"Look, I know you care for me too. I can see it in your eyes. Don't we deserve a chance? Shouldn't we pursue this? Can we really go on about our lives without pursuing this?"

Oh, I did care all right. As Tuscany had pointed out, I would have sent Harvey the story already if I didn't. No, Malcolm would never have to find out I'd written it, but I'd have to tell him we'd met before—and *how* we'd met before. I'd have to come clean, and I would. Once we were on solid ground as a couple.

I took a deep breath. "I'd be honored to be your date tomorrow night," I announced, deciding to put aside all the misgivings and let myself celebrate my good fortune. For one night anyway.

Chapter Twenty-six

||||||||||||||||||||||||||||||||||||||||||||||||||||||||||||||||||||||||||||||||||||||||

I floated through the rest of my shift, handing out magazines to anybody with a pulse. I was so excited, so jazzed, so overstimulated that when I saw Nadine without her harp, I grabbed her and hugged her.

"You look like you've just witnessed a miracle," she remarked.

"I have," I said. After thinking Malcolm was a lost cause, thinking I'd never experience the all-consuming joy of being enthralled with a man at the same time that he was equally enthralled with me, a miracle was exactly what I'd witnessed.

I was in such a good mood that I decided to call Isabelle before I left the hospital. I wasn't thrilled about the prospect of hearing more of her complaints, but I didn't want to leave her hanging. "It's the difficult ones who need us most." That's what Nadine had said.

"You're so nice to return my call," said Isabelle after answering the phone.

"My pleasure," I said. "How are you?"

"Determined," she said. "You told me to get my pathology report and I did. Now I'm suing the hospital."

"What?" I said, wondering if I'd heard her correctly.

"They removed my reproductive organs because they said I had a tubal infection. But the pathology report said there was no infection. The doctor I went to for a second opinion confirmed that."

"Wait, Isabelle," I said, still reeling from the word "sue." "Let's go back to the beginning. When we met, you were in a lot of pain. And the pain continued even after you went home. You must have had something wrong with you."

"Absolutely," she said. "I have endometriosis, not an infection, and it can be treated with drugs. The new doctor said my surgery was a complete mistake. And not an innocent one, according to my lawyer. He says the hospital makes the same 'mistake' with other unsuspecting women, just for the money."

"The same mistake?" I repeated, hoping she was wrong and had simply been given misleading information.

Yes, I was only a volunteer, but I had come to feel an allegiance to the hospital, the way you feel an allegiance to an employer who's been good to you. Heartland General saved lives. It had certainly brought purpose and meaning to my life in a very short time. And, of course, it had brought Malcolm back into my life. It wasn't easy to listen to Isabelle's claims. I was bewildered and frightened by them.

"Apparently, they perform hysterectomies on women who don't need them," she explained. "More surgeries mean more income for that place."

I held the phone away from my ear and stared at it, completely stunned now. Was she crazy? One of those litigious types?

"My lawyer put me in a class-action suit with other women who are suing the hospital," she went on. "He said Heartland General churns patients like stockbrokers churn their clients' investments to earn more commissions."

"I can't believe it," I said even as I asked myself if it was possible that something as mercenary, as sinister, was happening right under my nose. I knew Richard was concerned about the hospital's bottom line, but would he really look the other way if his OB/GYN surgeons yanked out a few healthy uteruses here and there in the interest of fattening the coffers?

Of course not. Doctors and hospitals were always getting sued, I reminded myself, and many of the suits were frivolous, only serving to drive up health care costs. But was this one frivolous? How could it be if an entire group of women was making the same claim?

As I was letting Isabelle's bombshell sink in, I flashed back to my own observation that there *were* a lot of hysterectomies being performed at the hospital. I'd had the suspicion that something might be amiss. I'd even raised the matter with Richard. Hadn't he mentioned that another woman was suing the hospital after her surgery? Wasn't that the call he'd taken from risk management when we were at the lake?

"I just wanted to thank you, Ann," said Isabelle. "Without your advice, I would never have found out the truth."

The truth. What was it? At the very minimum, her doctor at Heartland General had misdiagnosed her medical condition. At the very worst, she'd lost the ability to bear children because tubal infections were more profitable than endometriosis.

"You're welcome," I said, sort of dazed. Part of me wished I'd never offered my help; the other part felt proud—a Jewish Erin Brockovich, my grandmother would have called me.

After we hung up, I thought about marching straight down to Richard's office for answers and, hopefully, reassurance. But the last time I'd hinted at improprieties, he'd dismissed them out of hand. No, I needed more evidence before I confronted him. More information, at least.

That night, my laptop and I commandeered a table at the Caffeine Scene. I answered a few e-mails and then got down to work, doing a search for any class-action lawsuits against Heartland General. It didn't take long before I was poring over my screen, reading the very words I had been dreading. Isabelle wasn't wrong: There *was* a suit against the hospital, involving gynecological surgeries. Nine women were involved, and the likelihood was that all nine of them weren't crazy or litigious.

I needed to talk to Richard right away, and as fate would have it, I didn't have to wait.

"I had a hunch I'd find you here," he said with a chuckle, and, as per his usual cluelessness, he sat down at my table uninvited. It occurred to me then that he might very well be stalking me. He always seemed to turn up at the Caffeine Scene when I was there and he'd turned up at the lake when I was there too. For the first time, I understood what it must feel like to be a celebrity, followed around by someone—lots of someones, in that case—whose presence wasn't wanted. "Working on another interview for the *Crier*?"

"No." I decided not to beat around the bush or waste time making pleasantries. I launched into an account of my conversation with Isabelle.

Richard fiddled with his bow tie and did some more chuckling, and yet there was a toughness in his expression as I spoke, a narrowing of his eyes.

"Jeepers, Ann. I sure do admire your compassion for this woman," he said. "But what made you tell her to ask for her pathology report?"

"Why shouldn't I?" I said. "If her doctor wouldn't give her the facts, she had to get them herself. I thought asking for the report would reassure her, not open a can of worms."

"Can of worms?" Another chuckle. "You must be confusing all this with a Hollywood movie. But there's no plot. No intrigue. No soundtrack. We're just trying to practice medicine here in good old Middletown. Your friend is obviously another patient with buyer's remorse."

Buyer's remorse? Suddenly, I looked at Richard in a whole new light. There was more to him than the harmless nerd, I realized—more to him than the smart, ambitious striver too. There was a mocking tone I hadn't heard before, a sharper edge. "What could you possibly mean by that?" I asked.

"I meant that they want the hysterectomies and then they're sorry afterward. It happens all the time."

"Isabelle didn't want the surgery, Richard. She was given the wrong diagnosis by her surgeon and was forced into having it. A surgeon who reports to you, now that you're in a position of authority."

"I'm not responsible for this woman's ravings, Ann, if that's what you're suggesting." He said it with a shrug, as if he was being dragged into a hopelessly ridiculous discussion.

"What if they're not ravings?" I persisted, asking the questions that had to be answered, just as I always did. "She underwent a procedure she didn't need."

Back came the chuckle. It was a nervous tic, I saw now. There was nothing happy-go-lucky about it. "I can't be expected to stay on top of every operation performed at the hospital. I trust my staff. They're excellent doctors."

"Most of them probably are," I said. "But what about the ones who aren't? The ones who are conning patients with unnecessary surgeries? The ones who are in it strictly for the money? Wouldn't you agree that it's more lucrative to cut somebody than to try and heal them?"

" 'Heal' them," he said, nodding. "That's a real L.A. word, isn't it. We must seem like quaint country docs compared to—I don't know—Deepak Chopper."

"Chopra. But getting back to the patient, I've just done a search and there's an active class-action suit against the hospital involving nine women who had hysterectomies," I said, eyeing my trusty laptop. "You've got to be more worried than you're letting on."

He straightened his already ramrod-straight posture. He'd had enough of my interrogation. "We have a legal department. They'll handle whatever it is. I'd rather talk about us."

Us. Back came the yearning in his voice, evidence of the crush, the infatuation, or whatever it was he felt for me. It was as if he couldn't believe he'd managed to succeed professionally but still couldn't manage to win my heart.

"Look," I said. "I don't know if the hospital is guilty of negligence or of something even more criminal, but I do know that you're in the hot seat as assistant chief of staff. So I'd pay attention if I were you and stop acting like what I've been saying isn't your problem. Because it *is* your problem, Richard."

"Right. Okay." He held up his hands in surrender. "You've made your point and I'll pay more attention."

"Good move." Maybe he was guilty of something and maybe he wasn't, but it wasn't up to me to sort it all out. I was just glad I'd spoken up.

"Now," he said after clearing his throat, "I'm getting myself some coffee and when I come back, I hope we can segue into a more personal subject. I was thinking of getting tickets to that play over in Center Creek for tomorrow night. It's not like the splashy musicals you're used to seeing—your job at *Famous* probably took you to Broadway shows and Las Vegas shows and all kinds of—"

"I'm busy tomorrow night," I said, wishing my date with Malcolm could start right then, so I wouldn't have to deal with one more invitation from Richard. He was relentless.

"Busy?" He seemed surprised. "Anyone I know?"

"Yes. In a way." Oh, why not? I thought. It was time he understood once and for all that he and I were not going to be a couple and that the man I was busy with on Saturday night was Malcolm. I'd spent the past several weeks trying to tiptoe around his feelings, and yet all I'd gotten in return was his refusal to take mine into consideration. And now with the lawsuit and his possible complicity, I was done tiptoeing.

"Does this person have a name?"

I was about to tell him, but he answered his own question.

"Ah, it's our celebrity, isn't it," he said, minus the chuckle. "Jonathan informed me that you've hardly left his side."

Small town. Small talk. I should have remembered there'd be no secrets. Except that there were things Richard didn't know. I thought he might finally leave me alone if he heard the truth.

"Malcolm was the reason I got fired at *Famous,*" I began. "Well, my fear of flying was the reason I got fired, but he exploited it to get out of having to do the interview." I went on about Harvey's obsession with the story and my half-baked efforts to cure myself of my flying phobia and the scene at the airport that led to my flameout at the magazine.

"Was he contrite when you told him he was the one who'd ruined your career?" he asked, still taking in my news.

"He doesn't know I ever worked at *Famous,*" I said. "I haven't—"

"He thinks you think he's Luke Sykes." He shook his head in amazement. "You do take our patient-confidentiality rules seriously."

"No. Actually, he confided in me about being Malcolm Goddard."

Richard tried to make sense of my admission. "So *you* know who *he* really is but *he* doesn't know who *you* really are?"

"In a nutshell." I took a deep breath. "I intended to write a story about him. That's the reason I became a volunteer. I'm not proud of that, because I've come to love volunteering, but initially I needed an excuse for getting close to him. The plan was to write a story without his consent, e-mail it to my editor, and get my job back."

"Jeepers." He was shell-shocked. "I figured you missed your life in L.A., but I was hoping I could change that."

He still didn't get it. "No. I'm sorry. But just so you know, I would never have named the hospital in the story or given away anything about Malcolm's medical condition. And I never let him suspect that you were the one who tipped me off about him."

"Very sporting of you. But what happened to the story? Did you send it or is that why you're seeing Mr. Goddard tomorrow night? To pull more quotes out of him."

"The story's still in the computer." Another deep breath. This was the part that would throw Richard. "I decided not to send it."

"Too bad. It probably would have leaked out that he was a patient at the hospital and we would have gotten all that national publicity," he clucked. "So what happened? Cold feet?"

"Warm heart. I have feelings for Malcolm. Deep feelings. It's too early to call them love, but they might be."

No more clucking. Or chuckling. He didn't say a word. Not for several seconds. He just stared at me, his face contorting so he wouldn't cry or yell or something.

"Are you okay?" I asked, because he had turned very pale.

"No, I'm crushed." He put his head in his hands. "And I could really use that coffee now. I'd go and get it myself, but I don't trust my legs at the moment."

"I'll get it for you," I offered. Well, it was the least I could do.

I rose from my chair, walked over to the counter, and took my spot in line. The place was crowded that Friday night, and there were several people ahead of me, the most irritating of whom was the person who couldn't decide between decaf and regular and then had to fish around in her purse for the exact amount of her purchase. After ten minutes, I came back to the table and set Richard's mug down in front of him.

"Thanks," he said as I sat. His lower lip was quivering, as if he was still trying to hold in his hurt and disappointment.

"Feeling any better?" I said.

"It's not me I'm worried about, Ann. He'll dump you the minute he finds out who you are."

"No, he won't, because I'll explain everything to him," I said. "He'll understand."

"Nope," he said. "You wrote the story behind his back, let's not forget."

"But I didn't send the story, let's not forget *that*. I changed my mind because I care about him more than I care about my job."

He sipped the coffee. Slurped it, actually. A drop dribbled down his chin. "I say he'll drop you when he finds out that you're not the innocent volunteer you're pretending to be."

Okay, I didn't need him to rain on my parade. I had plenty of doubts of my own about how my truth-telling session with Malcolm would go.

I shut down my computer, packed up my things, and stood. "For the last time, I didn't send the story. And when he hears that he helped get me fired, he *will* be contrite. It'll all work out. We've both changed since our encounter in L.A., both made mistakes, both grown. He'll see that."

He shrugged. "If not, you can always come back to me."

"Richard."

There was nothing more to say. He was like that woman who kept showing up at David Letterman's house in Connecticut no matter how many times he called the cops on her.

"Wait. What do I owe you for the coffee?" he asked as I was leaving.

"My treat," I said and hurried out the door before he found another way to keep me there.

||||||||||||||||||||||||||||||||||||||||||||||||||||||||||||||||||||||||||||||||||||||||||||||||

Chapter Twenty-seven

On Saturday I forced Richard and Isabelle and everything unpleasant out of my mind, and concentrated solely on my date with Malcolm. It had been a long time since I'd felt so alive, so invigorated, and I was determined not to let anything bring me down.

My first mission was to get myself looking my very best for the date, which meant a morning appointment at Middletown's one and only house of beauty, Maggie's Hair and Tanning Salon, for a trim and a manicure. I hadn't ventured into the bustling, always packed place since my high school prom, but I viewed my date as an equally momentous occasion.

Over the years, Maggie Jacoby, the salon's fifty-seven-year-old proprietor, had tried to adapt to the latest trends (hence, the lone tanning booth), but she still "set" hair and she still used rollers to do it. When I'd called and asked for a cut and a blow dry, there was a momentary hesitation before she said, "If that's what you want."

Actually, she did a good job on me. She lopped off about two inches of my straggly ends and then dried my hair into a do that had bouncy little waves in it. The other women in the salon weren't shy about expressing their approval. They had watched the entire production (women in Middletown with nothing better to do often hung out at Maggie's to exchange local gossip) and pronounced me "a glamour girl." They especially liked my nails, which Michelle, the manicurist, had filed into an oval shape (square was considered trampy, as were French manicures) and painted a soft pale pink. Of course, they all thought I was getting dolled up for a big date with Richard, because he'd told anyone who'd listen we were dating, and I didn't want to start anything by correcting them.

Next I stopped in at Bettina's Fancy, the Victoria's Secret clone whose owner I'd profiled for the *Crier*. Not that I was anticipating a scenario in which Malcolm would see me in my underwear, mind you. I just wanted to wear something special beneath my clothes, something daring. And so I bought a black bra and black panties. They weren't silky, weren't satiny, weren't even lacy. They were just black, which, for Middletown, was daring enough.

Oh, and I bought a pretty black knit dress at a new store called Illusions. The clothes were more conservative than what you'd see in L.A., but they seemed to be well made and—here was their biggest selling point—they didn't smell of disinfectant. Grandma Raysa regularly sprayed all the closets in the house with antibacterials, some of which had fragrances. As a result, my stuff had alternately taken on the scents of Mountain Snow, Melon Burst, and Lavender Meadow.

"What's with the shopping bags?" asked my mother when I returned with my purchases. She and my aunt were sitting at the kitchen table playing gin rummy. "And your hair. It looks so glamorous."

So. It was unanimous. At least with the females who'd seen it. I just hoped Malcolm thought it looked glamorous too. Not movie-star glamorous, but a step up from volunteer tidy.

"I sincerely hope all this isn't for Richie Grossman," Aunt Toni muttered.

"Don't interfere," my mother scolded her sister. "If Ann ends up liking that boy, she just might stay in Middletown."

"She doesn't want to stay in Middletown," snapped my aunt. "Besides, Richie Grossman isn't good enough for her."

"Actually, I'm meeting my friend Jeanette for dinner tonight—the volunteer from pediatrics," I lied, hoping to end their bickering, for the moment anyway. I wished I could tell them about Malcolm, but I'd promised him I wouldn't tell anyone that he was a patient at Heartland General and I'd kept my promise, not counting Tuscany. Soon, after he was back in L.A., I would fill them in. On him. On us. I smiled as I pictured their stunned faces. Their stunned, delighted faces.

"See? She has friends in Middletown," said my mother. "She's happy here."

Aunt Toni scoffed. "If she was so happy here, she wouldn't be getting all fixed up for this Jeanette, as if it's some hot date."

"She's a big girl," Mom said. "She can fix herself up for whomever she pleases."

"Look, I'm fine with it if she turns out to be a lesbian," said Toni. "She should just be a lesbian back in L.A. where she'd fit in better. They have more of them there."

I laughed, both at the way they never ceased to discuss me in the third person and at the fact that they were still trying to figure out why I was single. "You guys enjoy your card game," I said as I headed for my room. "And no cheating."

I DRESSED AS carefully as if I were about to walk the red carpet at a movie premiere. I wasn't big on makeup, as I've already said, but I applied some foundation and blush, some eyeliner and shadow, and some glossy lipstick whose promotional material claimed it stayed on for hours and was "kiss proof."

Kiss proof. I couldn't believe I was even thinking in those terms. This was only my first date with Malcolm, for God's sake. What's more, it was taking place in a hospital room at Heartland General, not at his estate in the Hollywood Hills. I'd be lucky if he felt well enough to hold my hand again.

Once I was satisfied that I looked okay, I hurried out to the car and drove to the hospital. Malcolm had invited me for seven o'clock. I entered the building at six fifty-nine. Since the volunteers office was closed, I didn't have to sign in or explain to anybody what I was doing there on a Saturday night or why I was in a dress instead of a uniform. There weren't any doctors around, naturally, and the nurses were unfamiliar to me since I always worked the day shift. Nobody would recognize me, just the way nobody recognized Malcolm.

I had butterflies in my stomach as I rode up in the elevator to the sixth floor. Nah, forget butterflies. These critters were as huge as bats the way they were flapping around in there.

When I got to 613, I stopped in the hall and gave myself one last check in the mirror of my compact. No lipstick clinging to my teeth. No booger hanging from my nose. No crud stuck in the corner of my eyes. I was ready.

I was about to knock on the half-open door, issue my standard greeting, and ask for permission to enter, but I reminded myself that I was off duty. I was a visitor, not a volunteer. And it was my date inside 613, not just another patient. And so I simply knocked and said in what I hoped was a low, sexy voice, "It's Ann."

I heard shuffling and the door opened and there he was: Malcolm Goddard, the man whose whereabouts were a mystery to everyone in Hollywood. He was upright and free of needles, and he looked as handsome as, well, a movie star. He had shaved and showered and spritzed himself with some wonderfully citrusy cologne, and he was wearing a fluffy white terry-cloth bathrobe with HG, the hospital's initials, stitched on the front pocket. (The robes were sold in the gift shop, along with the HG hats, mugs, and bib overalls. The merchandising had been Richard's idea.)

While I was taking Malcolm in, mentally pinching myself that the date was really happening, he ran his eyes over me and whistled. "You do clean up nicely, but I kind of figured you would."

"Look who's talking," I said. "Very Hugh Hefner in that robe."

He smiled as he played with the ends of my hair.

"I put waves in it," I said, keenly aware of every single cell in my body. Suddenly, everything felt heightened, more vivid, in Technicolor instead of black and white.

"I like you with waves," he said. "I like you without them too."

We stood there on that threshold, gawking at each other like two stupid teenagers, for an entire minute before I finally asked if he was going to let me come in.

"Oh, right," he said with a goofy shrug, as if he'd completely forgotten his manners. "Please, enter."

With that, he swung open the door and gave me my first glimpse of the room. He'd transformed it. Gone was the IV pole and any other hint that he'd been ill, and the overhead fluorescent lights had been dimmed to the level of a cocktail lounge. But it was more than that. Much more. With some ingenuity and cash, he'd turned his quarters into a romantic setting for dinner. I was amazed and totally seduced.

There were a couple of beige chenille throws spread across his bed, making it look like a comfy sofa, and there was an identical throw draped across the top of the window, framing it as if it were a curtain. The round table where the vase of flowers still rested was now arrayed with blue-and-white-checked linen place mats and matching napkins and, between the stainless-steel utensils, there were white plates that weren't the hospital's usual plastic but were actual porcelain. Also on the table were cut-glass serving platters covered with pieces of aluminum foil, which he'd shaped into tops that resembled fancy silver domes. And there was an ice bucket of sorts—he'd converted a small metal wastebasket in which two bottles of spring water were chilling—along with two fluted champagne glasses. Oh, and there was music playing from the portable radio on his bedside tray table. He had it tuned to our local golden-oldies station. James Taylor was singing a song I was too overwhelmed to name.

"This is so, so beautiful," I said. "How on earth did you manage it?"

"I bought out the gift shop," he said. "Who knew they sold all this stuff in hospitals?"

"You didn't go down there yourself, did you?" I said, concerned that he shouldn't do too much too soon.

He shook his head. "Rolanda was my personal shopper. We made a deal before she left for the night. Basically, I told her I was having a guest and needed her help. My specific instructions were: 'If it's not a stuffed animal or a Mylar balloon with "Get Well Soon" on it, buy it.' "

I just stood there, admiring everything, appreciating that he'd gone to so much trouble for me. "I honestly don't know what to say, Malcolm."

"Good. You *are* impressed. That's exactly the effect I was going for." He took my hand and escorted me over to the table. "Now, let's eat. We can't let this feast get cold, can we?"

"Feast?" I said skeptically. He had a personal chef at home. The hospital's kitchen was hardly up to his standards.

"I had a talk with the dietician," he said. "We'll be dining on paillard of chicken, potato purée, and a medley of spring vegetables, with chocolate mousse for dessert."

I laughed. "I don't think I've met this particular dietician. Are you sure she works here?"

As I sat in the chair he'd pulled out for me, he whispered in my ear, "The truth is, I didn't get anywhere with the dietician, except that she agreed to have the food delivered at six-thirty instead of the usual five sharp."

I looked up into his face, inhaling his cologne in the process. I felt

light-headed from pure excitement, not panic, as if my body might levitate off the chair. "So what is the menu?"

"We're having leathery chicken breast, gluey mashed potatoes, and
tasteless succotash."

"And the chocolate mousse?"

"Pudding. The stuff that comes in those little cups."

I laughed and surveyed the offerings on the table. Yes, they were the
same old hospital staples, but he'd actually made them look appetizing.
He'd put everything in the serving dishes with the foil domes, and if I
hadn't known better, I would have thought I was dining anyplace other
than a hospital. "You're very creative," I said as he poured the bottled
water into our glasses.

"Maybe it's all that time I've spent on movie sets where people are
paid to make things look more appealing than they really are."

He was about to sit down next to me when he stopped in his tracks.
"Oh. I forgot the pièce de résistance."

He walked over to the closet, grabbed something, hid it behind his
back, and returned to the table. "Ta-da!" The secret object turned out to
be a flashlight. He flipped it on and set it down on the table, light side up.
"Since candles are a no-no here, we'll have to use our imaginations."

Oh, I was using my imagination, all right. As he sat beside me and began to spoon the various items onto my plate, I pictured myself in Beverly
Hills, eating with him at Spago. I also pictured him raising his champagne glass and toasting us, toasting our future. I pictured him stroking
my thigh under the table. And I pictured him doing all this with a thin
gold wedding band on his finger—the same ring I wore. Yeah, I was totally hooked, and the evening had only just begun.

We spent the entire meal in each other's thrall, the radio station turning out song after song in the background. For some reason—maybe because we knew that Malcolm would be going home in two days and there
wasn't much time for mundane chatter—we went straight to the heart of

the matter, which was that we were two people who'd connected in a way we'd never connected with anyone else before. He stated unequivocally that his heart condition and subsequent infection had changed him profoundly and that what he was looking for in a partner had changed too; that if we'd met earlier in his life he wouldn't have been ready for someone as straight talking as me. (I could hardly bring up the fact both that he *had* met me earlier in his life and that I wasn't as straight talking as he thought.) I stated unequivocally that volunteering at Heartland General had forced me to confront my fears and put the needs of others ahead of my own. (I could hardly bring up the fact that one of my own needs had to do with my career as an entertainment journalist and that a story I'd written about him was still sitting in my computer's Drafts folder.)

And, of course, we talked about his former significant other. He told me he'd called Rebecca to state clearly that they were finished and that she'd handled it better than he'd expected, and I admitted that I hadn't liked her very much.

At one point, our conversation drifted back to the hospital. He asked me about the other patients I visited regularly and I told him about Bree Wiley, about her positive attitude and inspiring courage, particularly in the face of her prolonged, desperately frustrating wait for a new liver. "She never gives up, never complains," I said. "All she wants to do is go to Hollywood and meet movie stars."

"Here's a promise," he said. "As soon as she's well enough, I'll fly her and her family to L.A.—all expenses paid."

"Really?" I gazed at him as adoringly as I'd once glowered at him. "You said you didn't have much direct contact with fans."

"That was the old me. I was a selfish, reclusive ass. But the new me is making a promise that I'll keep—a promise I never would have made if I hadn't landed in this place and met you, Ann."

It continued on like that—the trading of compliments, the flirtatious glances—right through to the chocolate pudding. And then Malcolm suggested we take a walk together. Hand in hand, we strolled down the nearly empty hall, stopping only to peer out the floor-to-ceiling window near the elevators. It was a clear night and the stars were dotting the sky and we could see a sliver of the lake glistening in the distance.

"I used to think the Midwest was one big cow pasture, but this is pretty country," he said. "How would you feel about leaving it?"

I turned toward him, my heart pumping very fast. "Leaving it?"

"Not permanently, but we've got to make some plans," he said. "If we're gonna keep this magic going, either I'll come here to spend time with you or you'll come to L.A. to spend time with me. Or both." Ever so lightly, he brushed my hair back with his fingertips. "You do want to keep it going, don't you?"

"You know I do," I said, feeling limp whenever he touched me. I also felt like a world-class fraud. If I went to L.A. to visit him, I'd have to pretend that I'd never been there.

"Then we'll have a commuter relationship for now," he said.

So I'd go from avoiding airplanes to practically living on them, talk about a turn of events. "I'll do whatever it takes to make sure we can be together after you leave the hospital."

"Glad we're on the same page about that."

Page. I tensed when I thought of how I'd almost blown my chance at a relationship with Malcolm for a chance at a second career at *Famous.* There was no contest as to which I would choose now. Still, I knew I'd have to tell him the truth about my former life, as I've already said. I wasn't completely without a conscience, nor did I believe we could succeed as a couple unless I told him. I just couldn't bring myself to do it on our first date, couldn't break the spell. Not yet.

I'll tell him tomorrow, I vowed. I'll apologize for deceiving him and allay his concerns and make him understand that I too have changed. Yes.

When we returned to 613, I asked him if he was tired, considering that he was recovering from an infection.

"My battery's draining a little," he admitted. "But I've got enough juice for a dance."

I laughed. "A dance?"

He turned up the volume on the radio. The song was Sam Cooke's "You Send Me," one of the great love ballads from the fifties. "I couldn't have said it better," he murmured, taking me in his arms.

There wasn't much room for dancing, but we carved out a little space at the foot of his bed. We held each other and swayed to the song, our bodies moving in perfect sync. Malcolm hummed the soulful melody in my ear as we danced, and I gave myself over to the music and to him. I couldn't imagine ever having felt so absolutely, incontrovertibly happy. I didn't want to be anywhere else, with anyone else. I was in a bubble of bliss.

"'You send me,'" he whispered, echoing the lyrics. "'Honest you do.'"

And then he lowered his head and kissed me. I'd been wanting him to kiss me, had been craving the kiss, and when it finally came I thought I'd pass out from sheer relief. The fact that it was also a luscious, stirring, seemingly endless kiss only added to my rapture.

So much for my No Actors rule. Oddly, it didn't even occur to me to obsess about all the movie goddesses he'd kissed on screen. Those images of him became irrelevant the instant his lips met mine. I was too engrossed in the moment to feel jealousy or insecurity—too captivated by the exquisite sensations of his mouth, his tongue, his skin, his smell commingling with my own.

I was so carried away that I reached inside his bathrobe to touch his chest and his back. I was not a physically demonstrative person and yet I was desperate to touch him everywhere.

Breathless, I said, "I never expected—"

He silenced me with another wave of kisses, and again I lost myself in him.

We were going at it with such passion that we toppled onto the bed in a heap, laughing as we groped each other. We must have been so oblivious to the outside world that we didn't hear the knock on the door.

"Just takin' the dinner away," said the woman in the shower cap whose job it was to collect everybody's dishes. Her eyes widened as she walked in and caught us in bed (*on* the bed), and she started waving her hands in the air and shouting, "This ain't right! I gotta tell a nurse!"

I sprang up and tried to calm her down, explaining that the patient and I were just saying good night, that there was nothing to bother a nurse about. Malcolm employed another strategy with her, which was to offer her one of his many gift-shop purchases in exchange for her silence. The idea of a freebie appealed to her. She chose the portable radio and left without incident.

After she was gone, I told Malcolm about the time I'd walked in on a randy couple and how I'd called a code gray on them. "There's a certain symmetry to this," I joked.

"There's a certain symmetry to *us*," he said, wrapping me in his arms. "I know this sounds crazy, but it's almost as if we had a history together. Maybe in a previous life or something."

Yes, I would tell him the truth in the morning, but for the rest of the night he was mine.

Chapter Twenty-eight

I woke up on Sunday morning with a love hangover. Instead of getting out of bed and starting the day, I luxuriated under the covers, indulging myself with replays of Saturday night. I blushed as I relived it all, every second, every kiss, and could only shake my head in wonderment when I thought about how unlikely it was that Malcolm Goddard and I were speaking to each other, let alone planning our future together.

It wasn't until the phone rang in the hallway, just outside my bedroom door, that I decided to rouse myself and get some breakfast. Now that my mother had taken the giant leap of leaving the house to walk to the mailbox, she was fielding offers from friends who were eager to drive her wherever she wanted to go. I figured the call was from one of her would-be chauffeurs.

"My, my. Someone slept late," Grandma Raysa tsk-tsked when I finally appeared in the kitchen. The ladies of the house were all in attendance, cleaning. Mom was scouring the stove. Aunt Toni was wiping down the counters. And my grandmother was spraying every visible surface. "It's almost noon. We thought you died."

"You came home after we were all asleep, so we couldn't see what condition you were in," said my aunt, giving me the once-over. "Did you and this Jeanette do a little too much partying?"

"No," I said dreamily. "I was just being lazy this morning."

"You're entitled to be lazy, sweetie," said my mother, who had traded in her bathrobes for polyester workout clothes.

"I think your lazy days just might be over," said Grandma Raysa.

"Why?" I asked.

"Your former boss called," said my mother. "I told him you were still in bed and couldn't be disturbed."

"What?" I grabbed the arm of a chair to steady myself.

"Harvey Whatever-his-name-is," said Mom. "Your boss at the magazine."

"He called here?" I said, not believing my ears. "And you told him I couldn't talk?" I vaguely remembered leaving my mother's number with his assistant, but I'd assumed he'd tossed it.

She nodded. "He said he tried your cell phone too, but you must have had it turned off."

Harvey had tried to reach me? *Harvey had tried to reach me?* It had to be important, given the two-hour time difference; he wasn't usually such an early riser. And he almost never called an employee on a Sunday.

"You made him sound like a monster, Ann, but he was perfectly polite," said my mother. "He asked me to have you call him on his cell phone as soon as it's convenient."

As soon as it's convenient? That didn't sound like Harvey, who was never on anybody else's schedule but his own. And why on earth was he calling me in the first place? Was it about Malcolm? Had Tuscany let it slip that I had information about where he was? Not possible. She knew how much Malcolm meant to me. She also knew how much legal trouble I'd be in if I blabbed that he was in a hospital in Middletown. What's more, she didn't travel in the same social circles as Harvey and wouldn't ever have seen him over a weekend. So why had he contacted me from out of the blue? I was completely mystified.

"Maybe he wants to hire you back," said Aunt Toni. "You never know."

"I doubt it," I said. "Maybe he just forgot how much fun it was to yell at me."

"Even so, you must be curious about what he wants," she said.

More than curious, obviously. I was dying to know, but I was dreading the answer too. For so long, I'd prayed he would call, prayed he would summon me back to the magazine, but things had changed. My priorities had changed. Now my main concern was preventing anything and anyone from coming between Malcolm and me, including Harvey.

"Are you going to call him now?" asked my grandmother as they all waited with bated breath. In Middletown, a call from the editor of a national magazine was like a meteor falling through the ceiling.

"Yes," I said and started for my room so I could use my cell phone.

My aunt barred the doorway and nodded at the wall phone next to the refrigerator. "Oh no you don't," she said. "We didn't spend the past few hours speculating about this, only to be deprived of the action. Call him from here."

With my audience looking on, I dialed Harvey's cell number, which I'd committed to memory along with his home numbers in Brentwood, Malibu, and Lake Tahoe, as well as the numbers of his various spiritual advisors. He picked up after the first ring.

"Harvey, it's Ann Roth," I said, my voice quivering out of habit. "My mother told me you—"

"Ann! I love you! I bow down to you! You rule!" he shouted.

I feared for any possessions he had nearby, but I also wondered why he was praising me. "What's all this about?" I asked. Could the explanation be as simple as his realizing that I wasn't such a loser and that he'd been hasty in letting me go?

"What's it about?" he repeated with a laugh. "Like you don't know. Like you aren't the hottest entertainment journalist in town. Like you aren't getting your butt on a plane and coming back to work here—with a promotion *and* a raise."

I was stunned, speechless, nonplussed. The words matched the ones he'd spoken in my fantasy. The problem was that I was no longer invested in the fantasy. What's more, the fantasy involved my sending him the story about Malcolm, and I hadn't sent it. Why was he going on as if I *had* sent it? "I still don't understand," I said as my hands started to tremble.

He laughed again. "When I think of how I kicked you out of this place. What a jerk I was, huh?"

So this *was* about him admitting he'd made a mistake by firing me? He was just being humble? "Yeah, you were a jerk, but I won't hold it against you," I said, trying to inject some levity into the conversation.

"Listen to you. So feisty. That fresh air in Mississippi must be doing you good."

"Missouri," I corrected him.

"Whatever," he said. "The point is, I made a stink about how you didn't have what it takes to get the big get, that you weren't a killer, and look how you proved me wrong."

Oh God. This was bad, very bad. There was only one big get in Harvey's mind and it was Malcolm. Something had gone terribly awry, but what? How? Had Tuscany betrayed me after all? Had she told Harvey I'd met Malcolm in Middletown and written a piece about him? Even though I'd begged her not to?

"We're crashing out the issue as we speak," he went on. "I've got everybody in here working their asses off. We were going with Camilla on next week's cover, but not anymore." He smacked his lips with glee. "Are we ever gonna blow the competition out of the water, thanks to you."

Oh God oh God oh God. I didn't have to ask whose face was replacing Camilla's. It had to be Malcolm's. And now it was clear that Harvey was talking about an actual story, not some gossip Tuscany or anyone else could have passed along to him. But how *could* the magazine be crashing out what I'd written? The story was still in my computer, unsent. Nobody had read it except me.

"Harvey," I said, forcing myself to stay focused. "I need to hear you tell me one more time exactly why you called this morning."

"To congratulate you, for Christ's sake!" he shouted. *"To hire you back! To tell you I think the piece is sensational, especially the part about how you had to conduct the interview at an 'undisclosed location!' Love that to death!"*

Yes, it was as bad as I feared. Somehow Harvey had my story about Malcolm in his possession—a story I had not sent him. I didn't know how it could have happened, didn't think I could survive Malcolm's reaction to it. How would I explain that I was the writer who'd ambushed him at Spago? The writer who'd been on his tail for an interview? The writer who'd taken advantage of his sickbed delirium to concoct a magazine piece about him? How on earth would I explain that I wasn't who I pretended to be? I thought I could have made him understand, thought I could have said, "Yes, I tried to be a killer and get my job back, but I didn't send the story because I only want you." Not now. Not with the story in Harvey's hands. Now I didn't have a leg to stand on.

"Please don't run the story," was all I could think of to say. My entire body was rigid now and extremely cold.

"You're too much," he said, then yelled at some underling without bothering to cover the mouthpiece.

"I'm not kidding," I said, feeling all the blood drain out of me, all the joy too. "I don't know how you got it, but you can't run it."

"You don't know how I got it?" Roars of incredulous laughter flooded my eardrum. "I woke up this morning and there it was, burning up my inbox, the best damn e-mail ever. I know you must be crowing—it's not every day someone gets a pat on the back from mean old Harvey, huh?—but you did great work, Ann. Now come on home and we'll figure out who's next for you after Goddard."

After Goddard. How aptly put. Once the story hit the newsstands, there would be no more Malcolm and me, only life *after Goddard.* He would be crushed when he learned about the article and would shun me forever, no matter how hard I pleaded with him to believe that I hadn't sent the e-mail, that there had been an awful glitch. How could I expect him to forgive me? *I* wouldn't forgive me. Lying to him about my past was one thing, but exploiting his celebrity for what he would rightfully perceive to be my own gain was quite another. Which was why I hadn't sent the story. I could never have sent it. Not when my heart had done a complete one-eighty. Not when my resentment and bitterness toward him had turned into the kind of love I'd always dreamed of.

After Harvey hung up with his typical abruptness—he was incapable of ending a call with the universally accepted "good-bye"—I stood there in my mother's kitchen, staring at the headset as if it were alive, listening to the discordant *beep beep beep* the phone makes when it's off the hook, wondering how a magazine story I hadn't sent had managed to find its way through cyberspace and land in his computer.

"Sweetie? Are you okay?" asked my mother. "You're as pale as a corpse."

"What was all that talk about 'running it'? Running what?" my grandmother chimed in.

I recounted both sides of the conversation for them. I also revealed that Malcolm was a patient at the hospital and that it was he, not Jeanette, who'd been my dinner companion the previous evening. "I wrote the story about him before I got to know him, before I came to care about him," I said, ignoring their gasps and other gestures of shock and awe. "I wrote it in the hope of getting my old job back, but once I realized I had feelings for him, there was no way I could send it." I paused to catch my breath. I'd been talking very fast, I realized. "But it did get sent. Somehow. Or by someone."

"I'm not a computer person, so what do I know," said my mother, "but maybe you hit the wrong button or something."

"I don't hit wrong buttons," I said, frantic, thinking of all the possibilities.

"Well, then maybe someone else hit it," said my grandmother. "You carry that thing with you everywhere, Ann. Maybe somebody hit something by mistake."

My grandmother couldn't even work the microwave, never mind understand the logistics of operating a computer, but she had a point. I did carry my laptop everywhere.

And everywhere I carried it Richard seemed to follow.

Of course. It had to be Richard, the lousy bastard.

My temples throbbed and my hands curled into fists as I replayed Friday night at the Caffeine Scene. After I'd told him about Malcolm and me, he'd asked me to get him some coffee. *I don't trust my legs,* he'd said. God, was I an idiot. Like a good little soldier, I'd trotted off to the counter, leaving him alone with my computer. I knew he had no qualms about blabbing other people's private business, knew he thought nothing of checking out what I was writing either, knew he felt jilted and even enraged by my admission of my feelings for Malcolm, and yet I'd still handed him the opportunity to ruin my life.

"Ann, sweetie," said my mother, who rushed to hug me and try to soothe me. "What is it? From the look on your face, I'm guessing you figured out who did this."

"Oh, yeah," I said, pulling away and punching the air like a mini-Harvey. "And I'm about to go find him and give him hell."

"Him?" said my grandmother.

"Richard," I said between gulps of air. "He had access to my computer on Friday night. And he knew about Malcolm and me, about the story I wrote, all of it. He predicted that I'd lose Malcolm once he found out the truth. I just didn't expect him to speed up the process."

"Richie Grossman did this?" said my mother, as stunned as I was and just as angry.

I nodded. "And he's gonna hear about it."

"Fancy job or no fancy job, he's scum," my grandmother spat out. "I've got a rifle in the attic if you want to borrow it, Ann."

"No guns," I said. "But I'm putting on some clothes and driving over to his house and by the time I'm done with him, he'll be sorry he ever trespassed into my life."

I started to storm out of the room, but Aunt Toni stopped me.

"Wait," she said, literally blocking my path with her arm. "You can't."

"Why not?" I said. "You've never been a fan of his, so what do you care?"

"I'm not a fan of his, no," she said in an uncharacteristically soft voice.

"Then what's your problem, Toni?" said my grandmother. "Ann has a right to chew the boy out. We have to help her, support her."

My aunt looked at me with tears in her eyes suddenly, and I was bewildered. I'd never seen her cry in my entire life. Not when my father died. Not even when Uncle Mike left her. "I thought I *was* helping you," she said. "*Was* supporting you."

"We have enough drama, Toni," said Mom. "What's your point?"

"I'm the one who sent the story to Ann's editor," she said.

"Don't say crazy things," my grandmother scolded her.

"It's true," said Toni. "I did it."

Well, we all just froze, naturally. I mean, my aunt could go off the track at times and was more than a little opinionated, but I would never have thought her capable of interfering so brazenly.

"Why?" was all I could think of to say as I sank down into a kitchen chair, all the fury and rage toward Richard drained out of me.

"Linda wanted you to live here forever," she said, her head bowed. "I love having you around too, of course. But I didn't want you to end up like me, a bitter divorcée with no children of her own and a good-for-nothing ex-husband who sleeps with sluts. That was your future if you stayed in Middletown. I knew how much you wanted your old job back, Ann. One night—I keep my bedroom door open because of the claustrophobia—I heard you talking to your friend Tuscany on the phone about it. You were telling her how the Malcolm story was your revenge against him *and* your way to get rehired at the magazine. When you said it was in your computer but you hadn't sent it, I thought you were stalling because you didn't want to let your mother down by leaving us. Since I know my way around a Mac, I just figured I'd move things along."

"But you've destroyed my relationship with Malcolm," I said. "Don't you get that?"

"I had no idea you'd changed your mind about him," she said. "I would never have meddled if I'd known how much he meant to you. I swear it."

"Still, how could you do that to my daughter!" my mother lashed out.

"Because you were content to sit around watching her waste her life!" said Toni, regaining her old fire.

"I was not!" said my mother.

"You were so!" said my aunt.

It went on like that until Grandma Raysa stepped in and told them both to behave or she *would* go get that rifle in the attic.

Still reeling from her revelation but nonetheless seeing how visibly shaken she was by what she'd done, I got up and put my arms around my aunt. She meant well, I knew that. She wanted me to have a better life. But how could it be better without the man I loved?

"Would you like me to talk to Malcolm for you?" my mother offered. "I'm well enough to go to the hospital by myself, and I'd do anything for you, sweetie. I do want what's best for you, no matter what your aunt thinks."

"I could talk to him too," said my grandmother. "I've seen all his movies. He's practically family. He's not Jewish, by any chance?"

I shook my head, inconsolable. Part of me wanted to run to Malcolm and beg for mercy. The other part wanted to crawl into a hole and die. I didn't know where to turn, what direction to take, how to make things right. It all seemed too much to handle.

Everyone watched me in silence, until my grandmother couldn't stand it anymore and rapped on the kitchen table with her knuckles.

"Enough of this, Ann," she said with authority. "You've got to show some nerve. Go and plead your case to the movie star. If there's any justice in the world, this'll turn out okay."

I didn't know if there was justice in the world, but she was right. I couldn't just sit there sucking my thumb.

Chapter Twenty-nine

||||||||||||||||||||||||||||||||||||||||||||||||||||||||||||||||||||||||||||||||||||||||||||||||||||

I showered and dressed and pulled myself together. I checked my cell phone, listened to Harvey's message, and deleted it. There was also a message from an overwrought Tuscany, who was trying to warn me that the story had somehow fallen into his clutches. I deleted it too. And there was a message from Malcolm, telling me how much he enjoyed Saturday night, how optimistic about the future he was now that I was in his life, and how he couldn't wait to see me. Choking back tears, I called him to say I felt the same way and that I'd be over as soon as I could.

"THERE YOU ARE," he said when I finally showed up at the hospital at two-thirty. He was relaxing in a chair watching the Weather Channel when I entered his room. "They just gave tomorrow's forecast for L.A.: sunny and eighty degrees. Wanna come with me?"

I closed the door and hurried over to him, planting myself on his lap and burrowing into his arms. I held him tightly, pressed my ear against his chest, listened to the beating of his heart. I wanted to block out everything but him, if only for a little while.

"Hey," he said, tilting my chin up. "You're shaking. What's going on?"

"Just the thought of you leaving tomorrow," I said, swallowing the lump in my throat. "I can't imagine what it'll be like around here without you."

He kissed me. "You won't have to imagine it. You can fly out to see me this weekend. I'm waiting to hear from my publicist, but I don't think I'm expected back on the set for another two weeks. Maybe you could come Friday and stay until Monday or Tuesday."

Monday or Tuesday. The new issue of *Famous* would be on sale by then and his publicist, my pal Peggy, would be seething. Yes, he and I could celebrate the issue's publication together—right before he hurled me into oncoming traffic.

I had to tell him. I couldn't let him amble by some newsstand and see his face on the cover of the magazine, only to open it and find my byline. I couldn't do that to the man I loved.

And I did love him. Why kid myself? Actor or no actor, I adored him, adored the man he'd become, and would do anything if I could rewind the tape and start over again with him.

"You can talk to your supervisor about taking some time off, can't you?" he said. "And then I'll fly back here as soon as I can." He nuzzled my left earlobe. "I'm sure there's a quaint little hotel in the area, isn't there? Some Stepfordy bed-and-breakfast where you get a free muffin in the morning and a free glass of sherry in the afternoon?"

I nodded. "With lots of lace doilies too."

We sat together in that chair and kissed and talked and gazed out the window. He said Jonathan had given him a clean bill of health. He'd have to continue the oral antibiotics for another week and check in with his cardiologist in L.A. regularly, but he was in good shape, physically and mentally. I, on the other hand, was falling apart.

As the clock ticked and the afternoon gave way to dusk, my resolve weakened. The more I realized how deeply I cared about him and he about me, the harder it became to broach the subject of the story and my role in it. At one point, I even tried to talk us both out of our relationship.

"You actors have flings on movie sets as if it's part of the job," I said. "How do we know this . . . this . . . connection of ours isn't like one of those flings? Just a matter of same place, same time?"

"Because you're the real thing, not somebody playing a part," he said, rocking me in his arms. "And you've made me into the real thing too. I'm a different man now. I know what I want, and she's sitting right here."

So. You see why I couldn't tell him on Sunday, why I couldn't break the news that I *was* playing a part. It was too damn hard. I couldn't bring myself to break his heart and my own. Not yet. Instead, I decided that we should enjoy each other for one more day, just one more. He was being discharged in the morning. I would tell him then.

Yes, during our tearful good-bye, I would explain that there was something important that he needed to know, and present him with the facts. No sugar coating. There was always the chance that he might accept my apology for writing the story as well as my assurance that I wasn't the one who'd made it public; that he would see that I was a victim just as he was; that he would acknowledge his part in the mess—that it was his own nasty game of chicken that had contributed to my getting fired in the first place. And if not, he would be leaving anyway. He could curse me throughout his entire flight back to L.A. and I wouldn't have to hear a word of it.

"You sure you're okay?" he asked after we'd taken a walk down the hall and returned to his room. "You seem so gloomy."

"I am gloomy," I said. "They'll have to cordon off room 613 after you leave because I'll never step in it again."

"Is that the only reason?"

"Well, my family situation isn't always a laugh a minute, as I've told you. My mother and her sister were going at it this morning, in fact."

"About what?"

Another opportunity to tell him. Another opportunity wasted due to my cowardice. "The usual," I said. "They love each other but they don't see the world in the same way, especially when it comes to me and my happiness. My grandmother referees these battles and gets them to back off, but it can be pretty rowdy around our house."

He kissed my cheek. "I'm sure they drive you nuts, but I'm still envious of you."

"You said that once before."

"Yeah, because they care enough about you to fight over your happiness," he said. "Some of us aren't so lucky."

Lucky. Well, yes. I may have lost my father, but I still had a family who cared deeply about me. I could forgive my aunt for going behind my back—hadn't I gone behind Malcolm's?—because she only wanted the best for me, more than I'd ever realized. I just couldn't figure out how to cope with what she'd done, with the consequences of what she'd done.

"Hey, you," he said. "Perk up, please?"

He smiled and I took a mental photograph of him, a snapshot that would burn in my memory forever, a "before" picture. How he would react toward me "after" was too awful to contemplate.

MONDAY WASN'T MY volunteering day, but I arrived at the hospital that morning in my pink-and-white-striped smock. I felt as if I should be wearing black. My mood was funereal.

"Here she is. Our candidate for volunteer of the year," said Shelley. "You just can't stay away from us, can you?"

"There's a patient who's being discharged," I said. "I've become kind of attached to him. I wanted to give him a nice send-off."

Kind of attached. A nice send-off. Was I ever full of it.

Before taking the elevator up to six, I hid in the magazine storage room for a few minutes. I needed to rehearse what I planned to say to Malcolm. It was the only place where I could gather my thoughts and try out the speech I was about to make without anyone eavesdropping or passing judgment.

I intended to start at the very beginning, with the bulletin that I was an entertainment journalist, not a dental hygienist, whose first and only job as an adult was with *Famous*. Then I would proceed with Harvey's insistence that I interview him before the Oscars, Peggy Merchant's refusal to grant the interview, my confrontation with him at Spago, my freak-out at the airport, my dismissal from the magazine, and my return to Middletown. I would mention but not dwell on how much I'd resented him for his divalike behavior and his preying on my phobia, on how much I'd blamed him for costing me my career. I wanted him to understand my motivation for the payback but not lay a guilt trip on him. As for the rest—how I'd viewed his stunning appearance at Heartland General as a chance to reclaim my job and then changed my mind about writing the profile—I would be honest about it, straightforward, the way he'd expect the "real" Ann to be, the Ann to whom ethics used to matter. And then, of course, I would explain about the complete turnaround in my feelings for him and the accompanying realization that I could never, would never, send the story to the magazine, even though it presented him in the most flattering light and would surely burnish his already shining star. I would take him through the shocking discovery that it was my aunt who'd hijacked my computer and e-mailed the story without my knowledge, and that I'd tried to persuade my boss not to publish it—to no avail.

"I love you," I would say in my defense. "I wouldn't hurt you for anything in the world. I thought there was some justification for writing the story while you were a patient, but I shouldn't have done it. And I didn't send it. I hope you believe me, Malcolm. And I hope you'll forgive me."

There. I was as ready as I'd ever be. I flipped off the light in the storage room, closed the door behind me, and, forgetting completely about the cart, went to meet my destiny.

When I got off the elevator on the sixth floor, I passed the nurse's station. Rolanda winked at me and whispered, "Good thing you got here. You almost missed saying bye-bye to our favorite patient."

Almost missed him? I thanked her, but her comment gave me pause. Malcolm was supposed to call me on my cell as soon as Jonathan discharged him. If he was that close to leaving, why hadn't he called?

I reached into my pants pocket and checked the phone. No messages. Maybe he had business to conduct, I thought. Yes, he was probably discussing the plans for his return to the set of the movie he was shooting and was intending to call me once he'd dispensed with all the details.

I hurried down the hall to 613, rehearsing my key talking points one last time and telling myself that everything was going to work out. And then I stopped at Malcolm's door, breathed deeply, and knocked. "I'm here," I said and entered.

He was standing next to the bed with his back to me, not in his hospital gown but in the black leather jacket and jeans he must have worn when he was admitted. *His* uniform. He was stuffing his things into a Prada knapsack. He didn't so much as turn his head to greet me.

"Hey," I said, walking over to him. "Presto change-o. You're a movie star this morning."

"Am I?" he said, finally wheeling around to face me. His voice was flat, without any of the enthusiasm I'd heard in it over the weekend. Something was wrong.

Maybe he's nervous about having to lead a normal life with a defibrillator implanted in his chest, I thought. Patients were often a little anxious about leaving the hospital, where every physical need was met. It could be daunting to go back out into the world.

I reached out and hugged him. He did not return the hug. "You're going to be fine," I reassured him, even as I worried that he wasn't fine at all, that there was a new distance between us. "Your doctor wouldn't send you home if he wasn't convinced of that."

In response, he opened his mouth wide. "How about my teeth?" he asked after exposing them all to me. "Do they look fine too?"

"Your teeth?" I said, wondering why he'd ask me about them.

"Sure. You're a dental hygienist," he said. "Do you see any plaque? Any gum recession? Am I due for a cleaning?"

Yes, of course, I'd told him that lie, just as he'd told me he was a real estate developer. But why was he bringing it up now in such a snide tone of voice?

"Malcolm," I said. "Let's close the door and spend some private time before you leave. There's something I need to—"

"I already know," he cut me off, his eyes blazing now. "And I've got a limo coming in ten minutes, so why don't you take your little candy-striper self and find some other sucker to milk for a story?"

I staggered back as if I'd been slugged. "What is it you think you know?" I managed, my throat closing up. It was a rhetorical question, obviously. Somehow, he *knew*.

"My publicist—" He stopped himself and laughed derisively. "I forgot. You and she are old buddies. Anyhow, Peggy called this morning with some news I wasn't expecting. An understatement."

I stood there motionless, heart thumping.

"She heard through her sources that *Famous* is running a cover story on me that goes on sale next week," he said. "They claim they interviewed me for the story, that the words came directly out of my mouth. But I was here. Right here. Can you believe those parasites?"

"I—"

"So I asked Peggy how something like that could have happened, because it was sleazy even for a rag like that, and do you know what she told me?"

"Yes, because—"

"She told me that you wrote the story." He poked me in the chest. "*My little candy striper.*"

Thanks again, Peggy, I thought. I'd wanted to be the one to tell Malcolm and I hated that she'd done it instead, but it was my own fault. I'd waited too long to tell him. I couldn't blame her. Not for this one.

"Malcolm," I said. "I did write the story, but I didn't—"

"Stop." He looked at me as if he were seeing me for the first time, and in a way he was. "You were the chick at the restaurant," he said. "*'Ann Roth, like Ross, only with a lisp.'*" He shook his head at me, as if I were beyond parasitic. "How come I remember that but I didn't remember you? Lame, huh?"

"Not at all." I reached out to touch his arm but he shrank away from me. "What happened that night was in an entirely different context."

"Really?" he said, his eyes full of pain and betrayal now. "What's different about the context? In L.A., you were after me for an interview. In Middletown, you were after me for an interview too. Only in this case, instead of buying me a cheesecake to get what you wanted, you pretended to care about me."

The tears came then, because I couldn't take the hurt in his voice. They sprang out from beneath my lids and rained down my cheeks. I batted them away and kept going. "If you never trust me about anything else, trust this: I didn't pretend to care. I love you."

He shivered. "If lying to people is your way of loving them, you're a scary, scary lady."

"And you love me too, I know you do," I said, forging ahead in spite of the insult.

He turned away. I was forced to talk to his back. I delivered my speech just as I'd rehearsed it in the storage room. When I got to the part about his making me do the interview on his plane, about his testing my ability to overcome my fear, he seemed remorseful but defensive too.

"Yeah, I knew about your flying phobia and yeah, it was wrong for me to play that card," he conceded, turning around to face me, "but I told you people that I didn't want to be interviewed and I meant it."

You people. That again. "Yes, but anxiety disorder is serious business, Malcolm," I said. "I tried to get over it myself—oh, did I try—but it wasn't until I came home and started volunteering and helping others that I discovered a sort of bravery I didn't know I had. The experience here changed me, made me stronger, made me rearrange my priorities."

"Priority number one being me?" he said with a mean smirk. "Getting me on the record while I'm delirious with fever is your idea of changing?"

"Look, in the beginning I thought you deserved whatever you got," I said. "You were as difficult and demanding as you were in L.A., and I was very angry with you. But then you developed the clot and the infection and you realized you were human just like the rest of us, and you changed too. You were so much more open."

"Much too open, obviously." He snickered. "But then I had no idea you were writing down everything I said."

"You treated people badly in L.A.," I said. "You treated me badly. I thought it would serve you right if I wrote the story."

"And getting your job back wouldn't hurt."

"Yes. But once we started spending time together—once I fell in love with you—I knew that you meant far more to me than that job or any job."

"Bullshit. You wrote the story, sent it to your editor, and sold me out."

"My aunt sent the story, Malcolm."

He cocked his head at me. "You're blaming this on your aunt? The one who's divorced from the body-shop guy?"

"She wanted me to have my job back," I said. "She didn't want me staying in Middletown and ending up as miserable as she is. While I was here with you on Saturday night, she took it upon herself to go into my computer, find the story, and e-mail it to my editor. That's what she and my mother were fighting about yesterday."

He let my words sink in, but not deeply enough, apparently. He glanced at his watch, zipped up his knapsack, and set it on the floor. "Maybe your aunt sent it and maybe she didn't. It doesn't matter. What matters is that you never told me you worked for *Famous* or lived in L.A. or any of it. You misrepresented yourself, just like you did at Spago that night."

"You misrepresented yourself too," I countered. "You ran away to Middletown and told everybody you were Luke Sykes, a real estate developer from Miami. Was my lie that much worse?"

"You bet," he said. "I wasn't masquerading as someone else to hurt anybody or take advantage of anybody or—here's the big one—advance my career. Can you say the same?"

No. I couldn't. It killed me to admit it, but he was absolutely right about the comparison. It didn't line up. Mine *was* the greater sin.

He shook his head again, as if he still didn't believe what I'd done. "I don't even know who you are."

As the tears flooded my face now, making it one big soaking eyesore, I shrugged, feeling like nothing, and said, "I don't know who I am either."

He waved me off. "The irony of all this is that you could have gotten the interview the old-fashioned way—by asking," he said. "As I told you the other day, my experience in the hospital made me reevaluate everything, including my attitude toward the media. I still hate those tabloid dirt bags who'd follow me into the bathroom if I let them, but I plan to make myself more accessible to the mainstream media now. I just had that conversation with Peggy. So if you'd only been the honest person I thought you were, it could have worked out perfectly. You would have had your story, your job, and me. A trifecta."

"And you?" I said, wiping my cheeks with the back of my hand. "Would it have worked out perfectly for you?"

"Oh, yeah," he said. "I fell for you, Ann. We could have been great together."

"We still can be," I protested, searching his face for even a hint of hope and not finding any. "I love you. You love me. We've been through a challenging situation, but we can—"

At that moment, Rolanda appeared with a wheelchair. "Time to go, Mr. Sykes," she said, motioning for him to lower himself into the chair. "You're a free man."

He nodded at her, lifted himself and his knapsack into the wheelchair, and sat. "Free as a bird who can't wait to fly away," he said with emphasis, in case I didn't get his drift.

Rolanda looked at me with puzzlement, then grabbed the handlebars of the chair. When she started to steer him out of the room, I moved toward the door, essentially blocking it.

"Could I just have another word with him?" I asked her.

She looked down at Malcolm, even more puzzled. "You wanna stay or go, Mr. Sykes?"

He hesitated before answering, but only for a second. And even then, his answer was directed at her, not at me, to show me just how insignificant I was to him now. "Go," he said. "I'm more than finished here."

And off they went. No good-byes. No we'll-talk-about-this-when-I've-had-a-chance-to-settle-downs. No overtures of any kind. Just an exit.

I did not cause a scene and run after them. There wouldn't have been any point.

Chapter Thirty

I had another phone conversation with Harvey later that day. I pleaded with him to pull the story and he pleaded with me to come back to work. Well, he didn't *plead,* exactly, but he did remind me of the hefty raise I'd be getting to reward me for a job well done. "You gotta earn a living," he said. "Might as well earn it here, huh?"

Tuscany said the same thing. Her take on the situation was that what was done was done; that I may have lost Malcolm but I had gained a new shot at my career; that I should seize the moment and pick up where I left off at the magazine; and that I should spend my raise on a fancier apartment than the one I'd been renting. Oh, and a new car too.

As for my family, they were also pushing me to return to L.A.—all three of them. I couldn't remember a time when they'd agreed on something so unanimously, but they were really rooting for me to reconcile with Malcolm and figured I stood the best chance of doing that if he and I lived in the same city.

"It wouldn't be the worst thing if you ran into each other at some swanky party and kissed and made up," said my mother, who was very excited about the possibility of boasting to everyone in town that her daughter was dating a movie star.

"Besides, that story you wrote is very flattering to him," said my aunt, who knew firsthand. "Once he gets over his snit, he just might thank you for it."

"I doubt that," I said, recalling all too vividly that "snit" didn't begin to describe Malcolm's reaction to my undercover caper.

"You'll never find out unless you hustle yourself out there," said my grandmother.

"And if I were you, I'd hustle myself out there before the story goes on sale next week and the shit really hits the fan," said my aunt, whose language prompted a sharp rebuke from my mother, whose criticism prompted a snide remark from my aunt, which provoked another round of bickering. Some things never changed.

"You go get your man," said Grandma Raysa while her two daughters traded insults. "I'll hold down the fort here."

So it was all decided: I would pack my stuff and head back out west as soon as possible. But there was one more piece of business to clean up before I headed anywhere.

I DROVE TO the hospital on Tuesday morning and met with Shelley. She was as happy to see me as always—until it registered that I was not wearing my uniform.

"I came to give you this," I said somberly, laying my photo ID on her desk. We were sitting in her tiny cubicle of an office, just as we had on my fateful first day at Heartland General when I'd appeared for my interview. Back then it was winter, and the dry heat blowing out of the ceiling vents had nearly suffocated me. Now it was early spring, and the air-conditioning blowing out of those same vents was turning my lips blue.

"What's going on?" she said with surprise and concern, her long upper torso leaning toward me. "I was so sure things were going well for you here, that you enjoyed being a volunteer."

"I loved it," I said, heaving a sigh of regret. "I didn't expect to, didn't think I'd last more than a day, didn't know what an uplifting experience it would be. But I'm leaving, Shelley. Before I do any more damage."

"Damage? What are you talking about? The patients adore you."

"I've done something I shouldn't have," I said, forcing myself to meet her eyes. "I didn't break any laws, but I committed a major lapse in judgment. I can't tell you how sorry I am."

I told her about Malcolm, about writing the story, about falling in love with him, about his discharge from the hospital. She was stunned.

"First of all, I had no idea we had a celebrity in our midst," she said with a shake of her snowy white head. "Which means that some people around here actually follow the rules."

I nodded and waited with dread for her to beat me up about the rest. I respected her and valued her friendship, and I was kicking myself for betraying her trust right along with Malcolm's.

"As for what you did," she said, her expression sorrowful, almost as if she was disappointed in me rather than angry with me, "I would have had to dismiss you if you hadn't quit first. You crossed the line, Ann. We can't have our volunteers selling a patient's story to a national magazine, whether that patient is a movie star or a farmer. The only reason you won't be disciplined further is that you weren't the one who sent the infamous e-mail." Another shake of her head. "Your aunt is lucky Mr. Goddard hasn't pressed charges or she could have been looking at jail time."

Again, I just nodded, humbled by my guilt and by my desire not to screw up any more than I already had. I also thought it was ironic that Aunt Toni and Claire Honeycutt might have had prison stripes in common in addition to Uncle Mike.

"If only you'd come and talked to me," she said. "I told you my door was always open to my volunteers. You could have confided in me that you recognized Mr. Goddard, that you were tempted to write about him to get your old job back, that you were developing romantic feelings toward him. I could have been there for you, offered my advice, maybe even prevented all this."

"I know," I acknowledged. "I wish I'd taken you up on that offer, believe me. I just want to say that this hospital has been wonderful to me and I shouldn't have even contemplated doing anything that might put its reputation at risk." I cleared my throat as my emotions threatened to overwhelm me. "I may have become a volunteer under false pretenses, but working here has given me back myself, my belief in myself, my belief that we can and should donate our time in the service of others. A flowery speech, I know, but I mean every word. I owe you so much, Shelley. I feel like slitting my wrists for letting you down."

She relaxed into a smile. "This is hardly worth killing yourself over," she said. "When you come through a serious illness the way I have, you learn that nothing is so god-awful important except your health. Did you make a whopper of a mistake? Yes. Should you stop with all the self-flagellation? Yes."

"Thank you for that," I said, touched yet again by her kindness and compassion. "Thank you for everything. You've been an inspiration to me. Truly."

We continued to talk for a few minutes about the hospital and the other volunteer programs she was trying to implement.

"While we're on the subject of making this place better," I said, "I also want to share a suspicion I have about Richard Grossman."

"Tight Ass?" She scowled. "What's he done?"

"I'm not accusing him of anything," I said. "Well, not directly."

"Come on, Ann. Let's have it."

I told her about Isabelle and the class-action suit and how unconcerned Richard had seemed. "Whether he's in denial about the situation or he's deliberately turning a blind eye to these surgeries, I couldn't begin to say. He doesn't strike me as a criminal, but my reporter's instinct suggests that somebody needs to take a closer look."

"Consider it done," she said. "Thanks for the tip."

When it was time for me to go, we hugged each other warmly.

"You did good work here. Never forget that," she said in parting. "When you're out there in la-la land, try to hang on to whatever it was that made you whole again."

"I will, I promise," I said, and bid her a poignant good-bye.

BEFORE LEAVING THE hospital, I went to pediatrics. I had to see Bree Wiley again, if only for one final time. Jeanette was working her shift that day, so I was able to see her too.

I gave my friend the *Cliffs Notes* version of why I was leaving and ended the story by expressing how much I wanted her and her husband, with whom she had recently gotten back together, to fly out and visit me.

"You've come a long way," I said as we stood together in the hallway. She looked so much stronger than the person I'd met at the orientation, the woman who'd lost her baby and nearly her marriage too.

"What about you?" she said, nudging me affectionately. "You once told me you were afraid of being around sick people."

"I guess Heartland General has worked its magic on both of us," I said.

My visit with Bree was brief—she had just returned to her room after having some tests and was quite groggy—but I told her I was going away for a while and didn't want her to wonder what had happened to me.

"Away where?" she asked through half-open eyes.

"Hollywood," I said as I played with her blond curls. "I'll be back in Middletown a lot because my family lives here, but I also want you to come and see me in Los Angeles as soon as you're better, okay?"

Her eyes drooped even more and her usually expressive face was a blank. "If you meet any movie stars, maybe you'll get me their autographs."

"Of course I will," I said, aware that for the first time since I'd known her she didn't press the issue of a trip to Hollywood. She ignored my invitation, seemed content to have autographs, wasn't imbued with her old zest and fighting spirit. I hoped she hadn't given up on getting her transplant. It was her positive attitude that had kept her going. "Please be all right," I whispered as I kissed her forehead, watched her fall asleep, and tiptoed out of the room.

I WAS PLANNING on making Bree my last patient, as I said, but as I was walking toward the elevator I came upon a black teenage boy in a wheelchair. He was out in the hall, spinning around and around in that chair, a big grin on his chubby face.

"Hey," I said as he continued to whirl. "What's got you so wound up today?"

"Nothing much," he said, bringing the chair to a stop. It was only then I noticed that both of his legs were missing just above the knee. His lower body was draped with a blanket, but there was no mistaking the fact that there was very little flesh underneath it. I'd seen a lot in my stint as a volunteer. Brains had been sliced open. Backs had been broken and braced. Bodies had been teeming with cancer cells and then injected with drugs equally toxic. But this young man—this boy—was my first double amputee.

What I thought as I approached him was that we all have handicaps, some more incapacitating than others. It's how we push through, how we climb over our obstacles that makes us brave. And this boy was brave. There wasn't a hint of self-pity about him.

"Nothing much, huh?" I said, wishing I'd had my cart. All the teenage boys loved car magazines. "Then why the big smile? Did you hear good news from your doctor? Or did you have a special friend visit you this morning?"

"Nah. Nothing like that," he said. "I just smile a lot."

"I'm impressed," I said. "Most people don't smile enough."

"Not me. I was born with a smile on my face," he bragged.

"Oh, yeah?" I teased. "And how do you know that?"

"Ask my mother," he said. "She'll tell you."

"Fine," I said, enjoying our little game. "Bring her on."

"She works on the sixth floor," he said. "Go on up and talk to her. Name's Rolanda."

Rolanda. So Malcolm's nurse was this kid's mother. She tended to everybody else's pain and suffering and never once let on that she had her own to deal with. Once again it was brought home to me that the hospital was filled with people to admire. I just hadn't anticipated how torn I'd be about leaving it. Or them.

"I think I'm gonna believe you," I said. "You were born with a smile on your face, and that's all there is to it."

"You here visiting somebody?" he asked.

"Yes," I said. "Bree Wiley. Have you met her?"

"Blond girl?"

I nodded. "She could use a friend—especially one with a smile like yours."

"No problem," he said. "I'm on it."

He waved and wheeled himself back down the hall toward the entrance to pediatrics. As he disappeared from view, it occurred to me that I had Malcolm to thank for exposing me to the "heart" in Heartland General. If he hadn't come to town, I would never have tried to pass myself off as a do-gooder—and then realized how much satisfaction there was in becoming one.

Part Three

Chapter Thirty-one

||||||||||||||||||||||||||||||||||||||||||||||||||||||||||||||||||||||||||||||||||||||||||

I loaded up the Honda with everything I had loaded it up with on the last trip (plus the black dress and the black underwear I'd bought for my date with Malcolm), and, after a tearful farewell to my mother, aunt, and grandmother, I hit the road. Before heading out of town, I stopped at the lake and sat on the beach and thought about why I was returning to *Famous* and Harvey. What I decided was that I must have really wanted my old job back if I wrote the story about Malcolm in the first place and that I owed it to myself to give it another try. Besides, what better way to mend my broken heart than to throw myself into my work? It was the right move, the sensible move. I would repair my professional reputation, earn some real money after my time-out, and be closer—at least geographically—to the man I loved. A no-brainer, as Tuscany would say.

I stayed with her once I got to L.A. three days later. She'd insisted that I be her houseguest while I reacclimated myself to the city, settled back in at the magazine, and searched for an apartment, and I took her up on her offer. We had dinner together every night during that period. Well, except for Tuesday nights, when she had her shift at a clinic in West L.A.

Yes, she had become a volunteer in their magazines program. She said that my success in overcoming my fears had motivated her to follow in my footsteps; that she hoped to conquer her own fears, which included getting married and getting fat. She had made strides with the former; she was dating a nice male nurse. But she was still struggling with the latter; she couldn't shake the idea that people who aren't a size 2 should have gastric-bypass surgery. She was as zany as ever, but I didn't realize how much I'd missed her until she was back in my life on a regular basis. She was a wonderful distraction and helped me not to think about Malcolm every minute of the day—no mean feat. Knowing he was nearby, seeing the occasional images of him in the newspaper or on television (he really was making himself more accessible to the media, and he was no longer wearing the hairpiece or the contact lenses), hearing through the grapevine that he was seeing Rebecca again . . . Well, it hurt, to put it mildly.

I found an apartment my first week in town: a light, spacious upper unit in a Spanish-style duplex in West Hollywood, only two blocks from my old place. It was exactly what I wanted, so I grabbed it. A week later, I moved myself and the things I'd been storing at Tuscany's into my new home, then bought some snazzy furniture. The neighbor who lived downstairs was hardly ever there, and when he was, he was extremely quiet.

The same could not be said for Harvey, unfortunately. While he welcomed me back with great fanfare, he hadn't lowered his decibel level at all.

"Sales of the Goddard issue were off the charts!" he raved a week after the story had run. *"So now the question is: What does Ann Roth do for an encore?"*

"What about an interview with Téa Leoni?" I said, since she had a new movie coming out. "I could talk to her about her humanitarian work. And, of course, I'd get into her marriage to David Duchovny—how they raise their kids in the glare of the spotlight, what it's like to be half of a Hollywood couple."

"Please," he said dismissively. "People don't even know who she is, let alone how to pronounce her name."

Why does he bother to ask me for suggestions? I thought. He always ends up assigning me the person *he* wants me to interview.

"Who's a big get now?" he said, rubbing his hands together as if he were about to tackle a meal. "Who's fresh? Who's hot? Who's everybody talking about?"

"Neil Young had a brain aneurysm," I said, giving the game another whirl. "Survival stories are uplifting to readers."

"Aging rocker?" He rolled his eyes. "I think we'll let *Rolling Stone* have him."

"Right." Okay, I would officially shut up now.

"So who's a big get? Who? Who? Who?" he said, sounding like an owl. *"Wait! I got it!"* He bolted up from his chair, waved his arms in the air, and knocked over the porcelain miniature of the pope that was resting precariously on his desk. *"You'll do Danny Moder! Mr. Julia Roberts! Everybody wants to know what it's like to be married to her, what it's like to have those twins with her, whether she really broke up his first marriage! He's perfect! He hasn't done any interviews with anybody!"*

"He hasn't done any interviews because she's the star and he's the behind-the-scenes guy," I said. "He won't do it, Harvey."

"Like Goddard wouldn't do it?" He laughed demonically. "Come on, you'll figure it out. You're my little killer."

His little killer. I should have been thrilled.

I spent the next few days making calls, trying to cajole various publicists and managers and assistants into letting me interview Danny Moder. Nobody was saying no, absolutely not, but they weren't giving me a green light either. It was clear that the wooing would be a long, drawn-out process, and I was finding—to my increasing surprise—that I couldn't care less how it turned out. Nothing against Danny Moder, mind you. It was just that the hunt, the chase, the conquest of him, of any celebrity, wasn't interesting to me anymore. I still loved L.A., loved being smack in the midst of the entertainment world, but the idea of expending all my time and energy on trying to extract pearls of wisdom from the stars or their spouses no longer held the same allure for me. Had I really blown my chance at happiness with Malcolm for *this*? I kept asking myself. This new apathy worried and confused me.

"I'm pursuing the interview, doing my best, but there's no kick in it for me now," I confided one night to Tuscany and James, who'd had a chin implant after his breakup with Walter. "I feel like I'm in a crazy competition over nothing."

"It's Malcolm," said Tuscany. "You're still mopey about him."

"I am, but that's not it," I said.

"It's Harvey," said James. "He's probably even harder to take in comparison with your terrific boss at the hospital."

"He is, but it's not that either," I said. "It's that none of this seems important. Not when there's a girl back in Middletown who'll die if she doesn't get a new liver."

My friends nodded and gave each other looks and tried to be supportive. But they didn't understand what I was going through. *I* didn't understand what I was going through, not after wanting to be around celebrities my whole life, wanting to be part of the action. I chalked it up to rustiness, to having been out of the rat race for so long. The rush would return once I got back into the swing of things, I decided.

And then came a panic attack—my first in a long time. I was supposed to meet an old high school buddy of Danny Moder's for lunch at the Polo Lounge. Infiltrating a celebrity's inner circle was Harvey's favorite tactic for nailing an interview.

I pulled the Honda up to the hotel's entrance, handed it off to the lone valet-parking attendant who'd deigned to park it, and proceeded up the stairs, only to come upon a crowd of people in the lobby. There must have been a special luncheon—a birthday party or a corporate function—and all the participants were leaving just as I was arriving. I found myself try-ing to squeeze through their mosh pit. Suddenly, my heart took a dive and I thought I might collapse. I looked for something to hold on to and saw nothing. And so I stood there amid the revelers, sweating, nauseated, dizzy, the works. When I realized what was going on, that I had relapsed, I started to panic even more and felt my legs turn to spaghetti. I lost the ability to swallow. I felt a thundering in my chest. I couldn't think straight, couldn't think of anything except getting out of there. Picturing Danny Moder's high school friend sitting at the table I'd reserved for us, waiting impatiently for me, wondering why I was late, only made me suffer more. I was never late!

Unlike the disaster at the Santa Monica airport, this one didn't involve me running away. Once the crowd dispersed and I found a wall to lean against, I rallied, collected myself, mopped my wet face, and hurried out to the restaurant, full of apologies having to do with—what else?—traffic. But the episode did force me to ask myself whether it was a coincidence. The timing, I mean. I'd been nearly panic free when I was volunteering. And yet now here I was, back at *Famous* and panicking again.

I may not have been the most self-aware person, but even I figured there had to be a connection. Especially when the attacks continued over the next few weeks—at the supermarket, on the freeways, at movie screen-ings. Clearly, my return to the magazine was triggering them. I'd been attempting to be the kind of journalist Harvey demanded I be, a woman I no longer recognized. That could cause someone to panic, couldn't it?

It could. The question was: What was I going to do about it?

I CALLED SHELLEY, that's what I did about it. No, she wasn't a shrink, nor had we ever talked at any length about my anxiety disorder, but she was the most levelheaded person I knew and she was a survivor, my role model. If only I'd availed myself of her wise counsel when I was working at the hospital, Malcolm and I might still be together. I would not make the same mistake twice.

"Remember what I said the last time we saw each other?" she asked after I chronicled my setbacks and conveyed how discouraged I was. "I told you to hang on to whatever it was about Heartland General that made you whole again."

"I remember." It was so good to hear her voice. She always had a calming effect on me, a way of setting my mind at ease. "And I've tried to hang on to it."

"What's the 'it?'"

"I guess it's the feeling I got whenever I'd find a way to lift a patient's spirits. A feeling of giving to others instead of obsessing about myself and all the catastrophes that could happen to me."

"But from what you just said, you *have* been obsessing about yourself. You've lost sight of what made volunteering so rewarding for you."

"The giving part, you mean."

"Exactly. Look, Ann. I know you love being a writer for *Famous,* but where's the giving in that?"

"Well, I'm providing readers with a light, entertaining distraction," I said. "I saw how much the patients enjoyed the magazine, and it made me realize that the kind of fluff we put out has value. It takes people's minds off their problems."

"Fine, but is that the kind of giving that will nourish your soul?" She let the question dangle in the air for a few seconds.

"Not really," I admitted. "Not anymore."

"Then what if you could combine your familiarity with celebrities, your contacts, your experience in Hollywood with a cause of some sort? A program that helps people the way you helped them here at the hospital?"

"I'm not sure what you mean," I said, trying to follow her thread. There were plenty of charities in Hollywood, but they were all about raising huge sums of money and I had no experience doing that.

"You know how we have occasional visits from local luminaries? They're not celebrities the way you think of celebrities, but they're a big deal for Middletown."

"Sorry, Shelley, but I still don't get it," I said, thinking that Malcolm had been the only celebrity in Middletown and nobody had even recognized him.

"Yes, you do," she persisted. "For example, we had those players from the Royals come to offer encouragement to the patients in physical rehab. I told you about it. The team sends them to us every year as sort of a goodwill mission. It's great PR for them and for major-league baseball in general."

Right. I hadn't seen the players that day, but I'd read articles about their visit in both the *Crier* and the *Kansas City Star*. It *was* great PR for the team and had a positive effect on the patients too.

"You might be on to something," I said, an idea dawning. Well, a germ of an idea.

"No 'might' about it," she said. "Just think of the goodwill missions *you* could arrange. That Rolodex of yours must be bulging with the phone numbers of celebrities and their publicists."

"It is," I said, nodding to myself, my excitement building.

"So? What about quitting your job at the magazine, since it's obviously making you sick, and starting a company that serves as a liaison between celebrities and hospitals around the country? You'd be using your know-how to help others, to *give,* and in doing so your panic attacks will vanish, I'll bet on it. And of course, those famous people you've been writing about would probably love to be photographed comforting patients. Talk about great PR. They'll be beating down your door, Ann."

Me, a liaison between the stars and the hospitals. Why not? Who better to do it? And how better to combine my skills and interests? Only the week before, *People* had a photo of Nicole Kidman visiting a girl with leukemia at a hospital in Sydney. And the week before that, *20/20* had a piece about Matt Damon and his friendship with a brain-damaged boy at a Boston hospital. My company could function as a clearinghouse of sorts. The hospitals could request specific celebrities, and I could get in touch with their publicists to try to bring them together. Or it could work the other way around. If Catherine Zeta-Jones wanted to meet with AIDS patients or Ben Stiller had a personal stake in seeing how stroke victims recover, I would be the one to make the connection for them. "It's definitely something to chew on," I said, feeling almost giddy with the idea, liberated. "I'd have to figure out how to earn a living from it though."

"Couldn't the celebrities pay you a fee for matching them up with the hospitals and patients? Lord knows, they make enough money to pay you."

"I suppose my company could function the way other freelance businesses do in Hollywood—the party planners, the stylists, the personal trainers, the life coaches."

"Life coaches?" She groaned. "Do they really have those?"

"Oh, yeah. Celebrities don't need a good reason to hire people. It's part of being famous. You have to have a posse."

"Then there won't be any problem for you financially," she said. "You'll be just another service provider, only the service you'll be providing will be helping people. Really helping them. And in doing so, it'll help you too."

It was a genius idea—a career opportunity about which I had no ambivalence whatsoever. I felt energized and optimistic that I could make it work once I figured out the details and tested the waters.

Shelley and I wound up the conversation with me thanking her profusely and her promising to hook me up with Heartland General's public-relations coordinator whenever I was ready.

"We get first dibs on Malcolm Goddard, seeing as we cured him," she teased.

"I wouldn't count on him becoming my client," I said. "He won't even take my calls." Yes, I'd tried to reach Malcolm since I'd come back to L.A. Many times, in fact. I'd left messages on his cell phone but had never heard a word in response. And I'd given my name to assorted assistants and housekeepers and not gotten anywhere there either. He had frozen me out.

"His loss," she said. "You're a lovely lady, Ann. You'll find some-one else."

I didn't want anyone else, but that was a subject for another discussion.

OVER DINNER AT my apartment, I tried out the general idea on Tus-cany and James. They loved the concept, so we batted around ways it could be implemented. It took an entire pitcher of margaritas, but we finally decided that my company would be a specialty public relations firm dealing exclusively with celebrities and hospitals. I would acquire a contact list of PR coordinators from every major medical facility around the country, and the celebrity publicists looking for positive media atten-tion for their clients would subcontract out to me the job of placing these clients with the appropriate hospital.

"It's perfect," said Tuscany. "Publicists are much too busy dealing with the media to handle something as unique as this, right? They don't have the time to go running around chasing down hospitals and patients."

"Absolutely," said James, nodding his head, which now resembled that of an albino. He had recently bleached his hair plugs platinum. "And I can think of a million celebrities who could use good PR. The ones com-ing off a movie that bombed. The ones coming off a divorce that got ugly. The ones coming off a DUI conviction whose mug shots were posted on the Internet."

"You're both being a little cynical," I said. "There *are* some celebri-ties who genuinely enjoy reaching out to those less fortunate, and maybe they've been looking for a simple, straightforward way to do it. I'd be catering to them too."

"You're right," said a semichastened Tuscany. "There must be stars who want to do more than promote their latest project and don't know how. Which is all the more reason for your business going gang-busters."

I was encouraged by my friends' enthusiastic reactions and more convinced than ever that the company would be successful after talking to them about it. "I'll start small," I said. "I'll work out of this room in the beginning. Then I'll find office space and hire a staff as needed."

"What's needed is a name for your enterprise," said James. "A clever play on words."

"Something catchy," Tuscany agreed. "Medical, but with an entertainment twist."

"I have it, Annie," said James, clasping his hands together. "You should call the company PRx."

Tuscany and I looked at each other blankly.

"Come on, you two," he said. "It's PR, as in public relations, but with the little *x* on the end, to look like a doctor's prescription."

"Oh," I said, getting it. "That's cute." I scribbled the name down on the pad of paper I'd brought to the table.

"Wait. What about CPR?" said Tuscany, pointing at herself as if she'd just won the lottery. "It's a play on words too. CPR, as in the lifesaving thing, but it stands for Celebrity PR too."

"I like it," I said, adding her suggestion to the list. "I like them both." There were a few seconds of silence while we kept thinking. "How about Star Shifts?"

James rolled his eyes. "Too down-market. Like the celebrities would be working at a coffee shop or something."

"Okay. What about Celebrity Stripers?" I offered. "It's a takeoff on candy stripers."

Tuscany stuck her tongue out. "Sounds like a reality show about celebrity felons. How about Hollywood Medical?"

"A one-hour drama on NBC starring Heather Locklear," sniffed James.

More silence. More thinking. Then I jumped out of my seat and lifted my arms in victory. "Code Gold."

Tuscany smiled. "As in code blue?"

"And code gray and code red and all the rest," I said.

"Code Gold," James murmured, trying out the name. "To tie in with the gold statuettes they hand out at the Oscars."

"And the gold statuettes they hand out at the Emmys and the Grammys," I said. "And the gold medals they give to athletes. Gold, as in the gold standard. Gold, as in glitz and glamour. It works, doesn't it? It combines a medical phrase with entertainment and fun. I think we've got a winner."

My friends demonstrated their approval by raising their empty margarita glasses. "A toast to Code Gold," they said in unison.

I raised my glass too. "Here's to the first company that encourages celebrities to show their caring, compassionate sides."

"Even if they never had caring, compassionate sides before!" said James. "To Code Gold!"

"To Code Gold!" Tuscany and I repeated.

We clinked glasses and congratulated each other for coming up with the right concept and the right name.

"I hate to bring this up while we're celebrating, but when are you planning to tell Harvey you're leaving the magazine?" Tuscany asked me with a shudder. "I don't want to be anywhere in the building when you drop the bomb."

"It'll be fine," I reassured her. "I know just how to handle him."

"Since when?" she said skeptically.

"Since I figured out that if I give him the exclusive on every celebrity who visits a hospital, he'll be a happy man," I said. "Jennifer Garner goes to see a patient in Phoenix? I make sure *Famous* has the first photo."

She smiled. "You're right. That'll totally shut him up."

"Any other questions?" I asked my pals, who'd been helping me brainstorm my new venture for the entire evening but were probably ready to call it a night.

"Just one," said James. "Where's that music coming from?"

"Music?" We'd been talking so animatedly and uninterruptedly that I hadn't heard anything but the sound of our own voices.

"Yeah, listen."

We listened. Sure enough, my neighbor downstairs had his stereo on. Not blasting the way James used to blast, but definitely loud enough to make it through my hardwood floor. And I'd thought I'd escaped this time.

"Oh God," I said. "And it's Cher."

"He has good taste," said James.

"Come. I'll introduce you," I said.

I DIDN'T WANT to leave *Famous* without completing the task Harvey had assigned me, so I continued my pursuit of Danny Moder, even as I plotted the launch of Code Gold, and ultimately got the go-ahead from his battalion of gatekeepers to conduct the interview with him. He and I spent a very cordial two hours together at the Chateau Marmont, discussing everything from Julia and the twins to his first job as a cameraman. I wrote up the story, e-mailed it to Harvey, and received kudos both for my perseverance and my writing. My boss was so pleased with the piece that he sat me down in his office and started badgering me about my next one.

He was in the middle of one of his "Now who's the big get? Who? Who? Who?" interrogations when I took the opportunity to break the news that I was quitting.

"What?" he yelled, getting the red kabbalah string he had tied around his wrist caught in the cord of the six-line phone on his desk.

I explained about Code Gold, as well as how the magazine would benefit from it, and he stared at me as if I'd truly lost it.

"Why would you throw away the chance to interview the people everyone wants to know about?" he demanded. "And why wouldn't you want to beat out the competition to do it?"

"Because there are more important things in this world than beating out the competition," I said.

"Like what?" he yelled in such a clueless way that I actually felt sorry for him. *"The big get is what it's all about!"*

"No, it isn't," I said, getting up from my chair and going around to his side of the desk. "What I've learned, Harvey, is that *the big give* is what it's all about." And then I did something that really unnerved him. I wrapped my arms around him and planted a huge wet one on his cheek. While he stood there gaping at me, I told him I looked forward to working with him in my new capacity and wished him luck finding someone to replace me on the staff. "You were right. I was never a killer," I said as I walked toward the door. "But not to worry. This town is full of them."

Chapter Thirty-two

IIIIIIIIIIIIIIIIIIIIIIIIIIIIIIIIIIIIIIIIIIIIIIIIIIIIIIIIIIIIIIIIIIIIIIIIIIIIIIIIIIII

Suddenly, *I was* a big get. I'm serious. I launched Code Gold and became the one everybody wanted to know more about.

Almost immediately after I'd sent out press releases about the company to hospital PR departments, entertainment publicists, Hollywood trade publications, and the general media, celebrities clamored to come onboard. And once they did and the hospital tours began, I was besieged with interview requests. Me. On the other side of the questions this time. It was odd and wonderful simultaneously. I was profiled in Oprah's magazine. I appeared on Jill Rappaport's *Today* show segment. I sat down for a long conversation with a writer from the Calendar section of the *L.A. Times*. And then came *Access Hollywood* and *Entertainment Tonight,* and before I knew it, Code Gold was on the map big time. I sent Sean Penn to a hospital in Washington state and Courteney Cox to a hospital in Alabama and Queen Latifah to a hospital in the Bronx. Movie and television actors, sports stars, celebrity CEOs—they all wanted in. Reaching out to the sick and downtrodden was good for their images *and* good for their souls, they were discovering.

As for me, those first six months after I'd left *Famous* and set up my company represented the happiest period in my professional life—with virtually no panic attacks, I should add. Once I was away from the pressures of having to sink to Harvey's low level and threw myself into a career that nourished me, my mental health improved dramatically. No dizziness in crowds. No wobbly legs in supermarkets. Not even a fear of vomit. Tuscany had a stomach bug, and I was right there holding her head. I was becoming so well adjusted that I was scaring myself.

Although I still hadn't flown. In fact, I hadn't been near an airport since the day I was supposed to fly with Malcolm on his Cessna. I'd been able to arrange all the celebrity events via phone, e-mail, and fax. But I knew I would step on a plane and tackle my last lingering phobia as soon as the situation warranted. I wasn't avoiding flying, really. I just wasn't rushing to do it. Everything was going so well that I didn't need to.

Not that I want to paint an overly rosy picture of my life. Yes, my business was thriving, but my love life was pathetic. Instead of accepting dates from the reasonably nice men who asked me out, I sat around pining for Malcolm. When I was in a particularly masochistic mood, I'd stick one of his movies into the DVD player, curl up in bed with a bag of Fritos, and watch him, recalling the anecdotes he'd told me about the making of each film and remembering how easily he'd shared his experiences with me. Because he'd trusted me. Because he'd fallen in love with me. Because he and I had connected in a way that didn't happen every day. No matter what had come after, I wasn't wrong about that.

Sometimes, I'd schedule a Malcolm double feature and watch two of his movies back-to-back, long into the night. Seeing him on screen was the closest I could get to the real thing. I ached for him during those exercises in self-torture. I wondered where he was and with whom as I stared at his flickering image on television, but mostly what I wondered was why he wouldn't forgive me. Surely he'd heard that I was no longer a media parasite. Surely he'd read about Code Gold along with everybody else in the entertainment community. His own publicist, Peggy Merchant, called me often, as sweet as could be, asking if I'd send Pierce Brosnan and some of her other clients out into the trenches. And every single time she called, I could feel myself tense, hoping against hope that she was calling on behalf of Malcolm. She wasn't.

Still, I didn't give up on him, on us. Well, not until I ran into him and witnessed firsthand his complete and total lack of interest in me. One of the most important aspects of building Code Gold was to network at industry events. Toward that end, I attended a party at Morton's restaurant, the spot where *Vanity Fair* always holds its Oscar soirée. This occasion was a birthday party for Sidney Lumet, the director who'd given Malcolm his first big break in New York. Since my status in town had risen considerably, I was able to score an invitation.

I was chatting with Harvey, who was now treating me with grudging respect, when I spotted Malcolm across the packed room. He was not alone; Rebecca was holding his arm. The sight of them together was a kick in the gut, but I hung on.

I continued to listen as Harvey pontificated, even as my gaze remained fixed on Malcolm, almost willing him to make eye contact with me. *Come on, come on, I'm over here!* I thought as I followed his every step, his every handshake, his every nod of the head. *Look at me, Malcolm! Remember how you loved me! Tell me you want me, not her!*

Finally, there was a moment. He saw me amid the sea of bodies, I know he did. Maybe I was reading something into his expression that wasn't there, but I could have sworn he looked happy that I was in that room with him.

But it was only a moment, as I said. The hint of a smile or whatever it was faded quickly, only to be replaced by a blank face and, just as quickly, a turn toward Rebecca and a directional shift away from where Harvey and I were standing. No kidding, he literally steered her away from me, to avoid even the possibility of having to talk to me. Another kick in the gut, yes, but it served a purpose. After that party, I realized it was over and the pining had to cease. What's more, I realized that despite how betrayed he felt and despite how much I'd deserved his anger, he couldn't have loved me. Not really. If he had, he would have made some effort to bridge the gap between us, some attempt to work things out with me. But no. He hadn't cared enough to make even polite conversation at a social gathering.

I felt tears prick at my eyes, made my apologies to Harvey, and hurried off to the ladies' room to regroup. I was at the sink, freshening up and vowing to stop feeling sorry for myself, when Rebecca sauntered in.

"If it isn't Ann," she said cheerfully as I was wishing I was anywhere else but in that bathroom. She was wearing a very strange outfit—a black silk pants thing that was configured like overalls and wouldn't have been out of place in Middletown if it had been denim—but she managed to look as beautiful as always. "Lovely to see you again."

"Same to you," I said, wanting very much not to appear like a sore loser. Besides, I had to think about Code Gold. Rebecca was a potential client after all. "Enjoying the party?"

She smiled. "I have a veddy, veddy, veddy handsome escort. I enjoy going 'round with him no matter where it is."

"I'm sure you do," I said, feeling my spirits sink lower with each "veddy." Hadn't he told me he'd broken up with her because she wasn't me? Apparently, not being me was now a good thing.

"And of course, Malcolm and I are so comfortable together after such a long friendship," she went on. "We finish each other's sentences."

So he really was hers. They were a couple. I had to accept it and take the high road. "I wish you two all the best," I managed, "but I do have to get back to the party. If you'll excuse me."

"Oh, dear. I'm afraid I've—" She hesitated. "Never mind. Enjoy the party."

"You too."

I held my head up as I walked out of that ladies' room, but I was dying inside. I couldn't shake the nightmarish vision of them finishing each other's sentences, including the ones in the wedding vows they would undoubtedly be composing to each other soon enough. After all the things he'd said to me, after all the things he'd said about her, she'd won. She'd won and I just had to face it. It was time for me to forget Malcolm Goddard and move on.

ABOUT TWO WEEKS after the party, I got a call from Jeanette. She and I had kept in touch since I left Middletown, just as we'd pledged we would. She'd been updating me on Bree Wiley, and the news hadn't been encouraging. Bree continued to languish in the hospital waiting for a new liver, while her parents continued to look for full-time jobs. My heart went out to all of them.

"I have good news this time," said Jeanette, sounding very upbeat. "In fact, I'm calling from Bree's room here at the hospital."

"What's going on?" I said, cautiously optimistic.

"She got the transplant, everything's fine, and she's going home in three or four days."

"Jeanette! That's fabulous!" I exclaimed, knowing what a long road it had been. Bree had spent most of her childhood in hospitals and doctors' offices and hadn't even started to live her life. Now she would have a future. Now she would have the chance to do and see and experience all the things the rest of us took for granted.

"She wants to talk to you. Do you have a minute?"

"Absolutely," I said. "Put her on." I smiled as I imagined Bree in settings other than Heartland General—going to school with other kids, making new friends, getting crushes on boys, all of it. Everything was possible for her now.

"Ann?" she said when she came on the line. Her voice was weak, but I could practically hear the grin on her face. "Isn't it great?"

"So great," I said. "I wish I could be there to see you leave that place. I couldn't be happier for you."

"Thanks," she said, then hesitated before continuing. "Um, I was wondering if I could be part of your new company, even though I won't be in the hospital anymore."

"Part of my—Oh, you mean have a celebrity visit you at home?" I'd tried and failed to put her together with a star, ever since the day I'd launched Code Gold. She was the first patient I'd wanted to help, given my personal connection with her, but she'd been too sick to have visitors over the past few months, too prone to infection.

"No. I mean have me and my parents come to Hollywood," she said. "Remember how we talked about that?"

"Of course I do," I said, flashing back to Malcolm. The night I'd told him about Bree and the horrible ordeal she'd been through, he'd promised to fly her and her family to L.A. and foot the bill for their entire trip. What good was that promise now? He was out of my life. Bree's too. Well, it was his loss, as Shelley pointed out. "You concentrate on getting your strength back and I'll surprise you with the most star-filled vacation you could ever imagine. How does that sound, Bree?"

"Awesome," she said with a giggle.

It sounded awesome to me too. All I had to do was make it happen.

Chapter Thirty-three

||||||||||||||||||||||||||||||||||||||||||||||||||||||||||||||||||||||||||||||||||||||||

The following week, during a scheduled appearance on KNBC-TV's *Six O'Clock News,* I promoted Code Gold and talked about Bree. "This is about more than just a hospital visit by a celebrity," I told the reporter and the viewing audience. "This is about reaching out to a young Missouri girl whose dream of coming to Hollywood sustained her through her long battle with liver disease. Her parents are saddled with her medical bills and can't afford to finance her trip, so my mission is to find a celebrity who will fly all three of them out here and fulfill her dream."

The next morning my phone rang at nine o'clock sharp. When I heard Peggy Merchant's voice on the other end, my heart did a little dance. Yes, I'd given up on Malcolm, but hearing her voice still triggered a reaction.

It's probably about Pierce Brosnan, I reminded myself. Not that I wasn't touched by the generosity he'd shown since I'd started the company. He'd been one of my best clients, offering to visit countless patients in countless hospitals, and I was extremely grateful to him. It was just that I—

"Malcolm saw you on the news last night," she said. "He remembered about the little girl in your hometown."

So this *was* about Malcolm? I was so startled that I had to ask her to repeat what she'd just said.

"He told me he'd made you a promise about her," she added. "He has his faults, as we all do, but when he makes somebody a promise, he keeps it."

So he did remember, I thought, my spirits buoyed by this new development, this new hope. If he remembered his promise about Bree, he had to remember his feelings for me, didn't he? They were bundled together in my mind, his promise and his feelings, part of the same place and time. It suddenly seemed more than possible that he did love me in spite of our estrangement and that this call from Peggy was his way of letting me know. Maybe he'd been trying to figure out how to approach me, how to say he was sorry for holding on to his anger for so long, and that it was his pride that had kept him from actually doing it. Maybe this was the excuse he'd needed—and the opening I'd been praying for.

"So Malcolm is offering to fly Bree and her parents to L.A.?" I asked, the crack in my voice betraying how much her answer mattered to me.

"Yes," she said. "They'll have full use of the Gulfstream to bring them here and take them back. It seats up to fourteen people and is quite luxurious. And he'll have it outfitted with any medical equipment the little girl may need."

I was so thrilled I could hardly speak. Malcolm had reached out, not only to Bree but to me. It was a miracle on both counts.

"Ann? Are you there?" asked Peggy.

"Yes, sorry," I said. "I'm just very moved by Malcolm's desire to get involved."

"He's glad to do it," she said. "Just give us the date of departure, and the plane will be fueled and stocked and ready to leave from the Santa Monica airport." She paused. "I'm assuming you *will* show up for the flight this time around? I mean, you do want to be there to accompany the girl, right?"

"I wouldn't miss it for the world," I said. I *would* show up this time. I had more than enough incentive. Not only would I be able to personally escort Bree to Hollywood in grand style, but I would be able to do it with the man I loved by my side. Sure, I'd be nervous about taking my first flight in a while. But I'd get over it. I'd have plenty to distract me.

"And did I mention that Malcolm will pay for the girl and her parents to spend a week at the Four Seasons?"

"A week? Wow. That's wonderful, Peggy." I couldn't wait to thank him, couldn't wait for us to be together again, couldn't wait to hold him and kiss him and—

"As I said, he's glad to do it. The only thing you'll have to do is set up their itinerary while they're here. If she wants to meet celebrities, you'll have to arrange it."

I laughed. "Malcolm doesn't count as a celebrity? I think flying halfway across the country with him will go a long way toward satisfying Bree's expectations."

"Oh, my," said Peggy, sounding suddenly as if she'd just been told of a death in the family. "I see our wires are crossed."

"I don't understand."

"Malcolm won't be flying with you, Ann, nor will he be meeting the girl and her parents."

"Why not?" I said, feeling my shoulders sag.

"He said he promised you he would sponsor her trip. He's leaving the rest of it to you."

Her words were so painful that I winced. "Sponsoring it?"

"Taking care of the bills, yes," she said. "He suggested that with all your contacts, you'll be more than capable of finding other performers for the girl to meet."

Other performers. I was finally getting it now. Malcolm hadn't forgiven me after all. He was merely fulfilling an obligation. A financial obligation. He couldn't even bring himself to hold his nose and spend a few measly hours with me.

Well, I wasn't going to throw myself off a cliff over it. No way. Maybe I'd earned his scorn and maybe I hadn't, but my overriding concern at that moment was Bree Wiley. Malcolm had offered her his private plane? We'd take it. He'd offered her the Four Seasons? We'd take that too. He didn't want to be a part of the celebration of her new life? *His loss.*

"Tell Malcolm I'm very grateful for his participation in Code Gold," I said crisply. "I'll get back to you with the dates."

ON THE MORNING of my flight to Kansas City to pick up the Wileys, Tuscany and James tried yet again to load me up with pills. This time I popped a Xanax. If it would take the edge off my anxiety without impairing my ability to function, why not? I'm telling you, I was so much braver than I used to be. For the most part.

When I arrived at the airport, I parked the Honda in the very same lot where I'd parked it the day I'd been too paralyzed to board the Cessna, and walked toward the pilots' lounge as per Peggy's instructions. Once inside the lounge, I was greeted by a broad-shouldered, craggy-faced man in a navy blue uniform. After a little salute, he introduced himself as Captain Jim Johnson, Mr. Goddard's pilot. He was pleasant and professional and made me feel as relaxed as a person with aviophobia on one tablet of Xanax can feel.

"Ready to board?" he asked as we headed out to the runway where a shiny silver jet was waiting for us.

I swallowed the lump in my throat. "Ready as I'll ever be," I said. "I'm not wild about flying, to be honest."

He smiled. "Nothing to worry about. We'll take good care of you."

"We? So there's a copilot?"

"Plus a flight attendant. There'll be four of us on the outbound leg and seven on the return, with your passengers."

"Great," I said, forcing myself to look adventurous. But as he stepped into the cockpit and I stepped into the cabin, it dawned on me that I was actually about to do the one thing I still feared: spend hours on an airplane. This was happening. This was not a computer-simulated exercise at some virtual reality clinic. Once Captain Johnson hit the ignition, I'd be helpless.

Back came the what-ifs, the catastrophizing, and the stirrings of outright panic. With my heart beginning to pound, I glanced furtively at the cockpit, which was now sealed off, and considered making my escape out the cabin door, which was still open.

You are *not* skipping out on this! I scolded myself. You're staying right where you are! Bree and her parents are waiting for you in Kansas City, you've planned a wonderful week for them in L.A., and if *she* can fight through a life-threatening illness, then *you* can fight through your fear!

I inhaled deeply then exhaled, mopped my sweaty brow with a tissue, and continued on through the cabin, where a pretty blond flight attendant in a honey-colored skirt and blazer that matched the plane's interior welcomed me.

"I'm Nell," she said. "Feel free to sit anywhere. May I bring you something to drink?"

I was dying for a Bloody Mary—for six Bloody Marys—but asked Nell for bottled water. I figured I shouldn't mix the Xanax with alcohol. I also figured I shouldn't show up in Kansas City with booze breath and a headache.

I sat in one of the four plush leather chairs inside the cabin. They were as big and swivelly as Barcaloungers. At least I'll die in the lap of luxury, I thought as I buckled myself in and surveyed my surroundings.

Malcolm certainly hadn't scrimped. In addition to the comfy chairs, there was stunning, wall-to-wall carpeting decorated with a golden sun motif, a brightly upholstered sofa, an office-type work space, and an entertainment center that included Bose speakers and a plasma TV.

"Here's your water," said Nell. Even the glass was fancy; it was heavy crystal—a far cry from the plastic I associated with air travel. "Is there anything else I can do before we take off? Captain Johnson tells me we're good to go."

Good to go. An oxymoron when it came to me and flying. "No, thanks. I'll just clutch this glass with my white knuckles and hope we make it to Missouri in one piece."

She laughed. "I have a feeling this will be the best flight you've ever had."

"Right."

I watched Nell depart for wherever flight attendants hang out when they aren't serving up platitudes, placed my glass in its slot on the nearby table, and lowered my head so that it was practically wedged between my knees. I was in crash mode. As Captain Johnson revved the engines and we started to taxi along the runway, I whispered to myself, "You can do this. You can do this."

"You *are* doing this," said a male voice.

I glanced up, petrified that the pilot—or maybe it was the copilot?—had somehow forgotten that he was supposed to be taking charge in the cockpit as opposed to chewing the fat with me in the cabin, and gasped. Really. I kind of made this noise that people make when they can't believe what they're seeing. Was my panic causing hallucinations as well as palpitations?

"Malcolm?"

He looked so handsome in his black leather jacket and jeans—larger than life but as familiar to me as a member of my family. I couldn't be conjuring him up, could I?

He sat down and buckled himself into the seat next to mine. "You can do this because you know from volunteering at the hospital that we're all vulnerable. Every one of us. Down on the ground. Up in the air. Doesn't matter. There's no such thing as 'safe.' All we can do is count our blessings."

So he'd shown up to give me a pep talk? Why? Since when did he care? He'd left it to his publicist to fulfill his so-called promise to Bree. "I don't understand . . . Peggy said you weren't—"

He pressed his forefinger to my lips. "But I did come. I had to. I need you to forgive me for staying away, Ann."

I was as astonished by his declaration as I was by his appearance on that plane. He wanted me to forgive him? Now? After so long?

"Why *did* you stay away?" I asked, the lump in my throat returning.

"I thought you sold me out, just like everybody else who was important to me," he said, gently brushing aside the tear that had trailed down my cheek. "I thought you were like the others."

"What changed your mind?" I managed, trying to rein in my emotions, in case he really was an illusion.

"The story you wrote about me." He swallowed hard. He seemed to be choking out his words. "I never could bring myself to read it, because the idea of it hurt so damn much. But then I saw you at that party and I couldn't get you out of my mind and I forced myself to read it." A tear trailed down his own cheek then. "It was beautiful, and it totally knocked me out. Nobody ever got me the way you did."

I smiled ruefully. I'd been able to "get" him, to capture the positive side of the Hollywood bad boy, because I'd made the effort. And I'd made the effort, not because it would ensure me a second chance at *Famous,* but because I loved him. I knew that now.

"I was wrong to doubt your feelings for me," he went on, "but I couldn't find a way to tell you I was sorry. Sorry about what happened the last time we were at this airport. Sorry about what happened the last day I was in Middletown. Sorry about what happened over the past few months." He lowered his head, humbled by his mistakes. "You may be the one with the panic attacks, but I'm the one who didn't have the nerve to apologize to you—until today." He looked back up at me. "Will you forgive me, Ann?"

Just then, the plane's engines roared in earnest and we started speeding down the runway at two hundred miles an hour.

Instinctively, I grabbed Malcolm's hand and squeezed it hard enough to cut off his circulation. I was both ecstatic and unstrung, pumped with enough adrenaline to lift the plane in the air myself. He loved me. He wanted us to be together. My life was going to have a happy ending after all, except for one tiny detail: I was about to die in a plane crash!

"I'll forgive you under one condition," I said.

"Name it."

"Promise me your pilot didn't get his license from one of those schools that advertise on matchbook covers."

He leaned over and kissed me on the mouth. The kiss was wet and hot and instantly erased all those months of yearning, of fantasizing.

"Jim used to fly for Delta," he said. "Forgive me now?"

"What about Rebecca?" I asked.

"She doesn't have a pilot's license."

"I meant, what about *you* and Rebecca?"

"We were just each other's arm candy," he said. "Forgive me now?"

"Yes, but I should tell you I have a No Actor's rule when it comes to romance."

"Can't you waive it?"

"Maybe, but how do I know you're good in bed?"

He laughed and kissed me again. We held the kiss as the nose of the plane reared up to meet the hazy white sky over Santa Monica.

"Oh God," I said, because I was both deliriously happy and absolutely terrified.

"Hey, I've got you," he said, holding me tightly in his arms. "I've got you."

Malcolm Goddard had me. It's true that there's no such thing as "safe," but suddenly I felt safe. Well, as safe as I was ever going to feel in an airplane. It was as if his statement, the pure simplicity of it, had flipped

my fear switch to the off position. To my great relief, I stopped catastrophizing. I embraced the idea that it was more than likely that everything
would turn out all right. I focused on the positive probable that he and
I would get married someday, preferably sooner rather than later. I even
relaxed my head against his shoulder as we ascended and I exhaled a sigh
of pleasure.

"Here we go," he said.

Sure enough, up, up, up we went, bouncing and shimmying through
the wispy clouds, over the ocean, above the mountains, into the great unknown.